The Valedictorians

Also by David Annandale

Crown Fire

Kornukopia

The Valedictorians

by

~~David Annandale~~

David Annandale (signature)

RaveN
STONE

Turnstone Press
Artspace Building
206-100 Arthur Street
Winnipeg, MB
R3B 1H3 Canada
www.TurnstonePress.com

Turnstone Press gratefully acknowledges the assistance of the Canada
Council for the Arts, the Manitoba Arts Council, the Government of
Canada through the Canada Book Fund, and the Province of Manitoba
through the Book Publishing Tax Credit and the Book Publisher
Marketing Assistance Program.

This novel is a work of fiction. Names, characters, places and
incidents are either the product of the author's imagination or are used
fictitiously, and any resemblance to actual persons living or dead, or
events or locales is entirely coincidental.

Cover design: Jamis Paulson
Interior design: Sharon Caseburg
Printed and bound in Canada by Friesens for Turnstone Press.

Library and Archives Canada Cataloguing in Publication

Annandale, David, 1967–
The valedictorians / David Annandale.

ISBN 978-0-88801-372-9

        I. Title.

PS8551.N527V34 2010   C813'.6   C2010-904972-1

Mixed Sources
Cert no. SW-COC-001271
© 1996 FSC
FSC

For Margaux, with love.

The Valedictorians

prologue

She should have snapped his spine.

Joe Chapel said, "Kill her on sight."

In Caracas, Major Alejandro Olano decided it was a question of honour.

Never listen to mercy, Jen Blaylock thought. It was a mantra that should have been as natural as breathing by now. But she had listened to it. She had listened to Kelly Grimson, had listened to her best friend, had listened at the worst possible moment. Joe Chapel, body smashed to pieces, had been strapped to a hospital bed in front of her. A quick twist and he would have been done, the CIA Deputy Director of Operations dispatched to black-ops hell. But Grimson had pleaded for his life, and Blaylock had listened. Grimson, who had every reason to see Chapel burn. Grimson, whose husband and unborn child had been killed by dirty bombs in Davos, useful collateral damage in a power play designed and executed by Russian organized crime, aided and abetted by the president of the United States. The plan, corpses notwithstanding, was dismal economics and expedient politics on a grand scale. Stepan Sherbina, crimelord and capitalist extraordinaire, had a notion of running the World Trade Organization. President Sam Reed wanted a piece of that action. Simple as that. Blaylock had brought Sherbina's dream down in a smash of burning building and slaughtered forces. And then she'd killed him. Her war had damaged Reed, too. The war had been spectacularly public, and the revelations were pouring out, a horn of plenty spewing corruption to the light of day. Chapel had done the dirty work for his boss, and now was receiving his loyalty's reward. He was in traction, was the designated scapegoat for the fiasco, and his career was doing the *Hindenburg* dive.

These were great and good things. But Reed was still president. Chapel was still DD Operations. And they were both still alive. They were paying now, but Blaylock knew they'd skate home. That's what their kind did. Even at each other's expense. Within hours of walking away from the crippled Chapel, giving in to Grimson's plea not to kill a man who could barely move, she'd known she'd made a mistake. Yes, she could spare Chapel, then watch him and Reed go to war and hurt each other. But that would be letting political bread and circuses obscure the big picture. As long as Chapel was alive, he could and would act again. There would be more wet jobs. Blaylock pictured new and worse variations of the Davos firestorm on the horizon.

She had listened to mercy. She hadn't finished the bastard

when the kill would have been easy. Now he had protection. Now she had to find a way to get at him. Always doing things the hard way.

"I don't even know what she looks like," Louise Meacham told Chapel. "We don't have any pictures."

Chapel grunted, fighting frustration and pain. He was in a clinic in the US mission in Geneva, doped to the gills on painkillers, though the aches were still sharp enough to cut through the drug fog. Only his eyes and mouth had mobility. His tongue, swollen, spelunked a landscape of absent teeth. At least Sherbina wasn't still breaking his bones. Sherbina was out of the game, and that was good. That left the woman. She called herself Baylor, and pretended to be a journalist. Her file nickname was Scary Lady. She had burned Sherbina. She was dangerous. He wanted her retired and on a slab. "Find a sketch artist," Chapel told the station chief. "I'll give a description."

Meacham shook her head. "No."

Chapel glared. "You didn't say that."

"I did. No more black bag jobs on my watch. There's enough of a shitstorm already."

"You seem to have forgotten the chain of command."

Meacham snorted. "Read the papers, Joe. You're radio-active. I could be putting my ass in a sling just talking to you."

"You sure enough about that to disobey a direct order?"

Meacham matched him stare for stare. He saw no wavering in her grey eyes, only a weary, disgusted cynicism. She had thirty years in the Agency, easily a decade on him, ten extra years of learning how to gauge the direction of the wind. "Whatever," she said, and the word was a deep statement of belief. Her head gave the smallest, most tired of shakes. "Dig your hole. I don't care. I'm walking away." And she did.

Chapel turned his eyes from the empty doorway. Gene Kemmerlin was still in the room. Kemmerlin only had three years' active service under his belt. He was still green enough to be shocked pale by Meacham's insubordination. "You still with me, soldier?" Chapel asked.

"Sir!" Kemmerlin looked like he wanted to snap a salute.

"You understand what I'm asking you to do?"

"Yes, sir."

"This woman is a threat to the national security of the United States of America. Anything unclear in what I just said?"

"No, sir."

"Good. Then let's do it. Immediately."

"Sir, finding her might take some time."

"I don't think so," Chapel said. He tried to smile, couldn't quite manage it yet. He knew how the woman campaigned. *Get well soon*, she had told him. He didn't think she'd wait. He wouldn't.

Tracking Chapel's whereabouts was easy. He had a pack of rabid media on his trail. Blaylock knew where he was. If he moved, she'd hear about it, along with the rest of the beautiful wired world. The problem was access. She couldn't storm the Mission. Too many civilians. But she'd caught a break earlier in the day. Half the press contingent split away to the airport. A leak had Chapel flying out of Geneva at 2300 hours. Back to the US, to face the music, or to counterattack. Blaylock liked her location. Likely route to the airport, a patch of countryside, no houses nearby. She crouched in the night, ignored the throbs of recent wounds, and waited for the coda to the last war.

"Where is she?" Kelly Grimson demanded. There was urgency in her voice, but also fatalism, as if she were facing a battle long since already lost.

Mike Flanagan asked, "I should tell you why?" They were standing on the Route de Pregny, half a block down from the cameras and mics. The weather had turned foul again, and a cold end-of-February rain drizzled down in a fine, clammy spray. Flanagan wiped the water from his face, wishing for an umbrella.

Grimson touched his sleeve. "I know why you're here. Do you really want to be doing this?"

Yes. He was watching for any departure from the US Mission that might be Chapel. He would radio Blaylock when the target left his lair. She was guessing some time around 2200. Yes, he knew why he was here. He was in the fight with Blaylock, all the way in adrenaline and fire. The stump of his left ring finger, his war wound from the Geneva campaign, tickled with anticipation. He was going to learn war, and he was going to like it. *Yes*. To Grimson, he said, "Why are you trying to stop her?"

"Because this is *wrong*. I'm trying to save her from herself."

"And who's going to save the innocent from the likes of Chapel? She's doing this for you, Kelly."

Grimson let go of his arm. "She's brainwashed you, too."

"No. I've just seen enough to know that if you're going to fight these people, this is the only way that will work. Not by waving placards." He regretted the shot at Grimson's brand of activism as soon as he'd said it.

Grimson didn't seem to notice. "Jen's not doing this for some fine cause," she said. "She's doing this because she likes it. And she's sucked you in."

"That's not true." His voice wasn't as steady as he would have liked.

"Prove me wrong."

They faced each other in silence.

In Caracas, honour dictated action.

Grimson borrowed Irina Zelkova's car. Progressive lobbyist and wife of Stepan Sherbina, Zelkova was hospitalized for severe shock, and wouldn't be needing wheels for a while. Grimson drove towards the airport, and tried to think like Blaylock. She should be able to do that. She knew what Blaylock was up to. They'd been soldiers together. So she called up the old training, and planned like the predator her friend had become. She thought *ambush*, and the location was obvious when she saw it. She pulled over to the side of the road. Traffic flashed past her as she stepped out of the car and scanned the darkness.

At 2150, an ambulance pulled into the grounds of the US Mission. There was something in Flanagan's gut. It was the excited need to see another bastard go down, and it felt like hunger. Twenty minutes later, the ambulance re-emerged onto the Route de Pregny. Flanagan radioed Blaylock.

Nothing. If Blaylock was here, she was part of the night. Grimson thought about calling out, but knew how futile that would be. She waited by the car, praying for the opportunity to stop more slaughter. She put the hood of her jacket up against the rain. Then she saw red and blue lights flashing in the distance.

Blaylock was soaked, cold and cramped. The discomfort evaporated when she saw the ambulance approaching. She turned her attention away from Grimson, fifty yards down the road from her. She grieved for the wound she was about to inflict on their friendship. I'm doing this for you, too, Kelly, she thought. Even if you don't believe me. Even if you don't want me to. She set her C7 assault rifle to single-shot, and sighted. The ambulance had just passed Grimson when Blaylock fired twice, blowing out both front tires. Brakes squealed. The ambulance careened left and right, sparks flying, as it swerved to a halt. The timing was good, no traffic. The driver hopped out of the ambulance and ran like hell. Blaylock rose to her feet.

Grimson was far ahead of her, streaking for the rear of the ambulance, spreading her arms, already in human shield mode, yelling "*No!*"

Blaylock hesitated, wondering how she would make Grimson step aside. And then she realized that there was still *no* traffic, in either direction, and there hadn't been for the last five minutes, and the ambulance had *no* escort, and finding out Chapel's travel plans had been *so* easy. "*Kelly!*" Blaylock screamed, and then her dark history was repeating all over again as the ambulance exploded.

Chapel's plane had flown out three hours earlier. Kemmerlin sat beside his gurney and took the call when it came in. "Got her," he told Chapel.

Blaylock cradled Grimson's body. There wasn't much to it, not much at all.

The next day, Blaylock and Flanagan were on a flight to the States. Blaylock was in the window seat, motionless, eyes unblinking, Gorgon-staring into the middle distance. Flanagan touched her hand once or twice, but her skin was too cold to comfort, and her joints were fused solid with guilt. He turned back to his paper. He unfolded the front page, and President Sam Reed gazed back, his hand gesturing with magisterial damage control. Blaylock stirred, and stabbed a finger at the picture. "Him, too," she said, her voice a flatline death sentence. "He's going down, too. Understand?" Flanagan nodded, throat dry.

In Caracas, Major Alejandro Olano made ready to serve his general.

1

April in Washington, DC, when the threats of winter were no longer real, but were fresh enough in memory that the slow warming was welcomed. Springtime in Washington, when the threats of summer and its clammy fist were too distant to be taken seriously. Springtime in Washington, where new wars and old, and hatreds deeper than God's provided the beat for the dance. Springtime in Washington, but the season had no effect on the dance. The dance went on, winter to spring to fall to summer, round and round and round again, a hermetic tango with no meaning other than itself. Economies teetered, governments fell and people died with every beat of the dance, but to the dancers, who were deafened by the drums, those events were distant phantoms, mere cues for variations in movement. The only true communications were between the dancers, who had eyes only for each other. Opponents and partners, they sought each other's doom, but not outside the confines of the dance. To do otherwise might threaten to throw off the beat, and the dance must never stop.

Trial by media was death by a thousand cuts. It will make me stronger, Chapel thought. But he played weaker.

The cuts that festered, that did him real damage, weren't the ones inflicted by *The Nation*, *Salon*, or even *Frontline* and the *New York Times*. The exposés and enemies in those quarters were known and welcome. If they had risen to his defence, he might have been more worried than he was. The serious wounds were the backstabs coming from Fox and the seamier precincts of CNN, where bow-tied blowhards and neocon blow-up dolls puked their venom over his name, and from talk radio, where the void of thought created a deafening echo chamber. Chapel had never had any illusions about the news media's three-ring freak show. He didn't feel concern over any notion that something vaguely recognizable as the truth was being distorted. That was a ludicrous irrelevancy. But he was on the losing side of the spin war. His optics were all bad, thanks to Charlotte Taber. The undersecretary of state for Public Diplomacy was the supreme dark goddess of PR. She and the White House's mouthpieces were the legion of doom. They had him in their sights, and bombarded him with all the artillery of a desperate president's publicity machine. The NASCAR dads and the security moms, who hadn't even known he existed until now, were rising against him in the righteous fury of their stupefied fear. Perception created reality, and his new reality was a countdown to oblivion.

From within his room in the George Washington University Hospital, he responded with silence. He didn't have the means for full countermeasures, yet. He wasn't sure what allies he had left, if any. He thought he had some. Kemmerlin was solid, sticking close and mounting guard, the loyal hound.

Where there was one good soldier, there would be more. There were still men of principle out there, Chapel believed. He had to, or he would despair for his country, and he wasn't ready to do that. So he would fight back. Not for himself. For his country. Always for his country.

For now, then, silence. He threw no morsels to the slavering packs of the press. He let them speculate, but gave them none of his own rope with which to hang him. He concentrated on healing. He made progress, but not as far as the outside world was concerned. The odd time that cameras surged past Kemmerlin, Chapel submerged his dignity and wrapped himself in his wounds. He didn't hide from the lenses. He turned to them. He let them and their audience feast on the madness of purple and smash that was his face, the wreck of angles that were his limbs. He was a Picasso collage of wound and white sheets, a corpse that didn't have the decency to seek its final rest. The image worked for him. For every three stories and pundits and editorials that called him a criminal (on the left) or incompetent (on the right), there was one that hesitated, and each one of those used the phrase *kicking a man while he's down*. They used the phrase *unable to defend himself.* And so the calls for his dismissal were qualified by *if this* and *if that* and *in the fullness of time* and *in due course*.

When the whole truth comes out.

Yes, and pigs would escort Air Force One, instead of being transported by it.

He nursed his silence and worked his injuries. He healed. He rested. He embraced the agonies of physio, loving the burn that would give him power. Movement gradually returned. So did the ability to think coherently for more than half an hour at a time. He used these gifts to do deep searches through papers, through the TV channels, through the Internet. He was looking for cracks to exploit, levers to pull, the perfect little unravelling thread to yank. He didn't work the phone yet. He didn't want his feelers to attract unwanted attention.

And through it all, he reminded himself that his position was not the worst it might be. He only had two principle antagonists: Sam Reed, and CIA Director Jim Korda. Stepan Sherbina was dead. So was that woman. These were good things.

Two other factors called his attention. One was a wild card. The other had the smell of opportunity, though he didn't know how to shape it yet. The first was getting a fair bit of face time on TV, and went by the name of Senator Daniel Hallam. The second factor was a small story buried on the BBC website. Chapel read it over and over, thought about it as he fell asleep at night, and woke up with it at dawn. He wondered why it excited him so, and why he wished he could make it down to Caracas.

The target was in a hospital, again. Surrounded by civilians, again. Blaylock eyed the facade of the building, took in just how much glass there was, and knew she was stymied. Again. She could storm Kornukopia's fortress, but she could not bring her violence into this place. She thought about the ripple effect of devastation that accompanied any act of war, pictured the maternity ward, and shuddered. She was relieved the decision was so easy to make. She turned her back on the hospital, gave Chapel his safety, and walked down Twenty-third Street to the bench where Flanagan sat. "I can't," she told him.

"That's too bad," Flanagan said. "He's weak." He gestured

at a newspaper box. Chapel and Kornukopia were still above-the-fold news, and showed no sign of dropping from the top of the hit parade. "At this rate, Reed will finish him off before you do."

"Reed won't kill him." Career immolation was not justice. That was simply part of the dance. Blaylock gazed into the middle distance, seeing strategy. "Just as well I can't get at Chapel for now."

"Why?" Flanagan stared at her with concern, as if he suspected mercy.

"Taking Chapel out now would make life too easy for the president. I don't want that, either."

"So what do we do, then?"

Blaylock went over to the newspaper box. "More intel collection. I need to find levers on them both." She dropped some coins and fished out a *Post*.

"And me?"

Blaylock looked back at him. "Have you thought this through, Mike? You're sure you want in? You know what helping me will mean?"

"I do."

"Think you're up to this?"

He smiled, and his face was unlined by doubt.

Blaylock felt gratitude and unease. She let gratitude win. "All right. For now, I want to know what's happening in New York. Check your place. Let me know what you find. If you think it's safe, go back to InSec. The Agency had interests there before Sherbina took over. So here's the question: who's minding the store now?"

Blaylock hit an Internet café. She did some preliminary research. She wanted some sense of where the actions she had in mind would lead. She looked up the United States' laws of succession.

Sam Reed decided to meet Jim Korda in the Oval Office. He doubted the aura of the room would do much to cow Korda, but he liked the feeling of gravitas it gave him. He would have home turf advantage. The king spook was due now, but at this moment, Theodore Ferryman was on Reed's case. The chief political strategist was a hard man to keep happy. That was why he was so good.

"All I'm saying," Ferryman repeated for the fifth time, "is that the announcement would be a good diversion from the Sherbina flap." Ferryman was in his late fifties. His hair, blond once upon a long and innocent time ago, was a receding, wispy grey. He was soft-looking, the bespectacled incarnation of colourless civil service. His suits were conservative, and still had more character than his round, fleshy, middle-aged-baby face. He disappeared in a crowded room. He was one with the faceless and the shadows. That was where he did his best damage.

"A diversion is exactly what it would look like," Reed answered. "Fuel to the fire, that's all it would be. Anyway, the flap is close to being under control."

Ferryman frowned and pursed his lips, the image of angry constipation. "I'm not so sure. Lawrence Dunn is still flapping his mouth to anyone who will listen. He implicates you pretty directly."

"You and Charlotte did a great job of making it look like he was duped. That was a gorgeous move, not actually attacking him. Made me look very, very clean."

"I just don't think that was enough. Too many people are still listening."

"None who matter. Look, Teddy, get it straight. I am *not* appointing a vice-president. Especially this close to an election."

"Why not? Never mind the WTO mess for a moment. Given everything that's happened over the last couple of years, can't you see how reassuring it would be for the public to have that hole in the succession plugged?"

"Of course I can. That's why I won't."

Ferryman blinked. His mouth fish-gaped. His spin instincts were flummoxed.

"I'll spell it out for you," Reed said. "The gap is a psychological plus for me. Nobody consciously thinks through the order of succession beyond the veep. So you're right. Having one would make everyone feel better. Safer. Stability would be assured." He paused, pleased with his strategy. "But without one, I'm it. I'm the ball game. We are living in a Time of Crisis." He grinned. "The country needs to unite behind its president. The country needs to *protect* its president." He leaned back, folded his arms. "You follow?"

Ferryman nodded, his lips unpursing into a tight smile. That was his version of wild enthusiasm. "I follow."

"Good." Reed checked his watch. "Now I need to deal with Korda."

Ferryman let himself out. Reed kept Korda waiting another five minutes before he called to have the man shown in. If Korda was ticked by the wait, he didn't show it. He was a beaming

17

cherub, almost twice the size of Ferryman and three times as confident. He didn't wait to be asked to sit. He plumped himself down in the chair opposite the desk. He folded his hands over his belly and twinkled at Reed. "Sam," he said.

"Jim. Thanks for coming by. I appreciate your making the time to see me."

"Of course you do." Korda twitched a little finger, flicking away the niceties. "We've had our differences," he went on. He spoke slowly, drenching each syllable in understatement and sarcasm. He was talking with a young, stupid child. Reed felt himself bristle, fought down the instinct to rise to the bait. "I thought," Korda continued, "what with the way circumstances have evolved, we might … oh, I don't know … iron things out." He winked. He actually winked.

"I'm sure I don't understand what you're—"

Korda shook his head. Sadly. Gently. "Sam, Sam, Sam. You don't, I mean, you just *don't*, bullshit a bullshitter. Especially not this one."

"Tell me what you want." Reed tried to freeze his tone, but he knew anger showed, and impatience. He hoped worry didn't come through, too.

"What any man wants. Job security. A nice pension when he retires. The respect of his peers." Korda chuckled, amused by his own joke. He gave Reed the cheery look of a player holding five aces and happy to broadcast his hand. "Look," he said, "I don't see why we can't work together."

"I do."

"And why is that?"

"You've asked me, so I'll tell you. I can't respect a man who doesn't see the world except through a filter of greed. You don't have your job because you're qualified for it. You have it because my predecessor was a friend of yours. And you don't want your job because of the good you think you can do for our country. You want it because of the good you know you can do for yourself."

If Korda was offended, he didn't show it. Instead, he eyed Reed with genuine curiosity. "That's quite rich, coming from you," he probed.

"Every action I've taken while in this office has been to help America." Pure truth.

"Really." Korda dragged the word out, turned it into an expression of supreme skepticism and contempt.

"I didn't say all my decisions were equally successful." Or legal, for that matter. Many people died, yes. Plenty who wouldn't be missed, perhaps a few that were unfortunate bystanders. He would do it all again if he had to. Hard decisions came with the job, as did the acceptance of hard facts. Facts such as other people paying for his decisions with their lives. Too bad. The way of the world was not his fault.

"So tell me this," Korda said. "Joe Chapel is the biggest true believer born. He's family. And you're hanging him out to dry."

Reed sighed. "Not an easy decision, but the right one."

"He's a necessary sacrifice," Korda suggested.

Reed hesitated, not liking the corner he felt himself being backed into. But he nodded.

"The loss of one good man," Korda said, clearly enjoying his extrapolation, "being balanced by the greater good you'll be able to accomplish by staying in office. The country, after all, needs you. Especially now."

Reed had just used almost the same words with Ferry-man. And he had meant them, even if they were the weapons of political hardball. He winced as Korda threw them back at him, emptying them of all conviction. "That's right," he said, and he was firm, trying to restore some dignity to the thought.

Korda cocked his head. "My God, I think you really do believe that." He shrugged. "Whatever. I'll say again that I think we can still work together. Productively. For both of us. Sorry, for me and for the country." He smirked.

Reed let the silence stretch to what he hoped was an uncomfortable length before he answered. When he spoke, he held his voice to a monotone barely above a whisper. It was the sound of venom, and it had always taken septic chunks out of his opponents. "Everything I know about you, and everything you have said here today, tells me to demand your resignation, written and signed before you leave this office."

"You'd like that, wouldn't you?"

"Yes. I think I would."

"Well, you can't have it. I'm in this job for as long as I want it."

"Those are brave words."

"Hardly. I'm the man who knows where the bodies are buried. I'm the man who has Dean Garnett's files."

Reed's pulse dropped to zero. "His files," he repeated. His lips were numb. Garnett had been his man twice over. He'd been Reed's insurance in the CIA, sticking close to straight-arrow untouchable Joe Chapel, and keeping the collaboration with Stepan Sherbina on track. More damaging yet, he'd been Reed's appointee to the Dispute Settlement Board of the

World Trade Organization. The idea had been that Garnett, along with Lawrence Dunn, the blackmailed left-wing economist, and Sherbina's right hand, Yevgeny Nevzlin, was going to make sure the WTO danced to the tune Reed and Sherbina piped. What Reed hadn't known was that, if Garnett had been his man twice, he was Sherbina's boy three times. None of that mattered, now. Garnett was dead, throat ripped out in a Geneva apartment washroom. Nevzlin and Sherbina were dead. Lawrence Dunn was alive, shouting the tale of the plan to suborn the WTO. Overwhelming counter-spin had held the damage to a minimum, so far. But if Garnett had kept files…

"They're very complete," Korda went on. "They'd have to be, just so he could keep his double-crosses straight. And a man with his experience would know a thing or two about covering his ass. Especially if he's dealing with such loyal employers." Korda showed his teeth, pleased with himself. "To be honest, I don't know what to do with the files myself. But I bet the media would. And Chapel, for that matter."

He knows how to dance, Reed thought. Korda might have been an incompetent intelligence director, but he danced like Gene Kelly. "What do you want?" Reed asked, aware that he was showing weakness, but was too fatigued now to care.

"To help you. That's all. I really don't want to fight with you, Sam. There's no reason why we should. After all, we have some shared interests."

"Such as?"

"Such as Joe Chapel. He is a bit of problem, isn't he?"

"I wouldn't say that. I think we have that situation well in hand."

"That's only because he hasn't started to fight back. He

knows at least as much as Dean did, and I don't think he likes you very much anymore, Mr. President."

"I already explained that sometimes, hard deci—"

"I thought we were past the bullshitting," Korda interrupted. "Listen. Joe would as soon shoot me as look at me. Do you see what I mean about having something in common?"

After a moment, Reed nodded, slowly.

"I *know* we can help each other," Korda said, and he wasn't joking now.

Yes, Reed thought. Maybe we can.

Daniel Hallam, senior senator for Illinois and president pro tempore of the Senate, said, "That's a hard question."

"Was it? I think it's a rather obvious one, given some of your recent statements."

Hallam returned the reporter's gaze. Her look was neutral, but the neutrality seemed like a mask, as if she were barely holding a weapon in check. Formidable, he thought. Striking, too, though she had clearly been through some kind of hell, to judge by the traces of scars on her face. Former freelance war correspondent, he guessed, who had gone a few too many extra miles for her story. What was her name again? There was that memory of his again, a sieve when it came to names. At least he knew that wasn't the curse of his seven decades. He'd always been awful at remembering people, and that had been his biggest handicap in his political career. "Ms. Baker," he began, thinking he had the name.

"Baylor," she corrected.

"I'm sorry. Ms. Baylor. I am on record as saying that I believe that the administration's line on the tragedies in Davos and

Geneva are too pat. I find the notion that this is all the doing of a deputy director of the CIA who has gone off the reservation, or is criminally incompetent, or both, hard to swallow."

"So you think Joe Chapel is the scapegoat."

"I think more answers need to be demanded."

The woman smiled. Her eyes didn't. Their coldness made Hallam uncomfortable. "You're being cautious, Senator."

Cautious, the political slur, the euphemism for *cowardly*, for *evasive*. The tag of a politician, the one Hallam had never wanted to wear, and intensely disliked every time he was forced to do so. That wasn't why he had come to Washington, carried in on the wave of '60s idealism and rebellion. He'd been in his thirties—young for a politician, not quite beyond the pale for the marching youth. It had taken a recklessness born of ambition and belief to think he could be elected. It had taken a careful, cool, and pragmatic head to make sure he *was* elected. The dreams had been eroded by realism before the first ballot had been counted. But he had never given up on the principles. Not completely. By Washington standards, he knew he was borderline revolutionary. "I am being precise," he said, irritated. "I am not about to make accusations without solid evidence."

"That's a rarity in this town. You'll excuse me if I'm skeptical."

"That's your right."

Now there was a hint of amusement in the eyes, cold light twinkling in the darkness. "You're angry."

"I apologize. I react that way when I feel I'm being called a liar."

"Then I apologize also. To return to my question, though—"

Hallam cut her off. "It is one thing to doubt a story, and to ask for better answers. To go from there to a call for impeachment is quite a leap."

"But you said the question was difficult."

"I don't rule anything out. These are early days."

"You don't trust the president."

"I don't. But that's hardly a secret. We're not in the same party, after all." Hallam's team had a hairbreadth's control of the Senate and, by virtue of being the most senior member of the majority, that meant Hallam was president pro tem. The House, though, belonged to Reed, by the same zero margin. The Supreme Court, stacked by predecessors, was more securely owned by Reed. The struggle was uphill and dispiriting. Having recaptured the Senate was a victory, but an accidental one. It hadn't happened at an election. A moderate from Reed's party had been revolted by the Ember Lake disaster, when the leaders of the G8 gang, along with a corrupt Multilateral Agreement on Investment, had been incinerated. He had defected, taking the balance with him.

Baylor looked at her notepad, "And what are your feelings about Representative Pratella?"

"The Speaker of the House?" Hallam fumbled, braying the obvious as he tried to catch up. The woman's tone was innocent, but the question was such a non sequitur that his threat antennae screamed a warning. He knew very well what his feelings were for Patrick Pratella, "Pee-Pee" to his enemies and to more than a few who were obliged to call themselves his friends. Hallam killed the urge to vent and played for time. "I'm afraid I don't understand what that has to do with anything."

"Would he make a good president?"

"*What?*" The idea was grotesque.

Baylor smiled again—a third time, and now the smile was a sweet lie. "In the absence of a VP, he is next in the order of succession."

Hallam shook his head. "We're a long way from even openly calling for impeachment. The process takes a long time. I really don't see why my opinion on such an unlikely hypothetical matters at all."

The smile was still there, and now the eyes were smiling too, but were filled with a knowledge that chilled Hallam and made him squirm. "These are very uncertain times, Senator. Anything can happen."

2

nSec, decapitated twice, stumbled and flailed. It was in limbo.
It needed a saviour.

Chapel knew InSec needed a saviour. He also knew he might
need one, too. How long would he have the Agency as a base
of operations? Not long, in the dreams of Korda and Reed. ·
He thought about InSec's fire and manpower. Its collected
mercenary force and security service could run a small country.
It had serious potential. And he had made himself known there
in the wake of the Ember Lake fire, when the CIA had brought
InSec's rogue dog to heel. Time it performed some tricks.
Time it heard its master's voice. These were his thoughts as he
picked up the phone.

Viktor Luzhkov hadn't realized that he was looking for
redemption until he encountered its possibility. When he saw
that hope, and experienced the epiphany, he also knew that the
prior lack of self-knowledge hadn't been simple ignorance. It

had been a necessary defence mechanism. When redemption was impossible, it was crucial not to look for it. Redemption had been thin on the ground in Chechnya.

Still, the search for redemption, or something very like it, had been behind enlisting in the armed forces in the first place. Not redemption for himself, not at this stage. Rather, redemption for the motherland, or some such other idealistic notion reserved for the young and the naive. He came by his romanticism honestly. His father was a frustrated retired major, too young to have fought in the Great Patriotic War, too old to see action in Afghanistan, dismayed to see his beloved Army defeated in a specious cause. His mother was a committed, never-say-die Marxist. She was born under Stalin, whom she despised with the memory of blighted youth, and pined for Lenin, whom she worshipped with the special nostalgia reserved for utopias not experienced, and therefore perfect. She held unwavering faith in the unfulfilled promise of the Revolution, a promise she saw the Soviet Union betraying with every passing day. Between his parents, there was a perfect union of thwarted dreams, as grand as they were broken. Their grandeur was seductive. Flush with the everything-possible glow of early adulthood, a young Viktor enlisted, his gesture part of a half-articulated goal to work for the fulfillment of both his parents' hopes. He would be what his father dreamed the Army should be again. He would work within the system to transform it in his mother's vision.

At the time, he didn't understand why they didn't seem happy when he donned his uniform. A year later, they were killed by a patch of black ice, so he didn't have to see their reactions when his excellence and quick rise brought him to the attention of the Spetznaz. He did well there, too, even as he felt his illusions taking the same pickaxe blows his parents' had. But the action, he discovered, was an addiction, and he couldn't open enough veins for its high.

Then came Chechnya, and there were no more illusions. He understood his parents completely, and was relieved, for their sakes, that they were dead. The muck piled high, and on the verge of drowning, he left. Anything was better than following these orders. Even the private sector.

And so he came to know Kornukopia. And then, in the death throes of the Kornukopia One corporate headquarters, he saw redemption, and she was explosive.

Evangelized, he looked for friends.

Luzhkov found Peter Vandelaare in Sierra Leone. He was in his usual Freetown bar. It was a nameless, ramshackle exercise in corrugated tin. The merc sat in the back, boots up on a burn-scarred table, nursing a beer and staring absently at the thirteen-inch TV that sat on the countertop. Snow danced over a soccer game. Vandelaare was a wiry blond, his skin weathered by sun and war into taut leather and tendons. He saluted with his beer as Luzhkov approached. "There's the man himself," he said.

Luzhkov sat down opposite Vandelaare and leaned his chair against the wall. "You look gainfully employed," he said.

Vandelaare snorted. "Hardly. But from what I hear, the man himself has been busy. I say, now, hasn't he? His phone call made me think so. I'm sure he has tales to tell. How are the wounds?"

"Healing." And yes, he had tales. Tales of the apocalypse come to visit Stepan Sherbina's fortress in Geneva, of

28

everything going south, and of being shot in the side by a teammate he had then drilled in the head. But most of all, he had tales of a woman. She hadn't brought the apocalypse to Kornukopia One. She *was* the apocalypse. "The man has been busy," he agreed, "but now he's unemployed, too."

"Sad times," Vandelaare sighed. "No stability anymore."

Luzhkov nodded. When Arthur Pembroke had fused the various mercenary outfits into the conglomerate that was Integrated Security, the future had seemed bright from an economic, if not ethical, standpoint. When Kornukopia had swallowed InSec, the future had become blinding. Luzhkov had seen good money in a way he hadn't once in his years in the armed forces. The money was the crutch he used, to his shame, to keep going when the jobs were little better than what he'd been called on to do and witness in Chechnya. Seeing Sherbina and his dreams brought low had been a singular pleasure. "I want to tell you a story," he said, and he spoke about the woman.

When he was done, Vandelaare asked, "Where's the man going with this?" His eyes were glinting with interest and the potential for excitement.

"I think the man's going to see her." Luzhkov said.

"To ask for a job?"

"Yes."

Vandelaare did the slow burn. His eyes were growing brighter, though. Luzhkov thought, I really see excitement there, now. Yes, I do. "She sounds like a solo operator," the South African said.

"Solo can be lonely. She might be more open to the idea than you think."

More of the burn. Vandelaare lit a new cigarette, inhaled, held. He leaned back and exhaled. "I'm interested. Why is the man thinking of doing this? He doesn't even know if there's money involved. Hell, he doesn't even know if the lady is sane."

"Are we?"

Big laugh. "I should hope the hell not."

"The man's sick of the scum, Peter. I'm sick of being dirty. You should have been there. She fought a good fight. When was the last time we did that?"

"A long time." Vandelaare's smile faded. "We being honest? Good, we are. It's been nice not to be receiving any orders from head office lately. They always stink worse than my shit, and I don't eat as my mother would like."

"How are your contacts?" Luzhkov asked.

Vandelaare's smile was back, big and broad. "What are you thinking?" he said, but it was clear he already knew.

Home again, home again, jiggety-jig.

Flanagan walked toward his building on Albany. He wasn't feeling quite so cocky and take-on-the-world now that he wasn't with Blaylock. But the ice-blood terror that had been the sum total of his being for so long was gone. His heartbeat was fast, and there was the jazz of an adrenaline buzz, but he was thinking. He was in control. He could do this thing. He had his very own body count now, and that moved him up the food chain. A personal vow: he would never be on the defensive again.

He didn't try to approach his home by stealth. Anybody who was watching would be professional, and would see him no matter what he did. So he brazened it out. Strolled right up. Cocked a big smile and a wave at Bernie Walmsley. The last time he had seen the doorman, Flanagan had been on the run, dead CIA muscle all over his apartment. "Mr. Flanagan," Walmsley said. "Good to see you. Been on holiday?" No hint of concern or surprise. And Walmsley was a man who had lost every hand of poker he'd ever played. If he looked like the day was normal, then it was.

"A working one, Bernie," Flanagan answered. He took the elevator to his apartment, braced himself for the stink, and let himself in.

He had half-expected what he found: nothing. No mess, no bodies, no blood on the carpet or on the walls, no shotgun damage to the plaster. The suite was cleaner than he had ever seen it. Someone had wiped out all traces of the embarrassment, and there was no one waiting to make him pay. How many bugs are here? he wondered. Best behaviour here from now on. He made some Puritan promises.

Shower, change of clothes. Next stop, the office, five minutes away. InSec had lost two masters. Anybody filling the vacuum yet? Business as usual at the world's biggest arms dealer when he walked in. Whether this was stability or inertia, he couldn't tell. No challenge from security when he arrived, and no funny looks as he made his way to the fortieth floor. All good. He reached his office and sorted through the backlog of memos and e-mails. One from yesterday stood out. It was a message sent out by Nick Brentlinger of the board of directors to all heads of departments, asking for a moment at their convenience. Time for Flanagan to put on his head-of-shipping hat, be the team player. He called Brentlinger. The director asked him to come by.

The top floor of the InSec building was the realm of the Gods, but the throne of heaven was vacant. Pembroke's old office, which took up half the acreage, was empty. The last time any of the directors had jockeyed for the top job, Sherbina and Kornukopia had stepped in and culled the herd. Flanagan imagined uncharacteristic caution reigning in the ambitions of demigods. Brentlinger's office was three doors down from the CEO's pad. Brentlinger's space was big, but spartan. Flanagan had seen the inside of Pat Forbes' office once, before he was whacked, and the Texan had done his walls up with an orgy of antlers and pictures of him pressing flesh with politicians. Brentlinger was an ascetic Mormon, at least on paper. The walls of his office were blank. His desk was small, and had zero intimidation factor. His suits were funeral-crisp, and he was as thin as hope. "Won't you sit down," he said when his secretary showed Flanagan in.

Flanagan sat. "What's up?"

Brentlinger steepled his fingers. "I'm sure it's no secret that these have been difficult times for the company."

"True." *And for me*, Flanagan added. He wondered how much Brentlinger knew about him. He wondered if he knew how much Flanagan wanted to burn InSec to the ground.

"I'm hoping," Brentlinger said, "that we can avoid the turmoil of the last transitional period, and move on to a more stable regime."

"Agreed." *He doesn't know a thing about me. He wants something, that's what's going on.*

"I think the best route to stability is through unity. Don't you?"

"Absolutely." *So that's what this was about. Brentlinger*

was jockeying for the top spot, and he wanted the department heads behind him.

The director smiled. "Thanks, Mike. This is one of those times when we really need to pull together as a team."

Pink Floyd's "Have a Cigar" started playing in Flanagan's mind. He kept a straight face. "No problem, Nick." Brentlinger's eyes flickered, but Flanagan put all the warmth of lies into his smile, and he saw the other man dismiss the sarcasm as an illusion.

Weeks of attacks, and not a single opening for a counterattack. Weeks on his back, plastered into immobility, playing possum but feeling like a sitting duck. But he was out, now. Months of physio in his future, and a cane in his hand for the rest of his life, but Chapel was released. He hobbled from the hospital entrance to a waiting taxi. Took goddamn forever, but he was vertical again. That counted for something. Time to work now on landing some of his own blows.

First thing: a bit of intel. Get a sitrep on Caracas.

Blaylock followed him home. She drove a Corolla with hot licence plates she'd picked up for cash in New Jersey. Around her, the seat of Empire made ready for bed. Chapel lived in a row house in Foggy Bottom. She'd already paid the place a visit. She watched him make his way from the cab to his door like an arthritic crab, and wished she had done that damage instead of Sherbina. (*You shouldn't have let him live, Stepan. I shouldn't have, either.*) Chapel unlocked his door, stepped inside, switched on a light. A second later, all of Blaylock's listening devices went dead. She wasn't surprised. She'd expected Chapel to have a pretty secure sanctum, but she'd taken the stab in the dark anyway. Keeping tabs on the man was going to be difficult. That didn't matter. They were going down. Both of them. She was going to see Joe Chapel and Sam Reed to their funeral pyres. The trick was means. And the trick was consequences.

Blaylock's interview with Daniel Hallam had been interesting, but not conclusive. The man seemed honest and genuine enough, as far as it went, but that could only be so far. He was still a politician. He might be useful. He might be good for information. He might also be good to feed information to. He went into her file as a potential asset. His reaction to her question about Patrick Pratella had been instructive. His answer had been cautious, diplomatic. His expression, for just a second, had been naked disgust. Remember this, she told herself. If Reed goes, Pratella ascends the throne. She'd checked into the Speaker's record. Bleak stuff. Perpetual re-election despite a career that gave pandering a bad name.

One mission at a time, she told herself. Don't lose focus. Right now, it was time to see if she could make another train jump its rails.

He would give them nothing but his contempt. That was all they deserved.

General Jorge Quintero held his face rigid as his posture. He sat beside his lawyer, but did not address him. He watched the prosecutor and the judge with half-lidded eyes. He hoped they felt his disdain. The prosecutor was saying something. Quintero paid no attention. The man had nothing worthwhile to say. This was a jumped-up monkey court. It meant nothing. Any court that thought it could sit in judgment on him was by definition a farce.

Colonel Ernesto Maldonado was in the witness box. He didn't appear to be listening, either. Quintero caught his eye. Maldonado gave him the smallest of nods. Respect.

"I find it odd that you are protecting a man who is the reason you are facing a prison sentence yourself," the prosecutor, sounding frustated, said to Maldonado.

"I have nothing to say against my general," Maldonado replied. His voice was the sound of calm, of certainty, and of discipline. Lost values, Quintero thought. Maldonado was a good man.

Not that his silence mattered. The formality of a trial was pointless. There was too much evidence against Quintero. And when the prosecutor and his jackals were done with his lion's corpse, they would go after the smaller prey like Maldonado. Quintero's attorney, recognizing a lost cause, had bowed to his demands and wasn't mounting a defence based on innocence. Quintero had done what the prosecutor claimed. He was proud of his actions. So the defence was arguing for their necessity. They would lose, but they would lose with honour. Quintero was not going to hide. He was not going to pretend he was ashamed of how he had tried to save his country from itself.

The ingratitude galled him almost as much as the stupidity. It shouldn't even take a brain to see that the president was an unreconstructed Communist and that his policies were going to destroy Venezuela long before the next election. There wasn't time to wait. The man had to be dislodged now. For a shining forty-eight hours, Quintero had seen his operation succced. The conservative opposition had rallied to his side. So did the major corporations. The UN had quivered ineffectually, but the US had made all the right noises. The Americans were just as glad to see the back of that lunatic. And then everything had collapsed. Quintero hadn't managed to secure the media fast enough. That was the one thing he would admit to having done wrong. He had made a stupid assumption, had thought any Venezuelan with an ounce of responsibility would have seen that the coup was salvation, not a threat. But the main TV networks gave the president his airtime, and he had summoned his army of malcontents to the streets. The visuals were spectacular. The marchers looked like the will of the people made flesh. Bullshit, Quintero thought. Bullshit. But the tide turned. The churches spoke against him. The momentum slipped, and the army did not follow him. That was the worst betrayal, the one that hurt more than the idea that the public might not have been for him. Ungrateful bastards. To the man.

The Americans, too. Fair-weather friends of the worst kind. The right noises in retrospect looked like cautious ass-covering. They didn't lift a finger to help. If they had sneezed the right way, they would have saved him and his country. After all the heavy lifting he had done for them, they were hanging him out to dry. This trial, he had learned, wasn't going to be his last. His lawyer had given him the bad news yesterday. Once the prosecution for the coup was over, and he was sentenced, he was in for more. Once he was down, once he was deprived of influence and couldn't fight back, they were going to bring up the past.

Bastards. *Bastards*.

Part of the past was his involvement in the 2002 coup against Chavez. He hadn't led it, and when it went south, he'd been able to insulate himself against the most damning of the direct evidence. His career had survived, but barely. Striking out twice meant that the old sins were going to come back, and circumstantial evidence would be good enough this time around. And then there was the deeper past, and here was where the American betrayal was doing the most damage. The deeper past was the '80s, the Reagan dirty wars, and the School of the Americas.

It wasn't called the SOA anymore. Now it was the Western Hemisphere Institute for Security Cooperation. It was still based in Fort Benning, Georgia, though, and it still did the same good work. Its official line was that it was all about "promoting democracy, human rights and civilian control of government." In fact, like any good school, it was all about its graduates and their success in the larger world. The larger world, for the SOA, was Latin America. Success meant the support of American interests. Support of those interests meant dealing with those who would oppose them. Like governments who would nationalize industries or strike off from acceptable policy paths. Like inconvenient liberation theologians. Like students. Sometimes like entire villages.

Counterinsurgency. Sabotage. Torture. Death squads. The SOA had the complete curriculum. It took the education of its graduates seriously. Quintero had heard the cries and the protests often enough to know them by heart. *Finishing school for dictators* was the most common refrain. He hadn't worried about the name-calling. He had known a good thing when he saw it. The training had been first-rate. He had put it to good use, and not just in Venezuela. He'd lent a hand in Guatemala, El Salvador and Nicaragua, too. Were his hands dirty? Of course they were. Would people have preferred a Communist alternative? Ridiculous. Did the work pay well? And if it did? Compensation for the hard work. Only his due.

All gone to smash now. Bastards. *Bastards.*

Prosecution and the witnesses looking at him like a virus under glass. The hell did they know about doing the right thing? About *belief*? Belief had been piped in with the tap water at the SOA. He had never acted except with absolute conviction. One of the central tenets of that belief had been the unwavering backing of the Americans. What was in their interest was in the interest of all the Americas. So where were they now? Where were they when it was time to walk the walk, when the loyal and the faithful were being taken to task for the necessary dirty work? The Americans were walking away, that's where they were, waving Pontius Pilate hands in the air, dripping with innocence. Don't ask, don't tell, don't want to know. Easy.

No, Quintero though. No. It will not be that easy. It will not.

Rome is burning, Chapel thought. Stop fiddling.

He'd thought Sam Reed was what his country needed. He could remember the visceral relief he'd felt when Reed stepped up from VP to take the place of the incinerated Walter Campbell. Finally, a leader instead of a politician. Campbell had been born for the main chance and couldn't see anything else. Reed was a true believer. That's what Chapel had thought. And maybe there was some belief behind that deal with Sherbina, but the result was more damage and more of the same same same Washington game. Fiasco all round, flames and death and embarrassment. American prestige curb-stomped. And meanwhile, look at this. Just look at this. Jorge Quintero going down in Caracas. What kind of justice was that? The whole of Latin America had shifted left. All the good work of the '80s undone, and was anyone paying attention?

He was.

Quintero felt eyes on the back of his neck. He ignored the gaze at first, but it was insistent. He gave in and turned around in his chair. Sitting in the audience was Alejandro Olano. He was another good man, but unlike Maldonado, the major was far enough down the chain of command to have escaped the dragnet that had swept up the leaders of the coup. Olano gave him an almost imperceptible nod. Quintero responded in kind. He turned back to face the puppet prosecutor and sellout judge. A man still has friends, he thought. He held the smile inside.

He was paying attention to burning Rome, and seeing in the flames the possibility of salvation. Not just for himself, but for his country. There would be bitter medicine to swallow, and a painful purging. But the renewed strength of purpose would be worth the price. Not to mention the punishment America's betrayers would suffer.

Chapel stood up from his desk and strolled to his living room. Nothing much there since the divorce, but he had kept the drinks cabinet. He poured himself a large scotch, swallowed the smoky burn and made himself think the possibility through again, weigh the costs again. He thought about his resources. What friends he still had. What other friends he might acquire. Then he considered the costs of not acting. The balance sheet result was obvious. Still, he stood by his front window, watched the street, and sipped the rest of his drink, giving himself time to see the flaws and change his mind. He didn't. The risks were high, but could be minimized if he had control of InSec. The prize was higher still, the perfect capstone of his life and career. He raised the last of his drink in a toast, and with a final swallow, he was committed.

He would be the saviour.

3

It was shortly before 0900 hours. There was the promise of spring glory in the air, and Blaylock stood outside a nondescript walk-up on Fourth Street, in the southwest of the city, holding her bag of tricks, waiting for her chance to kill the president. A young man stepped out of the building, briefcase in hand. He had the beaten look of a low-level civil servant who saw nothing ahead in his life but arid decades of cog-dom. He didn't even blink as she caught the door before it shut and locked behind him. She stepped inside and began to mount the stairs.

She had begun her surveillance of Charlotte Taber and the State Department headquarters the day after arriving in Washington. She'd meant what she'd told Flanagan on the plane. Reed was going down, and she wouldn't be satisfied with impeachment. He had too much blood to answer for. Reed was going to die, and Chapel was going to be fingered for the hit. This was the way the world would work.

It had taken her a while to find the woman she wanted.

The State Department was housed in a long, five-storey exercise in bland government architecture on C Street. Blaylock hung around the parking lot and entrance at the beginning and end of each workday, blending with the drones swarming in and flowing out. She watched the drones carefully. By the end of the first week, she had identified a half-dozen women who were close to the right physical type. They were about her age, close in height and weight, colouring not too far off. She spent another week winnowing down her short list. The one who most resembled her she ruled out. The woman marched toward her workplace with purpose. Too much fire in her belly. She wouldn't be as suggestible as Blaylock needed. There was one she thought was promising, one who eyed the building with a glazed look of bored hatred, but when Blaylock followed her after work, she saw the drone shake off the dead weight of her career with one party crawl after another. No good. Too many people who would miss her. A third, who looked almost as harried, turned out to be a mother of five. Even worse.

The fourth was the magic. Her name was Cynthia Kawin. Her clothes looked harried even when she didn't. There were bad creases in her slacks, and her blouse looked like it had had a bad encounter with another colour in the washing machine. She wore her hair tied back, but there were plenty of loose strands that hovered around her head, a frazzled aura of static electricity. Her face was pinched, on perpetual guard from blows always expected and too often received. Blaylock felt sorry for her, and with her pity, she felt her optimism grow. On a Friday, Blaylock trailed her to her car, and saw her crouch over the steering wheel, weeping. Kawin went straight home, and barely stirred from her apartment that weekend. All this was good.

The clincher was Monday, when she showed up with a black eye.

Kawin hated her job, hated her life, and the world hated her right back. She was perfect.

Blaylock abandoned the other targets. Kawin lived on the top floor of the walk-up, and Blaylock set up shop on the roof, spending two nights lying prone, dangling a mini-mic and fiberscope just far enough over the balcony to peer into the living room. She heard a lot of shouting, just like the last time she had used this technique. But that had been in Ciudad del Este, and she had been spying on gangsters. Now she was just watching slime. The boyfriend was a power-suited oaf. He had the look of a former college jock living off a trust fund of perpetual entitlement. He saw himself as a player, and would drown out with roars or worse all evidence to the contrary. Blaylock hated him on sight. She was lucky that, on the nights she watched, all he did was yell. If he had hit his girlfriend again, Blaylock didn't think she would have had the restraint to stand by, and the operation would have been flushed but good.

On Wednesday, Blaylock hit a travel agent's. She booked a Carribean cruise and airfare, for one, departing on Monday, under Kawin's name, and paid for it in cash. Next stop was a print shop. Concocting a phony contest logo took half an hour. Writing the CONGRATULATIONS WINNER! letter took half that time. All she had to do was crib from *Reader's Digest* junk mail, sprinkling block capitals, exclamation marks, and tiny legalese. Then she FedExed the package, and the gamble was on. Would the boyfriend open the envelope first? Would Kawin tell him about her win? Blaylock's palms were slick when she took up her surveillance post that night.

More yelling, more tears, but not a word from either party about the Carribean. Blaylock saw good things heading her way, bad things looming for Sam Reed. In the deep-sleep time between Sunday night and Monday morning, Blaylock saw Kawin creep into the living room and hide a suitcase under the sofa. Congratulations, Blaylock told herself. You're a winner.

Now, Monday morning, the apartment would be empty. The boyfriend was at work, slaughtering old ladies or selling insurance to cows, or whatever it was he did. His girlfriend, did he but know it, was gone for two weeks. The building was clean, but not recent or high end, and though there was a deadbolt to overcome, the apartment door didn't meet flush with the jamb, and she was inside in under a minute.

Kawin might have been shacking up, but the suite was clearly hers, not his. Boyfriend must have his own pad, preserving his space while occupying Kawin's. Unicorns of porcelain and crystal pranced on end tables and the stereo cabinet. There was a painting on the wall facing the sofa. It was abstract, a layering of oils and sand. The colours were brilliant yellows and oranges, bursting from a core of many-shaded reds. There was energy there, a hope and a cry for freedom that Blaylock had seen nowhere else in the woman's life. It was far more true and vital than the sad kitsch of the unicorns. Enjoy your cruise, honey, Blaylock thought. And don't come back. She allowed herself the brief daydream that she had handed Kawin the key to her liberty. She didn't believe it, but the wish that Kawin would be collateral benefit, and not damage, made her feel better.

In the bedroom, she rooted through Kawin's closet and picked the plainest suit she could find. The clothes were a bit too big, but that was their look on Kawin, too. The shoes didn't fit at all, but Blaylock had bought a pair of her own that matched the sensible economy of Kawin's. She sat down at the makeup table and opened her bag. She pulled out a wig that was close enough to Kawin's brunette colour for government work. She tied it back, teased out individual strands, worked until she was just dishevelled enough. Then the makeup. After a week, Kawin's shiner was fading but still obvious, no matter how she tried to blend it away. Blaylock discoloured her eye. It took a while, but she wasn't in a rush. Kawin wasn't expected to show up at work. She started over several times, and it was almost noon when she was satisfied with the result. She stood in front of a full-length mirror and gauged the effect. From a distance, she would pass. None of Kawin's friends or co-workers would be fooled, but Blaylock was banking on not having to deal with them. She'd checked the directories. Kawin worked in the Bureau of Legislative Affairs, same building but another world from Public Diplomacy. Blaylock liked the black eye. It was a useful blemish. She knew how people would respond. They would look, then look away, anxious not to deal with what the bruise meant. It would also distract from her own faint webwork of scars.

She heard the metal grind and chunk of a key in the door. Here we go, she thought. Had she been hoping for this? She might have been. She very well might have been. She waited in the bedroom, drawing the blinds. She wasn't quiet about it. Footsteps in the living room paused. A call: "You home?"

"Yes," she said.

Silence. Her voice would be confusing him. She listened to him stomp his way to the bedroom. He stopped in the doorway and stared at her. "Who," he demanded. "The *fuck*. Are you?" His fists balled.

Blaylock looked at his hands, then held his gaze with hers. "You going to hit me?" she asked. She stepped toward him. "Are you? You like hurting? Makes you feel big and strong?" She was in his face now. "It's okay," she purred. "I like it, too."

The instinct was to cat-play with him. The urge was to make him suffer and whimper. She made herself stay on track and avoid the diversion. He swung. She let him do that much. She let him lean back to grab the space he needed to hand her a first-class roundhouse. But before his fist came forward, she struck with her palm, grounding herself and swivelling her entire body to power the blow. She collapsed his ribcage and punctured his heart. He dropped to his knees. There was a second where his eyes were wide with surprise and the knowledge of his death. Then he fell forward, and his violence was over and done.

Now she had a body to deal with. She thought about the mess for a minute, looking for a solution that wouldn't endanger her operation and still be humane for Kawin. She grabbed boyfriend under the arms and dragged him to the bathtub. Kawin's vacation was for two weeks, her alibi absolute. Worry about this later.

In the drawer of Kawin's bedside table, Blaylock found her ID tag. She hung it around her neck, and left for work.

When she reached the State Department building, she settled her face into a frown. She approached security, creasing her brow with permanent distress. As she flashed her ID at the guard, she gave him a pleading look. She saw emotional panic flicker over his face, turning it into stone, and he turned his gaze forcefully to the man behind her. She was sending out pariah vibes, and the social sea parted before her. Nobody wanted to know. They especially didn't want to catch her infection.

She made her way down endless corridors. They were the marble and fluorescent impersonality of bureaucracy made flesh. Humanity streamed through the building's veins, so many red blood cells of the nation-machine's heart. Blaylock picked up fragments of conversations as she travelled. Gossip was a virus, turf warfare generated competing antibodies, management descended as white corpuscles, and the entire system was self-contained, going through its motions with only tangential and hypothetical connections to the outside world. When she reached the realm of Public Diplomacy, the last vestigial connections with reality evaporated.

Along with Kawin's briefcase, she was carrying a gym bag with the clothes she would need later. She ducked into a women's washroom and locked herself into a cubicle. She checked the ceiling, saw what she'd hoped for. Another cubicle was occupied. While Blaylock waited for the woman to leave, she removed the equipment she wanted now from the bag and slipped it into a pants pocket. Sounds of running water, washing hands, heels clicking by, door opening and swinging shut. She was alone. She climbed onto the toilet and moved a ceiling tile out of the way. She tucked the bag up, then replaced the tile. She opened the briefcase, took out a sheaf of papers. She creased a few to dishevel the pile, make herself look that much more harried and unappealing. Then she hit the hallways again.

Blaylock located Taber's office. The door was open. Bored

secretary in the reception area, solitaire on her monitor. Blaylock held up the papers and grimaced. The secretary nodded in sympathy. "She in?" Blaylock asked. The secretary shook her head. Blaylock sighed with the weight of an unfair world.

The secretary granted her a brief glance of sympathy. "Can you leave those on her desk?"

Blaylock played pained reluctance. "I guess."

No second helping of sympathy. Solitaire started clicking again. Blaylock walked past and into Taber's private office. She took in the monitors, acknowledged the woman's skill as a warrior on her own turf, and set about causing damage. She pulled the bug out of her pocket. It took less than thirty seconds to attach it to the phone line. It was invisible in the tangle of cables that ran from the TVs. Blaylock checked out Taber's window. The view was of the parking lot. Perfect to set up her listening post. She had to be within three hundred yards of the bug to pick up its transmissions.

She made some noises with her papers, then left, grunting a "Bye" to the secretary, and grinning inside. Her work was well begun.

That night, Blaylock pulled up in front of a three-level Victorian semi-detached on Thirty-third Street. The lights were off. No one home yet. She screwed a silencer onto her SIG-Sauer P-228. She waited. Around two, a limo stopped in front of the house and dropped off a passenger. Blaylock pulled on a balaclava. The limo drove off. Blaylock left her car, crossed the street and stood at the bottom of the steps as Charlotte Taber, fumbly with drink, worked to unlock her front door. The latch clicked. Blaylock opened fire.

4

Sometimes, the work was fun.

Back at the job, while he still had it. Time to marshal the resources, man the defences, and put the wheels in motion. "General Quintero," Chapel said, "it's an honour to speak with you."

"Who is this?" Quintero growled.

Chapel didn't answer. "I thought I should touch base with some old friends, just to let them know that someone was thinking of them." He hoped Quintero would take the hint. Chapel's end was encrypted, his voice unrecognizable and untraceable. Quintero was speaking from prison. If he had a brain, and Chapel thought he did, he would know not to speak freely.

"Very kind," Quintero said. His growl calmer, less hostile.

"Actually, I was hoping to quote you for the benefit of our readers." Chapel made his tone so light, the lie was transparent. "They feel you've been unfairly treated."

"I like your readers." Amusement in the general's voice. He was playing along.

"They believe our country has a certain responsibility."

"It does."

"Do you feel you've been let down?"

"I have been betrayed."

Good man, Chapel thought. He glanced at the files on his desk. Quintero's psych profile, dug up from the archives, showing true. Good analyst, whoever put this together. "I'm sure our readers would agree," he said. "They would also like to know your opinion about some well-known individuals."

"Such as?"

"Jim Korda."

Silence for a moment. Then: "*Hijo de puta*. I don't care who is listening. No more games. That man is a coward. He knew all of the planning. And now he hides and lets true men be dishonoured."

"I'm sure our readers would agree," Chapel repeated, staying with the game.

"Then let them show it!" Quintero shouted.

"They would like to. They would like to make a contribution."

Another silence, this time more congenial. Chapel could hear Quintero thinking. "What kind?"

"They think you should be able to afford the best defence." Chapel waited to see if Quintero would read between the lines.

He did. He began to laugh.

"Thank you for your time," Chapel concluded, smooth gears running. "If our readers would like to learn more, is there anyone else we should speak to?" Give me a contact. Who isn't in jail.

"Alejandro Olano," Quintero said. "He gets around."

Perfect.

Sometimes, the work was a lot of fun.

Being alive was a terrific thing. Nick Brentlinger had never thought about existence in those terms. But lately, as the prize flew toward his grasp like a bride-tossed bouquet, he felt a new perspective coming on. Change was on the way, and he welcomed it. He knew his image: New England Mormon and bureaucratic mortician. The other directors treated him as such. So did his wife. He dealt with it. His cautious conservatism had kept him alive. When Arthur Pembroke had come in like the Sun King to bring the other arms dealers to heel under the InSec monopoly, he hadn't kicked. Result: a smooth transition, and a fine working relationship with the boss. Exit Pembroke, enter the Feds of every description. Brentlinger had co-operated, worn the sackcloth of contrition as InSec had been made to pay for the G8 wipeout. He'd done as he was told, but he tailored the extent of his helpfulness to the individual. His mode was triple-max damage control. If the inquisitor was a junior FBI agent looking to make bones, he cranked the politeness, but constricted the info-flow to a stone-squeezed trickle. If the authority seemed like someone with a nose for business and mutual favours, he made himself more useful. Take Joe Chapel. There was a man who knew the lay of the land. There he was, in the middle of a domestic investigation, Agency man treading all over Bureau turf. Brentlinger sensed he was only half interested in what had happened, but twice as keen on potential. Brentlinger cultivated him. He opened files. He also watched. He saw Chapel give special attention

51

to Flanagan, realized he was making Flanagan his boy in the corporation. Brentlinger had no objections. He just liked to know who was who. If Chapel could work with Flanagan, so could Bretlinger.

Then the Russians moved in. Scary times for the ornamental board of directors. Worse for those who thought Pembroke's death meant they could flex their own muscle at long last. Pat Forbes pulled the Texas cowboy thing, took his attitude all the way to an East River grave. What an idiot. Then things changed again. There were still Russians around, but they seemed just as rudderless as everyone else. They had lost their Pembroke.

Brentlinger didn't think of himself as an initiative man. He'd gone into arms dealing as a hereditary obligation, carrying on the family firm whose history had stretched from the Civil War to the InSec amalgamation. He knew how to manage, within reason, and he knew how to balance books. Most importantly, he knew how to survive. But that, he felt now, was what his life had been: the grey safety of survival, with no risks to either terrify or elate. But in the weeks following Sherbina's death, he'd felt a restlessness that terrified him, because he knew it was the temptation of initiative, and he was worried it might actually be ambition. Then Joe Chapel called and pushed him off the cliff.

There were very good arguments for not taking over InSec's top spot. The best one was the hundred-per-cent mortality rate of the previous CEOs. Brentlinger countered that fear with the knowledge that he was different. He didn't have grand plans beyond reaching the summit. He wasn't out to piss anyone off. And if his regime was a facade, with Chapel the real force, he didn't mind. In fact, he was pleased. He'd have the title, he'd have the smell of power, but none of the headaches.

That was his fantasy. It was a fantasy brought about by a chorus that had grown from irritant to torment over the course of the last couple of years: *If not now, when?* He was sixty-two. He was still healthy, give or take, but he could feel entropy setting in. Every day, there was one more minor thing that required conscious effort, or simply couldn't be done anymore. The lesson that triggered the chorus had come when he tried to run for a subway. He'd been out of breath immediately, and his heart had *hurt*. The shock that this was happening to his body was worse than the pain itself. Worse yet was the lesson. You're getting old, Nick. You're going to die. Anything left to accomplish?

Yes, now that you mention it. Something. Anything. What did he have to show for his life? Full mastery of second-best. A career that paid well but meant nothing, with the last twenty years spent as a corner-office lackey, an expensive figurehead bowing and scraping to visionary madmen. His marriage had lasted, say that for it, say nothing more for it. He and Miriam had no children, or much else other than neutral coexistence. He was leaving no footprint. But if InSec became his, even if his reign was more in the nature of a regency, he would have reached the top of this one thing. He would have a tangible sense of what power meant. The mere thought was rejuvenating.

There were details to sort out. Obstacles to flatten. He could think of at least three other members of the board who were preparing their own gambits. He wasn't worried. His competition was cut of the same cloth as he was. That was why they had survived, Pembroke eliminating all but the most loyal courtiers. Sherbina had put the fear of God into any pretenders by whacking Forbes. None of the boys was going to make a move without being very sure of his personal survival, never mind success. Brentlinger had a better hand. He had Chapel as an ally. He had Chapel *telling* him to take over. So the man was taking heat these days. He still had juice. He was still big-time Agency. Brentlinger figured a bit of weakness on the part of his patron was no bad thing, either. Chapel needed friends, too. The balance could not be more perfect. Time for Brentlinger to grab that brass ring.

If not now, when? The chorus wasn't the nag of guilt anymore. It was a goad. Grab life. Give it that good squeeze. Enjoy yourself, for Christ's sake. He hadn't even taken the action yet, only planted seeds and put small wheels in motion, and he was already feeling power's rejuvenation. With it came a recklessness that he had managed to bypass in adolescence. Fifty years late, here it was, and with it, temptation. Indulge, he thought. *If not now, when?* So he'd left the InSec building in late evening, and taken the subway uptown, coming up at Forty-second Street. The street was a long way from the utopia of sleaze he had given wide berth to in early adulthood, but it stubbornly resisted full regeneration. He strolled along, grin big and uncharacteristic. Two blocks off Times Square he saw it. The strip joint had a black window and a disappointingly vague name: *JoJo's*. But it had the purple neon of LIVE GIRLS in the window, and that was good enough. There were plenty of high-end clubs, he knew, but where was the fun in that? If he was going to sin, he should feel dirty. He was laughing as he stepped inside, laughed harder when he thought how much impunity he had. No one he knew would ever believe he was here. He could tell Miriam the truth and she would shrug it off as sarcasm. He grabbed a seat at the splash rail. He watched the girl with the dead eyes and felt gloriously alive.

Mary Bottomore looked unhappy when Flanagan returned from lunch. She'd been his receptionist since his days in lower management, and he'd brought her with him when he'd ascended to head of shipping. Her face was a precision guide to the way his day would turn. "There's a gentleman inside," she said. Her unhappiness was a mix, half outrage at the presumption, half fear. "I don't know him."

"Thank you," Flanagan said, bracing himself. An unknown. Not Chapel, then. Maybe a minion?

"I tried to stop him."

He smiled reassurance. "I'm sure you did," he told her. "It's just harder to look out for me these days."

"You're telling me," she muttered.

Flanagan stepped inside. The man was making himself at home, balancing his chair back against the wall, tapping martial rhythms on the armrest. At least he wasn't sitting at Flanagan's desk. He stood up and held out a hand, and Flanagan felt himself dwindle. The man wasn't any taller than Flanagan, but he filled the room. He reminded Flanagan of Blaylock. He had some scars, too, one a bright red just to the left of his nose. His face was lined with the weathering of hard knocks and deprivations. "Viktor Luzhkov," the man said. His handshake was firm, and he didn't blink at Flanagan's missing finger.

Russian, Flanagan thought. Kornukopia, Flanagan thought. Sherbina, Flanagan thought. Flanagan tried not to panic. He gestured for Luzhkov to sit, and, while he settled himself behind his desk, worked on his breathing. The Russian didn't look like he was packing, at least. There was that. "What can I do for you?" Flanagan asked.

"I'm looking for a woman."

"I don't understand."

"Sure you do." Luzhkov grinned. He was comfortable with English, his syntax as good as native, but it came from the throat, and had a Slavic growl. It put Flanagan on edge.

"Humour me." Listen to Mike, talking tough.

Luzhkov was still grinning. "Okay. You know Bill Jancovich?"

Flanagan frowned, genuinely puzzled this time. The name rang a faint bell. "I don't think so. Should I?"

Luzhkov shrugged. "Doesn't matter. He used to work here. Computers. Maybe you never met. But he knows you, and the company you keep."

The name clicked. Arthur Pembroke had mentioned him as the hack who had killed Flanagan's back-door access to the NAVCON program. "Go on."

"Didn't meet? No? You'd remember. Frightened kitten, all the time. The man has yellow bones. He was transferred from here to Geneva."

Flanagan's anxiety levels climbed higher. How much did this guy know? "When was this?"

"After Sherbina took over."

Oh, shit. Big swallow. Slight nod. His throat had seized up.

"Anyway, he survived Kornukopia One. So did I."

"Not many did," Flanagan said softly. There was no point in pretending ignorance. He thought of the explosion that had made Blaylock into God. He thought of the twisted statues that had once been human. These were memories that didn't bother him the way they would have, once upon a time. Sometimes, they were even pleasant.

"No," Luzhkov agreed. "Pretty impressive. So was the lady."

"You met?"

"That's right."

"And she didn't kill you?"

Luzhkov shook his head. "The terms were good."

Flanagan relaxed a notch. "Why do you want to find her?"

"I'm looking for work. Some friends are, too."

Listen to your instincts, Flanagan thought. His instincts were saying *opportunity*.

Sometimes, the work was *too* much fun.

"Calm down," Sam Reed said.

"What do you mean, 'calm down'?" Charlotte Taber demanded. "Have you just been shot at? No, I think I would have read about that. So I don't need you on a high horse telling the silly woman to calm down. Don't you start." The anger made her forehead vein throb, a good way to trigger a migraine. But the throb was almost welcome. The beat was regular, moving her pulse away from panic arrhythmia. She was in her office, banks of TV screens flashing news channel infoscreams, and there was gold there for the taking, all the ore necessary to turn into weapons against Chapel and any other enemy of the administration, and she couldn't work. She couldn't concentrate. Her mind was trapped in a stuttering porno-loop of the night before. The spectacle was the same few seconds, slowed down, blown up, frame-by-framed for maximum terror. Each moment came with the booming crash of a clock-beat. Her key in the door. The wood of the door frame exploding out at her as she heard the crack of a bullet. Turning around to see the shadow standing on the sidewalk, its hands wrapped around a pistol, and no one, no one, *no one* around. Another shot, blowing in the stained glass on the door. The echo of the attack bouncing tumbleweed down the street that was a ghost town nightscape. The cold, zero comfort of the streetlights, showing her the shape of her assassin. Her scream, a howl that didn't belong in her body. Her whirl back to the door as her hands became sweat-soaked and cold-numbed, clumsy paws that banged at the key and didn't know what to do with it. The third shot, the one that tore her dress, the one that made her close her eyes. The key turning, but not like salvation. Instead, the movement was a tease, inanimate objects spitting in her face by showing her the safety she could never reach, because the next bullet would be the end. Her clawing at the door as her howl turned into a sob. The suspense before the blow. Her body splitting into disconnected pieces as her mind shut down. Her right hand turning the doorknob. The door opening. Her fall as the fourth bullet shrieked through the air where her head had been. The mirror in her entrance hall a shattering laughter of flying glass. Her spastic crawl inside. Then the missing second. Not a blackout, because she could remember the white glare of panic and her thrashing limbs. But the terror was so bright it blotted out knowledge and sight. The last image was her, curled in a ball, back against the shut door, trembling infant waiting for the bogeyman to smash his way in. But the silence of the street returned, and there were no more bullets.

There had been nothing but fear since then, with only very sorry relief when the police arrived. Daybreak didn't help, because night would come again, and with it would return clawed shadows. But for the moment, for just this moment, she could vent at the president, and a little miracle of alchemy turned her fear into anger. Especially when he told her to calm down.

"Hysteria isn't going to solve anything," Reed said, and she wished he were in the room so she could slap him when he said *hysteria*. She couldn't believe he actually used that word. "It certainly isn't going to make you safer," he went on. "What will make you safe is that you're going to have a full security detail at work, in transit, and around your home."

"Easy for you to say."

"Yes, it is. Welcome to my world, Charlotte." And he scored a real point. "Now focus. We have to work out how to use this."

"We don't even know who tried to kill me!"

There was silence on the other end of the line, one that Taber knew. It was the quiet of Reed mastering impatience. "Maybe not the precise individual. But I think we know who ordered the hit, don't you?"

"No, I don't. No one hates me that much."

"No one? You can't think of anyone whose reason to live is threatened by you?"

No, she began to say, then caught herself. Chapel. That thought made her say, "Oh, no." The panic built again.

Reed sensed it. "Easy."

"Right. Easy. I don't have a random nut after my ass, but the CIA director of wet work. I feel very relaxed."

"He had his chance. His operative blew it. I doubt he could take the risk of trying again. Once you're protected, any attempt would be hugely public. What he's actually done is hand us a huge club. Think of the spin."

She did. Life became brighter. Chapel was going to rue the day. He couldn't be accused directly. There was no evidence yet beyond obvious common sense. But they could kill him with innuendo. Beautiful. The attack unfolded before her, a heavenly plain. "I have work to do," she told Reed.

"I think you do."

The day changed from cocooning terror to shock-and-awe counterattack. She worked with a purpose, and with inspiration. She was very good at what she did, and Chapel was going to know it. She made sure the attack on her was news, and then she encouraged speculation. When the media came calling, she kept the interviews short and enigmatic. Come the evening, she had ordered the first leaks. Informed sources close to the story were dropping poison pellets for Chapel. When she left for home, surrounded by security every step, she felt good. She felt strong. Hear me roar, you bastard.

And when the work was too much fun, that was when the guilt would try to make some headway. That was when a voice that might have been her mother's, calling from the depths of a far well, would ask, *Do you know what you just did? Do you really? Are you happy with the kind of person you've become?*

Yes. Yes. And... Blaylock wasn't sure about the third question. She was encrusted with filth, she knew. But if there was such a thing as destiny, then she knew she had found hers. She was very good at what she did. When she took the enemy down, she felt the satisfaction and justifiable pride of the artist who looks at her work and knows that it is good. She had a gift, and she was using it.

But sometimes the headlong rush into the muck had its own appeal. It was the draw of to-hell-with-it, nothing-left-to-lose recklessness. She was locked into the ride now, bloodied beyond any hope of redemption, so why do anything but plunge in headfirst and enjoy the fall? For a while, she had looked to Flanagan as some kind of moral anchor point who would yank her back if she plummeted too far and fast. That was a wish as unfair as it was unrealistic. Oh, he had tried, he really had. Her chest still constricted when she remembered the way he had looked as they sat amidst the carnage at Ember Lake. In the charred aftermath of the forest fire, surrounded by the wreckage of the lodge and the bodies of G8 leaders and InSec mercenaries, Flanagan had gazed at Blaylock as if the worst threat of them all had survived. There were three-in-the-morning moments when she wondered if he might have been right. But Flanagan had failed to hold her back. Instead, she had pulled him down with her. He was learning to enjoy war. His aesthetic sense was tuned into hers, and he appreciated the art of the successful operation. He was learning to see the killing as her genius, and love the relentlessness of the execution, rather than recoil at the fact that lethal force wasn't anywhere close to being her last resort. In the crater that had been Stepan Sherbina's Kornukopia fortress, his eyes had shone with excitement. Blaylock knew she should feel guilty about that.

She knew this.

She should not be feeling gratitude and the enveloping warmth of not being alone. She knew this, too.

But. Oh, yes, *but*. And sometimes the work was just too much fun.

Like last night. Seeing Charlotte Taber dance, *that* had done her heart some real good. The woman was one of the Sam Reed's architects. She massaged the truth until it had no bearing to reality. She presented the worst lies as the most sincere gospel. She did it all with a sublime presumption of entitlement and innocence. She was as stained with the blood of Kelly Grimson and the murdered hundreds at Davos as Chapel, Reed or Sherbina. At least Chapel and Sherbina had had the stones to fight for their projects. Reed stood aloof and watched the massacres from safe distances and prime seats. Taber, though, was far enough removed from the slaughter to pretend she had nothing to do with it. She had faith in the concept of the abstract. Blaylock didn't think Taber believed her words and manipulations had no impact. But she was so far from the front lines that she could exist without ever understanding the reality of the word *consequence*. It was past time the front lines paid her a visit.

The dance last night had followed Blaylock's choreography. She'd experienced the pleasure of work well done even as anger was behind every trigger pull. The bullets had been close enough to convince and terrify, but not to kill. The difference between a con job and a botched assassination was perception, and she knew which version Taber believed. Blaylock had smelled her terror. She had heard it too, today, sitting in the parking lot, listening to Taber's conversations with Reed.

She thought she had done Chapel damage last night. She'd know for sure as the story played out over the next few days. But Taber wasn't frantic enough yet. Reed had calmed her down, at least a little. Next stage, then. She needed to goose Reed and Taber into a mistake. So she lay on an apartment rooftop two blocks down from Taber's home. She had a clear view of the street, and she watched through binoculars for the woman's car. She could see the security detail vehicles parked in front of the house, and the men lounging while they waited for their turn at bat. She'd watched them all day. No one had gone in the house since Taber had left in the morning. Good. That meant it hadn't occurred to anyone that the attempted hit hadn't been the first move. It also meant that she could make her next move with a clear conscience.

Yeah, right. What she was going to do was too much like what had been done to her. There was a sickness to the echo, but she was still going ahead. And, somehow, revolting herself distracted her from mourning Grimson. There were too many things there that hurt, too much guilt and blood and sorrow. She used the alchemy of anger to transmute all the bad elements to savagery, and she could go on. Despair was too easy an option, too tempting, and she didn't trust her ability to resist.

Dusk fell, then evening, then night. Taber was working late. Blaylock stayed on post, tensing and relaxing to ward off cramps, never looking away from the target site. Timing was important. She wondered if she had frightened Taber out of her home, sending her running to a sanctuary Blaylock couldn't penetrate. She didn't think so. The security detail would be a massive waste of manpower if Taber weren't returning. Blaylock didn't worry. She'd given Taber plenty of material to work with. She imagined the lie machine in full gear.

With darkness, she switched to infrared binoculars, reading the licence plates of every car that passed along the street. She saw the numbers she wanted around 2300 hours. Taber's vehicle was sandwiched between two dark sedans. Subtle, Blaylock thought. She stroked the button on the remote detonator. She'd broken into Taber's house three days ago and planted the C4 in the basement, along the exterior wall. Her welcome-home present. Taber's car stopped. The security personnel gathered around. Taber emerged from the passenger side. The car drove off. Taber started up the sidewalk. Braced but eager, Blaylock pushed the button.

The scorched-earth memory: her family's house fire-bombed; her mother, her father, her sister, instant coal; herself flying ass over teakettle, outside the house on a fluke and surviving to start a vendetta that swallowed up first all those connected to her family's death, and that now extended to anyone cut from the same cloth, all condemned by her jury of one. Now the echo: the streetside wall of Taber's house, the wall not connected to another home, blew out. The roar filled the street and expanded, shaking pavement and rattling windows. It reached Blaylock and surrounded her with a balm of destructive noise. Dust and plaster billowed into a choking cloud. Masonry collapsed. The house slumped in on itself with a groan of stone and the snapping of wooden bones. In the chaos, Blaylock never lost sight of Taber. She saw her knocked flat by the force of the blast and the trembling of the earth. Through the binoculars, the street was a swirl of dust and running figures. Taber was a tiny silhouette, one of Brueghel's insignificant victims, a stick drawing smacked around by a cruel God. That was me, Blaylock thought. That was me. She felt the stiletto stab of memory. She also felt the rush of divinity.

Fun.

5

Know your friends: Chapel's immediate mission as he prowled the corridors of Langley. Sometimes, that was more important than knowing your enemies. Having the enemies list down meant being able to choose the right defence. Friends you needed for offence. Allies willing to do the dirty, willing to let their hands drip the necessary blood. Willing to do the right thing. He needed this intel more than ever, after last night. Taber's house was up in smoke, and so were the rules of the game. The splash radius of the damage was reaching him. The spin of blame was pointing his way, and that rumble he heard was the guillotine being wheeled to his office. Problem was, he had no idea who had Taber on a hit list. Made no sense. No one with a motive in sight, at least no one desperate enough to want her dead. Except maybe him. It wasn't just his career on the line. So was his life. So was (he *believed*, he *knew*) the country. He could hardly blame Taber and Reed for the way they were using the attack against him. He'd suspect himself, too. Only he didn't do this thing. Who, then? The brazenness, the scary outside-the-box randomness of the attack made sense as the work of one person he could think of, but she was dead. His chest constricted briefly at the thought that her ghost had come to haunt him, and then he moved on. Could Taber and Reed be doing this to themselves, as a way of hobbling him? The idea had a certain perverted logic. Then he revised it. The concept worked better if Taber really was in the dark, and she really did think he was after her. So make it Reed as the player, sacrificing his pawn Taber to checkmate Chapel's king. Chapel liked that construct. He could believe in it. He was still walking funny from the diddling Reed had given him.

The noose was closing. Countermeasures were an urgent priority. He needed his friends. So find them, boy. Find them. He had begun the morning by making feeler phone calls to the other deputy directors. He was shooting in the dark and knew it, but the possibility of full Agency resources was worth the gesture. He spent a long morning twisting in the wind. He'd never been close to his opposite numbers—budget rivalry saw to that. But he'd been on good terms with a few. There had been a sense, at the best of times, of a passable imitation of *esprit de corps*, of fighting the good fight, whether the enemy was terrorists, foreign agents, or the Pentagon muscling in on their turf. His overtures collided with polite terror and sudden excuses. He was poison, a radioactive leper. The word was out: Chapel's ship was going down, so don't get caught by the suction.

Cowards.

Then there was his own fiefdom. In theory, as DD of Operations, he had the best weapons. The staff for Covert Action, Special Operations, Counterintelligence, Counterterrorism and the whole exploding black bag of tricks reported to him. In practice, he knew that survival instincts would be breeding disloyalty and mutiny. There would still be some good men around, though. He just had to find them.

There was Gene Kemmerlin, of course, and others like him. Loyal footsoldiers, but they weren't enough. They weren't even that useful. Loyalty was well and good, but Chapel couldn't count on it for the battle ahead. So he cut Kemmerlin out of the loop. He needed men with clout and balls. For that, Felix Jurado was his first, best hope. Chapel knocked on his door. Jurado had packed on the pounds over the last ten years, and he filled his suits like a wall of angry flesh. His face was heart-attack florid. His moustache and hair, both grey, were aggressive in their extravagance. His beat was Latin and South America. He'd been in the field during the Reagan dirty wars, old enough then to be a desk jockey with honour, but burning with the energy of the true believer and doing what needed to be done, weeping nuns and bleeding hearts be damned. He was spitting distance from retirement now. No one had ever controlled him, and now that there was nothing anyone could hold over his head, he was a sovereign nation unto himself. He wasn't what could be called insubordinate. That would imply he had bothered to hear the order he was disobeying in the first place. He looked up when Chapel appeared in his doorway and grunted. That was effusive by Jurado's standards. He stabbed a finger at a chair. Chapel sat, feeling like a supplicant, but knowing that the rest of the planet was in the same position when talking to Jurado.

"Do you for?" Jurado asked.

"What have you been hearing?"

"You're toast."

"That what you think?"

"Bastards." Jurado paused, then gave a curt nod, confirming his opinion.

"I have a plan," Chapel said. He waited for Jurado to tell him to leave, give any kind of signal that he didn't want to know. Jurado said nothing. "It'll change things up in a big way."

"Good."

"I'll be making some moves in your territory. I have the key personnel in place, but they'll need resources. I want to know if they'll have them." Chapel could give all the orders he liked, but if he was a lame duck director, nothing would happen.

"They'll have them," Jurado said. The old warrior had a gleam in his eye.

Patrick "Pee-Pee" Pratella knew he wasn't liked. He knew about his nickname. He wasn't worried. Being unpopular was his normal state of being. He'd been hated since grade school in South Carolina, and the nickname had surfaced then, so the funny-funny boys on the Hill weren't being original. Grade three was when he'd first been called a bully. Bullshit. He just didn't suffer fools. Being right wasn't the road to popularity, but so be it. People came around. He'd won every election since 1987. Victory was the other fact of existence that had been present since high school. His peers may not have liked him, but they knew it was smarter to be his ally than his enemy. He had never been lonely. And he'd always known what was what. He'd found his platforms easily. His first was just after high school. College had held no interest, an unnecessary delay in getting on with things. He'd marched into the office of the *Conway Trumpet* and demanded a column. He had things to say. The editor had resisted, but not long. Pratella was still a big man, and at eighteen, he'd been linebacker-huge. He had his soapbox. In no time at all, he had his voice: invective and innuendo presented as down-home plain talkin', facts be damned. Turned out he had a gift. His charging-bull methods that had seen him through school worked just as well in the new sandbox, and his enemies were just as quick to back down. He revelled in the impunity of print, worked the mojo for years against the dark forces of ethnic minorities, women and homosexuals, until he had the leverage he needed for his first run for Congress. Browbeating and threats never stopped being effective. He shook down whoever he needed, got his war chest, and got his election. Once he was in, the privilege of incumbency did the rest. He was unbeatable.

Being disliked was fine. That came with being feared, and that was the source of his strength. What was less fine was being impugned. The *New York Times* described his ethics as being somewhere south of Tom DeLay's. That was the kind of insult that grated, because it was a tactic Pratella was grand master of. Two good men's reputations used to sully each other's. That was wrong. Where possible, he moved against anyone who suggested he wasn't acting for the best interests of his constituents, his state, and his country. What was good for the country was good for him. That equation wasn't hard to understand.

As Speaker, he had clout, and there weren't too many bugs he couldn't squash. But clout could always be improved. He felt the same way about Sam Reed. The man knew a thing or two about putting steel in America's spine. Good stuff. He was still too diplomatic by half. Reed's problem was that he had an overload of education. That stuff feminized a man.

There was always room for improvement, for upward movement. So he was interested in what Joe Chapel had to say. The man was in political freefall, but his profession was information. There might be profit in giving him a hearing.

They met in Pratella's office. It was a domain of oak and old leather, framed pictures of the Speaker holding freshwater trophy fish, standing beside political big fish. The furniture was an image: old and solid, like the values Pratella stood for. He poured two scotch-and-waters, downed his, and settled back in his chair. "So?" he asked Chapel. "What do you want, and what do I get?"

"What I want is to save the country."

"Don't we all."

Chapel didn't laugh. The man sounded serious. "All right. In the immediate, I want allies."

"I bet you do, Joey. I bet you do. But you didn't answer my second question. Boy, you have to tell me why the hell I should tie my ship to yours, now that it's stove in and all. A man has to know why he's tying his shoes." He had no idea what that meant. He was always ad-libbing aphorisms. The habit had begun as a schtick, a building block of his image as a man formed by grassroots wisdom. It had become second nature. "Will you tell me why I'm tying my shoes?"

"Because of the first thing I said."

Chapel was being oblique. In this game, that meant being careful. Careful meant important. Pay attention, boy. Tie your shoes well. "What do you want to save the country from?" he asked. "Aside from itself, of course."

"From those who do not have its best interests at heart."

Oh. The man was gunning for Reed? Consequences and possibilities were suddenly enormous. "You sound," Pratella probed, "like a man who has lost his faith. You sound," he continued, "like a man on a Montana riverboat. You do."

"I am."

Reed gone. No veep. That meant he would be the one moving to Pennsylvania Avenue. Nice. Not a reason to lift a finger, though. Chapel was in a corner. He had to take Reed down or burn himself. All Pratella had to do was sit back and wait. If Reed lost, the presidency was his. If Chapel lost, he'd risked nothing. "It seems to me my shoes are slip-ons," he said.

Chapel's face darkened. "Mr. Speaker," he said, "I admire your voting record. You have fought for everything I value in our country."

"I try to keep the veranda well swept."

Chapel's smile was twisted. "Nobody's perfect, though."

"I don't pretend to be."

"Nobody's irreplaceable."

Pratella said nothing. His comfort level dropped to zero as Chapel opened his briefcase and pulled out a file. He slapped it on the desk and leaned forward. His eyes were unforgiving stone. "You didn't sweep under the veranda, you cornpone piece of shit. If you're going to surf the Internet, learn to cover your tracks."

Pratella's armpits were soaked. "I was only investigating a constituent's complaint about the kind of filth—"

"And all those bruised hookers were investigation, too. And your wife's broken arm last year. You try to feed me one more word and this file is on the six o'clock news. Feed me two and

71

I'll open up the file on some of your travel destinations." Chapel waited, giving Pratella a chance to hang himself. He nodded, capitulating. Chapel continued. "Good. So we're clear: we may be on the same page as far as the country is concerned, but that isn't enough. Not anymore. I thought Sam Reed was the man we needed. I made a mistake. I won't again. You're going to be the big dog, Mr. Speaker, but you'll be on a leash. I own you. Clear?"

Pratella nodded. "What do you want me to do?"

"I'll let you know." Chapel stood up to leave. "Meantime, tie your shoes."

Flanagan convinced Luzhkov to hold off talking business at the office. He didn't trust InSec's notions of privacy. He had plenty of reasons not to. He met the Russian the next day, over the lunch hour, on Broad Street. They walked north toward the Federal Hall, along the packed sidewalk. Luzhkov seemed amused. "Nothing is surveillance-proof," he said.

"No point making things easy," Flanagan answered. "So what's the score?"

"Our girl chopped the head off Kornukopia. Most of the torso, too."

"Anyone taking over?"

Luzhkov shook his head. "Sherbina was top dog. He's gone. Yvgeny Nevzlin was finance and organization. He's gone. All the lieutenants, gone. That explosion," he grinned. "Very beautiful."

"You were inside," Flanagan reminded him. "You just heard it. I saw it." He grinned back. "You have no idea how beautiful it was."

"Anyway," Luzhkov went on, "Kornukopia is finished. It's going to break up into little warring groups, until the next genius comes along."

That brought Flanagan up short. "You mean Jen?" His mouth was going dry again. He doubted she'd think much of him negotiating to set her up as an international crime lord. And yet... No. He shook free of the idea.

Luzhkov was way ahead of him. "No. But when an empire breaks up, some provinces are worth grabbing."

"The armed province, you're thinking?"

"I'm thinking."

Flanagan rolled the idea over in his mind, testing its weight as a wrecking ball. InSec's mercenary resources were huge, human product no different from any other weaponry, ready to be shipped on command. When Blaylock had whacked Pembroke, she'd left the stumbling conglomerate open to takeover. Sherbina had stepped in, and added InSec's forces to his enormous strength of ex-Soviet military. Soldiers, KGB, Spetznaz: anyone whose marketable skills were limited to combat had found a new and lucrative home. And now the collapse was happening again.

But not quite. "You think we can take over the merc forces."

Luzhkov hesitated. "Some, anyway."

"One problem. InSec's unstable, but still intact. The power struggle is on, and someone's going to win, I guarantee. Then business as usual. You'll see." The laws of inertia favoured the corporate beast.

"Then we split off what we can right now. I have names. They're eager."

"I'll try to get hold of Jen," Flanagan said. He wouldn't

commit, but oh, the possibilities. Build another little army, and not the lunatic canon-fodder survivalists Blaylock had used to bring down Pembroke. Maybe, maybe, maybe. It's a bit late, honey, but here's your Valentine.

Jorge Quintero watched the streets through the bars of the prison transport truck. He and Ernesto Maldonado sat on opposite benches, sandwiched between two guards each. Quintero had to lean forward to see through the narrow window. There was one police cruiser following. He could hear its siren syncopating with the lead car's. Two vehicles as escort. Not much for a man of his importance. And from what he could see on the sidewalks as they approached the courthouse, there were no spectators. The verdict was coming down today, and life was going on. No one knew or cared. He was yesterday's news, stale and forgotten. He leaned back. There was a time, he thought, when security around him would have been huge. There would have been the real threat of mutiny in his favour. He granted the regime some grudging respect. By waiting years after the coup attempt to prosecute, and simply keeping him in career wilderness during that time, they killed his profile. His men's loyalty faded with their memory. By the time the trial rolled around, he was a has-been in the dock. A fossil. The minimal escort was a slap in the face, a reminder of his steep fall.

The truck bounced over a series of potholes. Quintero knew the feel of the street by now. Bump, bump, bumpity, pause, bump. The last block before the courthouse. The truck slowed, then stopped. And here we are, he thought. Last trip before the sentencing. He felt no suspense. The verdict had been settled before the trial began.

He stood up before the guards could haul him to his feet. Maldonado did the same. Pride and honour. First, last, always. Posture vertical, uniform pressed, head up, a stance that expressed contempt for the handcuffs. Contempt in the eyes, too, for anyone who looked. I am a man, Quintero thought. The rest of you are vermin. No, not even that.

The door opened and they descended from the truck. Quintero blinked as his eyes adjusted to the sunlight. He took a quick look from side to side. The turnout was depressing. A couple of rag-tag protest groups, one wanting him president, the other wanting him drawn and quartered, both raising their voices when they saw him. But there were only a half-dozen people on each side, and the cheers and jeers were pathetic: tinny, thin parodies in the morning breeze. None of the foot traffic on the sidewalk even looked up. On the steps of the courthouse, there were the usual coffee huddles of reporters. There were a few more than recently, now that the trial was about to end, but still not many, and hardly any foreign press representation. They all looked bored. One journalist, an American, finished a cigarette, shrugged, and sauntered down the steps. The day was going to be warm, but the man wore his rumpled raincoat like an identity badge. Two guards, looking as bored as the reporter, stepped forward and held him arm's length from the prisoners. The man shrugged again. His face was hangdog cynical, his hair a thin grey web plastered on his greasy skull. "Are you feeling confident, General Quintero?" he asked in English. He held out a digital recorder for the answer.

"In the judgment of history, yes."

"What about the judgment of the court?"

Quintero said nothing.

The reporter jabbed harder. "Won't that have some influence on the judgment of history?"

Quintero still didn't respond. He held his gaze still and cold on the reporter. The two guards facing the reporter turned to look at Quintero. They had smirks on their faces. The reporter put his recorder back inside his coat. He withdrew a pistol. He moved with the casual speed of long experience. He rammed the pistol under the chin of the first guard and pulled the trigger. The bullet punched a hole through the cop's skull and helmet. The second guard was only just registering the fall of the corpse when he took it on the chin himself. Quintero and Maldonado dropped flat. So did the reporter as the two remaining guards brought their guns up. The doors of the police cruisers flew open.

Quintero's ears rang with the rapid bark of assault rifles. It was not the sound of the guards shooting back. It came from behind, from across the street, and the guards were cut in half before they could fire. That left four cops. Two gambled smart and piled out of their car on the courthouse side. They crouched low, their vehicle between them and the shooters. The passenger of the rear escort did the same, but the driver, too quick, was out on the streetside before the reporter had shot the second guard. Quintero heard him scream. He turned his head, sidewalk scraping his cheek, and saw the man writhing on the road. The shooters had ignored his bulletproof vest and blasted both his knees to pieces. He was clawing at the asphalt with his hands, moving nowhere, a sitting duck.

The reporter rolled to Quintero's left, came up in a crouch, two hands on his pistol and aiming at the two forward escort cops. He was very good. So was one of the officers, who had hit the ground shotgun in hand. He fired first. He was barely fifteen feet away, and the blast was emphatic. Buckshot slammed into the reporter. He flipped over backwards, ventilated but still twitching. His left arm was hanging by tendons. His blood pooled quickly, and his breath sounded like hiccups, not enough left for a scream. His eyes were shocked wide with disbelief. They didn't look bored now. His gaze locked with Quintero's. Even through the agony, Quintero thought he saw a pissed-off cussedness. The man was dying, and he still had the reserves to be mad at somebody.

There was a pause in the firing. The three remaining cops were sheltered by their vehicles, and weren't about to poke their heads up. The sound of screams and running feet rushed to fill the vacuum left by the gunshots. Life on the street had been disrupted by his presence after all. So much for the stale news, bastards, he thought. You don't deserve me.

The cop with the shotgun looked at Quintero. The general worried about the way the man was holding his gun. He seemed ready to make a decision based on expediency.

Crackle of a megaphone. "General! Incoming!"

Quintero and Maldonado curled up and rolled next to the prison truck. Quintero whacked his head against a tire as rocket-propelled grenades fireballed the police cruisers, flipping their burning wreckage onto the sidewalk. The cops died three times over. There wasn't silence, then, not really. There were still screams, and there was the hum and crackle of flame. But time paused for aftermath, and the end of explosions felt like three-in-the-morning quiet. The moment was at most a second, but Quintero savoured it. It tasted of vengeance.

Running feet, coming to a crisp stop beside Quintero. He looked up. Alejandro Olano saluted. The general and Maldonado stood. Still handcuffed, Quintero couldn't return the salute, but he gave Olano a nod of approval. One of Olano's men searched the guards until he found the keys to the cuffs and freed the two officers. "Well done, Major," Quintero rubbed his wrists.

"Thank you, sir."

"You have transport, I trust?" The battle had lasted less than a minute, but there were hundreds of witnesses. Quintero could hear sirens wailing through the Caracas traffic. If they weren't heading this way, others would be soon.

"Sir," Olano said, and led the way. There were three cars idling in the street. Quintero, Maldonado, and Olano piled into the lead one. A fourth man, a captain named Jiménez, joined them as driver. One of the other cars held four soldiers, the rear one three. Only nine men for the operation, Quintero thought, as they drove off. More than enough for the security detail, but he felt a twinge of regret. Was that it? Was this the sum total of men still loyal to him? Were memories so short? Was he worth so little? Or was it that courage was in such short supply? "You found some good men," he said to Olano. "Tell me about them."

Olano filled him in. They were all lower-rank officers. Three of them were Special Forces. All had trained at the School of the Americas. "That's a coincidence," Quintero commented.

Olano squirmed. "Actually, no sir, it isn't."

Quintero thought that over for a moment. He decided his pride had already taken so many hits, what was one more? "Go on."

"That was the connection that brought them together."

Not loyalty to me, he thought. At least, not principally that. Well, he should have guessed. Only half the names Olano rattled off had sounded familiar. Then there was the reporter, who had died for him, but had been royally pissed about it and no mistake. "Who was the American?"

"Agency. He said his name was Jim Blake." A shrug at the likely story. "He was the contact."

The rescue had barely been Olano's operation at all, then. Still, Olano had finished it. "Joe Chapel spoke to you."

Olano nodded. "Once. He asked me what I needed. After that, other people, mainly Blake."

Points to Chapel for making this possible, but Quintero wasn't going to swear fealty yet. He'd been down that road once already. You did not bend over for the Agency unless you were truly enthusiastic about the screwing. If all the men with him were SOA grads, then they had all been used and tossed away. Their enthusiasm would be long gone.

He listened for sirens, heard none. He twisted around in the back seat, and saw no one pursuing. "Is there a police scanner in this thing?"

"Yes, sir." Olano turned it on. The interior of the car filled with intermittent fragments of orders broken up by an ocean of static.

"Somebody's jamming," Maldonado commented.

Quintero agreed. "But it's not aimed at us." During the moments where the authorities broke through the jamming, all that came through was confusion and anger. Then the interference would clamp down again. There was war in the ether. There were other players out there, fighting for Quintero. Or setting him up as a pawn.

Deal with that in due course. First things first. "Where are we headed?"

"The harbour," Olano answered.

Good. For a moment, he'd wondered if Chapel had been brazen enough to arrange for extraction from the airport. The public spectacle at the courthouse was one thing. He was glad the world would know he was still a going concern. But if the actual extraction was too easy to track, then this would all be for nothing. He was not going down Pinochet's mud track of humiliation. No, thank you.

They raced out of the downtown area. The radio crackled its inarticulate rage. They were hitting the warehouse district when Maldonado said, "Trouble. Three o'clock."

Quintero looked, saw the flashing lights. All the electronic interference in the world couldn't save them from line of sight. A police cruiser had spotted them. It was barrelling down a side street their way. It was three blocks down. Jiménez hit the accelerator. He scythed through traffic. Quintero watched behind, saw the other two vehicles speed up. The cruiser shrieked onto the main road. Its driver was good, too. Maybe better. He gained ground. The traffic was middle-of-the-day heavy, and they kept hitting solid walls of cars in both directions. Jiménez would build momentum, then the coagulation would overwhelm even his aggression. The cop was having to slow down too, but he was catching up.

"He can't call for help," Olano said.

He might not have to, Quintero thought. The driver's partner had rolled down the passenger window. He was leaning out, cradling a shotgun. He was less than fifty yards away in the curb lane. "Captain," Quintero warned.

"I see it, sir," Jiménez answered. He shot the car forward. He rear-ended a dawdling Festiva in the median lane, sent it spinning to the right. Horns blared. There was the always startling shock-bang of metal against metal. Jiménez drove faster, and the cop fired. Quintero saw him raise the gun. He and Maldonado ducked down. The window shattered. The air in the car blinked black, not with buckshot, but with flechettes, tiny darts that flew further and penetrated deeper. They smashed and shredded Jiménez's neck and the back of his head. He dropped the wheel and lolled against the door. The car swerved, but went even faster, a dead foot hard on the accelerator. Olano yelled and reached for the wheel. They sideswiped a panel truck, and Quintero's door buckled. Olano steered them back into the lane one-handed. He stretched, trying for the driver's door handle. The traffic ahead went molasses again. They came up fast behind an SUV. Olano gave up on the door and yanked the handbrake. The car shook and bucked. Olano slammed a fist against Jiménez's leg, knocked his foot off the pedal, and the car slowed, but not fast enough. They hit the SUV hammer to anvil. The front of the car accordioned. Quintero's seatbelt held him, but his head snapped forward and back. The pain in his neck was a blast of white noise that shrank his vision to a narrow tunnel. His teeth felt piano-key loose. The engine stopped.

Quintero fought the clock and shock. "Out," he ordered. His door was stuck, but Maldonado, dazed, popped his open.

Quintero tumbled out after him. Olano was climbing over the seats to follow. His face was pouring gore.

Quintero saw the cop train his shotgun on the rear escort car. His target was a man leaning out the back passenger window, aiming an RPG right back. The cop fired first, catching the other man in the gut. The soldier slumped and fired at the same time. The grenade went wild and hit the ground in front of a car in the middle lane. The blast took out both the escort vehicle and the civilian. Fire bloomed over two lanes. The civilian car flipped onto the cruiser. It crushed the roof and squashed the men inside.

The remaining escort vehicle pulled up. Doors flew open. Quintero, Maldonado and Olano piled in, sat in the laps of the other passengers. They left a flaming barricade behind as they took off again. This car didn't have a police scanner. Quintero could hope the jamming was still on, but he couldn't know. The chaos of their passing was going to draw more attention soon in any case. His ears were still ringing from the collision, hearing was difficult, and everybody was yelling, but he still listened for more sirens.

He heard the wails, and plenty of them, as they reached the port. The driver careened out onto the docks, scattering stevedores. He stopped beside a filthy tugboat, its engine is already churning the water to foam. Another American stood beside the gangplank, smoking like he could speed them up. He was a big man, sloppy in jeans and sweatshirt. Quintero thought he belonged in a low-end bar, not on a covert op. "Where's Blake?" the man demanded as the car unloaded.

"Dead," Olano answered.

"So are other good men," Quintero put in.

The man shook his head in disgust. "Let's go," he said, and ground his cigarette.

Quintero watched the docks as they pulled out into the harbour. By the time the police arrived, they were out of firing range. The cars were hard to make out, their lights flashing frustration. "How long will the jamming last?" Quintero asked the American, thinking of aerial pursuit.

"Long enough," the man said, unconcerned.

"Where are we going?"

"There's a freighter. Then international waters." He belched, looked at Quintero with open contempt. "You better be worth all this."

You can't even begin to imagine, thought Quintero.

6

Run, Charlotte, Blaylock thought. Run to your master. Flush him out.

They were in the Oval Office again, but sitting on the couches, that much more comfortable with each other. Korda really was a man he could work with, Reed thought. He had the patriotism of a skink, but he was supremely pragmatic. Reed didn't trust him, but yes, he could work with him. And work well.

Reed put the phone down on his desk and returned to his couch. "That was Charlotte," he told Korda.

"I guessed. I could hear the hollering from here."

"Can't say that I blame her. What the hell is your man up to?"

Korda held up his hands. "*My* man? Let's not confuse chains of command with reality. I don't recall making that bastard DD Operations. He was your boy. You tell me what he's doing."

"I honestly don't know. I can't see what tactical sense any of this makes."

"It doesn't. Smells like desperation to me."

"If not outright insanity."

"There is that."

Silence, now, stretching long, each man waiting for the other to take the conversation to its next inevitable step.

"So…" Reed finally said.

"Yes," Korda agreed.

Reed took the plunge. This was how well he could work with Korda. This was how close their interests were. "Extreme liabilities call for … unambiguous responses."

Korda met him halfway. "And there should be no room for the liability to answer back."

"Exactly."

Korda fiddled with the lobe of his ear. "Some tricky bits. The war is a little too public. A flat-out hit might even make things worse."

"Worse than him remaining alive and active?" Reed prided himself on not flinching from the hard equations. Deciding who lived and died was part of the job. He took that responsibility seriously. He also liked it.

"Let me sleep on it."

"Don't leave it too long."

Korda laughed sourly. "You're telling me. You're the one living here. He's not about to blow up the White House, unless he's packing a nuke. You're the one who's safe. Physically." He let the qualifier sink in. "Now, what about Charlotte? She going to be a problem?"

Reed hoped not. She knew about too many skeletons, had too many toxic skills. He couldn't afford a second loose cannon. "I'd better go see her," he said.

"Good idea. She'll appreciate the gesture. Maybe you should put her up here temporarily."

Reed sighed. "If I have to." He knew he would. Just like he was going to have to face her fear in person now.

Christmas. Coming early.

Blaylock left the parking lot, jazzing. Action was looming, big bad risk coursed through her blood. She was going to do the bad thing that was the right thing, and she *wanted* it, couldn't wait for the filth that was going to pour down on her head. Every action had consequences. Reed should know that, too. *She* was consequences. He had acted. Here came judgment.

Listening to the call between Taber and Reed had been an entertainment and a half. Taber's amp had been cranked to eleven, but her blast hadn't been pure fear. Reed had made the mistake of trying to downplay her anxieties, a condescending move so stupid Blaylock had split a gut laughing. She'd felt a wave of sympathy for the woman she'd been terrorizing. Her fears were completely legit. Then Taber had struck back, and that had been a reminder that she was a power in her own right. She'd stopped just short of actually threatening Reed, but only just. The reminder of her juice had been enough. The president was on his way over. Sucker.

Once in Public Diplomacy again, Blaylock ditched the briefcase and loaded her arms with paper. She began a power wander. She moved like she had a destination, and wasn't happy about it, but she went nowhere. She was already where she wanted to be. She cruised the department, waiting for the big man to show, waiting to see if her extrapolations had been accurate. Trying for a shot at Reed out on the street was numb-nuts dreaming. With security the way it was, nothing short of an air strike would have a chance of servicing the target. So if you can't approach the prey, have him approach you. On turf he thinks is safe territory. See how many layers of security are peeled away.

The answer: quite a few. The man's presence announced itself at a distance. An expanding bubble of awareness moved through the building. Seeing the president in State's HQ was a long way from blue-moon rare, but he was still a big disruption of routine. Blaylock knew he was coming by the reactions on the faces she passed. She saw irritation, she saw concern, she even saw the occasional flash of excitement. But there was a reaction of some kind, no exceptions. Something's up, some-one big is coming, the comfort of tedium is being torn. You just wait, Blaylock thought. Just wait for it.

She kept her movements close to Taber's office, never los-ing sight of the battlefield. Two minutes after the reactions cued her to Reed's imminence, the man arrived. She almost whooped when she saw the opposition's strength. Reed had two Secret Service men with him. They looked relaxed, defences down now that they were in a secure environment. Their duties would resume when they stepped outside again. Right now they were on autopilot. Blaylock walked towards the trio, playing with fire. They weren't paying attention to her. A man five paces ahead brushed past the president, and the bodyguards didn't twitch an eyelid. Blaylock came up. She didn't look at Reed's face. They had spoken before. She doubted he would recognize her from Davos, not in this uni-form of the defeated, but there was still that opening to bad luck. The move was borderline stupid. It was also exciting. He didn't glance at her. She passed close enough to stab him, if she'd been armed. She could have reached out and crushed his throat with a fist. The temptation of the easy kill tingled her skin. She did nothing. Killing Reed was only one of two goals. The other was a successful retreat. She would leave the suicide runs to the religious.

Blaylock walked on. Behind her, Reed stepped into Taber's office. That started the clock running. Time to move. The washroom was down the hall and to the right. Blaylock went inside. The place was packed, the minor excitement of the president's passage triggering talk, slowing everyone down. The stall Blaylock wanted was vacant, a small mercy. She moved inside, locked it, sat down, and waited. The clock ran. Her frustration built.

Women came and went, but there were always just enough to keep the conversation going. Blaylock eyed her watch. The discussion looped back over itself and repeated its central premise every minute or so as the group renewed itself through turnover. The machine's motion began to look perpetual. She had to spanner the works.

"I say he's going to cut her loose," said one voice, speaking the majority view.

"Are you kidding?" said another, for the minority. "He wouldn't dare. She could burn him. I know she could."

Enough. Blaylock summoned a sob. The acoustics in the stall were terrific. The sound hit the conversation with a guillotine blade. Stricken pause. Then, a solicitous voice: "Are you okay?"

"Just leave me alone!" Blaylock wailed. And they did,

whispers of speculation beginning even before the washroom door shut behind them.

Up. Climb. Ceiling tile. Duffle bag. She took out the clothes. They were loose enough to fit over Kawin's slacks and blouse. Loose enough to hide her gender. She took off her wig, pulled on the balaclava and gloves, then replaced the bag. She stepped out of the stall, and saw herself in the mirror. Time stepped back. She was the same black-clad shadow she had been before her first assassination. That day, she had shot a man in a restaurant, splattering her future lover with her victim's blood. On that day, Flanagan had thought the world had opened up to show him the worst of hell. He'd been naive. He knew that now. She'd splattered him with so much blood since. And now she was going for her biggest hit yet, and her lover, far from ignorant or horrified, would bless her.

She took a breath, felt the fire of war, and there were no more doubts. She approached the bathroom door. No point in stealth anymore, dressed like this. She threw the door open. A woman on the other side recoiled. Blaylock ran down the corridor, took the corner hard, and picked up juggernaut momentum as she barrelled towards the door to Taber's office.

One of the Secret Service men was posted outside. He saw her but she was so out of place in her combat blacks and mask that she didn't compute, and his instincts were slowed by a critical second. He still had his pistol drawn by the time she reached him. But only drawn. Not aimed. He was swinging his arm forward when Blaylock plowed into him. She swept the gun aside with her left arm and slammed the heel of her right palm against his chin. His neck snapped back with a lights-out click and the back of his head banged against the wall. As he slumped, Blaylock snatched the pistol from his limp fingers. She could hear screams beginning to rise around her. The hallway was filled with panicky movement. She ignored the distractions, laser-focused on the mission, and burst through the door. The other Secret Service man was in the reception area. He was perched on the secretary's desk, just shifting into reaction mode when Blaylock shot him in the knee. He fell, yelling, but still had his own gun out, still fumbled for an aim, the well-trained protector. Blaylock kicked his arm. His shot shattered the glass of a landscape painting on the wall. Blaylock stomped on his wrist, breaking it, and grabbed the gun. She turned from the writhing agent. The secretary was reaching for her phone. Blaylock shot it. Leaving opponents alive, willingly giving up precious moments of uncontested action, she kicked open the door to Taber's sanctum.

The undersecretary and the president were facing her. They were frozen, poised for flight with nowhere to go. Reed's face was a portrait of terrified rage and denial. Blaylock remembered him in Davos. He'd been towering serene authority then, as the dirty bombs went off and the city burned. His impassivity then was cheap and easy. He'd known that the show orchestrated by Stepan Sherbina wasn't going to touch him. Different story now. The show was going to kill him, and how could God allow this? Because God was a reptile, and he raised Blaylock's arm. Reed grabbed Taber and shoved her in front. Blaylock held her fire. Reed ducked low behind his shield, holding her in place. Blaylock reached out, grabbed Taber, and yanked her out of the way. Reed had gained a second and rolled behind the desk as Blaylock fired. Her shot gouged the wall.

Blaylock moved forward, heard a noise behind her, spun and hit the floor. The agent with the shot knee and broken wrist was in the doorway, his left hand clutching a small pistol. Blaylock had forgotten, goddamn it to hell, *forgotten* to check for ankle holsters. The man was on the floor, crawling and trying to fire with the wrong hand, but still a legit threat, and Blaylock really didn't want to kill him. Behind him, his partner arrived, groggy but standing, and they both opened fire. They were clumsy from wounds and concussion, and they missed, but they drove her away from the desk, to the wall of monitors. Blaylock shot back, aiming over their heads. The one with the knee rolled back to the other side of the doorway and cover. The one on his feet roared into the room and jumped over the desk. He covered the president's body with his. Blaylock would have to shoot through Kevlar and innocent bone if she wanted her target. The operation had gone south. She faced the idea of a massacre, and it wasn't even a decision.

A bullet took out the monitor above her. Glass rained down. She rose to her feet, letting loose with suppressive fire, and ran from the office. She leaped over the agent as he crawled her way, and she was through the door to the hallway before he could turn around. She slammed the door behind her, took the second she'd gained to gauge the terrain. The corridor was deserted. Everyone in hiding, the lessons of Columbine and countless office slaughters well learned. Blaylock ran, shooting out security cameras, and in the time it took her to reach the first intersection, someone triggered the alarm. The building began to whoop and scream.

Back to the washroom. She tore off the balaclava and assassination gear, and turned back into Kawin. By the time she had retrieved her bag, tossed the guns and clothing inside, then hidden the whole kit again, there was the clamour of human voices joining the chaos of the alarms. Blaylock put herself back into character. She thought of the staff who had been close enough to hear or see her vortex. She thought of the secretary, who had done nothing to deserve the trauma Blaylock had brought down on her, who would be scarred by her actions, and who would be haunted by Blaylock in her nightmares to come. She thought of the pain she was spreading in the name of rationales each more dubious than the last, except for war in its own name. And when she had thought all this, she saw her works for what they were. But the awful thing was the realization that she would do far, far worse, and that was what summoned the wail. Her cry was so convincing she didn't know if she was acting or not. There would come a time, not now, but later, when she tried to sleep, when she would wonder, and fear the questions she would ask herself. But for now, the only thing that mattered was that others believe in her, and they would, since she almost believed in herself. She huddled in a corner, under a sink, and screamed for help. She worked herself into red-faced hysteria, exhilarated by the insane risk of the ploy. She hollered high-do fantastic for a solid minute before anyone came. She had honest-to-God tears in her eyes when two security guards burst in. They had weapons drawn and faces blanched. Their jobs were suddenly crucial, and they wanted none of it. When they saw that she was alone, one of them giggled with relief. "Come on," the other commanded, and grabbed Blaylock under the arm.

"What's going on?" she asked, and the quaver sounded damn good.

"We're getting you out of here, that's what's going on." He dragged her to her feet and began to haul her towards the door.

"I can't go out there," she begged.

"You have to," said the other guard, his fear as genuine as hers was counterfeit, and he still did his job. Blaylock gave him a mental salute, was glad he would be safe from her.

They herded her into a growing crowd, and the evacuees were led from the building. The hallways were an echo barrage of sirens, screams and yells. There was all the chaos of an ongoing war, but the war itself was over. The terror, did the good people of the State Department but know it, was being flushed from the system along with them. Outside, the afternoon was flashing red and blue from an ocean of police cruisers. Emergency personnel rushed forward. Someone threw a blanket around Blaylock's shoulders and hustled her to the back of an ambulance. Was she wounded? Was she all right? Was she sure? Yes? Yes? Okay. There's a therapist somewhere. You can speak to her if we can find her. Here's some coffee. And she was shuffled aside to make way for the next case. Posture slumped, wig hanging down over her face, Blaylock made her way to the background. When she reached the rear of the scene, she looked over the panorama of vehicles, armed SWAT members, sobbing employees, and media trucks and helicopters arriving pell-mell. She saw monster headlines being born. She saw what she had done.

For nothing.

7

Chapel was using the computer in Felix Jurado's office when the news came in. He'd been confirming landing sites and dates for Quintero's arrival, was feeling good about having his pieces in motion, feeling good enough, in fact, to push the gnawing worry about the previous day's big event aside for the moment. Then Jurado's phone rang. He answered, went pale, hung up and grabbed the mouse from Chapel's hands. "What is it?" Chapel asked, and his feeling good turned into big, bad, spooky intuition. Jurado didn't answer. He clicked over to CNN's Internet feed. Chapel watched the circus at the State Department. After a minute, as the implications sank in, he said, "Shit."

"Fuck," Jurado agreed. He slow-burned. "This your screw up?"

"Hell, no. You really think that?"

"Just want to know what's what." He gestured at the screen. "Doesn't look like a smart move."

"And it makes no sense, given what I *am* doing," Chapel put in.

Jurado shrugged his assent. "Had to ask." He turned in his seat to face Chapel.

"I'm taking the heat for this."

"Who else?"

Too right. He watched the coverage a bit longer, saw the walls close in. The speculation was all over the map for the moment, but that wouldn't last. If a car bomb had taken down the building's facade, if there had been bodies littering the parking lot, he might be okay, eyes turning to al-Qaida or homegrown whackjobs. No such luck.

Jurado worked the phone, calling contacts at State and the Secret Service. The picture took shape, and the noose around Chapel's neck tightened. A lone perp, in and out of security without a trace, this close to punching the president's number. This close. The work was good, had the earmarks of a covert op that hadn't quite come off. Chapel and Jurado both had seen plenty of jobs that failed a lot worse. "Christ," Chapel muttered. "Did I order this in my sleep?"

"You'd think," said Jurado. "So if not you, who?"

Chapel thought for a moment, drew blanks. "Makes no sense." Unless he cast himself as Suspect Number One.

"You like a link with Taber's house?"

Two hits on Taber, then an attempt on Reed in her office. No such thing as coincidence. Of course they went together. But he hadn't looked at that picture until Jurado pointed it out, and now he saw the pattern, and now he had gooseflesh. "Oh, shit."

"Who?"

Gambits for which you needed bigger balls than God. Massive property damage. The fingerprint was huge, couldn't be missed, shouldn't be possible. She's dead, goddamn it, blown to bite-sized chunks. He had what was left of her skull on file. He'd snipped that loose end good and proper. But ghosts didn't use c4. They didn't wear balaclavas. "Someone who's dead," he told Jurado.

The other man raised his eyebrows. "Then he's *really* good."

"She."

Jurado looked startled. Didn't happen often. "Your Ember Lake woman?"

"And Davos. And Geneva. If it explodes, she's nearby."

"But I thought you—"

"Exactly."

"So?"

So figure this out. Walk it back, see how she might be alive. "I need some time to think."

"Tick-tock, tick-tock. Bye-bye, Joe's security clearance."

Too right again. He didn't think he'd be arrested. There was no evidence. But in the court of politics, he was already drawn and quartered. He was about to lose his base of operations. He was honest with Jurado. "I'm going to need friends."

Jurado was honest right back. "You're poison. Plague. God-damn contagious."

"Don't I know it."

Jurado nodded, looked thoughtful, as if feeling maybe he did have one or two things to lose after all. "I'll do what I can for the Quintero boys. Arrange a safe house or two. I'll try to sit on a few things. Other than that…" He shrugged.

"Already more than I could ask," Chapel told him, and shook his hand.

He headed back to his office. When he stepped in, he wasn't surprised to see Korda ensconced in a chair, waiting for him. Korda looked grim, but there was a hint of satisfaction about his expression as well. "I can guess what you want," Chapel said.

"You might be surprised. So. What happened at State, you never saw it coming?"

"Did you?"

Korda pressed his lips together. He looked like a toad with a bad smile. "Cute."

Chapel moved behind his desk. He remained standing, maintaining height over Korda. Made him look up. "You're here for my resignation," he said.

"No," Korda said, "I'm not." Now the toad's smile grew broad, in anticipation of flies. "Surprised?"

Chapel said nothing. He stared at his enemy, refusing to play his game.

Korda went on. "You're not being shitcanned. You could be, but you're not." He paused.

"Are you waiting for gratitude?" Chapel demanded.

"Just a reaction. Thank you." The toad was amusing himself. "You aren't even being suspended."

"What, then? I'm receiving the Congressional Medal of Honor?"

"Har, har, and hee. No. You are remaining, especially as far as the public is concerned, very much the DD of Operations."

In other words, square in the spotlight, Chapel thought. Scapegoat. Anything that Reed or Korda threw at him would stick like tar. "That's so big of you I could cry."

"We believe in keeping our enemies close. We like 'em even better pinned and wriggling."

"You might be surprised, too."

"I doubt it. Did I forget to mention your working conditions? Your Directorate has new standing orders. Nothing from your office is acted on without clearance from me. You don't have the authority to order so much as a pack of Post-It Notes."

Korda was right to be toad-smiling. He had Chapel's balls in a vise. No unauthorized action meant he was being watched. Korda wasn't kidding about the Post-It Notes. Chapel knew he wouldn't be able to uncap a pen without the director knowing. He and Reed were boxing him in, to burn when they had all their kindling stacked up under him. Making his play with Quintero was going to be difficult with no resources. He needed an alternative. Time for Bretlinger to get off his ass.

She hunkered down in Kawin's apartment for a couple more days, boyfriend's corpse her only company. She brooded. It had been a long time since a mission had tanked on her. The mistakes gnawed, and the costs bit down even worse. The costs to Kawin bothered her the most. She could tell herself that the woman was better off without the son of a bitch in the bathtub beating her up, and Blaylock could believe that much. But the corpse, the stolen identity, those weren't big favours. Kawin was going to come back from her holiday to a world of chaos and trauma. Just another bit of roadkill on the side of Blaylock's highway to hell. And for what? The president was still alive. How useless is that? She could see from the coverage that Chapel was taking the worst of the fallout, which wasn't a bad thing, but worked out nicely for Reed, too. If anything, he was emerging from the fiasco with a stronger hand. She hoped he was a little bit nervous, at least. The Fates could afford to throw her that much of a bone.

She was stymied. She had no more moves to throw against Reed. Chapel was weakened; anything she did to him now would tilt the balance too far Reed's way. She was going to have to leave town and retrench. The idea of retreat tasted like bile. For the first time, she didn't know her next move. War had betrayed her, cut her adrift. She was going to have to go underground in the middle of a campaign.

With war gone, the loneliness came in like a cyanide fang. She missed Flanagan. She needed her comrade. She had held off contacting him while she set up the Reed hit. Even though he knew and approved of what she was doing, she didn't want anything to link him directly to the operation if it collapsed. It had, but she hadn't been caught. There was that little gift. She was pretty sure she'd covered her tracks well, but some of her camouflage was going to unravel once Kawin came home. There were still a couple of damage control measures she could take, and she would, once she started moving again.

She let the loneliness fester for two days. She knew Flanagan would be trying to contact her, but she resisted the temptation. Forty-eight hours of invisibility, she could be that smart. On the third day, she would allow herself to rise again, and minimize the harm to Kawin at the same time. She spent the last night in the apartment preparing to resurface. She wiped the place down, scouring her prints from the scene. She searched Boyfriend's pockets, found his wallet (Boyfriend had a name: Carter Wilmington, very posh), found his car keys. He was driving a penis extension of a Suburban. She located it half a block down from the building, and, just after 0230, she drove it round to the rear parking lot. In the suite, she debated trying to wrap up the body, or even just covering the man's face. She tossed the idea. It was pointless. If someone saw her, it would be obvious what she was carrying. She covered herself instead, changing back into her gender-neutral black clothes, and pulling on the mask again. See if you can do this one right, she told herself.

She found a bottle of Scotch, poured it over Wilmington to disguise the dead smell, pulled him out of the tub and hoisted him over her shoulder. He was dead heavy. She staggered under the weight to the door, peered through the peephole. The corridor was a bright wasteland of exposure, but was empty. She listened, heard nothing. She opened the door and made her way toward the rear staircase. As she wrestled her way around the first landing, one of Wilmington's feet caught the railing and Blaylock dropped him. The thumps were impressive and echoing. The corpse rolled down to the next floor. Blaylock scrambled after it, trying to listen for opening doors over the startled beating of her pulse. "Bastard," she whispered as she fought with the body. She won, and carried it out to the parking lot, where she shoved Wilmington into the back of the Surburban. She hid him with a tarp that was covering camping gear. Then she went back to the apartment, finished the cleanup, and gathered her equipment. She pulled off her mask and left Kawin's home behind. She climbed into the Suburban and took Wilmington for his last ride.

She made it a long one. She left the city, driving south, leaving the freeway when she could to catch the State highways and back roads down through Maryland. She followed the Patuxent River, watching it grow from minor effort to major force the further south she went. Dawn was an imminent threat when she finally found what she needed. A gravel turn-off led through woods to a rocky bluff overlooking the river. Here the current was fast and deep, and there was no shore to speak of. Blaylock drove the SUV to the bank's edge, got out. She opened up the rear and hit it lucky: Wilmington had a gas can. Mr. Prepared. The can and the camping gear didn't look as if they'd ever been used. Wilmington was the urban warrior who wore his equipment's outdoor pedigree as a fashion state-ment. Blaylock doubted he'd ever seen an outhouse in his life.

The camp gear included two air mattresses (folded in pris-tine creases, never inflated) and a foot pump. She disconnected the pump's hose, unscrewed the Suburban's gas cap, inserted the hose, and sucked until she had a flow. She filled the can, then splashed gasoline over the interior of the vehicle. She gave Wilmington's body a generous soaking. Everything she was doing was pure delaying tactic, and she knew it. When the body was found, it would still be identified. No point in making things easy, though. Might as well make Wilmington's murder look like three different kinds of overkill.

She checked the glove compartment, found emergency candles and matches, like Wilmington would ever have been snowbound. The dead man had gone out of his way to avoid the deeply unlikely. Blaylock thought, Never saw me com-ing, did you? She leaned in the driver's door and turned on the ignition. She lit the matchbook, tossed it in the back. The matches landed on Wilmington. The roar was dull but big, and the air filled with barbecued pork. Blaylock gave the fire time to build energy. The vehicle was almost a fireball before she reached in and threw the engine into gear. The Suburban went into a lazy roll over the edge of the bank. It plunged into the river, spun, guttering, in a molasses circle, and sank, not hurrying. Blaylock walked along the bank, a shadow in the trees, watching for any wreckage to emerge. The river's surface stayed calm. She stayed with the river until the sun rose. Then she made her way back to the road for the long walk to the nearest town. She still didn't have a plan, but she had a goal. If she had to retrench, she refused to be alone. She would head back to New York.

He walked the trail back in his sleep. The woman stalked through his dreams, a demonic wild card scuttling every strategy he threw up. Chapel's subconscious played back their encounters, especially the two in Geneva. The first was before the shooting proper had begun, when the body count was still, as far as he knew, zero, and Reed and Sherbina hadn't triggered the grand spectacle of their folly. The woman had stared him down, dared him to take her on. She called herself Baylor, and he believed no such thing, but he had never unearthed her real identity. The second time was during the end game, when the Kornukopia complex was wreckage and flame, and he lay in the clinic, his bones precision-smashed by Sherbina. The woman had loomed over him, and on her face he had seen an implacable math that zeroed his equation. His eyes snapped open then. It wasn't the memory of the woman's face that woke him. It wasn't even the fact that she hadn't killed him. He'd been rescued. That was what gave him the jolt. He remembered what he should have followed up long ago. Someone had stopped her from killing him. There had been a second woman present.

There were a lot of disappointed tourists in Washington. All visits to the White House had been suspended pending further notice. Jim Korda doubted further notice would ever be given under this administration. The man he met in the Oval Office was bone-rattled, and looked it. Korda have never even seen Reed off his stride, never mind upset. Scared? Full-eclipse rare. I have lived to see many wonders, Korda thought. "Let me guess," he said, as he settled himself in his chair. Reed was behind the desk again, sucking strength from its authority. "You want Chapel dead by sundown." He defied any recordings, guessing that Reed would be just as direct.

"Assuming we can't arrest him."

"On what evidence?"

"Why do we need any?"

"Because the man still has friends," Korda explained. Another sign of how shaken Reed was. The fully functional Sam Reed wouldn't need to be told. "Not many, but some. If we move on him with a weak case, we'd be handing them a weapon. You want to win this or not?"

"Then kill him." The president was frightened, but the scare was a combat scare. He'd had them in Vietnam, but had never stopped fighting. When he gave the order now, his voice was calm as stone, and as unyielding. Korda reminded himself to be careful around this man.

He still spoke truth to power. "Have you been listening? If you shoot first, do you have any idea how many questions will be asked later?"

"Questions I can handle. Chapel will be dead."

"Your career will be, too. Think it through. It's already on the public record that Joe is in the shit with the administration. My great-aunt's dog knows how much you two hate each other. An attempted hit on you goes down. Who's the first suspect on everyone's mind?"

"Exactly."

"Exactly right back. Chapel dies. Who does everyone think ordered the trigger pulled? You ever heard of optics?" You one-eyed bastard. Korda liked his joke. Make fun of the president with the glass eye. Good stuff. He almost giggled. He held the laugh in. "We destroy him publicly, shred his credibility, make every last one of his friends run screaming into the night, then we fire and arrest him. Voila. Neutralized."

"But not dead."

Korda shrugged. "You never know what could happen in the fullness of time. But it has to be when no one can remember who the hell he is anymore."

Reed shook his head. It was the only part of his body that was moving. The rest was immobile, a steel sculpture ready to spring. He was sitting with his hands flat on the desk. Korda felt a shadow of worry that those hands might suddenly reach across and grab his throat. Reed said, "This is taking too long. The war ends now."

"Try it and we lose," Korda pleaded. "We have him boxed in. He's paralyzed." He told Reed about the measures he'd taken at the Agency.

Reed stared at him in open disbelief. "You've never been out in the field, have you?"

"I know the game," Korda replied, on the defence.

"You know the chessboard. You don't know the field. Why do you think I want Joe dead? Because he's damned good at his job, and he was a first-rate field operative before he climbed the ranks. If he wants to move, he'll move."

"He'll still find it difficult. And if *we* act too soon, the whole thing *will* blow up in our faces. Plus there's another consideration."

"Which is?"

"What if Chapel had nothing to do with the hit?"

Korda was used to not being believed. That went with the territory. But the look Reed now gave him was of the purest disbelief he had ever seen. "Are you insane?"

Don't you wish. "No, and neither is Joe. What did this look like? Like a covert op. He wouldn't be stupid enough to mount an operation that *looks* like an operation. He'd have left leads pointing in another direction. If Chapel had tried to kill you, trust me, we'd be rounding up every male of Middle-Eastern origin in the country."

"So you're saying because the job looks like him, it probably wasn't."

"You did intel in Vietnam. Figure it out."

Reed looked equal parts thoughtful and alarmed. "If not Chapel, then who?"

"Your list of enemies that short?"

"No, it isn't. But you're the one who's supposed to know which ones are actually trying to do something about me."

"Working on it. In the meantime, we don't rule Chapel out. He's still dangerous. He might not have targeted you yesterday…"

"But not because he didn't want to," Reed finished. "Okay." He stood, ending the meeting. "He doesn't die tonight, but that's only so you can squash him. Fast and soon. Understood?"

Korda nodded, pleased. Say this for the man: he listened to reason. "What do you plan to do about the Hamptons?" The Reed family summer home, unto the umpteenth generation, was in the town of Petersfield. The president was supposed to spend the July long weekend there.

"I plan to see you there for my barbecue." Reed answered using the same steel that had demanded Chapel's head.

Korda swallowed. He liked the security he had built up around himself, and his house. He did *not* like sticking his head up for Chapel to play Whack-a-Mole. "If you're sure..." he began.

"I am. I will not cower in this office until the war is over. I will not grant Chapel or anybody else that victory. I will rely on the Secret Service to protect me and my guests. And I will rely on *you* to run our enemies to ground. Think you're up to the task, Jim?"

Korda wasn't going to give him any openings to replace him. "Of course I am."

Reed walked to the door and held it open. He looked at Korda expectantly. "Then why are you still here?"

8

He would have felt clever if he wasn't so pissed off and humiliated. Chapel couldn't do his research from home or the office. If Korda was watching him at work, every blink and breath he had at home would also be catalogued and parsed for subversive signals. What he was looking for shouldn't send up those kinds of red flags, but it might make Korda wonder. He didn't want Korda wondering. He hit the library instead. He surfed the net in anonymity. He searched for Global Response, references to and posts by, in the days and weeks surrounding the World Economic Forum in Davos. The group's website had been shut down in the aftermath of the Davos bombings. He and Sherbina had scapegoated them well. There was a wealth of material condemning and praising the group. Jonathan Alloway, blown to mist by his own explosive, came up over and over again, canonized and demonized as a cross between Che Guevara and Mohammed Atta. Chapel knew about him. He could also remember the names of the patsies who had been rounded up, held in the American Mission under the Agency's auspices, and whacked by Sherbina's plants before being shipped to Guantanamo. He looked for another name. He knew he was digging in the right place. The prisoners, before they had died, had babbled about a woman who had stayed with them in Winnipeg, a woman they had wound up fearing almost as much as the authorities. So Nemesis had been there. And she had a friend. The link wasn't steel, but it would do.

It took him five minutes to hit bingo with a blog excerpt. It was one of the minor anti-globalization websites, one that didn't coordinate the protests, but posted the author's heroic diaries and souvenir pictures of the marches instead. One of the rants was dated a week before the WEF. Joe Birkenstock was lamenting his inability to make it to Switzerland. He blamed the security clampdowns. Chapel doubted the joker would have made it through customs, but suspected a lack of job and money had more to do with his problem. None of the protests he had attended were beyond a two-hundred-mile radius of his house. As proof of the extinction of the right to raise hell, he quoted from a description of what protestors would be up against. The author of the worried sketch was Kelly Grimson of Global Response. Chapel popped her name into Google. Plenty of hits. She'd been one of the movers of GR, but hadn't been caught in the dragnet after the destruction of Davos. He tried to find a picture of her. No luck.

He drummed his fingers against the monitor, then left the library. At a 7-11, he bought a prepaid long-distance card. Two minutes at the payphone with directory assistance told him that there were only two Grimsons listed in Winnipeg. He cross-referenced with Alloway, and eliminated the phone number in common. No point calling Global Response's home base of Greenham Common. The co-housing project had been torched by Sherbina's proxies to goad the volatile Alloway into doing something stupid and violent. The best kind of scapegoat actually does the thing he's going to be blamed for. Alloway did take a bomb to Davos. He didn't know it was dirty, and he didn't know it was detonated by remote control and not by the bogus timer he played with, but he still carried a bomb to the protest.

One Grimson left. Chapel called. The woman who answered sounded like a senior. Chapel did his best to sound friendly and innocent. "I was hoping to speak with Kelly Grimson," he said.

"She's…" Hesitation. "She's not here."

"Oh dear, that is too bad. I was going to be in town only for a few hours and wanted to catch up. She is back from Switzerland, isn't she?"

"No." A tiny, beaten voice. "No, she's not. She's been missing for months." The voice collapsed in sobs.

Gotcha, Chapel thought, and hung up.

Quintero was expecting to meet Joe Chapel at Dulles. Chapel wasn't there, but an agent hustled them through Customs and into a minivan that drove them all to Langley. Even better, Quintero, thought. Straight to business. Now we'll get some things done. His antennae prickled, though, when they arrived and the agent had Maldonado and the others wait in the parking lot. "They're my men," Quintero protested.

"They'll be fine," the agent answered, as though that weren't completely beside the point.

They went inside. Quintero had been here before, back in the glory days of the School of the Americas. He'd come to know the Directorate of Operations well, and he'd *been* known, too. He hadn't needed an escort through the corridors. People had known him on sight. They had known to *respect* him on sight. Nobody knew him now. He walked the corridors as a supplicant, led as a child. The people he passed glanced at him with disinterest when they looked at all. He was wearing a cheap suit he'd been given on the boat. It had been wrinkled to start with, and he'd been in it over twenty-four hours. He wanted a shower, a shave, and a uniform. His uniform. He hadn't minded his appearance during the boat and plane travel. Here, he felt stripped of dignity, authority, and power.

Worse feelings, bad antennae pricklings, when he realized they weren't in Operations. The agent took him to the seventh floor and parked him in the waiting room outside the director's office suite. "Director Korda will be with you shortly," the man said, and left.

Quintero sat, worried, and fumed. No Chapel. Korda instead. Something had gone wrong. He knew a few things about quid pro quo. Chapel hadn't sprung him out of sheer idealism. There was something Quintero could do that would help Chapel, and since Korda had been mentioned in the phone conversations, then Chapel wanted him hobbled. So what was Quintero doing here? Not good.

He wasn't surprised that Korda kept him waiting forty-five minutes. That move was so old hat, he was surprised the director even bothered. Quintero wasn't fooled, and he wasn't impressed. Korda could play his social power games if he wanted. All they did was make him a little man. When he was finally summoned, Quintero marched into the office like the man he was: a general.

Korda was leaning back in his chair, swivelling it back and forth with his legs. He had a pen in his right hand, and was twiddling it over and around each finger. He was grinning. "Well," he said, "look what the cat dragged in. Hard times, eh, Jorge?"

"What do you want?" He would not banter with this man.

"Have a seat, have a seat."

"I will stand."

"Okey-dokey." The pen went round and round, in and out, back and forth. It was hypnotic. "So here you are. And here I am. Is this the conversation you were expecting to have? Let me guess: no. Where's Joe, you're wondering. Here's the thing. Joe's having a few problems. He really is going to have to sort them out before he'll be any good to anybody. Ever again. With me? Good. You always were a smart boy."

Quintero felt the insult. He didn't flinch. He promised himself extreme violence on Korda's person. "Get on with it," he said.

"Easy does it, boy. All in good time. I want to make a point, first. You want direct? How's this for direct: I wasn't supposed to know you were in the country. I wasn't supposed to know about the whole goddamn operation to free you. But I bet you knew that, being a smart boy and all. Good thing departments leak, wouldn't you say? Good thing I have loyal employees." He smirked. "Or at least employees who know how to cover and/or save their asses." He leaned his head back and gazed at the ceiling, making a show of thinking. "What do I want, you asked. Hmm. Yes. What *do* I want?" He looked back at Quintero and smiled again, Mona Lisa toad. "Let's try this. What do *you* want?"

Quintero hesitated. He saw the trap, knew he was going to lose at least a limb, probably his head, and couldn't see how to evade. He played for time, even as he resented having to do so. "Excuse me?"

Korda sat still. He stopped playing with the pen. His smile vanished. His face was cold cement. "'Excuse me,' fuck you. Don't play stupid. Answer the question. You want something. What is it? The next time I ask, you'll be back in leg irons."

All right, then. He had come here to be direct, so he would be. Especially with Korda. He was not going to let that game-player be the honest man of the two. "I want the best thing for my country."

"Which means you at the top," Korda put in.

Quintero ignored him. "When I had dealings with you in the past, you made promises of support. I want you to keep them now."

Korda began to laugh. "You want a coup, you cheeky monkey. What do you think this is, the 1980s?"

Quintero glared. "Yes," he said. "It is. Do you look south at all? Do you know what happens down there? Do you know the governments who are in power?"

Korda nodded. "Yeah, yeah, the bad old days are back again. Dominoes falling all over the place, leftists running the show—"

"Communists."

"Whatever. We have other things to worry about these days. Or maybe you didn't notice."

"You *should* worry about this."

"Is that a threat?"

Quintero didn't answer. Silence would give his bluff weight.

"I guess it isn't." Korda beamed contempt. "I mean, how could it be? You were just offering your best advice. Let me put your mind at ease, *General*." The title was libellous in its sarcasm. "If Venezuela or any other of your backwater, pissant countries gets too uppity, it will be slapped down. That's how things work. In the meantime, your countries are free to play in their sandbox. I guess you can relax now, right?"

"You made promises. I expect satisfaction."

Korda roared. "Jesus, you're priceless. 'I expect satisfaction.'" He laughed some more. "Do you really say things like that when you're speaking Portuguese?"

Spanish, Quintero thought, but didn't correct him. He wasn't going to rise to the insult.

"Did you misunderstand me? I said fuck you. Is that too vague?"

Quintero stared straight ahead, at a point on the wall above Korda's head. "I think we understand each other," he said. He turned to go.

"Where you off to?"

He stopped. He thought about killing Korda here and now. The thought was a good one, the impulse difficult to control. "There is nothing more to say."

"Sure there is. What, you think we say bye now, and I watch Chapel's latest bitch waltz off into the sunset? You that stupid? How the hell did you make it past private? Aren't you interested in your future?"

Quintero sighed. "What do you have planned for me and my men?"

"Listen to that esprit de corps. Leave no man behind. You know what I love about you army types? You're the last

113

of the unreconstructed sentimentalists." He paused, waiting for a riposte, or pausing before the execution. "The United States of America believes in the rule of law," he went on with a straight face. "It also believes in being hospitable towards its guests. You will be comfortably housed pending your extradition back to Venezuela."

"I will speak with the president," Quintero thundered. He had known Sam Reed back during the golden years, too. Reed had been on the SOA's board of directors.

"I'm speaking *for* the president," Korda said. His smile was quick, thin and smug. "He doesn't want your pain in his ass any more than I do."

Quintero hoped Korda could see the hatred on his face. The man should learn to fear it. "You are traitors. Both of you. Men of no principle."

Korda shook his head, completely unruffled. "We're just good at what we do."

Felix Jurado didn't get mad much these days. To be angry, you had to care, and there was just no percentage in caring. There was a time, far enough back that the memory was hazy now, when he had cared. That had done nothing but set him up for loss. After losing enough times, he had begun to see the black humour that ruled the universe. He hadn't thought much about principles in a long time. Chapel had stirred some embers for him. There were people he wouldn't mind seeing screwed, some things in America that needed a good blowtorch. Chapel was a good man to do the torching. He was taking his hits now, and Jurado had no intention of being caught by the splash damage of any explosion. But there were still one or two vestigial buttons that, when they were mashed, pissed him off. Stomping all over a man's turf was one. Leaks in his department was another.

He heard about Korda's intercept of Quintero from Sue Berg. She called him from the safe house, asking if he still wanted the place active, or could she shut it down, since the clients weren't coming. What did she mean, they weren't coming? Hadn't there been a change of plan? she asked. She thought Quintero was meeting with Korda. Jurado held his temper, asked her how she knew this. Matt Collins had called her from Dulles, told her he was taking it from there. Collins entered Jurado's shit list, never to leave. Korda cemented his position, bought himself the e-ticket to Painworld. Swearing, Jurado hauled ass down to the parkade and blew out of Langley. He drove into Washington, stopped at the first payphone he saw, called Chapel's, hung up, called back twice more and hung up again. The signal for them to meet. Stupid goddamn ball-busting tactics. This was what they were reduced to these days. Retirement, Korda's ass on a platter and Reed's head on a pike couldn't come soon enough.

They hooked up at the Lincoln Mcmorial. "You followed?" he asked Chapel.

"Probably. You're stretching your neck out."

Jurado shook his head. "Too stupid. What happens when I'm pissed." He looked around, disgusted by the clandestine clichés he'd fallen into. "This is pathetic." He was a grown man, after all. He glowered at the monument.

"Yeah, but it works." They were moving up and down the steps, cat's-cradling their way through the tourists, using the crowd and noise as cover. "What's up?"

115

Jurado told him. "If your op is screwed, you tell me now," he added.

"Going to jump ship if I'm sinking?"

"Got that right."

"Fair enough." Chapel was quiet for a moment. "No," he said. "The op is still good."

"You're sure."

"Watch them burn, Felix. Bring the marshmallows."

"So what do you want?"

"I'll set up a new safe house." His eyes twinkled, amused. "I think I can kill two turds with one stone."

"How long will that take?"

"I need a bit of time. Not too much. There's an ass that needs kicking, and after that, a couple of weeks, maybe. Do you think Korda will have shipped our boys off by then?"

"Bet he'd love to."

"Can you run interference?"

Really stretch that neck out. But he was pissed. "See what I can do."

"We'll need a good place to stash them. Surround them with friendlies so Korda can't do the grab again."

The idea popped in, bright and perfect. Jurado's mood went sunny and high. "How about a homecoming?"

Chapel caught on, laughed loud enough to make the nearby tourists stare.

New York and its vibe welcomed her back. Blaylock felt her batteries recharge from the ambient energy, and her mood lifted as the city juiced her up, made her ready for war again. She would find the strategy she needed. She'd kept up the rents on the SROs she used for caches, and had plenty of places to stay. Better: she had people to see. She called Flanagan at work midday. "Hey there," she said. That greeting meant she was at the Clinton location.

"How was your meeting?" Flanagan asked.

"Could have been better." They slipped into business-speak as innocuous as it was vague. As they talked, Blaylock heard her voice shake once or twice. They were going to see each other again. She was honest-to-God giddy. Little Jenny on the first date. Horny, too.

She was pacing by the time the evening rolled in. There was plenty of space for that. Her room held a mildewed mattress on a rusted and squeaking frame, and, stacked against the wall, weapon cases. Romance was in the air. War was an irrelevant distraction. She was going to hold and be held. She heard footsteps outside her door, and she threw it open. She was grinning, hungry and feral, as she grabbed Flanagan by the shirt collar. She dragged him inside, was already eating his face before she realized he wasn't alone. She released Flanagan and stepped back, nonplussed.

"I hope it's okay," Flanagan said. "You two really need to talk."

Not about a threesome, though, Blaylock thought, as she recognized Viktor Luzhkov.

Chapel in Pratella's office, putting the scare into the man, keeping him honest.

"I wish you wouldn't come here," the Speaker said. "You're bad to be around these days."

"Do what we talked about and I'll be gold before you know it."

Pratella's face was sour. "I don't have time. Why can't you go?"

"Because right now, I need my friends to act in my favour."

"A friend in need is a downturned nose," Pratella muttered.

"If that's what makes you happy," Chapel answered. He leaned forward into the older man's space. "Pack if you need to. I want you in New York by morning." He was slipping Pratella onto the hook and sending him out as bait. Bring her to me, he thought. Be that juicy worm.

Still horny, but war was hot, too.

When she first saw Luzhkov, Flanagan's security breach had infuriated her. What was he thinking? Who gave him permission to take such a foolish initiative? She was going to have to abandon this location. Flanagan must have seen the flare in her eyes. His eyebrows peaked in anxiety. He looked as if he were about to flinch away from a blow. His reaction burned away her anger. Her own insecurities spiked. Did he actually fear her? Still? Did he think she would hurt him? Really?

The question was too big. She recoiled from it, turned her attention to Luzhkov. The security breach wasn't terminal. He already knew her. He was another loose end she'd left dangling in Geneva, the one Kornukopia merc she hadn't killed. If she'd made a mistake, she could correct it now. But he had impressed her before, which was why he was still alive. She would give him the benefit of the doubt. And honey, maybe, just maybe, you should trust Mike's judgment. How would that be for a relationship's building block?

She locked the door behind them, gestured at the bed. "All there is to sit on," she said. She sat cross-legged on the floor.

Luzhkov seemed faster with certain realities than Flanagan was. "I could come back later," he said. Flanagan blushed.

Blaylock laughed. "That's okay. Mike looks like he'd think you were peering over his shoulder the whole time."

"I," said Flanagan, "am going to kill you both. " The embarrassment of the moment slunk off.

"Anyway," Blaylock went on, "I'm betting Mike is about to tell me why I should get into bed with you." She turned to Flanagan. "That about right?" She smiled, so he would know that she was not angry, and that she was receptive. The smile he returned made the evening a very good one.

"I think you should listen to the man," he said.

So she did. She was interested before Luzhkov began to speak. She was excited while he spoke. She was on fire when he finished. War, she thought. Better than chocolate.

"So?" Flanagan asked. "What do you think?"

She wanted this to be true. Her gut urged a leap of faith. Luzhkov had been wounded in Geneva, fighting *against* Sherbina, fighting *for* the right cause, and he hadn't even known her. She weighed the risk. The opportunity Luzhkov represented would be criminal to pass up. She asked him, "How many men are we talking about?"

"That depends. How important is trust?"

"Give me a sliding scale."

Luzhkov lowered his eyes for a moment. Blaylock could see him tapping through a mental PDA. He looked up again and said, "Six or seven I trust with my life. You can rely on them as you would on me."

Blaylock grinned. "Thanks for giving me something solid to measure by."

Luzhkov said, "I am offended," to show that he wasn't. He worked his way down his list. "A few dozen, I think more, who would act out of…" He hesitated.

"Conviction?" Flanagan suggested.

"Yes. Many more for the action."

"And for money?" Blaylock asked.

"Lots. But the action, I believe, will be the most important."

Sounding good. Sounding hot. The other big question: not if she could trust them, but if they would trust her. "What has Mike told you about the current op?"

"Nothing."

"We talked general principles," Flanagan said. "Not specific campaigns." Blaylock noted his use of the plural.

"How far would they be willing to go?"

After a moment, Luzhkov asked, "What happened in Geneva, is that typical?"

While Flanagan laughed, Blaylock said, "Remember when the G8 leaders were torched?"

Luzhkov's eyes widened. "That was you, too?"

"Indirectly. I wasn't targeting them." She shrugged. "Shit happens."

Luzhkov nodded slowly, visualizing consequences. "And now?"

Moment of decision. If she was going to trust the man, she was going to trust him. She had already revealed a lot, but the Rubicon was now. The Russian knew her past. Opening the door to her future was a big risk. For Luzhkov, too. "You know what you're asking?"

"I have an idea."

"People around me have a low life expectancy. I had some

forces with me at Ember Lake. The casualty rate was one hundred percent."

Luzhkov nodded Flanagan's way. "With an exception."

"Proving the rule." She was nervous, suddenly, at the prospect of responsibility and future loss. At Ember Lake, she had been prepared for the wipeout of her militia. She'd recruited people whose views and attitudes she'd despised, because she'd known she was leading them to slaughter. She had done her best to brainwash herself in the belief that she had set up one evil to fight another, that there had been a collateral elimination of a sample of the most dangerous strain of American subculture. Only she had lived with them, had grown to like them. And they hadn't been dangerous before she trained them. The guilt poisoned her nightmares. With what Luzhkov was proposing, she was opening herself up to something much worse. She was attracting goddamn *followers*. *Comrades*. How many losses could she face going through? How filthy would she demand they become? "I hope you're not planning to wash away past sins," she said. She gave Luzhkov a hard look. She thought he squirmed a bit.

"I have my shames," he said.

"Are you ready for more? I'm about retribution, not redemption." Her damnation had been complete and irreversible for a long time now. There was a certain liberation in that awareness.

"I'm ready."

"You'll love it," Flanagan said. To Blaylock he said, "You worry too much. We can take responsibility for our own psyches."

He was right, and still her heart sank when he spoke. The enjoyment she heard in his tone, and the excitement, were too familiar. They belonged in her, as part of her filth. In Flanagan, they sounded unalloyed.

(But you're not alone. How great is that?)

Too fucking great for words.

"I don't think you eat little babies," Luzhkov said.

"I did just try to assassinate the president of the United States." The confession was out before she realized she'd come to a decision.

Luzhkov whistled. "That was you?" He clucked his tongue in admiration. "When do we try again?"

The plural pronoun. Here we go, Blaylock thought, and really, truly, honest and for sure, war was so hot it was better than anything. Her mind began to snap and fizz with excitement and tactics. The really big idea took shape.

9

Nick Brentlinger ushered Patrick Pratella into his office. "Do sit down, Mr. Speaker. We're honoured to have you."

Pratella lowered himself into the proffered chair, sighing. The seat was big, leather, plush. It smelled very, very new. The whole office smelled new. Someone had been on a spending spree. Brentlinger's desk was littered with real estate brochures. There was an impressionist print on the wall next to Pratella. He looked at it more closely. He could see the relief of the brushstrokes. Not a print, an original. Beside it was a Mondrian. They clashed. Behind Brentlinger's desk hung a Fragonard. It didn't work with the other two. Nothing made sense with what he knew of Brentlinger's character, or at least the aspects of it that had made Chapel decide to anoint him the favoured son of InSec. Late-life crisis and power trip, Pratella guessed. He had had his own bouts with the symptoms. There was a time and a place for those indulgences. This wasn't it. Work wasn't being done, and Chapel was on his back. If Brentlinger didn't do his job, Chapel might dream up some way of forcing Pratella to become more active in whatever was going on. The Speaker didn't like that idea. He was happy living in the vague world of totally plausible deniability. All he needed to know was that Chapel's game was going to play out to his benefit. Having to haul ass out here to buck up a player who should know better than to dawdle was a pain and it was dangerous. Pratella said, "Do you know why I'm here?"

"I wasn't sure—"

"Then you should be, or what use are you? I was sent here. Do you understand? *Sent.* I don't appreciate being *sent.* Who, do you think, *sent* me? Who, do you think, is not happy with your progress on certain fronts? Since he isn't happy, he is making me unhappy. So where does that leave you? I will explain. Shit rolls downhill." Sometimes, the old sayings were the best. "So what I want to know is why you're still just one of several directors. Why," he asked, thinking of his own payoff, "aren't you first among equals?"

"I am working on it." Brentlinger's face had closed down, and was looking very much the outraged Mormon. "I'm almost ready to move."

"Prove it."

"Well, I—"

"*Now.*" He wasn't leaving until he saw some real momentum.

Brentlinger clasped his hands, beat them softly against his lips. His eyes were flicking with calculations. He tapped his speaker phone, asked his secretary to send for Mike Flanagan.

"Who is that?" Pratella asked.

"My head of shipping."

"What about the board?" Pratella didn't care about the peons.

"I … I was hoping Chapel could provide some muscle."

Pratella rolled his eyes. "Are you stupid?" He could see this much of Chapel's gameplan without even wanting to. "Why do you think he wants you, his boy, running InSec? What is InSec good at? *You're* going to be *his* muscle."

There was a knock at the door and a man let himself in. He was in his thirties, smartly dressed in executive bland, and at first glance reminded Pratella of the kind of junior assistant he regularly reduced to tears. Especially the male ones. Honest, eager to please, smart and decent, green as stupidity. It was the eyes that made Pratella change his mind. They were cautious, watchful, older and wiser than they should be. "You wanted to see me," he said to Brentlinger.

"Right, Mike, thanks for coming by. This is—"

Pratella cut him off. "I'm sure you didn't call Mr. Flanagan here for the niceties." He didn't want his presence here advertised any farther, if he could help it.

"Buying a new house, Nick?" Flanagan asked, eyeing the brochures.

Brentlinger stammered for a moment. Pratella wanted to bury his head in his hands. "Looking at getting a summer place," he said, his smile much too forced. "I'm not growing any younger, and the wife and I are thinking about retirement, you know."

Flanagan nodded, looking about as impressed as Pratella felt. "The Hamptons are the place for it, all right."

"The reason I asked you here is that," deep breath, "the time has come for those changes we talked about to be implemented."

"I see. We'll be ready in shipping. When's the big day?"

"Very soon."

"Right." Pratella caught the tone. Flanagan didn't sound any more confident in Brentlinger than he was. But he seemed ready to play ball for now: Brentlinger was still going to need much more solid support if he wasn't going blow the whole works.

"Thank you, Mr. Flanagan," Pratella said, dismissing him. Flanagan left, and Pratella said to Brentlinger, "Set a date."

"It isn't that simple," Brentlinger protested.

"Then make it simple." He pulled out one of the standard bully threats. It was a standard because it always worked. "Set a date before I walk out of this office, or we'll find someone else to work with."

Sometimes, you had to give the fear to generate results. Just look at the Old Testament. Good lessons from the Good Book. And here, results: Brentlinger with his eyes shut, rubbing his temples, for all the world looking like a man thinking as hard as he possibly could. "I suppose, as long as I put the order in first…" he began, then trailed off.

Pratella worried that the earth might fly off its axis if Brentlinger took an initiative. "Caution doesn't grease the wheel," he encouraged. "What are you thinking?"

"Using internal muscle."

There we go. The man was thinking.

Flanagan said, "He's buying property in the Hamptons, and he's fidgety about it." They were at Blaylock's SRO squat. He had suggested meeting at his apartment. "It's nice," he'd said. "It's known," she had responded.

"What is in the Hamptons?" Luzhkov wanted to know.

Blaylock didn't answer. She was staring at jagged pieces,

knew that the picture they'd form would have even sharper edges. "You're sure he was with Peter Pratella?" she asked.

"Positive. I've seen that smug face of his in the news often enough. That character bit he pulls gives him plenty of visibility. That and calling down the wrath of God on anyone to the left of Atilla the Hun."

"A man with ambitions?"

"Oh yeah. What are you thinking?"

She ticked off the points. "Pratella and InSec. Brentlinger about to move to take over the top spot at InSec. Brentlinger buying property in the Hamptons."

"What is in the Hamptons?" Luzhkov insisted.

"Damned if I know," Blaylock said.

"Oh," said Flanagan. Blaylock could almost hear the click in his head. "The president's summer home is in Petersfield."

The pieces snicked into each other. "Chapel," she whispered.

"What's he trying to pull?" Flanagan asked.

Blaylock lowered her whisper still further. The idea was almost too huge, too terrifying, to exhilarating to speak. "A coup."

Nightfall at Fort Benning. Chapel approached the quarters of Major General Bill Eastman, post commander and chief of infantry. The man was outside, sitting on his porch. He was in his late 50s, barely cracked five and a half feet, and was thin like rebar. He could cold-cock a bull. Charts covered the table at his right hand and spread out around his feet. He waved Chapel into a chair on the other side of the table. Chapel glanced at the papers. "Stargazing, General?"

"You know it."

Chapel looked up at the sky. There were more stars visible than in the city, but conditions still weren't ideal. "Can you see what you're looking for?"

"All I need is part of a constellation." Eastman had a notepad on his lap. Figures and symbols filled the first few lines of a page. The general was an astrology man. He took it seriously, approached the disposition of the stars the way he would that of troops. As hobbies went, Chapel thought it was nuts. He could deal with it, though. He'd seen action with Eastman in Kuwait, in Afghanistan, in Iraq. They had worked well together. The man was good, his beliefs solid, his ideology foursquare. He loved his country. That was what counted.

"What do the stars have to say about you and me?" Chapel asked.

Eastman didn't answer right away. He watched the sky for signs. He cleared his throat. "Interesting conversation I had with Felix Jurado," he said. Chapel waited. After a moment, Eastman went on. "Lot of things not working too well in this great republic of ours. Have to say Felix sees eye to eye with me on a lot of them."

"So you and I have a lot of common ground."

Eastman nodded. His face remained placid, but Chapel sensed a reluctance to commit himself to the conversation.

Chapel pushed the issue. "Did Felix tell you I'm trying to fix things?"

"Yes."

"And that I'll need your help."

"Yes." Eastman turned from the stars to face Chapel. "You understand, there are limits to what I can do."

"I know."

"Don't get me wrong. You're right as the Bible. That son of a bitch in the White House sure looked like he was going to make us shine on the hill once again, but he's only made things worse. He has to go. The whole rotten branch has to be cut before it kills the tree. But, you know, the army can't be seen to be changing the government, even when it's necessary. Just can't."

Of course not. Optics. "I know. You're right. I wouldn't think of asking you to violate your oath."

"Don't see how you're going to pull anything off without some troops."

"I have them. All I need from you is some gracious hospitality."

"You want to station them *here?*"

"Why not? They've all been here before. All graduates in good standing from the School of the Americas."

Eastman chuckled. "Can hardly turn away distinguished alumni. Anything else?"

"Nope. Just a place to stay, space to train. A little privacy."

"The less I know, right?"

"Right."

"How bad is this going to get?"

"Very bad. Serious casualty figures. Are you okay with that?"

"Omelettes, broken eggs, I'm fine. But if the blame police come looking for you, I'll burn you. Sorry, Joe, but that's how it is. You okay with that?"

"I'm perfect."

They shook hands.

It was a homecoming. Quintero thought they should have a reunion dance. It was only fitting, since the prize graduates were coming back to their alma mater. Quintero still thought of the place as the School of the Americas. The name change struck him as a capitulation, a cowardly retreat from the bad press generated by know-nothing NGOs and students who had too much time on their hands. He was proud of his time here. He was proud of what he'd learned. He was proud of what he'd done.

Pride in your school, however, did not mean being proud of being forced to go back. He was returning not as the valedictorian who had made good, but as the storm-battered refugee needing a port. At least he and his men weren't being deported. What they were, was being housed in a barracks tent. There were cots for two hundred and fifty, but the students had been moved out, and the old boys had the place to themselves. "Korda doesn't have any friends here," Felix Jurado had told them. They were safe here, for now. They were also powerless. Quintero sat on the edge of a cot. He felt diminished. The tent was halogen-sterile, its silver-grey fabric making him think of an operating theatre. There were high fences between the centre and the outside world. The difference between where they were and a prison was what? Quintero thought. He, Ernesto Maldonado and Alejandro Olano looked at each other. "Leave us," Quintero told the fourth man. Jaime Pérez was a good soldier, but he didn't need to hear this conversation. He would take and follow orders when they came. Pérez saluted and walked out the door.

"What now?" Olano asked.

Maldonado spat. "We sit here like dogs in a pen. Then Chapel loses his fight, and the last of his rats desert us, or

Chapel uses us as chips to play for time. Either way, we are going back to Caracas."

The same scenario had occurred to Quintero. He'd been stewing over it all the way to the compound. Hearing it articulated by Maldonado raised some doubts. A slight breeze of optimism fanned his anger. "I wonder," he said. "That was an expensive operation to free us. A lot of trouble to go through for some bargaining power. I can't see what value we would be to Korda. He's only interested in us because he wants to break Chapel."

"And why is Chapel interested?" Maldonado asked. "Why go to all this trouble?"

Chapel really wanted them stateside, that much was clear. He had his reasons, and Quintero knew they wouldn't involve a sense of the wrong being done to the SOA's finest and brightest. "I'll ask him," he said.

His chance came the next day. Chapel showed up at the dorm, looking tired but battle-ready. There was a set to his face that Quintero knew well. Chapel was a warrior who had taken hard hits, but had confidence in his planned counterattack. "Gentlemen," Chapel said. "I'm sorry for the inconvenience and the simplicity of the lodgings. Don't worry, your stay here is very temporary. Is there anything you need, in the meantime?"

"Uniforms," Olano said. Quintero silently thanked him for standing up for their dignity.

"Trust me, you're not going to need them," Chapel replied.

"Why not?" Quintero asked.

"Feel like a walk, General?"

Chapel led him away from the barracks and the training grounds toward the campus. Here the landscaping transformed from utilitarian to aesthetic. The main building was a tribute to the southward-looking orientation of the Institute, with its pink brick, orange tiles and central cupola. Quintero watched Chapel limp with his cane. His posture was perfect, his balance and movement were giveaways of his field training, but his grace had been tainted. He paused in the garden outside the portico, and eyed the American flag that flew from a pole to the left of the entrance. He said, "The injustices keep raining down on your head, don't they? I apologize on behalf of my country."

"Very nice. Now what do you want?" Quintero was tired of the coy dance.

"I want to know how angry you really are."

Oh, but he was good, Joe Chapel. A simple, direct statement, that told Quintero absolutely nothing, while suggesting some very big possibilities. Chapel was still dancing, which meant he had to be sure about Quintero. Sure in a final way. Quintero decided to encourage him. At this stage, he was ready for anything. "As angry as action requires."

Chapel didn't respond for a moment. He turned his back on the flag and faced Quintero. "I really want to know how far you're willing to go."

"You want to go very far, then." When Chapel didn't respond, Quintero made a conscious effort to stop the dance. "Your nation betrayed mine, and it betrayed me."

"I am not asking you to destroy my country," Chapel said, dead cold and hard.

Quintero nodded. He could respect this man's patriotism. It was real, and it had steel. "Then what are you asking?"

"To help me save it."

"So it can, in turn, save mine."

"I think that's a distinct possibility, yes."

They were understanding each other. Good. "We have enemies in common." That was hardly a revelation. "Sam Reed and Jim Korda."

"Bringing them down," Chapel said, "will not be a clean operation."

"Whatever it takes," Quintero said, meaning it. He dreamed of grinding his boot into Korda's smug cheeks.

"There's more to this," Chapel continued. "Removing two weak men isn't enough. The country is sick, and it needs total shock treatment. We've been on the wrong track for years. If we're going to find our way back to the right road, it's going to take a massive blow upside the head."

"What do you have in mind?" Quintero asked. He was imagining some very big actions.

Chapel began talking coup. He talked details. Quintero felt his face pale with shock, and his eyes widen with admiration. The operation was very big. He'd never heard of anything bigger.

Blaylock still wouldn't go to Flanagan's place. The security aspects were just too stupid. If he had pressed her, she might have admitted that there was more to her recoil. He had been attacked there, while she was in Europe, by CIA operatives working by proxy for Stepan Sherbina. She had left him a shotgun for defence, hoping that he would never have to use it. He had. He'd killed three men, splashing his walls red, and fled. The shadow armies had descended on his home and purged all trace of an operation gone totally balls-up. When Flanagan returned home, it was as if nothing had happened. He seemed fine with the situation. Blaylock wasn't. There was the practical side. His apartment might be clean of blood and bodies, but nothing short of burning the building to the ground and sowing the foundations with salt would convince her that it was clean of bugs. There was more. There was the thought of the attack. Every danger that descended on Flanagan was because he had crossed her event horizon.

No going to Flanagan's apartment. But a night in a decent hotel, that was fine. A permissible luxury and minor risk before the next engagement. She could afford the Plaza in cash many times over, her coffers overflowing with the riches of an exterminated crime family. They didn't aim that high. They chose the middle-of-the-road unexceptionalism of a midtown Best Western instead. They swam in the rooftop swimming pool, under the earthbound constellations of the Manhattan skyline. Later, in bed, they touched each other's wounds, warming old scars. Flanagan's fingers fluttered over the ridges on Blaylock's body, the Braille of conflict left by bullet traces, flying glass, impacts massive or surgical. Her body's memories of its injuries. They didn't bother her. They were part of the pageantry of being the war machine, scorching and scoring the world around her, carving out deeper scars than any she received. The wounds she inflicted were septic and did not heal. Hers closed. Her family's death was, she believed, a sealed wound. Everyone responsible for the explosion that erased mother, father and little sister had been dead for well over a year now, some themselves incinerated. She still felt the loss, but vengeance was over and done. The murder of her nearest and dearest had pushed her onto her path. She had needed direction. She had it. That much of life, at least, was simple.

Everything else was complex. Flanagan didn't have the scars she did. He had similar emotional losses, his sister and nephew executed by Karl Noonan, InSec's brute-in-residence. He also had a physical loss that Blaylock didn't. The ring finger on his left hand was gone, chopped off and used for a prop by Dean Garrett, who worked for both the CIA and Kornukopia, and Blaylock didn't think that was a case of divided loyalties, not at all. The absence on Flanagan's hand was a reminder, an accusation pointing its phantom at her. This happened because he knows you. Everything bad that has happened to him, happened because he knows you. She kissed his stump. The flesh was puckered over the nub of bone and rough against her lips. "I'm so sorry," she said, the apology by now an incantation.

"Don't," he whispered, stroking her hair. "You have to stop. I don't mind it. It doesn't hurt, and it doesn't slow me down." He demonstrated with his tongue.

Afterwards, as they held each other, she said, "I'm afraid of worse things happening to you."

"I'm not." Flanagan squeezed her tighter. He laughed. "I can't wait to see what happens next." He was adapting too well to her world. He was infected with her disease. She remembered when he had looked at her with fear, when he did what he could to hold down the numbers on her body count. What he could do was nothing, but at least he tried. Now he was looking for ways to facilitate her wars. She could see the damage she was causing, and he wanted more. All wrong, all wrong.

And it made her happy. Really happy.

The emotional spiral was a vicious one, the whiplash

collision between the joy of not being alone and the guilt of corrupting a good and decent man. Round and round, shame and happiness. Happiness always won out. It felt good, and she wasn't about to lay down her weapons. She was convinced she was doing the right thing, even—and especially—if she had to damn herself in order to do it. Plus, she was too good at what she did to quit.

A whisper: it's fun, too. Yes, it is. *Fun* was what she heard in Flanagan's voice. Untempered fun was what worried her. "Are you happy?" she asked.

"What a question."

"Answer it, please."

"Of course I am."

"Why?"

He sputtered. "What kind of specifics are you looking for? Is this one of those 'we need to talk' conversations?"

She punched his shoulder. "No. I'm not asking if you still find me attractive, or if a dress makes me look fat. I'm concerned about *you*, not me. You know what we're doing. You know the sorts of things that are probably going to happen."

"So?" Genuinely puzzled. Either not thinking consequences through, or worse, welcoming them.

But I want him with me, Blaylock thought. I want my comrade at the barricades. I want the higher-sex bond of war. She said, "This thing we're going to do with InSec, you know what it entails? You know what you're going to help me do?"

"Yes."

"And?"

"They have it coming, Jen. Think about how many hundreds of thousands of rounds of ammunition these people have shipped out and made hot spots even worse. Think about how many people they've killed and how those numbers haven't registered beyond accounting figures."

"Am I any better? Are you?"

"We are."

"How?" He had to think about these things. Even if he couldn't find good answers, he had to ask himself the questions. He had to take some responsibility, too.

"Because we're bringing the bad guys down," Flanagan answered. Simple as that. "And it's going to be beautiful."

"You weren't saying things like this last fall."

"You've shown me so much more since then."

The Coscarelli warehouse, littered with Claymore-shredded corpses. Stepan Sherbina's private train, derailed and blazing. Kornokupia One, levelled. Her opera of destruction. In spite of herself, she felt the pride of the appreciated artist.

"I want to see more," Flanagan continued. "I want to be part of it." He raised his left hand and stared through the darkness of the room at his mutilation. "I want to make more of the bastards pay."

"Sometimes," Blaylock said, "people who aren't bastards get hurt."

"I survived." She felt him smile against her cheek. "And I'm the nicest guy going."

"Irina Zelkova," she murmured. "Inna." Sherbina's wife and child. Blaylock hadn't touched them physically. But she had made Zelkova her friend, and then destroyed her house with a mortar bombardment. She had used them to insert herself into Kornukopia One. They had witnessed her apocalypse. She had taken away the husband and the father.

She hadn't seen them since she began her final assault on Sherbina's fortress.

"Oh," Flanagan said, checked.

"They didn't deserve what I did to them."

He was quiet for a bit. Then, "Would you take back what you did?"

"No. I did what I had to."

"What you wanted to?"

"Yes." No hesitation. She could roll with her filth. The rewards of the perfected war were what her life fed on.

"Irina loved Sherbina, even though she knew what he was."

"Thanks for the comparison."

Flanagan ignored her. "She told me, when everything was burning and ending in Geneva, that I had to make a choice. I have. You know I did."

Yes. He had come to her in the wreckage, eager to be embraced by her horror. His fear and revulsion at Ember Lake had been completely burned away.

"I want to help you do more," he said.

She smiled. She accepted his damnation.

And like all moments when great art happens, the elements, shaped by inspiration, fell into place, the Reptile God's gifts to Blaylock.

The next morning, Viktor Luzhkov heard from Peter Vandelaare. "Can the man guess who's coming to New York?" Vandelaare asked. Luzhkov couldn't. "I am," Vandelaare said. "Didn't the man get the word?" Luzhkov allowed as how the man hadn't. "Lots of the old InSec boys are being called in for Friday. Something big going down. Does the man think we should be excited?" The man thought they should.

Luzhkov spoke to Blaylock. She felt the excitement build, that heavy-metal will to violence that expanded out from the chest and forced the mouth into a feral grin. Luzhkov put her in touch with Vandelaare. "Are you the lady?" the South African asked.

"I am."

Vandelaare said he was looking forward to meeting her. Quite a few of the guys were. He'd been spreading Luzhkov's word. They were more than ready for her to lay down the beat.

Blaylock turned to Flanagan, and told him what he needed to do.

Flanagan swung by Brentlinger's office, all smiles and serious purpose. "About those changes," he said. "I want to help bring them about." Brentlinger was delighted. He foresaw a bright future for Flanagan, and told him so. He also told him how he could help.

Flanagan told Blaylock.

Her grin was permanent now. The energy buildup was huge. Only one way to release it. Bring on the power chords.

10

Summer had held fire until May, but impatient, it cut loose, and brought the hammer down. The blow was a humid squelch on Washington. The air stilled, turned brown and thick. Movement became sluggish as swimming. Existence became an enervating struggle from one air conditioner to the next. Those with no AC turned to torpid worship in front of placebo electric fans. The first day of the heat, the sunbathers hit the parks and were colour filler on the local newscasts. By the second day, sleep-deprived and sticky tempers were short. The novelty evaporated double-quick. The high temperatures settled in for the duration. The forecasts were a monotony of upper 80s. And only May. June became a terrifying prospect. July and August were suicide threats on the horizon.

When things were hot enough, Chapel could feel the clammy energy-suck on his skin and in his bones, even when he was indoors and the machines were fighting hard against the climate. Pratella looked even more unhappy. His eyes were sunken, his armpits sodden. He was a drooping pudding in his chair. He looked up at Chapel and gave him all the joy of a third-time audit victim. "Why do you have to keep coming here?" the Speaker asked. "This could be so damaging to me."

"I should say so." Chapel sat down, put his feet up on Pratella's desk and crossed his ankles. Pretended his shirt wasn't glued to his flesh. "Gives you incentive to see our project through to success, doesn't it? Failure looks like a worse and worse option."

Pratella closed his eyes for a moment. "Let's get this over with," he said. "What do you want?"

"I want to hear about New York."

"I did what you said. Gave Brentlinger the kick in the ass. He's calling in the help and making the move Friday."

"What about the real estate?"

Pratella frowned, puzzled. Chapel wasn't going to clear things up for him. He was going to throw him a few more non-sequiturs. Might as well have a morsel of fun in the day. "He's made the deal," Pratella said. "Sounds like he's in the market himself."

"He'd better be," Chapel commented, making Pratella frown even more. "What about pamphlets and literature. Was he showing off?"

"Are you kidding? The gentleman and restraint are ants in the rain. He calls people in just so they can see his dream home location."

"He mentions Petersfield?"

"All the time." Pratella looked so baffled his energy was perking up.

"Good." He didn't know where the woman was, so he was

throwing chum into the ocean. She had a track record of swimming around InSec. If there was blood in the water, she'd scent it. Get the info out there, show his hand just that little bit, and she'd come, sooner or later. And he'd have his harpoon ready. In the meantime, he would set up his alternate Agency. InSec had global reach, intelligence assets, and weapon muscle. InSec and the Quintero cell: hammer and anvil. In between: Reed and Korda. Chapel still felt the heat, but the opposition was going to melt.

Friday.

The enforcers answered the call. They arrived at the InSec building in strength.

So did the war machine.

Bill Jancovich didn't do sleep well anymore. Too many nightmares. He didn't do work well anymore. Too much not sleeping. He hated his life, because his life was doing him hard, and with no lubricant.

He could see the irony, but didn't appreciate it. Jancovich knew computers. He knew them with the instinct and expertise of a Casanova. When he touched them, they responded. He never broke sweat. They were the one thing he did brilliantly. Reality outside the circuit board was spooky and dangerous, always had been. He had never been athletic, and puberty had been the doorway to permanent gangliness. He had the coordination of splinted kiwi. Junior high through to graduation had been a social apocalypse of acne, clothes that wore him badly, and evergreen pranks aimed his way. The dogshit in the locker, man, that *never* got old. But computers were sanity and salvation. He could speak to them. They responded politely.

They didn't give him a hard time. They didn't require social skills. They were a valuable skill in themselves.

The pranks stopped in university. Outright victimization came to an end. A frozen social landscape still existed, but even that saw the occasional thaw as he ran into other outcasts. He found his digital community, morlocks illuminated by the 3 a.m. glow of their monitors. He communicated less through speech than through the touch of flesh to keyboard plastic. He graduated with his PhD in computer programming and from his parent's basement at the same time. He landed a job whose starting figures were in the high five-digits in less than a week. This wasn't gym class anymore. Being unable to dunk a basketball was an irrelevance. What he was good at was important. He was in demand. The company that snapped him up was InSec.

He had a short honeymoon at work. There was that happy set of days, enshrined and golden in his memory, when he believed, really believed, that there was no difference, as far as his job was concerned, whether he was working for Integrated Security or Microsoft. He could do his thing, be the well-paid but insignificant cog, disappear completely and happily into a world of code, and never re-emerge. Then Karl Noonan took an interest in him. Jancovich had thought he'd left the scary boys behind in high school. He was wrong. They were older, and they were worse. He had a brutal master to please. His first ulcer developed. But he did what he was told, did it well, and prospered. More money, more responsibilities, better title. Very nice. More contact than ever with Noonan. Not nice.

And then one day Noonan asked him to identify a woman's face, and the thug must have triggered some horrible spell, unleashing a demon from her tomb, because ever since, the outside world had become terror and blood, with no escape into the circuits. First, InSec losing its master. Then the reorganization conducted by Russians even scarier than Noonan. Then the false hope: transfer to Geneva. Away from New York and its lurking terrors, into the land of clockwork and safety, working in a super-secure complex, and feeling that testosterone boost as, being a member in good standing of the security team, he first strapped a gun he was never supposed to use around his waist. Superhero cool. He was working every day in James Bond Land. Another moment of Arcadia, but one that was only a sour memory because it was an even bigger lie than his complacent idea of InSec, and because he should have known better.

The demon followed him to Geneva, and descended on Kornukopia One. He wasn't working for Bond, he was working for Bloefeld, and the super-secure was super-destroyed. He saw that woman's face on the monitors, coming for his peace of mind, and she brought hell with her. Darkness and fire descended. He saw a man cut in half in front of his eyes. The demon appeared before him, not as a screen image but in the flesh. She had spoken to him. She had murdered his sleep.

At least he'd survived. He was one of the few. No injuries, either, apart from some minor smoke inhalation. Kept at a hospital overnight for observation, then released. Released right back into the nightmare, because he hadn't even left the hospital grounds when that scary Russian, Luzhkov, had collared him, asking questions about the demon. Afterward, he hid in a hotel room for three nights, waiting for her to come and punish him for talking. When he surfaced again, he didn't know what to do next. There was no one around to give him orders. It had been too long since he'd had to make his own decisions. He didn't know how anymore. So he called InSec, assuming the corporation still existed, and that he was still technically employed. He was. They called him back to New York.

Home for a couple of months now. Horror stories on the news, but not here, and not happening to him. He was being a very good and quiet boy. He hadn't become anyone's new protege. The remaining powers that be clearly saw him as tainted by doom, so welcome to downward mobility. No office anymore. Just endless code-crunching in the computer pool, another cubicle drone in the open plan hive. He loved it. Anonymity ruled. It was peaceful. Now if only his nights could be.

Friday, ten-thirty in the morning. Take a break. Little stretch of the legs while he thought about the weekend. He would spend it at home, in front of keyboard and monitor, but playing on-line games. He used to do role-playing fantasy and first-person shooters, like any good member of the *Halo* generation. Since Geneva, he stuck to virtual tennis and golf. He took the elevator down to the lobby, bought a coffee and donut from the sandwich counter, and strolled to the central fountain. He sipped his drink and watched the water jet thirty feet high. The roar and splash drowned out the background noise. The sounds relaxed him. He wondered if he should buy one of those ambient CDs, have the sounds of a fountain play all night beside his bed. Maybe that would help him sleep.

He finished his coffee, started on his donut. He turned from the fountain, thinking about picking up a paper for later. Ten feet away from him, heading for the elevator, was the demon. He choked on the pastry, his throat locked tight and dry forever. He coughed. The demon turned her head. She stopped. She looked at him, a small frown creasing her brow. It cleared; she knew him. She said something to the man she was with, and walked over to Jancovich. She smiled. "We've met before," she said.

Jancovich tried to swallow his mouthful of donut. No luck. Speech denied, he nodded.

"What are your plans for today?" she asked.

Now he had to answer. He worked his throat muscles, forced them into action, gagged the food down. He gasped. "Go home early," he whispered. I will not piss myself. I will not piss myself.

"Good idea. Let me see your wallet."

He handed it over without thought. There were authorities whose orders were commandments from somewhere above the Lord God Almighty. She was one of them. She opened the wallet, took out his driver's licence, looked at it for a minute, then handed everything back. "Be good, Bill," she said. She touched a finger to her nose: *I'm watching you.* He nodded, grateful lightning hadn't struck him where he stood, despairing because his sleep, he knew, was gone forever. "Don't run as you leave," she said.

He walked. He didn't look back. His back was tense for a death blow. He walked out the door, and kept walking with numb joints for a full block. Then he ran.

There was a sense of repeating history. It had been a couple of years since Blaylock had first penetrated the InSec building. She had been the warrior, come to slay the Hydra. She had decapitated it, but it had stumbled on, grown a new head, lost that one to her, too. It lived still, and she was back. She was in a different frame of mind, this time. She had projects other than vengeance. There was more than one way for the parasite to affect the host.

She and Flanagan passed through the security turnstile. She wasn't carrying. She had no metal on her at all, which was good. The guard was jittery. Blaylock scanned the lobby as they waited for the elevator. She spotted at least a half-dozen likely pros. Their weapons weren't obvious, but they wore suits that were just that little extra loose. The game was on.

Blaylock and Flanagan took the elevator to the top floor. Blaylock's first visit to the royal court. More security up here. The mercs weren't trying to hide their presence. Two were waiting as they stepped out of the car. One of them was strapping an SMG. She was searched. Flanagan too, though more as a formality. They gave him "good morning" and "sir." They expected him to be here. They walked down the hall toward the boardroom. At the other end was the throne room. Once Pembroke's office, then Sherbina's when he deigned to visit his new subjects, it was empty, waiting for the pretenders to the crown to finish their jockeying. For now, the power was in the hands of a collective regency, ruling from the boardroom. More security outside this door, and a clutch of civilians with food trolleys. Brentlinger's mission for Flanagan: arrange the catering for the lunch meeting. It would have been insulting if it wasn't so funny. The head caterer was making some kind of demand. The mercs were looking a bit overwhelmed.

Flanagan showed his ID again. "I'm running the food show," he said. "What's going on?"

The caterer turned to him. He was a big man with a bearded, overfed face and a bald scalp. "Are we doing this right or are we doing this shit?" he demanded.

"What do you mean?"

"I mean this!" He brandished a bag of plastic utensils. "These jerk-offs want us to set the places with these." He tapped a cutlery chest on one of the trolleys, then pointed at the merc at the door who wasn't carrying a weapon. "No metal objects, he says. So he's telling me we're going to do plastic forks with Limoges plates. Is that what he's telling me? Why the shit not go for paper cups and order in pizza while we're at it? I'm not serving my filet mignon without silverware."

"Brentlinger's orders?" Flanagan asked the merc. The man nodded. "Don't worry about it," he told the caterer. "I'm the guy who hired you. Give me that thing." He took the chest. "Once things are underway and everybody's happy, I'll bring the good stuff in. Good enough?"

The man still looked like a belligerent tenor, but he nodded. "I still say it's doing it shit," he said.

Flanagan shrugged and made a sympathetic face. "Tell me about it. But what can you do? Welcome to the new normal." Blaylock noticed how naturally the adlib came. When she first met him, Flanagan would have lost his shirt playing poker with the blind. His acting and lying were coming along. Aren't you proud, girl? He's learning from the best. "This is my assistant," Flanagan went on, gesturing to Blaylock. "She'll liaise. Any problems," he looked back and forth between the caterer and the mercs, "talk to her, she'll talk to me, and it all goes back up to Nick. That work for everybody? Good." He smiled at Blaylock, and Christ he was good, because there was nothing but the operating executive in that smile, not a trace of the developing brother to mayhem. "You good here, Gloria?" he asked her.

Gloria? Nice. "Perfect," she said, and that was true, because a minute later the boardroom doors opened.

Nick Brentlinger was worrying about his bowels. When he was anxious or excited, they became looser than he'd like. He had to concentrate holding things in. That was the kind of distraction that put a man off his stride. Today, he needed his stride. He needed to *strut*, but not for long, if he could help it. The pressure from Chapel was already a back-breaker. The Hamptons beckoned. He'd do his stint, assemble his golden parachute, and bail. The testosterone jolt he'd felt when Chapel first put him on this path had worn off. He wanted the power, but he would be ornamental, barely a constitutional monarch. He'd be a puppet, and he knew he wouldn't fight back. He'd make do with the money.

The dark lord was reading his mind. The phone rang. Brentlinger knew who was calling before he picked up the receiver. "It's happening," he told Chapel.

"You call me when it's done. Don't keep me waiting."

"I won't." He didn't sigh until he hung up. He looked at his watch. Ten minutes until noon. He should head over, be there first. His stomach gurgled. Swallowing hurt. Butterflies everywhere. He had the nerves, and that was stupid. He'd rehearsed the meeting in his head until he dreamed the moves. He had stolen the march on all the other directors by calling in the mercenaries. He had muscle to back his claim. Nothing to it. Go in there and be dominant.

He walked down the hallway. The directors' offices were on either side. Ahead was the T-junction: right for the boardroom. After today, he'd be turning left. As he approached the doors, catering staff was wheeling away trolleys. "All ready?" he asked the head of the security detail.

"Just about."

"That's fine." He grabbed the handle and pulled. The door was locked. He frowned. "What's going on?" he asked. He rattled the door.

"They're just finishing up," the merc answered. He didn't bother to look at Brentlinger, who bristled. The other man was tall, wide, built like a fist. Brentlinger was the thin old man here. It was the same physical pecking order he'd experienced his entire life. The merc was sending a message: you're paying for this gig, but you're still the lesser man. Brentlinger made himself a promise. The minute the show was over, the merc was being assigned to a security duty in Iraq.

Meantime, the door was still locked. Brentlinger pounded on it. "Hey!"

"Just a minute," a female voice called.

"Open this door *now*," he demanded.

"Can't," came the response. "Presentation, presentation. Let me do my job."

He let go of the door. He thought about ordering the guard to break it down. Now how would that look? Not good. He glanced at the merc. The man was trying to hold back a grin. He wasn't trying very hard. Brentlinger backed off and leaned against a wall, arms folded. Down the hall, he could hear doors opening and closing, shoe leather echoing on marble as the rest of the board arrived for the meeting. All going wrong. He wasn't just losing his stride. Someone had shoved an iron bar between his legs.

At least he was still at the *door* first. Whatever that was worth. He tried to look dominant. Barry Fish was at the head of the line, but the rest of the twelve-strong board was right behind. Fish was looking puzzled. "What's up, Nick?" he asked. "Why are you just standing there?"

Yay dominance. "Just giving the caterers a chance to finish setting up."

"Caterers?" Don Eagleton asked.

Brentlinger pressed his lips together in a smile. "I thought we should dine properly today."

Joey Martino was looking at the hardware on display. "You going to tell us what's going on?" Voice hard, eyes narrow.

"A little patience, please." Brentlinger sniffed a threat. His hackles rose. Chapel receded into the background, suddenly irrelevant. This prize was *his*, damn it. He *would* run InSec, like he'd run his own armaments before Pembroke's takeover. If Martino or anyone else begged to differ, Brentlinger would demonstrate exactly what the weapons in the hall were for.

He heard the lock click behind him. Thank Christ. "All done!" the woman called out.

Brentlinger turned back to the door and pulled it open. "Gentlemen," he said. He went in last, closed the door and locked it. He stared at the wood grain for a moment. Time to take his turn on the stage. He faced the room.

A buffet was laid out on the left-hand side of the board-room. Lobster to steak, warmed by gas-flame. Appetizers to desert. Meat to potatoes. Soup to nuts. All of it high-toned, hugely expensive, top-crust quality and piled-high quantity.

Brentlinger would take care of everybody well. That was the message he wanted the food to send. "Nice spread," Eagleton said. "Who's that?" he asked.

Brentlinger's question, too, the one he shouldn't have to be asking. There was a woman sitting at the far end of the board-room table. At its head. Where *he* should already be sitting. "I—" he began, but had no clue what he was going to say.

"Please sit down," the woman said. Brentlinger felt the nau-seating movement of control slipping away. "Thank you for coming," she said.

The slide accelerated.

They sat. Good boys. Blaylock smiled at them all, her expression genuine because she was having a very, very good time. Great thing about this room. Very, very private. Ultra-secure against surveillance. No bugs, no security cameras. A room where the masters of InSec could speak freely. She had a file in front of her on the table. It was open to a cheat sheet of the directors and their pictures, but she didn't need it. She'd memorized the who's who. She kept the momentum of normality going. Don't give the suckers a chance to think. "Mr. Fish," she said, and batted her eyes at him. He was a compact package of bald muscle. Big ugly scar running diagonally from his left ear to the corner of his mouth. One of the board members who had bothered to get his hands bloody directly, instead of by proxy. "Would you mind terribly passing the water?" Huge on the sweetness. Anticipation saved her from diabetic shock. Fish blushed, and did as she asked. The water jug arrived in front of her and she ignored it. "Thank you so much," she murmured, dropping her eyes and tone as if promising to go down on Fish as soon as the meeting was concluded. He turned max crimson. He stared at his fingers.

Bunch of goddamned innocents. The whole murdering bunch of them. Just like her.

"Not to be rude," Brentlinger began, "but—"

"Who am I and why am I here?" she finished for him. "Guys," she said, "meet the new boss."

Brentlinger coughed, but was suddenly sitting up straighter. "Oh," he said. "Fine, but that wasn't necessary. And you can tell Chapel that surprises like this aren't welcome."

The other directors were shifting, tensing, hip to the fact they were being had. The air charged up with anger and machismo. Fish's red was a different shade. He was staring hard at Brentlinger. His little eyes were twitchy and violent. Brentlinger, Blaylock thought, was a walking mercy kill. He had once had survival instincts. Flanagan had told her how he'd stayed flat to the ground during the Sherbina regime. Funny what the promise of power will do to a man. He'll hold his head up high for the bullet. She said, "Chapel is going to shit himself when he finds out how this meeting went." Eyes, twelve pairs, back on her. She wasn't smiling anymore. She'd stripped the sugar from her steel. Eyes, twelve pairs, nervous. "And I wasn't talking about you," she told Bretlinger. She had their attention in a fist. She was squeezing it with their nerves. "This is your basic hostile takeover."

"On whose behalf?" Tony Weart, who had a really bad moustache, didn't know how to match colours, but knew a thing or two about adding some bonus weapons to small orders to unbalance things just a tad more, about making a little local trouble into a big regional set-to. Weart knew how to make the market demand the supply. Weart was going to rip her heart out with his bare hands. Grandstanding bastard.

"Mine," Blaylock said. She let the silence stretch from disbelief to discomfort. Jim Makaryk started to laugh. "Shut it," she snarled, and he choked on a guffaw. Twelve pairs of eyes very, very worried. Fish was a former field man. So were Martino, Bud Connor, and Jeremiah Keesey. The rest were executives born and bred. Accidental fate was the only reason they weren't selling bad shares, inflating quarterly forecasts or speculating on currency. Four men happy to do violence to her. The others content to set up the deal. "I'm going to tell you once," she said. "Resign your positions, effective five minutes ago. Turn over all your interests to me. Walk away."

"Out of your fucking mind," Keesey said. He enunciated very clearly. He didn't want to be misunderstood. There were nods.

Brentlinger surfed the courage. He was reading the room. The man still had his delusions, couldn't handle seeing someone else step in to take his prize. In other circumstances, Blaylock thought he might cry. "Young lady," he said. "Who do you think we are?"

"Losers," she said. She reached under the table, pulled out the silenced Steyr 9 mm tactical machine pistol Vandelaare had duct-taped there. She stood up, raised the gun, flicked off the safety. Fish first, she thought.

"Wait," Bretlinger pleaded.

"I told you," she said with no apology. "Just once." She held the trigger down until the room was clear.

11

Wage war. *Quietly.*

Dan Pryor heard the sound of a day gone bad. The noise wasn't a big one, wasn't loud enough to be heard on the other floors, but it was plenty audible through the door to the boardroom. Rapid-fire spitting of a weapon, the thud and crash of bodies hitting the floor. Pryor exchanged looks with Sean McCourt. The two mercs posted at the elevator must have heard the noise too. They were pounding down the corridor. Pryor held his radio and stared at it as if the day were its fault. Command-decision time. He was point man for security on this floor. He hesitated. The firing had stopped. Couldn't have gone on for more than ten seconds. Wouldn't need to, against an unarmed group.

"We in or we out?" McCourt asked. The other two had their weapons up, ready to Swiss cheese the door.

Problem. Pryor didn't know if the bad day in the boardroom was part of his employer's game plan or not. Christ, he hated office politics. "Hang on," he said. Better try to speak to Brentlinger. He hoisted the radio.

It beat him to the punch. "Boardroom security, come in," it said with a woman's voice. That Gloria person? She didn't sound much like a personal assistant anymore.

Find out what's what. "Security," he answered.

"I'm giving you the same chance I gave your former employers. They said no. They're dead. You're taking orders from me now."

Pryor cocked an eyebrow at the others. Mean eyes and headshakes all around. Too right. Pryor didn't feel any loyalty toward Brentlinger or the rest of the clowns in suits. But the bitch had made him and his boys look bad. Professional honour dictated payback. Gloria was an idiot. She was outnumbered and boxed in. Where was she going to go? Out the window? Yes, and in pieces. He turned the radio off and raised his gun.

Blaylock switched channels, called Luzhkov. "Any of ours on the top floor?" she asked.

"No."

Their infiltration was still pretty limited. This was going to be messy. "Let's do it," she said. "And watch for civilians."

In the lobby, Vandelaare's radio clicked three times. He caught Nick Haasbroek's eye. They moved out. Special trick for his assignment. The space was crawling with potential collateral damage. Touch not one hair of their heads, and don't even let them know what's going down. Delicacy required. He could do delicacy. He had to do it fast, before word of the war reached the wrong ears. Besides him and Haasbroek, there were four other mercs on the floor. He didn't know them, but he could see them. He walked over to the nearest, an Angolan whose expression could pass for extreme boredom if his eyes weren't on perma-scan. "Spare a moment?" Vandelaare asked him.

"I'm listening."

"There's been a change at the top."

The man stopped scanning for a second. That was the only sign of surprise. "And?"

"You okay with a smooth transition?"

"How's the money?"

"It will still flow. Especially if we aren't looking at a big market correction today."

"What kind of work?"

"The kind that was done in Geneva."

A tiny frown. "Glad I wasn't there."

"I meant on the side that *did* the business."

The frown disappeared. There was a slight rearrangement in the face. This was what passed for excitement and interest. "Okay, then."

"Excellent. Peter Vandelaare, by the way."

"Abel Jamba."

"Know anybody else here?"

Jamba twitched his head to the right. Vandelaare spotted a wiry merc by the fountain. Vandelaare asked, "Will he play?"

"Depends. Bad discipline."

"Can he take orders from a woman?"

Jamba laughed.

"Right," Vandelaare said. He glanced around, pointed to the washrooms. They were in a small corridor recessed off the main lobby. Jamba nodded. Vandelaare hit the men's. He counted five civilians: two at the urinals, two at the sinks, one in a cubicle. He stationed himself at the entrance, stared hard at anyone who tried to come in who wasn't Jamba or the other man. They jumped back from the scary man and decided they could wait. The guys already in the washroom hurried up double-quick. He had the place almost to himself in fifteen seconds. The cubicle occupant was the holdout. Vandelaare heard the rustle of a newspaper. This boy was here for the duration.

The door opened again. The wiry merc stepped inside, hooked a thumb back at Jamba a pace behind him. "He says you need to see me."

A newspaper page turned.

"Yeah," Vandelaare sighed. Jamba pinned the man's arms. Vandelaare stepped in and hammered him in the throat, crushing the windpipe flat. The man made a flat, choking sound and slumped. Vandelaare felt his pulse, frowned. Jamba shifted his grip. Left arm around the throat, right on the back of the head. He leaned hard. Vandelaare heard the snap. No need to check the pulse now. He picked up the man's legs. He and Jamba hauled the body to the farthest cubicle, settled him on the toilet. Jamba, the bigger man, stepped outside. Vandelaare closed the door, locked it, then dropped to the floor and slid out underneath. He cocked his ear at the occupied cubicle. The man inside cleared his throat, grunted with an effort. Busy with his own troubles. He and Jamba headed back out to the lobby. Two more to recruit or lay off.

Blaylock hugged the wall to the side of the boardroom door. No answer to her offer, and no response was a response. The bigger response came a few moments later. SMG fire powered through the door at waist height. Bullets chewed up the table and punched out the window. Blaylock winced as the Plexiglas tumbled to the street below. That was going to raise a question or two. The wind whipped into the boardroom, blowing papers and napkins into a vortex. The door was kicked open. The first merc came in crouching low. Blaylock shot him in the head, dropped under the table as the next man fired around the corner. She nailed him in the gut, and then her clip was empty. The man tumbled over, fingers splaying open and dropping his SMG. There was a bottleneck of corpses at the doorway. The other two mercs stayed in the corridor and showered the room with bullets. Blaylock rolled to the side and scuttled back to the wall. She eyed the SMG. Almost in reach, but in view of the hallway. No more fire from the enemy: they were waiting her out. She backed up to the corner of the room, giving herself room to build up speed. She ran. Just short of the door, she dived for the floor. She grabbed the SMG in mid-somersault, propelled herself through the rest of the tumble as the guns started firing again. A bullet whined by the bridge of her nose. Her eyes teared furiously. She rolled to the far corner and rubbed her eyes clear.

The mercs still weren't coming in after her, but they knew she couldn't come out for them. The standoff could go on until next Thursday, as long as the men didn't call for backup. Which they would. She wished for a grenade, looked around the room, saw the furniture instead. The chairs were big, wheeled, padded affairs. Headrests and armrests, all the comforts for the modern executive. Blaylock wondered how anyone could stay awake more than ten minutes in one of those things. The seat nearest her had been Tony Weart's. When she had shot him, his legs had stiffened fast, and he'd knocked over the chair. She pushed his corpse the rest of the way off the chair and righted it. She dragged Weart out of the way, then, sticking to shelter, she hauled the corpses out of the doorway, and down to the window end of the office. She needed room. The occasional burst of fire from the hallway kept her head low, kept her honest. Then back to the entrance, where that chair waited. She hooked her elbow around the armrest. She gauged her space. The room was a generous one. There was plenty of margin between the wall and the table. She spun, whirling the chair around. It was heavy and awkward. Momentum built up fast. She danced, stumbling in her vortex, toward the doorway. She almost mistimed, had to dance back one step, and then she had the chair careening toward the entrance. She swung around the doorway with the world's most awkward hammer toss. The chair slammed into the nearest merc. It rocked him back on his heels and knocked his weapon high. He fired at the ceiling. The other man jumped out of the way. Blaylock pulled her trigger as she spun. She sprayed bullets around the hall. The second man yelped and fell to a crouch. He clutched his side. Blaylock let the chair hit the ground and she landed on it, rolling backwards down the hall. She raked fire across the width of the corridor. The man she had hit with the chair dropped, thud, bullets stitching finis over his heart. The other merc fired back. He was slumping, and his rounds were low. Blaylock raised her feet, heard the smack and *wing* of lead against plastic and steel. The chair bucked back and started to spin again. She kept firing, her aim thrown. She finished the job with quantity over accuracy.

The job wasn't a pretty one. There were scorch marks and

bullet holes in the walls, chips in the marble floor. Smashed ceiling tiles hung like gaping flesh, wires dangling like guts. Half the lights were out, and there was broken glass everywhere. I'm good because I'm delicate, Blaylock thought. She rifled the bodies, loaded up on ammo. Then she headed for the stairwell.

Flanagan saw the Plexiglas fall past his window. He winced. My girl, he thought. I guess she's around. He sighed. His job was containment: interface with the outside world as necessary, and keep it from looking in at InSec until the war was over. He left his office. Life on the fortieth floor was Friday routine. Nothing going on. There was one mercenary, not one of Luzhkov's, at the elevator, looking more bored than conspicuous. Nobody was expecting excitement in the shipping department. Flanagan made his way down to the lobby. He looked around for Vandelaare and Luzhkov as he headed for the exit. He didn't see them. He didn't see the other security men, either. Absence equalled war. Waged quietly. Good. He hoped.

Outside, things were less quiet. The window hadn't killed anyone, but it had hit Trinity Place like a meteor, cut a half-dozen people, and scared thirty more. Everyone down the length of the block was staring up, looking for planes and fireballs. My girl, he thought again. She passes through like a ghost. He turned to the man next to him. "Has anyone called 911?" he asked. The man nodded, not taking his eyes from the sky. Ambulance, fire engine and police were there a couple of minutes later.

Like a ghost, Flanagan thought. She's not even here.

Luzhkov knew what it was to be a virus. He liked it. He was having a sip of the draft that Blaylock had gulped by the tankard in Geneva. Intoxicating. Nectar of the gods. One taste was never enough. No wonder Blaylock was hooked. Especially since she was so good at it. The action fix was what had carried him down his path. But this, beyond covert and rogue, was one of the drugs he had been hoping Blaylock would supply. She'd delivered. The drip was hitting his veins and burning the wires.

They had divided the building's sixty storeys into thirds. Blaylock was starting at the top and working down. Vande-laare going from the lobby up. Luzhkov had floors twenty to forty to cover. The numbers sounded ridiculous. They weren't. Brentlinger hadn't called in InSec's full complement, just enough ornamental muscle to give him insurance, a show of force against unarmed board members. There wasn't a contingent on every floor. Numbers on the top floor for the board members themselves. Sentinels in the lobby to control ingress and egress. The others were scattered through the rest of the building as troubleshooters, monitors in more sensitive departments, and potential backup, in the unlikely event of trouble. And here came Blaylock and company, the unlikely event.

Luzhkov's earpiece was giving him the news as it broke. He and Blaylock had spoken once on a different channel from the InSec boys, then established radio silence. From Vandelaare, he was receiving patterns of clicks. They were the running tally of the infection. The numbers were good. The patient was growing very sick, very fast. His contagion was spreading well, too. No bad trouble so far. After the first couple of conversations, he'd been travelling with a posse of the converted.

That made his arguments, when the group converged on a man who was lone and bored, very persuasive. He was already on floor thirty-four. Next one up was R & D, and that would be better protected.

Trouble broke out on the radio traffic. Guys were trying to reach the posts on the top floor, and were hearing nothing back. Worried calls were going out. Luzhkov's recruits sent out words of calm, but some voices were just not being heard, and their silences were holes that couldn't be plugged with third-party reassurances. Someone ordered all hands to the top floor. Someone else belayed that, rattled off a half-dozen names to meet him there, told everyone else to hold their positions. Luzhkov didn't know any of the names. They weren't in his group. He guessed they were all stationed near the top of the building, and could reach their rendezvous point fast. The action in the building was looking to concentrate. At the landing to thirty-five, he split half of his group off and told them to head for the sixtieth floor. "Be smart," he told them. "Try to come up behind them. Avoid unnecessary combat. If we can intimidate them with numbers, let's." Four men jogged up the stairs. He took the other three with him through the door.

They came out on the floor and almost collided with another gang of four that was reaching for the stairwell door. Luzhkov thought fast. "Heading up?" he asked.

The leading man nodded. "I don't care what Henderson says. He should have backup. There's nothing going to go down here," he swept his arm to take in the cubicles and offices. "Bunch of goddamn slide-rule drones. No threat." The man was a shouter, his voice box muffler broken from too many years of barking orders. Luzhkov saw a couple of heads poke up like meerkats from within cubicles. *What's going on?* they would be thinking. Next they'd be growing nervous. Then a tiny nudge would spread fear through the building, and no one would recover from the mess. He had to contain Loud Boy fast.

Behind him, he heard footsteps echoing in the stairwell. Traffic there was picking up. No privacy. "Can I have a moment?" he asked Loud Boy, and started walking down the main aisle between the cubicles. His gait was unhurried, casual, and his arms at his side, far from his weapon.

Loud Boy kept pace, looked like he wanted to move faster, have this conversation done with and be where the action was. The two posses followed. Luzhkov's pack dropped just behind the other. "What's up?" Loud Boy asked.

"I have been hearing some things. The situation is much bigger than we've been told." Privacy, privacy, where was the privacy? The place was an open-form anthill. Ahead, the second half of the floor was a suite of offices. There was a bank of dens with massive windows looking out onto the floor. Even less privacy than a cubicle, and they were all occupied. The aisle became a corridor between the offices.

"Then what are we doing wasting time down here?" Loud Boy wanted to know.

"Contingency planning," Luzhkov said, keeping it vague. Two doors down to the right, a woman emerged from an office with a sheaf of papers. She was frowning at them, barely glanced at the mercs as she brushed past them. She left her door open, so she wasn't planning on being long. Luzhkov glanced back, caught the eye of Jean Decaux, who'd been part of the op from the start. Decaux gave a slight nod and peeled off to intercept and delay the woman. Luzhkov turned in to the office. It still had a window looking out onto the corridor, but it was much smaller. As good as the privacy deal was going to get.

"What's in here?" Loud Boy asked, but he and his men followed. Luzhkov's remaining two closed the door behind them and hung back. They were both new recruits. Loyalty test coming up. They'd jumped ship once. They might again, if the wind started blowing hard from the other direction. For the moment, they were looking solid. One of them, Mark Vrenna, stood in front of the window.

"There has been a takeover," Luzhkov told Loud Boy. "InSec is under new management."

The merc looked like Luzhkov had just farted in his face. "Bullshit."

Luzhkov said nothing. He held his face expressionless, waited for the other man to decide he was serious. He was standing beside the desk, and he played absently with a retractable ballpoint pen that sat on top of the computer keyboard.

Loud Boy said, "You're part of the new management, you dick."

Luzhkov shifted his stance, ready. He kept his tone level, non-threatening. He didn't meet Loud Boy's eyes directly. He was trying to pacify the bear without triggering deadly force. "No," he said. "But I do work for it. So can you."

"Traitor," Loud Boy said.

Luzhkov could have argued the point. He could have said he used to work for Kornukopia, and had never been part of the InSec structure. He didn't think the man he was facing would care for the finer points of debate. He tried one more time. "Good money," he said. "Good action."

"I'm no traitor, you fucking commmie."

A man of principle. Not bright, but he was loyal. There was a bit of shame to this. Luzhkov checked over Vrenna's shoulder. No one was passing by the window. "I wish we could cooperate," he said.

"We can't," said Loud Boy.

Vrenna flicked the lights off.

Luzhkov saw his opponent's weight shift forward. Luzhkov made a fist around the pen and swung his arm in a swooping arc. He rammed the pen into Loud Boy's neck. It went in deep, but missed the carotid artery. The man was choking up blood but still alive and struggling. He banged into Luzhkov and brought them both down in a heap, Luzhkov on the bottom. They fought and clawed. Luzhkov heard the bumps and scuffles of other fights, couldn't see past Loud Boy's bloody face. No one was yelling. The only sounds were thrashing and Loud Boy's wet, drowning breaths. The radio was crackling, and Luzhkov thought he heard Blaylock's voice being answered by a man's snarl. He wrapped his fingers around the merc's throat. Loud Boy tried to do the same, but Luzhkov ducked his chin to his chest, blocking access. Luzhkov squeezed harder. Loud Boy tried to tear away. He reared back, raising Luzhkov with him. His movements lost coordination. His hands slapped at Luzhkov's face, but there was very little force behind the blows. He flailed. His fingers caught a cord and yanked the phone down to the floor with a crash. *Shhh*, Luzhkov thought. *Shhhhh*. Squeezed. Loud Boy stopped struggling, started twitching. Then he was quiet.

Luzhkov shoved the body off and stood up. The other two fights were vicious love tussles. The fourth member of Loud

Boy's group stood off to the side, watching, not joining in. Vrenna was pinned down. Luzhkov started to move forward, froze as someone walked past the window, then lunged and hit Vrenna's opponent on the back of the neck. There was a good crack. The man fell over.

One more to go. He was grappling with Reggie McGee. He was also staring in fury at his aloof teammate. He broke free of McGee's stranglehold, opened his mouth for a big yell. Luzhkov and Vrenna piled on. They smothered his shout, then beat him to death.

Aftermath. Three bodies, blood everywhere, the office in disarray. The hourglass draining before Decaux's distraction would expire. How do you clean this up? Dispose of the bodies and evidence of struggle in less than a minute? Very likely. Oh, this is a war that is going very quietly, all right. First, the survivor from Loud Boy's party. "So?" Luzhkov asked him.

"Guess I'm working for the new team."

"You were waiting to see who won?"

"Yup."

Brave in either honesty or stupidity. "Can we count on you now?"

"Sure."

"What's your name, soldier?"

"Matt Dolinksy."

Well, Dolinsky, thought Luzhkov, you're on the front line first, last and always. Luzhkov wasn't going to kill him now, but he'd cut that life expectancy down to size. He turned to McGee. "Stay here. Keep everyone out until we can clean this." He looked at the chaos again, shook his head.

"Any idea what kind of excuse I can use to keep them out?"

"Say it's a security exercise," Vrenna suggested.

Nice one. Luzhkov cocked a finger at him. "Perfect." They still had to block sight of the carnage from passersby. He pointed at a shelving unit. It didn't have a back, but it had enough binders, paper stacks and reference books on it to do. "Help me with this," he said, and they dragged it in front of the window. Quick and dirty improv. "Let's go," he said, and they stepped out of the office.

They almost collided with the woman. Decaux was two steps behind, trying to slow her down. "What the hell are you doing?" the woman demanded.

Luzhkov spouted Vrenna's lie verbatim. "Security exercise," he said. He drew a blank for a good follow-up.

"Whatever." She wasn't buying. She stared at the window, now blocked by the shelves. "What does that have to do with redecorating my office?"

"We're using your space as a temporary command post for the duration of the exercise," Vrenna said. Luzhkov stood aside to let him spin his story. He was very smooth. "It's the nature of security in today's world. I'm sure you understand."

The woman's hard gaze didn't suggest that she did, but at least she waited for him to go on.

"We have to be flexible, and be able to, for instance, set up a secure command centre just about anywhere and with no warning." He smiled an apology. "You won the lottery this time. Someone else will have to put up with us for the next exercise." He paused. "There will, of course, be compensation for the inconvenience."

Sheer genius. The woman softened. "How long before I can get back to work?" she asked.

Vrenna made a show of looking to Luzhkov for confirmation. Luzhkov played along, made a thoughtful face, then nodded. Vrenna said to the woman, "Why not take the rest of the day off?"

She hesitated. "I have some deadlines…" she began.

"Believe me," Vrenna reassured her, "the top management knows and realizes the situation we're putting you into."

"In that case," she said, "can I just go in to get my purse?"

It took another minute of fast dancing and ad libbing before they had her things out of the office and the woman on her way. Too much delay. Luzhkov left McGee to start the sanitization. They'd haul the bodies out after hours. He wanted to run to the elevator, but he had to walk, look like nothing was up. He hadn't received any radio communications all the time he'd been stuck on this floor. What's going on up there? he wondered.

"Hi," Flanagan said to the fire chief. "I'm with the building. We're so embarrassed. We were in the middle of installing that window." He began the lie with that. He built on it quickly. He lied a whole epic, and he was barely aware of what his mouth was saying, only that it was doing so with a contrite smile, and with the assured tone of God's honest truth. His mind split into three. One part sectioned itself off and was devoted completely to the art of the laugh. A second gibbered panic. The third crowed, *Christ, I'm good.*

The stairwell door was next to the elevator. Blaylock opened it and listened. She heard boots pounding up the steps. And the elevator was humming, on its way up. It took priority. She closed the door and stood to the left of the elevator, gun up, finger already exerting pressure on the trigger. She spoke into her radio. "You in the elevator. You are ordered to stand down. Throw your weapons out before you leave the car."

"Who the fuck is this?" a man responded. "Screw that, I don't care. You made trouble, so that makes you a dead bitch."

They had their chance. She crouched low. The elevator dinged its arrival. She started firing before the doors had finished opening, crab-walked to the right, strafing the idiots to pieces. One of them managed to stumble out and get off a burst. His effort was a last protest against death, and meant nothing. He barely saw her. His fire didn't come anywhere close. The other three never left the car. Blaylock reached inside and turned the elevator off. No more arrivals by this method.

She gathered more clips, reloaded, strapped extra guns over her shoulder, and went back to the stairwell. She stood by the doorway, aiming down the stairs, ready for the next sucker. Every corpse she created made the cleanup that much more of a headache, but they weren't leaving her any choice. Sounds of boots coming closer. Hard to tell how many flights down they were. The concrete walls and steps conducted the echoes up and amplified them. She waited. The sounds changed. The steady marching up stopped. Shouts. Confusion. Men yelling at each other, the volume building from boiling to explosive. A meeting of factions, she realized. She ran down the steps to help her boys. She jumped two or three at a time, not worrying about noise. The cacophony below would cover an elephant's approach. She ran faster.

Too fast.

Phil Lambeck was thinking he was seeing a good idea go bad. He liked what Luzhkov had sold, and for the first while, the takeover had been smooth as silk. But now he and three buddies were in a screaming match with at least six other mercs, and those guys had the high ground in the stairwell. He really didn't want shooting to break out. There were only stupid reasons for it. But it was going to happen anyway. He was at the head of the group, pleading for reason, but he and everyone else had his gun drawn, and he should just end the suspense and open fire.

The enemy beat him to it. The bullets rained down, pinning them. Ricochets pinged a zigzag off the walls. "*Shit*," he yelled, dropping and firing back. He moved down a landing. He had no clear shot, but neither did the others.

"Now what?" Sid Wilson asked.

Like he knew. This could go on for hours. Then he heard sounds of approach from below. He and Wilson exchanged looks. "Friendlies?" Lambeck called to the rear.

"Aw, hell." Tony Earl, the furthest down the stairs, didn't sound happy at all, and then he was firing.

Lambeck's heart sank. They were between floors, with no way out of the stairwell. They were caught in a pincer movement.

Blaylock almost ran straight into the bullet stream. The forward guard was standing just around the corner from her, in the same position she had used on the men upstairs. She threw herself backwards, alive only because the man hadn't heard her coming and had been as startled as she was when she showed up. He wasn't surprised anymore. He stopped firing, waiting for her to do the dumb thing and try to take him. From just a bit further below, she heard the steady fire of SMGs. Then still more. The stairwell became a soundscape hell of spitting weapons, one huge rattling roar.

Not good, not good. She had to overwhelm the guard with firepower. She unshouldered the extra guns, picked one up. Double wielding, twice the damage, zero accuracy. She pulled the triggers. She unleashed a hail of bullets and cement chips as she whipped around the corner on her knees. Debris slashed her face. The guns marched all over the goddamn place, hitting everything except the merc. They drove him back. He stopped firing long enough to run down for cover. Blaylock pursued, dropping one gun, taking the time to aim. She nailed him as he turned around to fight back. She shoved past his body before it had finished falling, and around the next turn of the staircase, there were his buddies, firing down at the team that had given their allegiance to her. She brought the wrath. Bang bang bang.

The firing above Lambeck eased, then stopped. He turned to help the others. Earl was dead, but they'd taken out at least two of the attackers.

Luzhkov's head was spinning dizzy, his lungs were ragged from the climb, but the sound of gunfire pulled him like a lodestone. When he found the battle, adrenaline cleared the system. He and Vrenna piled in. Dolinsky did too, once he saw that the opponents had their backs to him. By the time they realized they were sandwiched, they were halfway to being dead. The last man cursed Luzhkov with creative fury before he took a round in the throat.

Ringing in his ears, then, Vrenna yelled, "Clear!" and silence descended. His lungs started complaining again.

"Come on up." Blaylock's call. It summoned his energy. He marched up, wading through bodies, and two landings up, there she was, above a bigger pile of the dead. The demon queen gave him a regal smile.

12

Washington, thick with heat and impatience. It was afternoon, when the air could be consumed with a knife and fork. Summer was going to be an abomination. Good time to get out of town. The Hamptons called. But meanwhile, what the holy hell was Brentlinger playing at? Chapel was at home, computer on, and was checking his e-mail every minute, had been since noon. No word. Brentlinger was supposed to use an anonymous server to send confirmation that the job was done. Nothing incriminating. Just a simple message: "So much spam these days." Totally innocuous. But it would tell Chapel that InSec was his. It was three-thirty now, and still no message. If Brentlinger had forgotten or was delaying, Chapel would make him wish he'd never been born with an ass.

He waited until four. His armpits were dripping, his body reacting to anxieties he refused to acknowledge. He gave up on the Internet, left the house and drove to the nearest Safeway. He bought groceries, doing the mundane for any surveillance, then hit a payphone. He punched in the number for Brentlinger's office. His secretary answered.

"I'm sorry, Mr. Brentlinger is not available," he was told.

"He is for me," Chapel told the woman. If he had to, he'd give his name, but he thought his tone would do the trick. She might even recognize his voice.

"I'm sorry," she said, and hesitated. "Mr. Brentlinger... Mr. Brentlinger is on indefinite leave."

Chapel had a moment of neon crimson rage. His vision was obscured by blood, and it was all Brentlinger's. His fist tightened on the phone, squeezing a throat. Then the secretary's tone registered. She was hiding it well, but there was a tremble in her voice. Brentlinger, he realized, wouldn't be jerking him around. The man didn't have the balls for that. "How is his health?" he asked.

Another pause, and then there was nothing but dial tone. He stood with the receiver to his ear, listening to the idiot whine of defeat. His body was pouring sweat, but not from the heat. Ice and fear were running through his veins. It's her, he thought, and the knowledge was as certain as it was bad. The silly hope that this was a counter-move by Korda stirred in his heart, and died. If Korda had beaten him to the punch, Brentlinger would still be around to answer his phone, and would be mealy-mouthing all sorts of cowardly platitudes. Chapel would have given his right arm to hear the pathetic pleading instead of the flatline tone. Indefinite leave, he thought. I'll bet. Bitch. Bitch. *Bitch*. He didn't have a right arm to give. She'd taken it from him, chopped it off hard and messy.

He replaced the receiver, picked up his grocery bags, and walked out of the store. The automatic doors parted and the heat took him, slamming in like walls. He thought about what he would have been capable of with InSec. He thought about the woman having the same power, and what she might do. He wanted to throw up. His knees were threatening betrayal.

Screw your country, she had told him in the ruins of Kornukopia One. *Screw your country, front, back, sideways, and down the middle*. Jesus Christ. Like the damage Korda and Reed were doing wasn't bad enough. He would have nightmares tonight.

He unlocked his car, and his fingers were anaesthetized, clumsy. He fumbled the door open and tossed the bags inside. He sat down, started up the engine. Cold air blasted out of the dashboard. He sat with his hands on the steering wheel, but didn't pull out. He stared at the parking lot and saw nothing. He forced himself to think through the panic, consider his strengths.

She didn't know his plans. The bait was still out there for her. Take her down, and InSec would be up for grabs again. And he still had his left arm. He'd give it a good workout. He'd always thought of himself as ambidextrous.

"Jesus," Flanagan said.

"Bit of a mess," Blaylock agreed.

Flanagan shook his head. He had joined the stairwell confab. He was looking at the bodies and the blood. The confined space was already starting to smell like a slaughterhouse. He saw serious problems. But he also saw more of Blaylock's seduction. He saw the death and the horror, yes yes, of course. But the recognition felt like rote duty. His stomach was twitching because of the stench, not because of its implications. "What now?" he asked.

"Can't exactly call the janitor," Blaylock said. She switched subjects for a moment. "Was anyone hurt by the falling window?"

"No, nothing serious."

"Fire marshals going to descend on us?"

"Not for the moment. They'll want to inspect things when the new widow is installed, make sure it doesn't happen again."

"I'll try to keep the gunfire in the boardroom to a minimum."

Flanagan touched a spent shell with the tip of his shoe. "I take it things weren't as quiet as we were hoping for."

"No," Luzhkov said. "We made noise. We will have been heard."

"But not outside the building," Blaylock pointed out. She looked at Flanagan. "Give me the Human Resources angle."

"I'll need to feel things out. But at a guess?" He thought it over. He thought about his own don't-rock-the-boat past in InSec. Most of the staff, he knew, would be coming from the same place he once had. Working in the arms industry wasn't a conscience-soother. The best tactic for sound sleep was tunnel-vision ignorance. It had worked for the cogs of the Nazi bureaucracy. It had worked for him. It would still be the operating principle for most of the people in the building. If anything, the instinct would be stronger than ever, thanks to the rapid regime changes. Every head with an ounce of self-preservation would be hunkered down low, hearing, seeing and holy-Christ *speaking* no evil. Scary bang-bang noises from the stairwell would have been a signal to reinforce the wall of ignorance. There would be plenty of sleepers with the covers drawn over their heads that night. "I would say," he ventured, "that as long as everyone knows that there is a boss, then everyone will be satisfied."

Baylock nodded. "A familiar face wouldn't hurt, I bet."

"Meaning what?"

"Meaning you're it. You're the new boss."

When she said that, the logic struck him as airtight, the conclusion inevitable. And yet he hadn't seen it coming. Somehow, he had pictured Blaylock in Pembroke's old throne room when she took the reins. But of course not. She belonged to the shadows. He could step into the light without drawing a walking artillery bombardment. He knew how the place worked. The job was his duty, no doubt about it. Still. Spooky. "Whoa," he said under his breath.

"Up for it?" she asked. She spoke softly, for his ears alone, giving him the dignified out if he wanted it.

"Yes," he said. He would prove it to himself as well as to her. This was where he could do the most good for the war effort.

"You know things will be messy," she said.

"Yes."

"Your hands will be dirty."

He laughed, and there was a walnut rattling around in his throat. "Like they aren't already?" He was standing knee-deep in bodies, and he'd done his bit to bring these men to their deaths. Blaylock had pushed him down a very steep slide when she'd stepped into his life, shattering its comfort and its lies. He was still picking up speed. The bottom of the ride was in a darkness tinged with flame. The impact could be severe. But the speed was exhilarating. The faster he slid, the better the thrill.

Blaylock kissed his cheek. "Thank you," she whispered. "All right," she announced to her army. "Let's cleanse and consolidate. Mike here is going to head into the staff areas and be the face of reassurance, stability, and continuity." She grinned with demon anticipation. "Peter," she said to Vandelaare, "take a couple of guys and go with him. You're the muscle of his authority, but don't be too intimidating. The message, for now, is relax. Business as usual. We clear?"

"Where will you be?" Flanagan asked her.

"Here," she said, looking at the bodies and the blood. "I'm on disposal."

Flanagan decided to work his way from the top down. He and Vandelaare's squad headed for the top floor and the offices of the board of directors. The marble was slicked red, and the walls were pocked with bullet hits, but there was still life on the floor. In the reception area of each office, they found a secretary, sheltering under a desk and waiting to die. Flanagan went through the same conversation until he knew every call and response by heart.

"Everything's all right," he would say, the reassuring minister.

The people: "Where is Mr. Brentlinger/Martino/Fish/ Eagleton/Weart/Makaryk/Keesy/ Connor/Whoever?"

The minister: "He's gone."

The people: "Is the board—?"

The minister: "There is no more board."

The people: Silence.

The minister: "I'll be moving into Mr. Pembroke's old office. I'll need all relevant passwords. Do you understand?"

The people: "Yes."

The minister: "There's no need to worry. Nothing will happen to you. Your job is secure. The transition will be smooth. Okay?" The minister smiles.

The people nod, Amen, and crawl out from under the desk.

"Why not stay here until I call you?" the minister suggests, sparing the people the sight of death.

There was one variation. He was an anonymous face for all but one of the executive assistants. They had no trouble buying him as the next avatar of absolute power. Brentlinger's aide, though, had seen him more than once. Donna Landis knew him. They'd been casual acquaintances before she'd risen to the top floor. When she realized what he was telling her, she looked at him as if tentacles were coiling out of his chest. "You're running the show, now?" she said. "Mike? *You* are?"

Flanagan shifted a bit to one side, so she could have a better view of the three men behind him. "Yup."

"But how...?" She gestured with her hands, seeking words adequate to the scale of her disbelief. She wasn't buying the scenario.

Flanagan couldn't blame her. She'd known him as the quiet team player, the corporation's eager-to-please puppy. She was right: the transformation made no sense.

Then she said, "Who—?" and stopped herself.

Too late. He understood. The transformation made no sense, but Flanagan as yes-man figurehead to the real power, *that* she could believe. The assumed emasculation pissed him off, made him even angrier because at one level she was right. Not all the way, though. He wasn't Jen's puppet. He was her partner. InSec was his now because he was the best man for the job. He had juice of his own. "Donna," he said, keeping his voice calm, reasonable. "Am I going to have trouble with you?" He glanced over his shoulder. Vandelaare, smart man, read the dynamic and gave his gun barrel a stroke.

Landis blanched. "No," she said. "No, Mike, I'm good. You know I am."

"I'm glad to hear it." Still very calm, but very serious. No smile in his tone, or in his eyes. He stretched out a second of silence, then gave her the smile. He kept it quick, a warning that it would not be granted often or easily. Then he and his posse left her office.

Butterflies in his chest as they headed for the elevator. Exhilaration and nausea fighting it out, then fusing as one. He'd just put the fear into another person. He'd never done that before. He'd always been on the receiving end. He felt the shame and excitement of first sex. Get out of your navel, he told himself. Think this through later. Do your duty, first. All the time for PTSD once the war was over. In the meantime, for the first time in his life, he had his own arsenal, to be used as necessary.

Blaylock found what they needed in the basement. Cleaning supplies weren't a problem. There was a custodial storeroom on every floor, and staff more than happy to find the keys for men with guns. She and her men made good progress mopping up the blood. It was the bodies that presented the problem. She didn't know how they were going to dispose of them, but on a hope she went downstairs, and there was the incinerator. She headed back up to the battleground, where the corpses were stacked and waiting to move out. When she told Luzhkov what she'd found, his wince was very slight.

"Is it big enough?" he asked.

"No other options," she said. She looked at the dead, pictured more unpleasantness to mark the day. "If we have to, we'll make them fit."

Luzhkov didn't sigh, but she did see him go through the same steeling process she had just done. "All of them?" he said.

She nodded. "Problems?"

"Not for the mercenaries. They aren't family men."

So no next of kin to wonder where daddy had gone to. But she saw where he was going. The board members were a different story. Pillars of the community to a man. Their absences would not pass without comment. "Good point," she said.

"What do we do?"

"Doesn't change anything. Burn them. Make them vanish. Make sure there's nothing to find when anyone comes sniffing around."

So they did. Blaylock manned the disposal squad with volunteers only. She did the worst of the work herself. Every crack of bone was another item on the scroll of her damnation. She didn't care. By this point, more entries could hardly make any difference.

So they were seven. Not much of a corps. Enough for a core. Chapel said there were other men loyal to the cause who were on their way. The left turn South America had taken had thrown plenty of soa graduates out on their ears. They were whipped dogs, abandoned by their trainers, now gone feral, eager to bite the hand that had once fed them. The first of them, Chapel promised, should be arriving within the next twenty-four hours. The others a few days after that. Quintero would have his army again. He would have his fist.

At the crack of dawn, Chapel arrived at the soa in a minivan and bundled the men off on a field trip to Petersfield. He drove them through the town, showing them the territory. Quintero saw deep money and quaint streets, antiques shops, galleries and a polo field. His gut twisted with envy and contempt. "The playground of your elite," he muttered.

"Of the complacent," Chapel corrected. He turned south onto Ocean Avenue, heading into reaches where the properties were sparser, and more immense. Towards the end of Farriers Lane, he touched a remote as he turned right. A wrought iron gate pulled back and gave them access to a long drive. At the end stood a restored farm house. It was a big two-storey home, almost large enough to be called rambling. It seemed small compared to some of the mansions they had driven past. It would still retail in the millions.

They climbed out of the van and Chapel took them inside. "Six bedrooms," he said. "Five and a half bathrooms." His voice echoed in the unfurnished rooms. The hardwood floors gleamed with new stain and polish an inch thick. The original rear of the house had been remodelled and expanded. The kitchen now opened into a second sitting room with huge bay windows that looked out toward the water.

Big for now. Not so large if the promised manpower showed up. "Could become crowded," Maldonado commented.

"No one here except the necessary personnel," Chapel said. "The bulk of the forces will stay at Fort Benning until needed."

"Why?" Maldonado didn't want to let it go. "Splitting up strength isn't a good idea."

"Neither is high visibility," Chapel said.

"You think we're going to be holding drunken parties here and cruising for girls in the local bars?"

"That isn't the point."

"Then what is?"

"Our skin colour," Quintero answered.

"*What?*"

"This is a very white town."

Chapel nodded. "Sorry, boys. Hispanics make up barely more than three percent of the population. What will we be at full strength? One hundred? Two hundred? More? Let's say only fifty. Pour that number into a centre with only fourteen hundred people grand total, and where everybody knows everybody. Figure it out."

"I'm delighted we weren't arrested upon arrival," Maldonado spat.

"We're hiding you in plain sight with the cover story. The general here really is a retired general."

"From Mexico?" Quintero asked.

"From Spain."

Of course. So much more upscale. Less evocative of cheap hired help, of desperate people brought in to do whitey's dirty work. Quintero nodded and said nothing. These were the realities.

"As for the house," Chapel went on, "there is plenty of room for work. The tools, cots and other supplies will be here later today. Weapons, too."

"What about vehicles?" Olano asked.

"You'll have two more like the one outside."

"One with a lead lining would be nice."

Chapel shrugged. "The extra precautions are up to you. Just don't draw any attention." He led the way out the back door and across the property. The rear grounds were as narrow as the front were spacious. The ground sloped almost immediately to a private beach and dock. Sunlight shone hard diamonds on the choppy surface of the water. Quintero squinted."The best part," Chapel said. "Location, location, location." He gestured across the arm of Mecox Bay. Quintero looked where he was pointing, and saw a huge mansion sprawling over manicured grounds. Its dock was almost swimming distance from the one where they stood. "The president's house," Chapel stated.

"A patient sniper could do the job," Maldonado said. "Easier, less risky, much cheaper."

"No." Chapel shook his head. "You're missing the point. An assassination wouldn't have the results we want. A week of headlines and some PBS specials aren't going to change anything. The president isn't the primary target. It's the act that's important. He just determines the location."

"It could happen here," Quintero said, thinking through the risks. "In this house." He liked the idea of an easy getaway.

Chapel nodded. "If necessary. But if this is really going to work, it has to be as close to the man as possible. I want it at his home. You'll have plenty of choice. Boat or van will get you there."

"And what will get us away?" Olano sounded suspicious. Quintero couldn't blame him.

"Common sense," Chapel retorted. "You'll have three vans. Can you count the boats?" There were two pleasure sailboats moored at the dock. Each was large enough to carry the complete team. "It's up to you to make sure you have enough time. Think you can handle that?"

Olano glared. Quintero said quietly, "If you recruited us, you must have some respect for our abilities."

Chapel eased off. "Sorry. Hard day at the office."

"You will do me the courtesy of deferring to my judgment in the field during the operation itself," Quintero said firmly.

"Are you saying I don't have field experience?"

"I'm saying that this will be a military operation, and these are my men. Yes?"

Chapel pursed his lips, nodded.

"If I determine the approach is too risky, then we do this thing from here. Yes?"

Chapel's look was sour. "As long as that really is the decision of last resort."

"It will be."

"And the date is firm."

"The Fourth of July," Quintero agreed.

13

The time was coming for all the ducks to be properly lined up. Some of the waterfowl were floating, tits up and dead in the water. Chapel still thought he had enough healthy birds to keep the others in line. There was really only one big risk between now and the Fourth. That was Quintero's worry, and he was a good man. What Chapel had to focus on now was preventing the political birds from flying off in panic. He walked into Pratella's office like the world was good. "So?" he asked as he sat down with casual dead weight. "Have you spoken with her?"

Pratella didn't answer the question. He was glaring at Chapel as if he'd just soiled the carpet. "Are you going to tell me what the fuck is going on?" No Dadaist folk wisdom. Pratella wasn't walking in a world that was good.

"What's going on is that we're close to ready."

"Is that right? Then why can't I get Brentlinger on the phone?"

"Don't worry about it."

"I do worry. That sorry old Latter-day Saint should be standing on my nerves, inviting me to barbecues and I don't know what at his fancy new home. But not a peep do I hear. I say to myself, this ant's off the clover. You tell me straight, my son, why isn't he calling?"

No point putting this off. "Because he's dead."

Pratella's mouth clapped shut. He drummed his fingers, nonplussed and slow-burning. Finally, he asked, "Did you—?"

"No, I did not." Irritated.

"And you didn't order it?"

"For Christ's sake, Patrick. Use your head." Though in all honesty, there had been times when he'd been tempted to plant a bullet between Brentlinger's funeral-director-spotting-the-main-chance eyes.

"So what happened?"

"We were beaten to the punch."

Pratella's eyes bugged out. This wasn't going well. "Someone else grabbed InSec?"

That's what I said, you stupid pol. He nodded. "Shit happens."

Pratella grunted his disbelief. He spun around in his office chair, shaking his head. "'Shit happens,' the boy says. Listen to him. Who did it?" he asked. "Korda?"

"No. A third party."

Pratella stopped his spin. "Better and better all the time," he spat.

"Don't worry. I have contingencies in place. Losing InSec is an inconvenience, not a tragedy. It's also only a temporary problem."

"I shouldn't worry, he tells me. All is well, he wants me

to believe. I'm sorry, my son, but I *am* worried. And I've had enough. The smart man knows when the pontoons are wet. Find yourself another playmate."

"That's funny."

"I surely didn't think it was."

"You sound like a man with no principles. You sound like a man whose love for his country is more hot air than deeds."

Pratella sighed. "Son, I'm too old for that bullshit. Don't try it on me. I'm a patriot, but I'm not an idiot."

"You'd be an idiot to think you can back out now. The operation is happening whether you're in or out. But if you're out, then you're really out."

"Is that a threat?"

"Abso-fucking-lutely." He wanted Pratella to take him seriously, because he wanted the Speaker by his side. Old whore that he was, Pratella still had what it took to be the right kind of president. And Chapel really didn't want to have to kill him. "I need to know you're in, or someone else is going to be in the top job when the time comes."

A snort. "Oh, really? You're going to bypass the order of succession?"

"I didn't say that."

A pause while Pratella digested that and worked out the implications. Some of the air went out of his balloon. He became smaller in his chair."All right," he said. "I'm in."

"I knew I could count on you. So, you didn't answer me when I asked you before. Have you spoken to Leadbetter?"

"Not yet. I'll get on it."

"Good man. The country's going to thank us, Pat. You know it will."

"I know," Pratella said. He sounded tired. "But what about this third party?"

"Being taken care of. As we speak."

The boardroom was clean, now. There were holes in the walls. Flanagan was making noises about having them plastered over. There were going to be other people coming into this room sooner or later, he argued. Can't be having them freak over the signs of war. She gave in, but not tonight. She wanted the moment. She was sitting in the heart of her old nemesis's empire, and it bore the signs of her conquering wrath. She hadn't thought of the takeover in terms of revenge, but the idea occurred to her now, and it pleased her. Johnathan W. Smith III had ordered the bombing of her home to kill her father. She'd shot him. Her family had died because her father was an inconvenience to Arthur Pembroke. She'd slit Pembroke's throat, slaughtered his foot soldiers and torched his plans and hopes. Now InSec was hers. That was a pretty complete vengeance, tidy in its irony. It wasn't closure, though. She didn't believe in the fatuous term. There was always more war, always more revenge. Nothing was every really tidy. InSec, enslaved to her will, was now at the service of another vengeance.

She sat at the head of the table, Flanagan at her right hand, Luzhkov at her left, the Reptile God at her shoulder, and called the meeting to order. Sitting around the table were the lieutenants of her army. Good men and hard, chosen with the help of Luzhkov and Vandelaare. Nick Haasbroek, too baby-faced to be real, his deceptive pudge a magician's sleight of hand, distracting from the grace of his movements.

Abel Jamba, carved-wood muscle and sphinx-impassive. Mark Vrenna, relaxed Montana posture, surprisingly blue-blooded New England accent. Reggie McGee, former Scots Guards and SAS, Danny Boy curls but Loch Lomond dourness, and God help the man who made the mistake of placing him on the west side of the Irish Sea. Jean Decaux, pale-eyed, shaven of head, could have been a shit-kicker for Skins de France if not for the rainbow tattoo on the back of his neck. Phil Lambeck, the perfect civilian, hair by Supercuts, clothes by Wal-Mart concealing the compact force of his frame. No distinguishing scars on this man. The ideal Mr. Bland.

Her team. And they all knew who she was. Her neck was out a long way. Her test was to see if she had enough trust to go around.

First business, the extent of her control. There had been a culling of InSec's mercenary forces. She had killed many. More had been siphoned off by Sherbina into Kornukopia. There had been still more splintering as the monopoly collapsed. But the manpower was still huge. As she and Flanagan dug through files, as secretaries surrendered passwords and accounts were unlocked, she was just beginning to grasp the potential size of the army.

She spread out some preliminary figures on the table. She looked from face to face. "Give me your best guess," she said. "How loyal are the troops?"

Vandelaare scratched his chin. "My boys are good.". He glanced at Luzhkov, who nodded his agreement. "True believers, most of them, likes us all." He swept his arm to take in the room. Jamba laughed. "Nobody believes like a new convert," Vandelaare said, acknowledging Jamba.

"That true?" Blaylock asked the Angolan.

"For some of us." He turned serious. "Mostly, we follow orders. A lot of the guys will never know management has changed. They get the money, they get the action, they get happy. Simple."

What she expected, but useful to have it confirmed. She had an army of mercenaries, not crusaders. "I don't have to ask how they feel about wet work," she said. She'd seen plenty of willingness to kill, and kill dirty, when she was up against Pembroke. "What about the American theatre? You know the kind of thing I have in mind."

"If they're not from here, no problem," Vandelaare said.

Blaylock wasn't surprised. There had been a serial disaster of administrations, each one more unpopular abroad than the last. Reed's domestic approval ratings were high. If he tried to run for election in any other country, he'd be lucky to get away without a lynching. Blaylock turned to Vrenna, who was looking thoughtful. "And if they're locals?" she asked.

"Depends on the mission, depends on the soldier," he said. "I'd screen pretty carefully."

"In other words, don't call in the boys from the Midwest to assassinate the President. Am I right?"

Vrenna nodded. "Some would be keen to get behind something like that, but not all."

"All right," Blaylock said. "Let's keep operational information on a need-to-know level." To Luzhov and Vandelaare, she said, "I want to haul in as much outside talent as we can."

"Not a problem," Luzhkov answered.

"Any particular deployment?" Vandelaare wanted to know.

"The Hamptons."

Luzhkov had been along for the ride for a bit already. He knew the target. The other men took a bit of time to digest the information. The mood in the boardroom was grave. Now you know I really mean it, Blaylock thought. You boys up for it?

They seemed to be. Decaux muttered an admiring, "*Putain.*" There was a nervous shake to his voice, but he was grinning, too. All to the good, Blaylock thought.

Flanagan spoke up. "Can I ask something? You think Chapel is moving into the Hamptons to take out Reed. Right?" When Blaylock nodded, he continued. "So why interfere? Why not let him do the job for us?"

"And let him pull off a coup?"

"You really believe that's what he's planning?"

Poor Mike. Still some traces of the innocent left. Aren't you tired yet of being maimed by your hellbitch of a girlfriend? "Chapel's a true believer," she said. "He loves his country." She couldn't help smiling when she said this. She saw Vrenna wince slightly, knew her smile was bad poison. "He wants to save it. He's no idiot. He knows that whacking the president isn't enough to change anything. You guys have a long history of shooting your leaders. You want something radical to happen, you need a follow-up to the assassination." She cocked her head at Flanagan. "Good enough?"

"Just making sure."

"Of what?"

"That this wasn't all about beating Chapel to the punch."

Several answers sprang to her lips. Only one of them felt like the truth. She hesitated, then went with that one. She'd led one army to its doom on a lie. She wouldn't do that again. If these men were willing to follow her, she owed it to them to let them know exactly what it was they were following. "In my perfect world," she admitted, "I have one hand on Reed's throat, and the other around Chapel's. I want to squeeze them both. I want my pound of flesh. I want them to burn because of *me*. So yeah, it's personal. But it also needs to be done."

"Isn't that what Chapel would say?"

She shrugged. "Probably." Nice try keeping me in line, Mike. She glanced around the table. "Any problems? Air them now?"

There were none. The boys were hungry for action. They shared her vibe. The InSec takedown was an appetizer. She was promising a Rabelaisian main course. Cool.

"So," she said. "Let's talk infiltration."

Another White House conference. Another lecture on loyalty. More security directives. Sam Reed put on the good show. He was the man of iron confidence and unassailable high ground. He was still in control. He was not changing any plans. He was not hiding. He was not running scared.

The giveaway: all these meetings. The control freak was gripping with white knuckles. Great facade. She could still see through it.

Secretary of State Meredith Leadbetter wasn't happy about that. The man was losing focus. She was just back from the Middle East, had briefed him about the vomit hole that was Iraq. He'd listened. He'd asked intelligent questions. The moment she was done giving her answers, the shutters went down over his eyes and it was as if she'd never spoken. He was forgetting as fast as he heard. Other things on his mind. Outside world be damned.

No way to run an empire.

Patrick Pratellá caught up with her in the underground car park. "What did you think of the latest performance?" he asked.

"A good one," she said, keeping her tone noncommittal. She wondered what the old toad wanted.

"I'd say the horse isn't weathering the barn door."

She'd reached her car. She paused and turned to face Pratella. The Speaker was watching her closely. He was waiting for something. His words were gnomic. His tone was limpid. "What are you thinking?" she pushed. She wanted all his cards face up before she showed a hint of her hand.

Pratella sighed an old man sigh. Deeply sad. "I just don't know if he still has the interests of our great nation at the forefront of his mind. Through no fault of his own, of course."

"Of course."

Pratella kept watching her. "So?" he prompted. Her turn now.

"You might be right."

"I think the interests of the country should come first. Maybe I'm old-fashioned."

"That doesn't make you wrong." She meant it. The toad was a smart one, and for all his warts had the right instincts for the country. She hated spending time with him, but she thought he was the best Speaker the House had had in thirty years.

Pratella smiled. He was transmitting something serious. "My inquiring mind wants to know," he said, "how concerned you really are. These are times for cards to be kings over aces. How worried are you about your great country?"

How worried was she? How worried should she be? What do we have going on, after all? Multiple attempts on Charlotte Taber's life. Serious explosions in the capital city. An attempted hit on the president, and in the State Department itself, how *do* you do? No one caught. No one even suspected. The ramparts of security doing a Jericho. The big man going AWOL in his head. Yes, she was plenty worried. This was not the strong America she'd spent her adult life helping to build.

Meredith Athena Epifania Leadbetter, née Birrell, old-fashioned enough to take her husband's name even though she made ten times his salary and it was only thanks to her intervention that the prince was able to hold down a job at all. Born to Atlanta Baptist stock, she was a daughter of the socially engaged and God-fearing upper middle class. Childhood was an idyll in a suburban tract home. Sundays were the communication of big values by a big man with a big voice in a big church. God and country. Render unto them both, for they are one and the same. God speaks through the destiny of His chosen nation.

The big lessons were learned. The big values stuck. They did more than follow her. They became the core around which her identity was shaped. The mould set hard. She was defined well before she graduated from high school. By sixteen, her shape was complete. Anything that followed was buffing and polish. The big values were her shield at Harvard, protecting her from any corrosive touch of namby-pamby liberalism and self-flagellating critiques of the nation's greatness and rectitude. Her PhD was poli-sci. Duty was the drive. The goal was a rescue mission. Too many of the wrong people running the country into the ground. Too many without the drive, the love, the purpose. America was losing her birthright. She was deviating from the path of her destiny. She was pulling away from the big values.

Leadbetter had the big ideas. After Harvard, a straight-line run from strength to strength. She took the big ideas to the conservative think tanks. The wonks creamed for her. She wrote well. She debated like a pit bull with charisma. Fox News discovered her, went porno in its enthusiasm. They put her on stacked-deck political debate shows. She could remember the first time she saw herself on TV. The studio pros had done well by her. The lighting created a platinum halo around her hair. Her cheeks glowed. Her lips were bad-thought red. She was a damned fine forty-five, if she said so herself, but on-screen she looked ten years younger. Superfine. She had felt a rush of pleased vanity. But what felt even better, what flushed the system with a crack-high, was her methodical evisceration of her opponent. The network execs had multiple orgasms. She was Ann Coulter who didn't need to make shit up. They fell at her feet and offered her the moon. She took it. For a while.

Strength to strength. The government took notice. President Campbell watched her show. Vice president Sam Reed read her papers. First one gig, then many as freelance advisor, first to the secretary of state, then to the Cabinet in general, then more and more sessions with the big boys themselves. They groomed her. She loved it. She saw the chance to do some real good. Then Campbell was killed. Reed came in and cleaned up the shop, brought some real iron back in. The secretary of state was Campbell's boy, and hadn't taken her advice often enough. Reed told him to clean out his office so Leadbetter could move in. Her confirmation hearings were the shortest on record. She had arrived. She would do her duty. She would save her country.

But now Reed was withering. If the man on top wasn't doing his job, her efforts were undermined. They were pointless. The country was at risk.

So? So answer Pratella's question. "I'm very concerned," she said. She faced him hard. "Tell me exactly what it is you want to know."

"I want to know if you agree that what's best for Sam isn't necessarily what's best for the country."

"Right now, I'd say there's a pretty big gap." And that was the God's honest.

The old toad held out his hand. She shook it.

14

"ll provide the means," Chapel had told Quintero. "You'll have all the intel you need, and as many resources as I can shake free. But you do the work."

It was time to work. Time for the alumni of the School of the Americas to put all that knowledge to good use. It had been a while for some of them. They might be rusty. The extraction from Cararcas had been nicely done, but now the recruits were descending on Fort Benning, and these were men he did not know. They came from Bolivia and Chile, from El Salvador and Nicaragua. Some came from countries that had voted in leftist governments, undoing all the craft of the 1980s. Others came from regions from which the United States had suddenly pulled in its horns and withdrawn its money, abandoning friends as it turned its obsessions to the Middle East. They had all been excellent students. They had all been betrayed by their teacher. They were all ready to teach a lesson in their turn, and make the world behave the way it should.

First, the lesson materials had to be gathered. Most of them were easy. Chapel had enough connections left to free up all the basic weaponry and transport Quintero needed. More specialized equipment was available in the private sector. He reviewed the troops, looking for the physical types he wanted: as fair of skin as possible, slighter of build, non-threatening. If the man wore glasses, even better. Captain Hernán Gonzáles, a Bolivian, was the prize. At fifty-five, he was older than most, and more bitter. He'd spent the prime of his life in the good times, and had a vivid sense of what had been lost. He met every item on Quintero's checklist, and then some. His glasses were bifocals. His voice was soft. He didn't look like a soldier. He was the faculty member who never made waves as he coasted towards retirement. He was already perfect, and on top of everything else, he knew a few things about chemistry. Quintero put him in charge of the team gathering the lab equipment, and told him to make most of the actual purchases himself. Quintero gave him a van and three weeks to get it done. Gonzáles's mission would be simple but monotonous. He would travel the country, buying no more than a single big-ticket item in any given city. The job was a glorified scavenger hunt. It would have minimum visibility.

Quintero kept the maximum visibility mission for himself and his boys.

He learned the territory. He studied road and elevation maps. He found opportunity. He sent an advance team down to be his eyes and prepare the way. "This will not be cheap," he told Chapel.

"Just tell me what you need."

Quintero rattled off the firepower he wanted for the operation itself, and the vehicles necessary for afterward.

"Easy enough," Chapel said.

"I also need a tanker truck."

"As well as a semi-trailer? Full of what?"

"It doesn't matter. It can be empty."

A bit of hesitation, then Chapel said, "Fine."

The finishing touch: "And two South Carolina state trooper cars."

Chapel kept a poker face, but he did frown slightly as he thought. "That's trickier."

Quintero shrugged. "They are necessary."

"I'll see what I can do."

And this was why the loss of InSec rankled. Chapel nursed black thoughts about the woman, hoped she was sniffing around his bait. Make his life difficult, would she? Let's see how she liked the trap. But before he could spring it, he had to work around the obstacles she'd thrown up in his way. He didn't have the money or the resources he wanted. His juice was limited. He was depending on the ambition and self-interest of others. He was depending on Pratella not noticing just how little leverage Chapel really had over him.

"You want *what?*" Pratella said.

"Can you get them or not?"

Pratella was shaking his head with melodramatic exhaustion. "The man wants a rainmaker in a high wind."

"I'll take that as a yes."

Pratella narrowed his eyes. He became pure predator,

gauging tough prey. "This means sticking my neck out," he said. "I'm going to have to call in some old markers."

"Can't win the prize without playing the game," Chapel said. He smiled.

Shit rolls downhill. Quintero's requisition made its way down to the suckers. Pratella weighed candidates, found a good prospect, saw a nice multitasking opportunity. He put his proposal to Chapel. Chapel said it sounded fine. Quintero gave it the okay, too.

"Good things to those who know," Don Mitchell said to Joe Baker. "You hear me, boy? How many times have I told you that?"

"Plenty," the younger trooper admitted.

"And? Was I right?"

"Looks that way."

Mitchell laughed and clapped both hands on his paunch. It hung like a half-pipe wave over his belt and strained the buttons on his uniform. "Feed me. I'm in need of more praise."

"Go fuck yourself."

The youth of today. No respect, and no mistake. He was trying to give his partner the benefit of his experience, teach him a thing or two about making the world work for *you*, instead of the other way around. And this was the thanks. He spared a sad thought for the state of society, then said, "Let's go." He climbed into his car. The steering wheel pressed into his belly, and he had to struggle to fit the safety belt around his girth. He watched Baker slide into the other vehicle. Baker was thin, but it was a metabolism thin, not a workout thin. He knew Baker was no more prone to rise from his couch and exercise than he was. He didn't resent the younger man's build. It would pass. In his late twenties, Baker was already showing the warning signs of the gut to come. He'd have his regrets over the passing of his youth, he surely would. Mitchell didn't. He'd never been thin. He'd been obese from childhood. His schoolmates had learned quickly not to taunt him, though, because he'd been big in every sense. He might have been fat, but he was stronger than any of his peers. He'd survived through intimidation and violence. There was one boy who wasn't afraid, because he was even stronger: Pee-Pee Pratella. It turned out that they shared a bullet-and-fist view of the world, and they formed an alliance, an axis of terror through school and beyond. When Pratella began to think politics, first in his columns, then at the ballot box, Mitchell plumped for the Highway Patrol. Stick and gun felt as good as his dick in his hand. When Pratella needed some strong-arm jobs done, and he could no longer afford to do the leaning and the kneecap smashing himself, he turned to Mitchell, who was happy to oblige. The work was fun, and Pratella paid well. Cash only, tax-free. Beauty. But in his advancing seniority and power, Pratella had used him less and less. Eventually, he'd severed all contact, dropping Mitchell like a bad memory. Mitchell lost his big political buddy, became just another fat highway cop. At least he was based in Charleston and not Conway anymore. His work was too sloppy, lazy and brutal to move him up in the ranks. He decided he would not retreat to the shadows without his pound of flesh. He knew where a goodly number of Pratella's skeletons were buried. He'd put a number of them into the ground himself. He reminded the Speaker of the things that, given the inclination, he could speak about himself. Pratella arranged for an ongoing honorarium. A tribute to friendship and services rendered. It wasn't huge, but it kept Mitchell in hookers and booze. Every so often, he would drop a friendly note to Pratella, just to say hi and make sure there was an appropriate but modest cost of living increase to the payouts. He wasn't a greedy man, but he knew his worth.

And then, out of the blue, Pratella called *him*. He needed a favour. Just like old times. Two highway patrol cars had to be delivered to a friend, no questions asked. That was a *big* favour, Mitchell opined. An expensive one. Pratella suggested a fee, and it was so generous Mitchell didn't bother to bargain. His pussy would be top of the line for the next six months. Ordered by phone, not picked off the street.

This was a two-man job, so he brought Baker in on it. They'd been partners for the last two years. Baker didn't think much of Mitchell, and the feeling was mutual, but they worked well together. Baker was a knot of white-trash resentment. Forty years earlier, he would have been torching churches. Instead, he made sure his suspects resisted arrest, Tasered them, and used his stick good and proper. He worked shakedowns with Mitchell for the violence and the money. Good enough reasons, as far as Mitchell was concerned.

The job was stupid simple. Mitchell had mounted a Broadway production for Pratella about the difficulties in getting hold of patrol cars that wouldn't be missed immediately. Bullshit, but Pratella bought it and jacked up the price. Mitchell began to develop a finer sense of his self-worth. Pratella was anxious about something if he agreed so easily. That made the man vulnerable. A vulnerable man was one who would be willing to pay through the nose not to be vulnerable again.

Mitchell had services to offer. For proper consideration, he could make sure the bodies never emerged from the ground. This was the lesson he hoped he was teaching Baker. A man should always know how to make himself useful, especially to people who wished he would go away.

The rendezvous was in the Francis Marion National Forest. The drive was barely more than twenty miles. An easy night's work, as long as he and Baker weren't having to thumb it home. Mitchell followed the memorized directions, turned onto a gravel road. It wound through trees that brought the dark in and threw cataracts over his headlights. He drove slowly. The road rose. At the top of a hill, the trees thinned out, and the road widened to a lookout. There was a pickup parked there. Two men stood beside it. One of them stepped forward, shielding his eyes in the lights of Mitchell's car, and waved. Mitchell pulled up. He opened the door and squeezed out from behind the wheel. He stumbled slightly as he popped free of the car. "You boys waiting for someone?" he asked. He heard Baker stop behind him. The other trooper stayed in his vehicle.

"Mitchell?" the man inquired.

"I am if you're Maldonado."

"Thank you for coming," Maldonado said.

Mitchell flicked a wrist at Baker. "Come on, youngster. Time to get what we came for."

Baker slid out of the car and joined him. His lips were tight and curled down. Mitchell knew why, didn't exactly blame him. Doing business with spics was a fact of the modern world, but it still felt like a hit to dignity. He didn't know why Pratella couldn't do this properly, with some decent whites. He supposed it was just another sign of how politics made a man just a little too flexible. These boys seemed to be pretty solid specimens, though. Held themselves straight. Hair very short. They were wearing T-shirts and jeans, but they were military, sure as shit. Maldonado pulled an envelope out of his back pocket and handed it to Mitchell. "Is this right?" he asked.

Mitchell flipped through the bills. They riffled pleasantly under his thumb. "Perfect," he said. He took a couple of steps away from the cars and gestured to them. "Gentlemen, your vehicles."

"Thank you."

Mitchell nodded at the pickup. "That for us?"

Maldonado pursed his lips and studied the ground, thinking. After a moment he said, "No. I think we still need it."

"Then what the fuck?" Baker demanded.

The hair on the back of Mitchell's neck stirred as he heard the crunch of a footstep on the gravel behind him. "Ah," he said, a slack-jawed fool, and that was that.

Cabezas nailed them both in the back of the head. One shot each. Both troopers down and dead. Maldonado nodded approval at work well done. He and his two men, Cabezas and Meiselas, stripped off the uniforms. Mitchell's was huge. Baker's was going to be sphincter-tight on the man who had to wear it. They would pass for the length of time they would be needed, though. The three men carried the bodies from the crest of the hill, into the woods and the large hole that was waiting. The corpses dropped and tangled at the bottom. Then the tedium: putting all that dirt back into the hole, and setting the forest floor to rights. By the time the soldiers were done, the grave was invisible. They drove off in the patrol cars and the pickup.

It took them three days to modify the transport truck. Then they ran the exercise through on the Fort Benning grounds for a solid week. Quintero threw as many spanners and twists into the sessions as he could think of, then had Chapel toss a few surprises his way. He wanted clockwork precision and high improv adaptability. There could be no fog-of-war excuses on this mission. One hitch and the entire operation, and every hope and dream, would be a smoking ruin. When Quintero was happy with the runs, he and his team drove down to South Carolina. They went in three SUVs with tinted windows, and the modified truck. They travelled on separate days to avoid the appearance of a convoy. They hooked up again on the first of June, in Allendale, not far from the Georgia border.

MOX. Mixed oxide fuel. Combine plutonium oxide with uranium oxide, and you have your nuclear reactor fuel. France, Belgium and the UK had been producing it for a while. France, Germany, Sweden and Switzerland used it. The US was new to the game, but it was a handy way to make use of decommissioned nukes. The plutonium was extracted from the warhead, then shipped to the Savannah River plant for the uranium to be added. The MOX was then shipped to reactors in the southeast. In the best of all worlds, Quintero would have been able to snatch the plutonium before it made it to the Savannah facility. He'd ordered the advance team to track delivery patterns and gauge transport security. The military grade material was an impossible nut to crack. The escort was too big, too heavily armoured. Grabbing the pure stuff would require an air strike. Not on the agenda. They weren't strong enough. Not yet.

The MOX wasn't a bad compromise. Separating the plutonium out again wouldn't be difficult, and they still had time. Quintero's recon team gave him the report he expected: military security going into the plant, civilian on the way out. The material wasn't weapons grade anymore, so why worry as much? Idiots.

He set up the ambush on Highway 3. There was a nice stretch of road between Martin and Estill with a big slice of nothing. Lots of wood cover on either side of the road. No houses, filling stations, or rest stops nearby. Traffic was light and could be cut to zero for the time Quintero needed. Close to ideal, one problem to solve. Route 125 was the only road that passed through the Savannah River site, so the transport's starting point was a given. About ten miles southeast of the site, just past Martin, 125 crossed paths with 3. A few more miles southeast and it intersected the divided lanes of the 301. If the transport was going to head southwest into Georgia, it would take 3 south and hook up with the 301 that way. The other common route involved taking the 301 north, in which case the truck would stay on 125 until it reached the highway. There was no pattern. No way to predict which way the target would choose. So take away the choice.

You get used to everything. How goddamn true was that? Take the lane-wide pothole just outside the site. The first time Burke Pallumbo had hit it with a truckful of MOX, he'd screamed. His mind's eye had seen him vanish in a scale-model mushroom cloud. Three beats later, his heart had started up again. His cargo hadn't cared. Now he hit the hole at speed to see how high he could bounce in his seat. Back then, he'd been excited as well as scared about the gig. He was moving *nuclear material*. Holy Jesus, James Bond and Tom Clancy. Knocked tinned goods into a cocked hat, better believe it. Now, he was just a tinned goods schlepper with an escort. He didn't do anything differently. He was bored all over again. The security guards in the cars ahead and behind him were just as zoned. The plutonium came in to the site in full military excitement, guns bristling and armour frowning, daring the bad guys to take a poke. On the way out, it was him and the muscle for rent. Pallumbo thought again about ditching the job. And do what? an interior voice that sounded a hell of a lot like Charlene's demanded. Rent to pay, two kids to feed, a third on the way. You go, Burke, you spread your wings and fly. He grunted, and shifted gears like he was trying to choke something.

Lights flashing ahead as he approached the junction with Highway 3. A tanker truck had jacknifed across the intersection, blocking 125. Oily smoke rose from the wreck. A state patrol car was on the scene, the trooper waving Pallumbo and his escort off onto the southbound route. Pallumbo shook his head as he made the turn. The road conditions were excellent, and there were no sharp curves. The idiot must have been doing a hundred and driving with his knees to pull off a boneheaded crash like that. He also thought the trooper was looking sloppy. His uniform was strictly sad sack. Christ, man, Pallumbo thought, show some respect for your job. We're all bored, here.

Maldonado was the poor bastard in Baker's uniform. He'd been right about how tight it would be. The pants squeezed and rode up his ass, clutched hard enough to trigger hemorrhoids. He couldn't wait to change out of them. Anything for the cause, though. He didn't want to delegate this duty. He wanted to see it done right. He was leaning against the second highway patrol car. The car was sitting across the road, a mile or so north of Estill. He was turning traffic away, smiling and nodding and firmly polite no matter what complaints, politely firm no matter what kind of questions and curiosity there were. He had a kind and jocular word for every driver. He wanted to get a look at each one. He wanted to choose carefully.

The clock ticked down. He still had a quarter of an hour, but he still hadn't seen what he needed. Too many commuter hatchbacks a strong wind would knock over. But now, coming down the road, something promising. He held up his hand and the van slowed down. Oh, this was nice. Not a minivan, an old-fashioned VW van that must have been around long enough to know both hippie shit and trailer trash. It was mud-caked and rusted. Duct tape sprouted from the chassis and wrapped around pipes. The sides had DAN BURROWS—HANDYMAN stencilled on. The lettering had faded. The van was white, perfect for showing off how filthy it was. Maldonado walked to the driver's side. The man inside wore a baseball cap the same crap-white as the van. It looked as if it been grafted to his head. He was in his late fifties, carried big flab in his gut, but his biceps were still hard. His stubble was three days and two beer binges old. When he asked, "What's the problem, officer?" his voice blasted old onions and older cheese in Maldonado's face.

"There's been an accident up head," Maldonado said. He

glanced behind Burrows' seat, saw a filth-caked clutter of tools and tarp. "We're having to turn people back."

"Okay," Burrows said. He stepped on the clutch.

"Just a moment." Maldonado opened the driver's door, hopped up into the van and squeezed a surprised Burrows over to one side. He held up a bottle of Jack Daniels. "Would you drink this, please?"

Burrows stared, not a thing computing. "Say what?"

"Drink it."

The stare carried on. Finally, Burrows shook his head. His laugh was uneasy. "Funny," he said, and turned away. He started to shift into gear again.

"No," Maldonado said. He raised Baker's gun. Burrows was more than uneasy now. He was white-face scared. "Please," Maldonado insisted. The handyman took the bottle. He uncapped it, took a swig. "All of it," Maldonado said. Burrows sobbed. He gagged on the whiskey. He choked it down. He was a good boy, and more and more of the liquid disappeared from the bottle. When two thirds was gone, Maldonado figured that was good enough. "Face the other way," he said.

"Please," Burrows pleaded.

"Face the other way," Maldonado said again, and he prodded with the gun. Burrows looked out the passenger window. Maldonado reversed the gun and brought the butt down with all his strength on the back of the other man's neck. The impact ran up his arm. There was a deep *thunk*. Burrows gurgled and sank forward, but Maldonado hadn't heard the sound he wanted. He hit Burrows three more times. The third time, the noise was there: *crack*. Vertebrae turned to dust. Burrows stopped breathing. Maldonado pushed him over the rest of the way into the passenger seat, then manoeuvred the van around the patrol car and headed north.

The transport had a security escort, but they weren't expecting an ambush. No one, Quintero knew, ever expected what had never happened before. Oh, they made a good show of preparedness on paper. They had to. It was all part of the new normal. Every living soul of the Land of the Free was supposed to be on the alert for ambush, ready aye ready to denounce the dark-skinned neighbour with an interest in chemistry or the cable customer who was receiving Al Jazeera. It made for stirring Homeland Security speeches. One and all Doing Their Bit. Belief in that illusion was not the same thing as true preparedness. Quintero had been in the field. He knew he couldn't really be prepared for what he had never experienced either. But at least he was aware of the gap. No way the trucker and his bodyguard had the same advantage.

He crouched as close to the roadside as he could get without leaving the cover of trees, looking north, waiting for the convoy. He had a good view of the staging grounds. Everything that was supposed to go down would go down here.

It began to go down. The escort vehicle appeared from around the far bend. It was a Hummer, which Quintero thought was perfect. Like everything else about the convoy, it was imitation military watered down to strategic uselessness. Behind it came the reinforced semi-trailer. The opening move came from Jose Cabezas, Maldonado's point man on surveillance. He had laser eyes. He had sniper skills. He could shoot out the front left tire of the Hummer blindfolded, and probably did. The tire blew out explosively, hit by a heavy calibre round. The vehicle wasn't burning road, but it was still moving at a fair clip. It swerved drunkenly to the left and started its roll.

Burke Pallumbo watched his escort turning into a bowling ball. It bounced over the road, crumpling metal and tossing glass shrapnel. Time was molasses. He was watching a movie. No other explanation. This couldn't be life. His reactions were a spectator's. He sat and did nothing, taking in the show. Then the camera zoomed in on the rolling wreck. Then the pressure of the steering wheel against his slicked palms and the pain of his whitening knuckles brought him into the movie, and though he didn't think he was frightened yet, and though he was watching the whole production with a dispassionate holy-shit, he began to move his foot off the accelerator. In terminal slo-mo, he began the movements that would bring his feet to the clutch and brake.

Someone tore the movie screen. His windshield frosted, then shattered. He thought someone was throwing rocks at his chest, very hard and very fast. His hands slipped off the wheel.

Fade to black.

It all went down. So smoothly, it was almost boring. Quintero had the scene memorized before he saw it. Everything ticked over like the exercise, with a few minor variations tossed in by reality to keep things interesting. He saw Olano open fire on the truck's driver. The transport was close enough for Quintero to see the man slump down, his face looking like he was killed more by surprise than by bullets. The truck lost speed and began to weave, unsure of its direction. By default, it plowed straight into the Hummer as it finished its roll. The cab rode over the wreck, a bucking crowd pleaser at a monster truck rally. It reared up, roaring, then lost momentum. It hesitated, then began to slide off the on the right side of the Hummer. Flip, Quintero thought. Come on, now, and save us the trouble. The truck listed. The cab fell on its side, and took the trailer with it. Metal crashed and roared as the beast died.

A moment of quiet as the dust settled. Then Quintero's machine clicked into the next gear. His truck came up from the south, and the men swarmed to the cab of the crashed transport. They weren't wearing radiation suits. This was the first of the real risks. If the MOX containers were breached, they were all dead, but Quintero was gambling on the fact that the seals were more than up to a traffic accident. Olano had the rear of the cab opened, and he gave the thumbs up. They transferred what they needed to the other vehicle. It was a pretty small proportion of the original cargo. Who would miss it? Quintero knew someone would. But he could stretch the time it took for anyone to be sure. When his truck was loaded up, it headed back south to make its way past Maldonado's roadblock and begin the long trek back to the Hamptons. There was one last trick to play. Maldonado arrived in his hijacked van. Quintero ordered the withdrawal to begin and walked over to the van. "Like it?" Maldonado asked.

"It's perfect." He looked around, made sure everyone was in the clear. "Do it," he said.

Maldonado put the van in neutral, let it idle, and climbed out. He wrestled the corpse back into the driving seat. He placed Burrows' foot on the accelerator. The dead weight made the engine roar. He threw the van into gear and jumped back. The van raced forward and slammed into the Hummer.

Vehicle eight-ball. The wreckage tangled and scraped along the road until it slammed into the transport. Now they had a cause for the accident. Quintero waited a minute, watching for sparks. There were some, but not enough to do the job.

"Guess we'll have to do it ourselves," Maldonado said, and he walked forward to start the fire.

A few minutes later, Quintero and Maldonado were driving down Highway 3. In the rearview mirror, a dark, oily rose of smoke bloomed. "That went well," Maldonado said.

Quintero grinned. The operation had been Swiss clockwork. He could almost hear the final timer ticking down.

15

Maybe things could have been different. Blaylock would think that later. Maybe, if she'd been a bit faster in getting her forces to the Hamptons. If surveillance had lucked out sooner. If she'd seen the right thing at the right time, if she'd only *known*. If she hadn't underestimated Chapel. If she'd realized his commitment to his cause, and that his willingness to do the unspeakable in its name was equal to her own, and Christ she *should* have realized that. If, if, if, an infinity of almosts and near misses paving the highway that blew past the gates and down into the heart of the inferno.

It was the little things that built the chain. The small links that finally locked out every other possibility but one. She didn't believe in fate. But the Reptile God, at whose war altar she sacrificed? Oh, she believed in him. She was his favoured daughter, blessed in slaughter above all women. But that was the point: slaughter. That was meat for the Reptile. That it took place was what mattered, and the Reptile's word was law. Given that, how could she have hoped for things to be different?

Little things. Coincidences. Tiny links. Small world. All it took was the right time, right place, right look. Right past. All of those things together. Not much at all.

There was no fate. But there was the Reptile.

"Jesus with a horse," Vandelaare said when he saw the man.

A week after the takeover, Blaylock began moving her strength to Petersfield. It had to be done gradually. Infiltration, not invasion. She didn't want to spook the locals, and especially not Chapel. If he was setting something up, she wanted him to carry right along so she could see him do it. She wanted to be able to judge when to step in. She smelled coup, and she would stop it, but if Chapel was targeting Reed, she might be able to use that. Reed was still hers to kill. She wasn't going to sacrifice her vendetta so Chapel could fulfill his, but she didn't mind surfing his wave to a sweet kill opportunity.

The night before the first move, she had a council of war with her lieutenants. Road and topological maps on the board-room table. Satellite imagery of the area on PowerPoint. "So," Blaylock said, "who here knows where the president's house is?"

Flanagan tapped a spot on the road map, then mouse-clicked to a photo of a mansion and large grounds. Viewed from the top down, the house looked like a Lego block. "There's your man."

"Nice work," Blaylock commented.

"Thank you, Mr. Google," Flanagan replied. "Amazing what you can find out with this Internet thing."

Blaylock eyed the location. Figure high security, every square inch of the grounds accounted for by camera, now factor in the Secret Service. The man would be under double and triple guard since her botched attempt. No approaches to the house with cover. Hard target for anything short of a battalion.

She had one. Did Chapel? She wasn't planning on throwing hers away on a charge so risky with a payoff of dubious value. She still liked her coup theory, but she stumbled over how Chapel was going to carry it out. What were his resources? And if he clipped Reed, what then? It's not like he was in the line of succession. Was he planning on storming the Capitol while he was at it? Too many questions, not enough intel. Get in the field, girl. Look at the site through Chapel's eyes. See what he sees. "Mike, do you know the Hamptons?"

"Some. Went there as a kid."

"Anyone else been there at all?" Negatives all around. Blaylock hesitated. "Give me a realist answer," she said to Flanagan. "I need you to run this place. Can it autopilot for a few days if you come out to Petersfield with me?"

"It's been doing that a fair bit these last couple of years. It keeps losing its CEO."

"How careless of it," she said, grinning. Then she turned serious. "There's more to the way InSec works now, though," she said. "I don't need it just to keep running. I need it to keep running for *us*."

"It will," Flanagan reassured her.

"Can you fucking believe it? Because I can't," Vandelaare said when he saw the man.

They drove to Petersfield in a Corolla that Flanagan bought, cash, at a used car dealership that was honest enough to sell quality, but still mobbed-up enough not to worry about customers that preferred the anonymity of outright purchase transactions. Into town they came, the happy young couple looking for an early summer getaway. Blaylock had kept her ordnance to a minimum: c-7 buried at the back of the trunk, sig-Sauer in the glove compartment. She wore a summer dress and sandals. Combat clothes were in the suitcase. Flanagan's eyes kept flicking from the highway to Blaylock as he drove.

"Whaaaaat?" she said, finally.

"Just wondering when I last saw you in a dress," he said.

"It's been known to happen." She sounded a touch defensive.

"Not often."

"So?"

"So nothing. You look good." Truth. He loved the story of her face. He could see the traces of scars, but only because he knew how to look. The diagonal line that was the legacy of her family's death wasn't disfiguring. It was an artist's grace note, underscoring the resilience of her beauty. Her bare arms bore what looked like scratches. He knew they were the echoes of harsher wounds.

She blushed. "Thanks," she muttered.

"What's the matter?" He didn't think of her as shy. He'd seen her strut when the spirit moved her. And in bed, she wasn't just aggressive. She invaded Poland. "Don't like compliments?"

"Don't know what to do with them." She shifted in her seat, looked out the passenger window.

"Want me to stop?" He reached out and finger-stroked her hair around the back of her ear.

She grinned, shook her head. "No," she said. "It's nice."

They descended on Petersfield, demon and her consort.

Flanagan negotiated the streets, eyed the quiet of an economy built on wealthy leisure, saw families, and grew anxious. "What are we bringing here?" he asked. "What are we going to do to these people?"

They stopped at a traffic light. A young woman crossed in front of them, a four-year-old in tow, stroller in front. Flanagan watched the unease colour Blaylock's features. "We're going to be careful," she said, firm. "We're here to stop something from happening, not cause it."

"We don't have a good track record when it comes to collateral damage," he said. He saw the little girl stumble as the family reached the curb. The mother caught her arm and lifted her to the sidewalk before her knees smacked the ground. Flanagan suddenly felt nauseated. His lunch crawled up from his gut.

"What do you mean 'we'?" Blaylock whispered. She was pale. They had the AC on high, but sweat beaded her forehead.

"My hands are dirty, too." He thought about Switzerland, and helping to set up the mortar shelling of Sherbina's home. Irina Zelkova and her daughter running from the flames in terror.

"I dirtied them," Blaylock said, still barely audible.

The full mortar memory: not knowing what he was helping her do until the first shell flew. Him screaming in horror. But he didn't let himself off the hook. He'd gone with her into the mountains knowing a bad thing was going to be done. He had gazed upon her killing fields, and felt joy and hunger. He was helping her now, with the full knowledge that one of her goals was the assassination of the president of the United States. He wanted to see it done. He knew all these things about himself, but didn't say them. She would only blame herself more. He took her hand and gave it a squeeze. The light changed to green. He drove on.

"I won't hurt them," Blaylock said. She twisted in her seat to look back at the mother and children. "We'll keep them safe."

"How?" Flanagan asked. He thought of all the people he and Blaylock had wanted to protect in the past, and how many of them had died. He really was going to be sick.

"By being careful." Her tone was a mix of firm resolve and desperate hopelessness. "This operation is stealth, not assault. We'll keep it that way."

"Do you think Chapel will let us?"

She didn't answer.

Flanagan scanned the sides of the road, forcing his thoughts off future horror and back on present need. "B & B or hotel?" he asked.

"Hotel. More anonymous."

He drove out of town onto Montauk Highway.

"How often did you use to come here?" Blaylock asked.

"We didn't actually stay in Petersfield," he said. "My mom's sister had a place a few miles down the road. We would town-hop, check out whatever was interesting that day." He was fifteen when that summer tradition came to an end, when his uncle, bombed behind the wheel of his BMW, wrapped the car, himself and his wife around a telephone pole. Flanagan hadn't been back to the Hamptons since, except once. A warm Easter in business college, he'd been talked into hitting the party scene here. It had been a gruesome weekend. The in-crowd was out in force, and he was not of it. The insiders were the native-born and the spawn of wealth. In the lineups outside nightclubs, they greeted each other with Masonic knowingness. Flanagan's friends, the ones who had dragged him out here, and who had passed for perfectly human at Harvard, morphed into the most inbred, ill-bred incarnations of the American aristocracy. He became the little people. The weekend was eternal. He prayed for escape. He prayed for the entire area to be given the Dresden treatment, followed by a healthy dose of Carthaginian salt. Now, here he was, green at the gills with the thought that he might be coming to answer his own prayers.

A hotel was coming up on the left. "There's one," he said.

"As good a place as any," Blaylock answered. "It's not like we're hurting for cash."

The hotel looked a bit like some of the mansions Blaylock had been researching on the web. It was a decent-sized building, but was still smaller than a number of the homes in the area. Flanagan noticed an outdoor swimming pool to one side. No slide. The joint was upscale and didn't cater to families.

They checked in using IDs that announced them as the O'Hagans, Andy and Madeleine. Then the question was how to mark time until the rest of the team trickled in. Blaylock wanted to reconnoitre. Flanagan said, "Let me take you to dinner."

They found a place on Shinnecock Road, not far from the Petersfield Golf Club. It had a sidewalk patio, and served good lobster. It could have been romantic, but Blaylock never turned off her radar. Flanagan watched her memorize the street and the people on it. She frowned more as the evening wore on. "What is it?" Flanagan asked.

She shook her head. "Too much data, no way to filter. I don't know what I'm looking for."

Flanagan glanced around. "Chapel won't have the decency to show up himself, I suppose."

"No. Inconsiderate bastard."

"So I guess there's not much you can do right now."

"No," she agreed.

"So, I don't suppose you might consider relaxing for the evening."

"No," she said, cheerful but firm.

"And later tonight?"

Her eyes glinted mischief. "I'll squeeze you in," she said.

She sent him back to the hotel alone. She wanted to walk and learn the streets. He didn't see her again until after midnight. He asked if she had any luck. No, she answered, but she had the terrain down. She was ready for urban warfare. So now what? he asked. This, she said, and stepped out of her dress.

The boys arrived. Good. Eyes on the scene, that's what she needed. Luzhkov and Vandelaare would triple the military evaluation of Petersfield. Flanagan would bring another viewpoint. He was civilian. Better: he had moved through enough of the cream of New England society to be able to detect anomalies.

"What are you talking about?" he had asked, in bed, when she told him this. "It's been over a decade since I was last here."

"And the reason you haven't been back?"

"Hate this place."

"Exactly."

"What's that supposed to mean?"

"Visceral memories are good. They stay with you. You're

watching and judging the place all over again, whether you know it consciously or not. Things might stand out for you."

"Such as how much I want to leave?"

"You're worried. I promised we'd be good."

"It isn't just that. It's also because I hate the place." Shuddering sigh. "I might want to be bad."

She knew about that. She knew about being bad and liking it. She also knew that being bad was her job, not his. "I won't let you," she told him. "I'll never put your finger on the button, Mike. I swear."

He'd gone to sleep after that, his muscles relaxing slightly. This morning, he was better. The way he looked at the town was still sour, though. Good. Use that hate.

They hooked up with Vandelaare and Luzhkov at The Roasting Den, a coffee shop on the main drag. It was the higher Starbuck's, twice as much dark colour and wood in the decor, three times the price. Vandelaare looked bemused. "So this is where the Great Republic is going to be toppled," he said.

"It's counterintuitive," Blaylock admitted. What's your angle, Joe? I know you're here. I can feel your vibe.

"Lenin had his share of coffee house meetings," Luzhkov pointed out.

"Yes, but *we're* not the ones doing the toppling," Flanagan reminded him. "We're here to *prevent* the toppling."

"Reed still dies," Blaylock said, doing her own bit of reminding. She watched Flanagan's reaction. She hadn't lowered her voice. She had used her normal speaking tone to commit her crime. She had uttered a threat against the president of the United States. Not a big leap, since she'd already tried to take him out, but she wanted to see how Flanagan dealt with her promise not as an act he heard about, but one that she committed to in public. He looked up, grinned, and drew his finger across his throat. My boy is solid, the war machine thought. She turned back to the others. "Give me your initial impressions," she said.

Luzhkov raised his hands helplessly. "You tell me where to look. Because I don't know."

Vandelaare nodded, agreeing. "Our man Chapel is a smart one. If he's here, he's not bringing tanks to the party."

Blaylock twirled a cinnamon stick in her hot apple cider. "Can't exactly shoot everyone in town until we smoke him out." She risked giving Flanagan a tease. "Much as we might like to."

"Funny," Flanagan said without anger. He looked thoughtful. "Don't know if my hate is quite what it used to be anyway. The place doesn't seem quite as nuke-worthy as I thought in my callow youth."

"Oh?" Blaylock raised an eyebrow. "That tune changed suddenly."

"I was just noticing when we were driving around today. The town isn't quite as wall-to-wall whitebread as I remembered."

Flags went up, all red. Blaylock didn't like that they did, but knew better than to suppress instinct. "How do you mean?" she asked.

Flanagan heard the sharpness in her tone. "Racial profiling, Jen?"

"From what you said the tradition here is partial to profiling itself."

"In the sense of self-selection, yes."

"So if that profile is being broken, colour me curious."

Flanagan's mouth sagged. "This is gross," he said.

"Completely," Blaylock agreed. She stood up. "Let's go for a ride," she said.

They piled into the Corolla. Flanagan drove. They prowled the streets, and Flanagan was right. This was gross. She was looking at every face that wasn't hardcore Caucasian. The slime on her soul thickened a little bit more. Plus you realize, she thought to herself, that your gaze could slide right over Chapel and miss him completely. Because you're not looking at the white faces. She tried to compensate, tried to widen her focus. She wasn't sure if she was successful. After half an hour, the tactic was turning into a distasteful dead end. Then Vandelaare said, "Jesus with a horse." He was staring at a man walking down the sidewalk with a bag of groceries in each hand.

"What?" Blaylock asked. She twisted around in her seat to watch the man as they left him behind. He looked Hispanic. Christ, she thought. I will not be happy if this leads somewhere. He was dressed for the holidays: shorts, sandals and a loose, buttoned shirt, untucked. His bearing was rigid straight.

"Can you fucking believe it? Because I can't." Vandelaare shook his head.

"You know him?"

"Oh yeah, I know the man. Alejandro Olano. We did some work together in the Democratic Republic of the Congo."

"Fill me in."

"He's Venuzuelan. Was in tight with the strong-arm generals. Very big unhappy when the country went left. I don't think he left the forces, though. The Congo jobbies were some kind of freelance. Busman's holiday doing some gun-running."

"Making himself feel useful," Blaylock said.

"Sure. He's one of those types who has to be busy all the time, you know?" He winked. "Get themselves and others into all sorts of trouble."

Yeah, she knew. "When was the last time you heard of him?"

"It's been a while. He went home. It's not like we promised to write. This was a few years back. Before you started shaking everything and everyone up."

There was a small bookstore coming up on the right. "Pull over," Blaylock told Flanagan. She looked back down the road. Olano was about two blocks down, still walking. "Viktor," she said, "pop into the store and buy a newspaper or something." Establish cover.

"Done," Luzhkov said. He opened the door.

"Don't be long."

"No worries."

Luzhkov disappeared into the store. Blaylock turned around to face forward, but moved the rear-view mirror so she could see Olano. She saw him unlock a pickup truck. "Okay," she said. "Mike, get ready to start the car again." The truck pulled out. It drove past them just as Luzhkov sauntered out of the store, newspaper under his arm. "Good timing," Blaylock said as he settled back into the car.

"I try."

"You ready?" she asked Flanagan.

"Always wanted to try this," he said.

"Not too close," she cautioned. "Hang on a sec." Another car drove past. She could still see Olano, but there was a buffer between them now. "Okay," she said. "Go."

They followed six car lengths back. When Olano turned a

corner, Flanagan sped up so they wouldn't lose sight. "You're a natural," Blaylock said.

"Played my share of *Grand Theft Auto* in my time."

Olano took two more turns in quick succession. Flanagan almost lost him.

"He's made us," Luzhkov said.

"Maybe." Blaylock cursed under her breath, hoped Luzhkov was wrong, knew that he wasn't. Olano's route was too twisty, too random. He didn't seem to be heading anywhere in particular. There was still a chance that this was SOP, a routine to shake off whatever tails there might be, a precaution without knowledge. A chance.

They hit a long stretch of Farriers Lane. The road ran straight. There were no other cars between them and Olano. Flanagan hung back as far as he could. If Olano checked his rear-view mirror, Blaylock wondered, would he be counting how many times he had seen the Corolla?

The truck's brake lights flashed, and Olano pulled a dime-grazing U-turn. He headed back their way.

"Ahhh…" Vandelaare began.

"… shit," Flanagan finished.

Blaylock almost told her mercs to duck low, then realized there was no point. The truck's penis-extension tires didn't seem quite as stupid now. They gave the truck elevation. Olano would see everyone in the Corolla, hiding or not.

"What do I do?" Flanagan asked.

"Keep going," Blaylock told him. "Faster." Don't give Olano time for a good look.

Flanagan accelerated, closing in on sixty. "Eyes right," Blaylock ordered as they crossed the truck. She turned her head, giving Olano a view of her hair, not her face. Ahead, the road hit a bridge. "Turn the car around and stop," she said. She looked back. Olano was turning around again. Flanagan got the car into position, then pulled onto the shoulder. Olano was also just off the blacktop. They faced each other, a hundred yards of showdown lane between them. On the east side of the road: stone walls, electronic gates and windscreen trees shielding extensive properties from the road. On the west: more walls, and the gentle rise of scrub-covered dunes promising the ocean. Not a lot of room to manoeuvre. "Not a bad place for an ambush," Blaylock muttered.

"Who's doing the ambushing?" Flanagan asked.

"Not us."

Olano was on his phone. "You're sure?" Quintero was asking.

"Yes. I'm staring at them right now. They're not moving."

"And your ID is positive?"

"I didn't get a good look at them, but one of them is a woman. Must be Chapel's. He said she would show up." Quintero said nothing to this, and Olano waited. Finally, he prompted, "So? Sir? Do we take them out?"

"We should get out of here," Vandelaare said.

"That would be the smart thing," Blaylock agreed, but she held Flanagan's hand back as he reached forward to put the car in gear.

"If we run, we lose this guy," Luzhkov said.

"Exactly." She reached into the doorwell and caressed her SIG.

Quintero visualized the terrain, saw the opportunity Olano had set up, came this close to leaping. He could send a strong contingent out, move fast to surround, contain and neutralize. Then he thought about what Chapel had briefed him about this woman. He reminded himself what she had done in Geneva. The odds there were even more massively unbalanced. If she didn't die, Quintero would be showing his hand. She'd know where they were based. Don't underestimate her, he thought. "Run," he told Olano.

"Where to?"

"Anywhere. All the way back to Georgia if you have to." So long as she was kept clear of the operation.

The truck started moving again. It tore past them at speed. "Tag, we're it," Blaylock said.

"Could be a trap," Flanagan said, but he swung the Corolla around and followed anyway.

"We should be so lucky," Blaylock answered. The truck barrelled over the bridge, picked up more speed. Olano wasn't relying on twists and turns anymore. No more stealth, no more silly games. This was flight. He was using raw horsepower to put distance between them. "He doesn't want to be caught," she said.

They raced to Highway 27, accelerated further as it became a divided highway. They were over the speed limit, but not yet enough to catch the attention of the police. Each time Flanagan tried to give it just a bit more gas, edge up to Olano, he sped up too. He was more willing to take his chances with the authorities than with them. Conclusion: he had some idea of the threat the Corolla constituted. Chapel knows I'm around, Blaylock thought.

She also thought: We're going nowhere fast. "Screw it," she said. She pulled the SIG out. "Try to get a bit closer," she told Flanagan. "Eyes on traffic," she instructed the other two. She lowered her window, focused her gaze on the truck's right rear tire, but didn't aim the gun yet. There were plenty of other cars on the road. This was going to be dirty. Blaylock's peripheral vision recorded the terrain. Woods blurred by on the right. "Now," she whispered. Flanagan overtook a subcompact, closed the distance just that bit more. He created a window for her. There were no vehicles between them and the truck. He pulled back into the right lane. "Rear?" Blaylock asked.

"Clear as it gets," Vandelaare said.

"Same for left," said Luzhkov. "Go."

She narrowed her concentration to the point ahead of her where the bullet would go. The universe contracted to that singularity. She barely felt the movement of her body. She lifted the gun with both hands and swung her arms and head out the window. She fired one shot and ducked back inside the car. The movement was a single one, a wave motion in and out. Two seconds. So short that anyone who happened to be looking wouldn't be sure they'd seen anything. A good act of war as long as the bullet went true. It did. She'd known it would. She'd seen its path and moved on to the next act before she'd even begun to lean out.

The tire blew. Olano was doing more than seventy. The truck fishtailed and careened onto the shoulder. It flipped with hard anger into the trees. Shrapnel saplings flew. The truck cartwheeled twice and crumpled around heavier trunks. Trees fell. Flanagan braked at the scene. Luzhkov jumped out, waved another car on that was starting to slow. The truck was resting on its side. Blaylock scrambled over it and ducked down, shielded from the road, to look through the shattered windshield into the cab. Olano was pinned by the steering wheel. There was a lot of blood. He stared at her with righteous anger. "Any point in my pulling you out?" she asked.

He spat blood in her face.

"You're not dead, yet," she pointed out.

"You are," he wheezed. "You are in the path of history." Triumph in his glare. He was fighting the good fight to the last.

"You want to tell me what history that is?"

He pulled his lips back.

She nodded, acknowledging the smile. "Good soldier," she said. "I admire your loyalty. You have friends, I take it." Olano kept grinning. "People who would miss you, who would seek retribution." He nodded, victory soaring. "That's what I'm counting on," Blaylock said, and shot him.

16

Building a bomb in the Hamptons. Easy peasy. They had the material, they had the base, they had the privacy. They could practically sit back and watch the bomb assemble itself. Hernán Gonzáles had aced the purchasing mission, and gone a few steps further, supplementing the lab with equipment Quintero hadn't ordered, but which might prove useful. The SOA boys had enough toys to start up a first-class drug lab, supply the idle rich with all the nerve joy they could purchase. Make big money.

Not even a temptation, Chapel saw, pleased. The dedication to the project was absolute. These were principled men. He toured the lab, looked upon the works, saw that they were good.

Building a bomb in the Hamptons. There was MOX and plenty of it. Gonzáles had bought an ion-exchange resin column. Chapel stood in front of it, admiring the magic. He didn't understand it, didn't care. Not knowing was what made the process magic. There were two tanks standing upright in a frame, connected by piping. Water was pumped in and out. MOX went in. Plutonium and uranium oxides came out. Magic. The plutonium was ninety-two percent pure. Sweet. Not good enough, Quintero declared. Each batch got the treatment a second time. Purity ninety-nine percent. Feel that radioactive glow.

The plutonium oxide was fine. It could form the basis of a bomb more than big enough to get the job done. But its predictability wouldn't be perfect. Make the boom bigger, the whole package more reliable? Why the hell not? The equipment's on hand, the process is dead easy. Convert that oxide into a metal.

Building a bomb in the Hamptons. It was like a jawbreaker: layers of sweet candy around a sour popper of a centre. The centre would be the sphere of plutonium metal. Seven kilos of the stuff in a ball not much bigger than a baby's fist. The next layer would be the reflector: a shell of beryllium as thick again as the sphere's diametre. Coat the whole thing with sugar: four hundred kilos of plastic explosive. It sounded big, but Chapel had seen the plans. The jawbreaker would be about the size of a basketball. Some kinda candy.

Small but heavy. It wouldn't be carried in a backpack. That's what vans were for.

Quintero was giving Chapel the tour and the sitrep. The construction was shaping up well. The bomb would be ready on the Fourth. Big finale fireworks. Chapel was grinning hard, clam-happy. The loss of InSec didn't even qualify as an irritant anymore. Quintero wasn't grinning. He was doing the motions, performing the necessaries for his superior officer, but where was the joy? Where was the love? Dead in the roadside woods, shot through the head beside his truck, that was where. Big local headlines. Lurid and spooky, but probably not the death of One of Us. Gang related, was the speculation. What do you expect from those people? said the gossip. The old money shuddered with delight. Chapel sympathized. He had those shivers, too. She's here, he thought. She'd taken the bait. The hook was deep in her cheek. Life was good. But you wouldn't know it to look at Quintero. "Spit it out," Chapel said.

"You know who killed my man."

"Yes, I do."

"It's the woman you warned me about."

"As I live and breathe."

"I want her dead."

"Get in line."

Quintero's storm cloud darkened. He wasn't enjoying Chapel's line in flip. Too goddamn bad. "She killed a good man."

"She's killed plenty of those."

"But not *my* good men."

They were standing in the middle of the basement lab. The SOA boys were stopping what they were doing and looking Chapel's way. They were loyal to Quintero, he reminded himself. "Let's go outside," he said.

Quintero's eyes went narrow and smug with a sense of scored points. He bowed and gestured for Chapel to lead the way. Fuck you, Chapel thought. Strut that stuff where it belongs, in your own country. He respected Quintero's ideals and accomplishments, but there were limits. He tightened the leash on his temper. Life was still good. The goals were within reach.

They walked down the slope of the grounds to the beach. Chapel stretched out his arms, letting the ocean breeze play in his shirt sleeves. "Are we on the same page here or not?" he asked.

"We have the same hopes and dreams," Quintero said.

Oh, you cagey bastard. "That's not the impression you were giving your men back there." *Your* men. I bought and paid for all of you, but I'll throw you that bone of respect. Maybe you'll think about that. I doubt it.

Quintero shrugged. "We are all loyal to Major Olano."

"I mourn his loss, too." When Quintero snorted, Chapel said, "Okay, look. All I'm saying is that we should be showing a united front."

Quintero crossed his arms, cocked his head at Chapel. He looked pissed, amused, cynical. Neat mix. "*You* look, *Señor* Chapel." Chapel caught the emphasis on the civilian title. He was being excluded from the brotherhood of arms. "You are using me. That's okay. I am using you. Our needs are the same, our project is a great one. Believing anything else would be to believe in an illusion, and that does no one any good. Yes?"

"I need to know that I can rely on you."

"You can."

"Because this project doesn't end on the Fourth. That's when it really gets started."

"We will be there for you." Something gleamed in his eye. It was a war thirst. Chapel saw it, felt reassured. His army was still his. Then Quintero said, "But I want her dead."

"She'll die. I told you she'd come. Now she's here. She'll be on site on the Fourth, don't you worry about that. Taking her out is no small part of this endeavour."

Quintero didn't look satisfied. "This is a matter of honour," he insisted. "Do you know what that means?"

Did he know what that meant? Jesus Christ. His life was about his country's honour. He turned on Quintero with death in his eyes. "Don't ever ask me that again," he said. His fist tightened around his cane. Sherbina had broken the fighter he had once been, but he would still pulp this tin soldier if he had to. "Why do you think I'm going down this road?" he hissed. "You think this is some goddamned personal power play? I would kill any man who would have that for a reason. This is about saving the nation. I'd say that's a matter of honour. Whaddaya say, Jorge?"

Quintero bowed again, without irony this time. "I say that I am satisfied."

"Good." Chapel started back up the lawn. More work to do. Places to be, people to prep. But he turned back and pointed his cane at Quintero. "She *is* going down," he said. "I owe her a thing or two myself."

Quintero watched him go. Idiot, he thought. Turning her into collateral damage wasn't payback. It was a lucky coincidence. Justice was more personal than that. He headed back to the house. Maldonado was waiting for him at the back door. "So?" he asked.

This was what Chapel didn't understand, Quintero thought. He wasn't the only one pissed and impatient. All of the boys were. No one here was going to brook delay. "He won't go for it."

"What do we do?"

"The right thing." He wasn't going to be stupid. He wasn't going to jeopardize the project. He wasn't going to underestimate the woman. He *was* going to exact the pound of flesh. "She's here and she's not alone," he said.

"We don't know what she looks like," Maldonado pointed out.

No, and Chapel wasn't going to help out on that front. Quintero had already demanded a picture. Chapel had refused, too quickly and with too much venom. *You don't even have one*, Quintero had thought. "We don't have to," he said. "Gather the men. Full briefing in five minutes."

They met in what would have been the house's living room. It had become the meeting hall. Quintero walked in front of the troops. There were twenty men on-site. Many more back at Fort Benning, but he couldn't call them in. That would be tantamount to staging an invasion of Petersfield. The idea was not to advertise their presence. Justice was going to be precise, surgical, silent. "We know what she does," he told his men. "We know she's not here on vacation. There are hostile forces in town. We watch for them, we locate them, we take them out. Quietly. The civilians don't even know there's a war going on around them. Am I being heard?"

He saw the tight grins. He saw the resolve. He was being heard.

Gather the forces. Shape the fist. Blaylock drew her mercs in. No groups larger than three, and those had damn well better look the part of rich frat boys. They filled the hotels and never spoke to each other. If she sent out the word, her fist could shut the town down. If she had to, she would. For now, no action. Not enough intel.

That was changing. Flanagan had a laptop with wireless Internet access, and they worked the Web. They trolled the news sites. The questions that needed answering: why was

Olano here? What was the link with Chapel? What the holy hell was up? She picked Vandelaare's brains. Any other known associates for Olano? Who was his commanding officer? She asked these questions. She found some creepy answers. The paydirt was the news story out of Venezuela. Would-be coup leader and hard-right strongman Jorge Quintero saved from prison and spirited away by armed men. Spectacular daylight action, mucho violence. The name rang the right bells for Vandelaare. "He's a centrefold for guys like Olano," he said. "Big hero."

Blaylock followed the lead. It disappeared with its subject. Quintero evaporated from Venezuela, didn't show up any- where else. "Where did he go?" she wondered. Warrants out all over for his arrest. Nothing. Dead? Not likely. Who had the means to make him disappear that effectively? Plenty of states and organizations. Who had the motive?

Chapel wanted InSec. She took it from him. He had plans in Petersfield. Olano was here. Olano worshipped Quintero. Quintero was missing. Connect the dots, look at the picture. Trouble.

More research. Go back, not forward. Look into Quin- tero's past. Human rights violations a-go-go, all documented and advertised by watchdog groups and NGOs. Another name began to show up: School of the Americas. Follow the threads, stumble over the bodies. She expanded her search, cross-ref- erencing the SOA with plausible Quintero KAs, and disgruntled Latin American army officers in the news after failed coup attempts or removals of hard-right regimes. The roll call was impressively long. She had photographs to go along with many of the names. Lots of glory hounds in the bunch, consumed by their own righteousness and happy to set straight any passing reporter. A fair number of other pictures were old, taken before the men behind the faces found their beliefs, their careers, their crimes. They were the smarter ones, long since gone to ground. But their traces remained. She made her list. She checked it twice. She consulted with Luzhkov and Vandelaare, factored in their knowledge of likely names that had passed through the merc world. Then she sent the word out. The list was distributed to the men who gathered in Petersfield, the soldiers who had come to the summer playland to prepare for war. Look for these faces, she ordered. Watch for the enemy. Keep things quiet but hurt them.

She met with no more than a couple at a time. The time might come when she would need a concentrated strike force, a battalion strength. If the time came, she could trigger a sudden condensation. For now, she wanted the spread and subtlety of a web. She waited for the thrumming struggle of the captured fly.

At night, the parties started. Summer was here, in temperature if not quite yet in date. Good enough. Fun was serious business. The nightclubs swelled with the young, beautiful in the promise of secure inheritance. The joy was raucous, and drowned out the footsteps of the hunting shadows. The sheep played hard. They didn't know the wolves were at war. They didn't even know there were wolves about.

Some of the sheep bleated. If they knew how close they were to being collateral statistics in the debit column of post-op debrief, they would have bleated in fair earnest.

"It's not fair!" The perfected whine of a fifteen-year-old.

"So you've said." Samantha Edgerton didn't have the energy to argue anymore. Apathetic sarcasm was the most she could summon.

"How come Krysta gets to go?"

"Because I'm twenty-one." Krysta was out of the car and on the sidewalk, but still leaning in the open door, arranging cell phone and makeup in her purse.

Twenty-one going on twelve, Samantha thought. "Would you mind not taunting your sister?" she asked to the wind.

Sienna didn't appreciate receiving an answer to a rhetorical whinge. "Just *stupid*," she grumped.

Krysta smirked, snapped the purse shut and strutted over to join the lineup for the entrance to the Octothorpe. Fragmented beats and sub-audible bass lines floated out of the doors, vibrating Samantha's chest. Didn't I used to go to places like that? she thought.

"Why *can't* I go?" Sienna demanded, as if a million repetitions of the question would change the answer.

"Apart from anything else, it's the law."

"Well the law *sucks*."

Through her fatigue, Samantha felt a twinge of sympathy. She could remember her own impotent rage at the arbitrary and perverse rules of the adult world. The girl just wanted to have fun, after all. She said nothing, though, and put the car in gear. As she pulled away, she looked at the lineup, was reminded again of the rush of decades. She kept thinking she was of party age. She was not. The people waiting to get in were all the age of her eldest daughter. Where's that fork? she thought. 'Cause I'm done.

The lineup stretched the length of the block, and lost

coherence with distance from the doors. People milled instead of queuing. They hung out. Car roofs became benches. Samantha almost didn't notice the woman sitting by herself on a car near the edge of the crowd. She was out of the glare of the nearest streetlight, shadowed, but Samantha could still see that she was older than the rest of the crowd. Samantha started to think, *Cougar*, then realized she was wrong. The woman was dressed casually, jeans and leather jacket, definitely downmarket for the venue. No leopard prints or stilettos. There were a few of the dudes hanging around the car, talking and laughing too loud, angling for attention. She was ignoring them. She wasn't even looking toward the Octothorpe. She was staring at the street. She looked like hard trouble. Samantha's foot twitched on the accelerator. She sped up, leaving the woman behind, whisking her younger daughter home to safe resentment. She wanted to drive back and haul Krysta away from there. She told herself to calm down. Krysta would already be inside. She had insider privilege. That woman would never get past the bouncers.

Matt Dolinsky stood in an alley between a souvenir shop and a clothing boutique. He was all the colours of bored. He'd been here since dusk. He could barely see the street from here. He only had the vaguest sense of what he was supposed to be looking for. He'd pumped Luzhkov for more, but the Russian had just said, "Someone who doesn't belong," and plopped him here. "Don't move from your post," Luzhkov had warned. Fine. He wouldn't. Didn't mean he had to like it.

"Screw this," he muttered. He'd been standing on point for nothing for hours now. Enough. The game was stupid, and he wasn't playing anymore. The work at InSec had been fun in the early days after he'd left the marines for more profitable muscle work. InSec gave you the maximum of toys and the minimum of rules. The orders were fun. Shut so-and-so up, however you like. Kick up a bit of trouble in the Ivory Coast, boost the sales figures. Then the shakeups came, job stability and fun diminished, and the takeover by this woman happened. He'd made the smart decision back in New York. He was still alive. But where was the action? Where was the fun? Why was he still in the States? When did he get to shoulder the white man's burden and an overheating M-16 in Africa? This gig was bullshit, and he didn't like the idea of taking orders from a Russian on American soil. The hell were they doing here, anyway? His deep shit antennae were twitching. Time to cut losses, leave town. He had enough money to get to Africa on his own. There were still enough indie outfits out there. He'd find some buddies, make some cash, raise some hell, shoot some people back into their proper places. So here's the deal. Get through the night, obey whatever stupid rules are in place, then take off tomorrow. Sound good? Sounds good. He leaned against a brick wall, lit a cigarette. After a minute, he sat down. Might as well be comfortable while he waited out the night.

He heard a footstep at the other end of the alley, where it opened into a parking lot behind the stores. He saw a male silhouette. Shift relief, he thought. Thank Christ.

Luzhkov lay on the roof of the souvenir shop. He'd been motionless since taking up position, watching the alley, watching Dolinsky. He saw the man light up and stop watching the street. He saw judgment confirmed. Then he heard the steps, and saw judgment coming. It was too dark to make out the other man's face. He was wearing dark clothing and a baseball cap. He walked casually towards Dolinsky, who looked up, but didn't stand. Dolinsky said, "Hey," a bored greeting. Then he said "*Hey*," and stood, but was slow and awkward and the other man held him close and plunged a knife into his kidneys. Luzhkov watched his bait sag onto the blade. That, he thought, is what sitting on the fence gets you. The killer dragged Dolinsky's body to an autobin against the wall of the shop and heaved the corpse inside. Then he sheathed his knife and walked out onto the main drag. Luzhkov scrambled off the roof, dropping down onto the lid of the autobin, then into the alley. He padded out onto the street, spotted the baseball cap, followed. The pipe dream: the man would head back to base. Worst case: Luzhkov would still kill him. Cut the numbers of the enemy by one. Blaylock's boys would still come out ahead. Dolinsky didn't count as a loss. That was pruning. Necessary to keep the tree healthy.

The man crossed the street. Luzhkov spotted another alley half a block further ahead. He speeded up to avoid losing sight of the target. The man turned into the alley. Luzhkov did too. The alley was a short one, dark. The other end of it was illuminated by a splash of glow from a streetlight. There was no sign of the baseball cap. The alley looked empty, apart from its own autobin and garbage cans overflowing with popsicle wrappers and greasy french-fry boxes. Luzhkov started to jog, wondering if he'd been made. There was the sound of sudden movement behind him as he ran past the garbage. He had time to think how stupid he'd been not to look closer, and the knife arm wrapped around his throat. He slammed his hands against the arm, holding it tight to his chest. The knife blade was flat against his collar bone, not going anywhere. He bent forward, flipped the attacker over his back. He kept his grip iron on the arm. The man hit the ground hard on his back, his arm reaching skyward and useless. Luzhkov held the wrist with his left hand, drove his knee into the man's ribs, heard breath whoosh out and bones crack. He rammed his right hand, fingers extended, into the attacker's throat, crushing the larynx. The man twitched and bucked, kissing breathing goodbye. Luzhkov stayed on him until he was dead. He heard shouts behind him. He looked over his shoulder, but it was just the drunken call of youth to youth. No one in the alley. He checked the dead man out. No baseball cap, and he was wearing a camo T-shirt. Not his boy. They were operating in teams. He was one lucky idiot. But he'd also lost his mark.

Silhouette at the other end of the alley: a head poking around the wall to see what was what. Luzhkov jumped up and ran. So did the baseball cap. Masks off now, neither of them being coy. They tore up the street, boots pounding tarmac. A well-dressed couple stepped out of a restaurant and Luzhkov plowed between them. The guy yelled blue. Ahead, the baseball cap was picking up momentum and distance. The guy was *fast*. Do better, Luzhkov told himself. He poured on the steam. He didn't close, but he didn't lose more ground.

The baseball cap ran across the street, playing with traffic. Luzhkov matched him. There was a big lineup on the sidewalk ahead. Luzhkov realized where they were just as he saw Blaylock leap off the car roof and join the chase. She was ten yards closer to the baseball cap. The man ran straight for the doors of the Octothorpe. He hit the lineup with linebacker force. The beautiful people went flying. A bouncer stepped forward and got himself clotheslined. The baseball cap disappeared inside the nightclub. Brilliant move. He'd be near impossible to find. Luzhkov didn't slow, and didn't feel bad. Watching Blaylock run in full predator mode, he felt exhilarated. You poor, sorry bastard, he thought. Here comes your pain.

The bouncers were pulling themselves together. As he and Blaylock reached the entrance, for a moment Luzhkov thought there was going to be an attempt to block them. Then one of the bouncers met Blaylock's gaze. He stepped aside fast.

And they were in.

Blaylock moved quickly out of the doorway and into the crush of dancers, blending with the crowd while she waited for her eyes to adjust. The Octothorpe had a split-level dance floor. A railing and a row of tables marked the edge of the upper level, keeping the dancers from tumbling down the six-foot rise. Another series of small platforms lined the walls at various heights, with room for three or four patrons to go-go behind neon-purple bars. The music was faux-edge: Top Forty pop hits given mild remixes and high volumes. Electronica for the Ikea shopper. The lights did the strobe thing, the disco ball thing, the multicoloured laser thing. The Octothorpe wasn't doing anything that hadn't been done and wasn't being done by thousands of other clubs, whether they be in the Hamptons or flyover America. But the Octothorpe had its location. Better yet, it had its clientele. People wanted in because people wanted in. The herd would move on, but for now, the club was pulling in the prestige and the cash.

Blaylock bopped with Luzhkov, scanned the crowd. She did a 360 look in the first thirty seconds of their arrival. Still slower than she would have liked. "See him?" she asked. She had to yell.

Luzhkov shook his head. "Didn't see his face properly," he said.

Blaylock had. She'd memorized his features as he had run past. Late thirties, moustache, military hair, military fit. He was trying to lose Luzhkov in here. Good choice. Where next? Out the back? "Stay near the front door," she said. She pushed her way through the dancers toward the rear of the club. A short corridor led past the washrooms to the fire exit. The door was closed, no smokers stepping out for a backlane puff. Blaylock saw why: opening the door would trigger the fire alarm. Their boy hadn't gone out this way. She hadn't seen any windows. Unless he'd doubled back very quickly and slipped out just after she and Luzhkov had come in, he was still here somewhere. In plain sight on the dance floor? Could be. There was a lot of risk in that decision, though. He might not be able to spot his pursuer first. Her eyes fell on the door to the women's washroom. She didn't think the man had noticed her join the chase. He thought he was running from a lone male. Two women stepped out of the washroom. They looked underage but with enough disposable income to afford first-rate fake ID. They were glancing back at the washroom and giggle-snorting into their hands. Blaylock pushed the door open, crossed paths with another woman on her way out, who looked pretty amused, too. The washroom was angular chrome and rounded plastic hard and smooth and white enough to be marble. It gleamed sterilization. At the far end, a young woman was haranguing someone in a stall. She was clutching her mauve purse like a blackjack. Her skirt and heels kept her stance sexy trim instead of authoritative. "I swear to God," she was saying, "if you're not out in ten seconds I'm calling security." She was vibrating with indignation.

Blaylock walked up to her. "What seems to be the problem?" she asked. But she knew.

"Are you security?" The girl looked at her, took in her age and clothes, assumed she was. "There's a guy in there. He won't come out."

Blaylock reached out, gave the door of the stall a slight push. It was locked. "Sir?" she called out, having fun with the role. "I'm going to have to ask you to leave." No response. Her boy was playing for time. He was in there, though. She could hear him breathing. She turned back to the girl. "What's your name?" she asked.

"Krysta."

"Krysta, will you do me a favour? Go hang outside the door and keep people from coming in here until I've dealt with this situation. Can you do that?"

"Sure." Pleased to be having an adventure, a touch disappointed she wasn't invited to watch the serious shit about to be dealt out.

"Thank you." Blaylock gave her a smile to show she appreciated the help. She waited for the door to close behind Krysta, then looked at the closed stall. "Sir," she said, maintaining the fiction, "I'm not going to tell you again." As she spoke, she ran her weapon options. She had her SIG and a combat knife. Neither good. The war had to stay quiet. Marks and blood would be bad. Couldn't stain the lovely white. All right, then.

She checked the hinges, saw that the cubicle door would open inwards. She grounded herself on her left foot, raised her right and kicked the door. The latch flew off and the door banged in. The man inside grunted as the door hit him. He recovered fast. He lunged out, knife in hand. His backhand slash was fast. Blaylock sidestepped left and brought both arms up to her chest and throat in a double block. She caught the handle of the knife against the back of her fists. She grabbed the man's wrist with her right hand, twisted it down. She hit up against his elbow with the palm of her left hand. He yelped and rose to his toes, off balance. Hammerlock time. She forced him forward and down, as fast as his own strike had been. His face smashed into the counter. It was still plastic, it was still white and fake, but it stood up to the impact and gave as little comfort as the marble would have done. Big crunch of breaking nose and teeth. The knife clattered to the ground. The man lost his baseball cap and crumpled, two hundred pounds of dead weight. He was still conscious, hands waving weakly to ward off Blaylock and a blackout. Blaylock dropped a knee into the small of his back, driving out his breath. She hit his neck with two spear hands, wrapped her fingers around his throat, squeezed hard.

She heard the washroom door open. Shit. A voice: Krysta's. "Hey, there's a crowd here, can people come—" A gasp.

"Give me a second," Blaylock said. The man was still alive. She could feel the pulse in his carotid, getting down and funky.

"Ohmigod what are you *doing?*"

"Almost done." No more struggling. No more breath. Flutter flutter of the pulse. Growing weak. There we go, flatline. Blaylock stood up from the body.

"Ohmigod ohmigod *ohmigaaawwwwd!*"

Smears of blood on the counter, minor pooling on the floor. Some cleanup required. Could be worse. She turned to Krysta. "Shut. *Up.*" Her look and her words brought the silence. "Stay there," she ordered, and brushed past. She opened the washroom door, poked her head out into the corridor. "Sorry for the delay, girls," she said. "You know how it is: male, drunk, disorderly." There were a couple of knowing nods. "We'll be out in just a few moments. Thanks for your patience." She shut the door. She grabbed Krysta by the upper arm and hauled her over to the body. She grabbed a handful of paper towels from a dispenser, turned on a tap. "Make yourself useful. Clean up the sink. I'll take care of the rest."

"Oh, God, no—" Krysta began.

"*Now,*" Blaylock clarified.

Sobs, but Krysta began to mop. Blaylock knelt, sponged up the blood from the floor, rolled the man onto his back and cleaned up the leaking from his nose. She checked her work. Some damage visible, but she thought he would pass as an idiot who drank himself blotto and whanged his face when he passed out.

Krysta was standing rigid, sodden and red paper towel clutched in a fist. Blaylock pried the clump from her fingers, tossed it in the trash. Krysta said, "Ohmigod ohmigod ohmigod he's *dead.*"

"No, he isn't," Blaylock lied. "Now give me a hand with him."

"He isn't?"

"No. We're taking him out of here and sending him home." Blaylock knelt and swung one of the man's arms around her neck. "Take his other side," she ordered. Krysta struggled under the weight, tottering on her heels, but was the good soldier. They lifted the heavy sag between them. It might have been easier for Blaylock to sling the body over her shoulder in a fireman's carry, but she wanted to maintain the illusion that the man was still alive. This way, they were hauling out a dead drunk, not a dead duck.

"He weighs a ton," Krysta complained.

"Be strong." They dragged him to the door. His head wobbled between them. A string of blood formed at his lips, dangled like slow drool. Blaylock fumbled the door open and they shuffled into the corridor. "All clear, ladies," she sang out. She grinned: look at this loser we have here. She did a big-theatre roll of her eyes: what a night I'm having. Laughter and applause greeted her. "Come on," she told Krysta, and they dragged and bumped across the dance floor. A young man in expensively ripped jeans and a YOUR PRAYERS HAVE BEEN ANSWERED T-shirt backed into Krysta, made her lose her grip. The corpse flopped her way. Blaylock leaned right, took the weight, but not before the man's head smacked Krysta's. She picked up her end again, but was staring now into the open, unblinking, dilated eyes. Her own eyes went terrified round. Even in the flashing purple-red-black of the club, Blaylock could see Krysta turning grey. Blaylock moved forward, forcing them on. Krysta stumbled to keep up.

They neared the entrance. Luzhkov was there. He stepped forward and took up Krysta's post. "Thank you for your help," Blaylock said to the younger woman.

Krysta wasn't listening. "He *is* dead," she said. "Oh shit, oh shit, oh shit, who *are* you?"

"No one you want to piss off." Blaylock snapped her free arm out, grabbed Krysta by the throat. She squeezed just hard enough to show she meant it. Around them, the good times pounded on. No one noticed. "Listen, sweetie. You're going to go find your friends, and tell them all about the obnoxious drunk, but you *aren't* going to tell them about the dead guy and the woman who killed him. And sure as the shit that would follow, you are *not* going to say anything to the police." Krysta was shaking her head, trying to croak out her agreement. Blaylock said, "I'm not done yet. You know why you're going to say some things and not others? Because you helped me, so you're an accessory. Want to meet more people like me in prison?" Weave that dark fairy tale. "And you know what else? If you cross me, I'll find you, and you know what that means. I didn't even know this guy. What do you think I'll do if you make things personal?" Krysta choked. She sobbed. Blaylock let go and pushed her into the crowd. "Let's go," she said to Luzhkov.

They emerged from the Octothorpe. The night was still muggy, but it was a release from the hepped-up sardine shaker of the nightclub. "Was that necessary?" Luzhkov asked.

"Christ, I hope so." Her conscience was the sharp beat of her pulse. Another innocent terrorized. Nicely done. Jen Blaylock: Asshole #1.

They hauled the body past the lineup. People hooted. "What do we do with him?"

"You said there were two?"

"Yes. I put the other one in a dumpster."

"Let's reunite them, then get a truck. Can't have bodies turning up all over town in the morning. Have you heard from any of the others?"

"Not yet."

No news, no action. Could be worse. "We lose anybody?"

"Dolinsky."

"And?"

"What I figured."

Luzhkov had tagged him as a weak link with fair-weather loyalty. No loss, then. And they'd taken out two of the opposition. "Go team," Blaylock said.

Reggie McGee cut across Petersfield's Militia Park. He'd lost track of time. He'd been in the same spot longer than was smart. He didn't think he'd been seen, hadn't seen any SOA goons, either. Time to trade rooftops, though. Get a different angle on his section of turf.

The sound of running. He turned his head, saw a jogger coming up. He moved a few steps out of the way, kept going. The jogger pounded up, then slewed hard into him. McGee flew off his feet, slammed into a tree. He staggered, winded. The jogger knocked him to the ground. He kicked at the man's legs, missed. Another figure stepped out from behind the tree. The jogger grabbed his legs, held him down. Someone grabbed him by the hair, yanked his head up. Wire tightened around his throat.

17

Blaylock and Luzhkov came into the hotel room. Flanagan took in their faces, felt a pinch of something bad. They were brother hunters. He knew the night hadn't been a banner triumph, but that wasn't what tweaked his gut. They were fuming, but they were high on battle. Bonding over bloodshed. All he'd done was tend the home fires. Blaylock wouldn't let him play. "Have fun?" he asked.

Blaylock gave him a sharp look.

Washington was hot, but Baghdad was worse. This was a no-mercy heat, fifty centigrade and up. Water was over halfway to boiling. Flesh curled up like bacon. Screw finding AC. It was rare, it was crap, it was killed by the power outages. Keeping cool was like staying alive: high risk, low payoff. The sane people were leaving.

It was good to be back in the field.

Chapel knew his trip was on Korda and Reed's radar. No way he could use a passport now without the flags going up.

No point using any Agency means to reach Iraq quietly. He couldn't raid company stationary without Korda knowing. Losing physical tails wasn't a problem. Korda could put all the men he wanted on his scent. Chapel would spot them, dance with them, shake them. He knew a lot of the operatives he made. He didn't think they were trying very hard. There was war in Langley, and everyone knew it. Chapel was poison, to be avoided. But Korda was king asshole, and commanded zero loyalty. Chapel was an intelligence soldier, not a manager parachuted in because he had friends and was owed favours. So Chapel had his breathing space.

Machines, though, didn't care about politics. They ready-aye-readied to whoever controlled the buttons, and that was Korda. The little big man wouldn't have Chapel's location pinpointed, but he knew he was here. Good. That would give him a few more sleepless nights. Chapel could use the paranoia. Channel it in the directions he wanted. Korda and Reed might sniff what was in the wind. Chapel hoped they crapped their pants.

He was sitting in a café off Monsour Street. He was all the way at the back, out of the sightline of sun, Korda and insurgents. He was sweating his way to dehydration. He didn't trust the water, and was chugging back warm Cokes. He checked his watch. It was 1445 Baghdad time, who the hell knew what it was by his body clock. His contact was half an hour late. There'd been a time when he would have been early. Chapel wasn't sure if that was a sign of how far his own stock had fallen, or of the total disintegration in Iraq.

The man sauntered in just after 1500, when Chapel was half-past pissed off. He sat down, grinning wide, big show of teeth, white against his leathered white-boy tan. His name was

Donovan Victor Donovan. Thank you so goddamned much, mum and dad, you shits. He went by DVD. He was English. After one year on his parents' money at the University of Leeds, he'd come out to Iraq in the lead-up to Bush Daddy's excellent adventure. He'd stuck it out through Bush Baby's bogus journey. He was still here, and didn't look like he'd bought new clothes since 1991. Chapel found him hilarious. DVD thought he was living *Casablanca*. He thought he was Bogart and Rains combined. He saw himself as a Friend of the People, helping them fight against neo-colonialism and American hegemony. He also liked the spy game. His fantasy world worked like this: he had contacts in forty different flavours of insurgent groups, religious militias, and al-Qaida cells, real and imagined. He would present himself to the Americans as invaluable HUMINT. He'd give them some bones. Then he'd report back on what the imperialists were up to.

Too funny. The man was da bomb. The stunt was so insanely stupid, it kept him alive. Neither side took him seriously. They used him as a conduit to pass on information they wanted the opposition to know. Giving DVD any kind of information was better than posting on the Internet. Especially for what Chapel needed.

"You look hot," DVD said. He didn't. He looked moron-cool in torn shorts, badly faded Nirvana T-shirt, ragged Nikes. "Sorry I'm late. Traffic was murder." He snort-laughed at what he obviously thought was the living end of Baghdad sick humour.

Chapel pulled a business envelope out of his pocket. He handed it to DVD. "I'm looking for a post office," he said. "Think you can help me out?"

DVD felt the thickness of the stack of bills in the envelope. "I can mail this for you, if you like."

"Thought you might."

DVD sat back, pocketed the envelope. "Anything else I can help you with?"

Time to play the player. "What are you hearing?" Pretend you're fishing.

The man's shrug theatrical blasé. Ooooooh, he's so cool. "The usual. Anything in particular?"

"Something juicy on the WMD front."

DVD laughed. "You mean, like are there any articles about sex in *Hustler*? That's practically all everyone talks about. Everyone wants one. That's news?"

Chapel made a show of looking disappointed and little bit anxious. "I was thinking of something more specific. Like about somebody who was doing a bit more than dreaming."

The other man stopped laughing. He sat up straighter. "What have *you* heard?" he asked.

"Come on. You think I can tell you that?"

"Can I ask some questions, though?"

"Knock yourself out." Chapel had his repertoire of silences and significant looks practised. He prepared to roll them out.

DVD marched along according to the script. The man was too easy. It wasn't sport. "You think there's a group that might actually have laid their hands on something?" Chapel looked serious. "Nerve gas?"

Maybe one sentence. Just to speed things up a little. "We should be so lucky," he muttered.

"Jesus." DVD mucho excited. "Not a nuke?" Chapel did the Very Worried look. "Are they going to use it here?" DVD growing pale, for a moment the fun leaking out of the game. Chapel shook his head. "The *States*?" DVD's excitement and joy back and maximum large.

Chapel's finale: the stony gaze, the determined set of the jaw, the faintest glimmer of absolute terror in the eyes. He'd worked on this one for hours.

DVD said, "Bugger me sideways." He exhaled the words like an after-sex smoke.

"I'll ask you again," Chapel said. "Have you heard anything?"

"Time is short?" Could the man become more excited? Apparently so.

"Yes."

DVD started nodding. His ankles were tapping little kid rhythms against the legs of his chair. "Maybe," he said. "Maybe." Chapel bit his tongue to stifle his laugh at the lie. The thing was, he was pretty sure DVD was at least half of the way towards believing his own bullshit. "I'll see what I can dig up. How do I contact you?"

"You don't. I'm flying out of here today."

"Back to the home front, then? Think they're already in-country?"

You have no idea, you happy idiot. "You'll pass on any intel through the usual channels. We clear?"

"Clear. So I had better get on this." Frisky puppy. Couldn't wait to leave. Places to go and people to see.

"America thanks you," Chapel said, and he meant it. He watched DVD scamper out of the café. The man might well start asking specific questions. The important thing was that, through him, the story was going to spread that a

Middle-Eastern group had a nuke in the States. The original source of the idea would be lost very quickly. Enough members of enough groups would believe the tale, and talk to each other about it. Scary chatter would be picked up by American intelligence. Paranoid eyes would turn in the wrong direction. *David Copperfield is a pansy,* Chapel thought.

The news almost beat him home. DVD did his thing, and the word was just too exciting. The Internet exploded. At the NSA, there was an outbreak of strokes. The CIA's ground troops caught the story from contacts and freaked. Korda was woken from a nightmare of darkness and flame and a female demon by howling analysts. Fuzzy with sleep, he thought at first that he was still in the nightmare. When he put the receiver down, he glanced at the clock, groaned, and wondered if he should be calling Reed. Probably yes. He was reaching for the phone again when it rang. It was Reed, beating him to the punch.

"What the holy hell is he doing?" the president demanded.

"I don't know."

Reed snorted. "You tell me Chapel is in Baghdad, reasons unknown. Next thing we hear, al-Qaida has the bomb. Don't tell me you don't know."

"It's not like he slipped over there with one in his pocket. How would he get one to them? Not to mention, why would he? He's not that crazy."

"What I want to know is, why hasn't he been neutralized? Why is he still capable of any kind of action?"

"We're working on it."

"*Faster.*"

Critical mass came a day later. One of DVD's contacts had a contact who had a contact who spoke to a reporter for the *New York Times*. Boom.

The night before the boom.

The spade hit roots. They weren't very thick. Blaylock put a boot against the blade, cut through. The hole became another shovelful deeper. Almost good enough. The *chinks* of her digging made a rhythm with Flanagan's. They were working in the dim light of a filtered flashlight. Ten yards away, another hole was being dug.

Another night of urban warfare on the ultra-QT. Neither side wanting the general populace to know it was going on. Another night of trackdowns and stealth kills. Another night of bodies scooped up and buried out of town. Shallow graves in the forests. Bad half-measures, Blaylock knew. Sooner or later, someone's dog was going to catch an interesting scent. The chain reaction would be a sight to behold. This was stupid. The war was dumb-ass stalemate. Her team notched up some numbers, and so did the enemy. They couldn't stop her harassment, and she couldn't find where they were. Futility.

"Thanks for including me," Flanagan said, deadpan.

She was tired. She was stressed. She was frustrated. She wasn't in the mood. She held it all in. Flanagan's anger was worrying. "Tell me why you're mad," she said gently. She kept digging.

"I want to be part of you," he said.

She answered, "You are." Then his phrasing struck her as odd. She wasn't sure what he meant.

"How? I'm hanging out in the hotel room while you're out playing with the boys."

She stabbed the shovel deep into the ground and let it stand there. She took a step forward into Flanagan's space. He stopped digging. His face was a shadowed blur. "What do you think this is?" she asked. "You, of all people, should know better than to call this a game." She wasn't being hypocritical, she told herself. She had her bad joys, but she monitored them. Flanagan was saying things that should never come from him.

"I just want to be—"

"Yeah, you said. What do you think that means?" She carried on before he could respond. She had a sudden instinct that she didn't want to hear the answer. "How can you be that if you're dead?"

"Oh. Is this the part where you tell me that you can function best in a battlefield knowing that I'm safe?"

That was true, but that wasn't what she had been thinking. "No, it's the part where I remind you that you don't have the training, and I ask you to use your head."

"I've done okay before."

"You were lucky."

He didn't answer. She'd stung him. She hated that. She hated him having illusions about his warcraft even more. She reached out to the blur, touched his cheek. "I need you *with* me," she whispered. "Alive."

His silhouette had been rigid. Now his shoulders slumped. He sighed. "Sorry," he said, then snorted. "I think baby's finished his tantrum now."

"Are you okay?"

"I'm fine."

She leaned in and kissed him. It was good. It was their first real kiss in a couple of days. With a jolt, she realized how much she'd missed those. She let her forehead touch his. "You'd tell me if there was something else?"

"You know I would." He squeezed her hand. "I just want to be with you in the trenches, that's all."

She started digging again. "Trenches is what it is. Just as useless."

Another five minutes, and the hole was deep enough. They scrambled out, rolled the body in, and began to shovel the dirt back. Chapel's man disappeared into the forest floor. Somewhere else, she thought and hoped, the enemy was burying her losses.

"How long can we keep this up?" Flanagan asked.

"We can't. This could blow up in our faces tomorrow." A thought hit her. "Damn," she said. "Maybe that's what he wants."

"Why?"

The idea was half-formed. It needed work. It needed more evidence. "Let me think this through," she said.

They finished burying the corpse.

The evidence turned up the next morning. It came in the complimentary morning paper. It came on TV, all networks singing the same song. Big news. Oh shit.

Council of war.

"What do you think?" Luzhkov asked. Flanagan was on the bed, surrounded by the spread-out paper. Luzhkov, Vandelaare and Blaylock sat cross-legged on the floor. Blaylock had her back against the exterior wall. She stared at the room's door as if it were an oracle.

"Can't be a coincidence," Vandelaare said. "Your boy Chapel's in this, too right."

Flanagan was shaking his head. "It's too crazy. It's all bullshit. Whatever Chapel's game is, he's not playing it in the Middle East. We haven't seen any evidence pointing to that."

"The man is saying this is a bluff," Vandelaare said. "Makes sense to me."

"Or it's misdirection." Blaylock nodded to herself. The idea was fully formed. She was feeling like a sucker.

Flanagan looked at her. "That sounds spooky."

"Think about it. Chapel can do a lot of damage to Reed just by making people think there's a nuke loose. He doesn't need to have one. Everyone looks in the wrong place. He makes his move. Checkmate. Like he's been doing to us."

"What?" Flanagan scrambled off the bed.

"We've been played. It's what we were talking about last night. This is a phony war. We're asking to be caught. He's drawn us out. He knows where we are, and he has us running around being useless and he has his hands free."

"But *something* must be going down here," Flanagan objected.

"He wants us to think that," Luzhkov said, picking up the thread.

Blaylock said, "I was trying to figure out what he wanted to do here. So Reed is going to be down here with Korda on the Fourth. Okay. So let's say Chapel's troops attack, and they kill Reed and whatnot. Terrific. Now what? How is this a workable coup?"

"Who becomes president?" Luzhkov asked.

"The Speaker of the House. Patrick Pratella. He makes Nixon look like FDR."

Flanagan snapped his fingers. "*That's* who it was."

"Who what was?"

"I was in Brentlinger's office when he was meeting with someone who didn't want to be introduced. He looked familiar, but I couldn't place him until you mentioned him. It was Pratella. I'm sure of it."

Blaylock nodded. "Joe's boy, ab-so-posi-lutely."

"So what does this mean?" Luzhkov asked.

"It means whatever happens here, he also has to make things happen in DC."

"A takeover bid makes more sense in the centre of power," Vandelaare said.

"Exactly."

"But what about Reed?" Flanagan insisted. "The rules of succession don't kick in if the president is still alive."

"Move while he's away from the White House. Isolate him here. Reed's already on shaky ground with the Geneva fiasco. He's not looking good with recent terror attacks on home ground."

Flanagan grinned. "Whose fault is that?"

"Thank you. These bomb rumours are even worse. It wouldn't take too much to force him out."

"Impeachment? You think Congress will go along with that?"

"With the right leverage and the right moment, why not?"

Flanagan was frowning. "I don't know. Feels weak."

Blaylock shrugged. "I'm not convinced, but when you come up with something better, let me know."

"What if al-Qaida really does have the bomb?"

"If they did, it would already have gone off. There wouldn't be all kinds of boasting ahead of time on the Net."

Vandelaare said, "So what, this man wants to know, is the plan?"

Blaylock didn't answer. She was frustrated. She was playing the game according to Chapel's rules, and that pissed her off. The game should be hers. Then, as she followed the desire, as she shifted from a reactive mindset, the plan blossomed. She would use Chapel's play to her own ends. She smiled. "We know where Reed is going to be and when. We know who Chapel's man is. The plan is we take both out."

There was a moment of silence out of respect for the plan's ambition. Blaylock appreciated the gesture. Flanagan spoke first. "By 'we,' I'm hearing 'you.'"

"With assistance."

"Good of you. So that means you'll be here on the Fourth."

"I want a second crack at him."

"This is a trap, you know."

"Yep."

"And how are you going to get at Pratella?"

She hadn't thought that far. "Any good ideas?" she asked the room. She was drawing a blank.

"Poison," Flanagan said, half-joking. "Do it old school."

Spin it. Spin it good.

Korda walked up to the mics. He was good at press conferences, but he'd been doing too many lately. Too many forced ones. He liked the angle he had on this one. He'd been chipper when he called it. Chapel had thrown the ball. Korda wondered how he was going to like the way it was batted back his way. Korda smiled, and read his statement. He'd consciously written the blandest, most platitude-ridden speech of his life. It was boring as hell. It said nothing. It was vigilance this and preparations that, Our Men in the Field and the War on Terror. He spotted a stringer from AP nodding off in the back row. He watched the reporters' hostility grow. They would be gunning for him. He was having fun.

"Well then," he said, putting his notes down, "I'll take a few questions. June?"

June D'Amato was with the *New York Times*. Korda was not her favourite person. He knew it. He expected a hardball from her. I'm at the plate, he thought. Let's see what ya got.

"Director Korda," D'Amato said, "how can you give us such a sunny picture of intelligence operations when we all know the CIA is riven by civil war. Aren't you more interested in fighting each other than potential terrorists?"

"I'm glad you asked that," he said, and he was. The setup was beautiful. He should put D'Amato on his payroll. "I'm not going to pretend that there haven't been some problems lately." Theatrical chuckle. "I guess you could say we've been doing some finger-pointing." Pause for the laugh. It didn't come. Screw them. He was wasting gold on these turkeys. "But whatever differences with, and concerns about, Joe Chapel I might have, I have never, ever had the slightest shred of doubt about the man's patriotism, or his ability." He'd done a fair bit to put both into question over the last while, but memories were short, attention easily distracted. "It is one of our strengths as Americans and citizens of a democracy that, though our opinions are diverse and we can argue with passion, when the security of the country is at stake, we all pull together. That is exactly what's happening. We are operating as a team to counter this threat."

"You and Chapel," D'Amato said with frosty disbelief.

"That's correct." Grin. Go folksy. "In fact, he'll be joining me at the president's Fourth of July barbecue."

"Since when?" Quintero demanded, turning away from the screen.

"Since two seconds ago, apparently," Chapel answered. He gave Korda a mental tip of the hat. Well played, you bastard. "This changes nothing," he said as Quintero raised his hands to the heavens, preparing a rant.

"So you are not going."

"Oh, I am."

Quintero looked at him askance. "I did not see you as one for a martyr's death."

Chapel snorted. "I'm not."

"Then you have delusions of immortality."

"I'm a planner. I'll get out."

"But why go?"

"I can't resist."

"That is the nature of a fine trap."

"Korda's sharp, but he couldn't trap a mouse."

Quintero rolled his eyes.

"You don't believe me?"

"I don't think you should have contempt for your enemy."

"He's not the enemy. Not the main one. Reed is. And the woman."

"But why are you going?"

"I want to see them for myself. I want to see all three of them there, so I know where they are when it happens."

"How do you know the woman will be there?"

He clapped Quintero on the back. "Because it's perfect. Me, Reed and Korda in the same spot? No way she can resist." He laughed big, picturing the boom.

18

Her army pulled out of Petersfield much faster than it had gone in. The Fourth was only a week away. The timing was going to be tight. Not much time to take up strategic positions in Washington. Blaylock and Flanagan had taken a room at the Watergate, because why the hell not? Blaylock knew she should care more. She was being a bad girl. She didn't care. The promise of a double hit was just that sexy.

June 29.

Progressive Solutions made its home in the industrial waste-lands of Bayonne, New Jersey. It had a small chemical factory and a warehouse. The buildings were grimy and covered by competing gang tags. That didn't worry Luzhkov as much as the number of broken windows the warehouse had. The air as he approached the complex turned sickly. His eyes watered as he climbed out of the car. He wished for a gas mask. He straightened his tie. He and Blaylock had spent hours shopping for the right look. The clothes were supposed to convey both money and sleaze. The suit was the money. The tie and the footwear were the sleaze. The tie was too bright, its pin too big. The boots were snakeskin. He might be oligarch, he might be *mafiya*. He was probably both. He called up his best shit-eating grin and walked through the front door.

The reception area had been painted an antiseptic white once upon a time. Now the walls reminded him of yellowing teeth. The scuffed tile floor hadn't been cleaned since the '70s. The seating possibilities were from the same era: a couple of plastic chairs and an old metal-and-vinyl bench leprous with duct tape. A coffee table was covered with the staff's discarded magazines: unfinished crossword collections and exhausted porn. The receptionist looked like she had been a package deal with the building. She had aged right along with it. Her hair went well with the walls. It wasn't blond. It was yellow, hard and brittle. Her mouth was a slash of Crayola-red lipstick. She was flipping through a copy of *Us* when Luzhkov walked up to the counter. The ash on her cigarette was getting long. The ashtray beside her was full and smelled of stale cancer. At least Luzhkov now knew the air wasn't flammable. "Yeah?" the woman said without looking up. Her voice gargled gravel.

"Gregor Deripaska for Mr. Girdler," he said, thickening his accent.

The woman picked up her phone and punched a button. After a moment she said, "Your two o'clock is here."

Howie Girdler's office wasn't far. He appeared at the counter inside of thirty seconds. "Gregor!" he hailed. "Great to know ya." His handshake was all-American hearty. His suit was shiny. It was permeated by an odd chemical bouquet. Its seams strained. Girdler was a big, soft man on the easy slide to diabetes if chemical death didn't get him first. "So," he said, leaning an elbow on the counter. "I hear we can do business."

"I hope so," Luzhkov said.

"Mind if I ask who recommended us to you?"

"Some satisfied customers who value discretion." Dealing with Progressive Solutions had been Vandelaare's idea. He'd run into the name several times in Sierra Leone.

Girdler cocked a thumb-and-forefinger gun at Luzhkov, winked and clicked his tongue. "Gotcha. And you'd be the same."

"Correct."

Girdler straightened up and clapped his hands, rubbed them together. "What can I do ya for?"

"I am told you can supply my firm with chlordane."

"Pesticiding, eh?" Girdler's eyes narrowed. His face became cautious. "You know the EPA banned the stuff back in '88."

"For use in the United States."

Girdler brightened, happy again. "Got some bugs overseas giving you problems?"

Luzhkov nodded. "Africa. We are trying to help some farmers, and—"

Girdler held up his hands. "Hey hey, gotcha gotcha gotcha. I know the score. We're all over the Africa thing, believe me. We're just trying to help, like the name says. How much ya want?"

"A thousand gallons, to begin."

"And more if you're happy. Believe me, you'll be happy and back for more." He reached over the counter and snatched a pad from beside the ashtray. "Okay," he said. "Let's talk details."

Luzhkov was back the next day to pay cash. The day after that, the shipment arrived at InSec's Washington warehouse. Luzhkov and Flanagan looked at the stacked drums. "How much do we actually need?" Flanagan wondered.

"Not much. A few drops. Maybe a bit more."

"What are we going to do with all this shit?"

Luzhkov shrugged. "Store it. Forget about it. Nobody's going to pay attention to an industrial purchase. Buying one bottle, that would have been noticeable."

MOTF FX had a studio in Brooklyn's Williamsburg district. They had been part of the early vanguard of artists migrating to the area, driven out of the Village by the gentrification of rents. They were proud of their underground street cred, but they made enough money on work-for-hire projects that they didn't have to move again. MOTF was Mortification of the Flesh. They were gore specialists. They made their own films. Their *Nekrotize* series had been thrown out of dozens of festivals and been banned in most of Europe. The films were hand-held, grainy, plotless video exercises in extreme depravity. They could pass for snuff, and often did with people who didn't notice that the same cast was killing and being killed in each entry. Blaylock was greeted by Suspiria De Profundis. That's what her card said. The woman was in her late twenties and was dressed in full Goth. She had rings in her nose, ears, eyebrows and tone. Her black hair was spiked, with a crimson streak on each side. "Come on in," she said.

Blaylock followed her into the studio. The open space was a hall of autopsies and sculptor's workplace worthy of Maldoror. There were a half-dozen artists at work. Some laboured over corpses on tables, arranging intestines and stomachs. At the far end busts of shattered heads were being constructed. A reptilian monster slouched in a corner beside a bookshelf stereo. Skinny Puppy snarled out of the speakers. The walls were decorated with movie one-sheets and ironic propaganda posters. One of them was a picture of Pratella, waving with his arm outstretched, grinning that corncob grin. He'd been photoshopped onto a swastika background. The wave turned into a cheery Nazi salute.

"You didn't mention what you need this for," De Pofundis said. She led the way to her worktable.

If the outfit had been mainstream, Blaylock would have ordered a butcher's shop worth of appliances, prosthetics and fake blood. She felt kinship here. She felt reckless. Screw it, she thought. She would go with just what she needed, and have fun with the truth. "Going to kill Peter Pratella," she said.

"Sweet." No way to tell if De Profundis believed her or not. "Let's start by taking a mould of your hands."

"You're nuts," Flanagan said.

They were back in New York. In Macy's. A girl has to shop. Big event coming up at Korda's. A girl has to look her best. "How am I more nuts than usual?"

"Reed *knows* you. You'll be shot on sight."

"He knows me from Davos. He didn't see my face when I tried for him at the State Department."

"I'm so reassured."

"Good." She ignored the sarcasm. "What do you think of these boots?"

More shopping. The outfit was coming together. But a girl needs a date. "What are you looking for?" Luzhkov asked.

"A good marksman."

"Abel Jamba."

In Washington again.

She caught him in hallway just outside his office. It had been a question of timing. The Senate was recessing for the day. She took a guess at how long it should take him to make it back, arrived in her press persona at the right moment to make the encounter look natural. She didn't want to be seen to be loitering in the hallowed halls. She'd made her way through security with a crush of reporters, just one name badge among many. She had to keep up the anonymity. "Excuse me, Senator," she called out.

Daniel Hallam stopped and turned. He frowned, trying to place her. "Can I help you, Ms. ..."

"Jen Baylor."

The frown vanished. "Of course. I'm sorry I didn't recognize you right away."

"It's been a while. Could I have a few moments of your time?"

Hallam sighed. He was looking harried. "What would this be about?"

"Joe Chapel and Peter Pratella."

A frown. "I'm afraid I don't understand."

She waited a moment as people brushed past them. She lowered her voice. "I have reason to believe they're about to stage a *coup d'état*."

A true Kodak moment. The Senator nonplussed, his face all over the damn place. Blaylock wondered if he would ever speak again. He did. "Let's talk in my office," he said. He seemed as conscious of the people around as she was.

His workspace was well lived-in. The books on the walls and the papers on the desk were constrained, but one all-nighter of work away from total chaos. His window had a good view of the city. When Hallam sat down with his back to it, he did so with the hardwired habit of a man who rarely had the chance to look out that window. "You'd better have a hell of a good reason to make that statement," he thundered.

"Chapel is supposed to be a pariah. So what's he doing meeting with the Speaker? Meanwhile, the president is looking very bad with this al-Qaida nuke scare, which is exactly the kind of story Chapel could cook up in his sleep. Oh, and Sam Reed is also going to be away from Washington, and thus the levers of power, on the Fourth. Connect the dots."

"How do you know Chapel and Senator Pratella have been meeting?"

"I've seen them."

"Can you prove this?"

"There's only my word."

The senator stared into an infinite space to the left of Blaylock's shoulder. Why don't you use your window? she thought. It's designed for moments like this. Hallam's eyes turned back to her, but they were still half-focused on the phantom zone. "What am I supposed to do with this?" he snapped. "You tell me something that has enormous implications, if true, but no real way of backing up your claim. Why?"

"Should I just keep it to myself?"

"You might as well, for all the good you can do with the information. And I'm not saying that I believe you."

"It's a cinch that someone else knows whether what I'm telling you is true or not."

"That would be…?"

"Peter Pratella."

Hallam raised his hands to heaven. "Of course. That solves everything, then."

"It might."

"Really." His eyes narrowed. "Just what, exactly, is it that you want?"

"To get the truth out, whatever that might be."

"I fail to see where I come in."

"Get me in to see the Speaker."

"We're not exactly drinking buddies. You might remember we belong to different parties."

"No, but you could do it. Which of his allies do you think would listen to me if I approached them?"

Hallam conceded the point. "So I set up a meeting. Then what? Convince me you're not setting me up for a major political embarrassment."

"We go in together. I tell him a version of what I told you. We watch his reactions. You decide what to do, if anything, from there."

"That's not much of a plan."

You'd be surprised, she thought. "If you want, I'll walk out of here and you can forget we ever had this conversation." She counted on a mix of principle and political opportunism to nix that possibility.

"Give me a number where I can reach you," he said.

Bingo.

At the Watergate, Flanagan asked her about Hallam. "What did you think of him?"

"He'll do."

He called the next day.

The Fourth of July rolled in. Its dawn was clear, a perfect deepening blue with a cloud or two for contrast. It was, Chapel thought, a beautiful day. A minor cold front had moved in, dropping the temperature to the merely hot, and the night had been cool. The dawn of promise. It was a great big American sky. Possibility was everywhere. Renewal was inevitable. This was the kind of morning, he felt sure, the Founding Fathers had seen and embraced before embarking on the grand experiment. He would do them proud.

The bomb was ready. It was gorgeous as the morning, its perfect outer sphere of Semtex featureless as a canvas, but as ripe with potential. It was waiting for the artist. He picked the remote detonator off the worktable. He ran his finger over the button. He jazzed.

"Here," said Quintero, "is where we must exercise the greatest trust."

Chapel pocketed the remote as he turned to the general. "Meaning what? That you don't trust me?"

Quintero's eyes had followed the detonator and were fixed on Chapel's pocket. "I did not say that. But please appreciate my position. I must trust that you will not detonate the bomb early, thus removing inconvenient witnesses such as myself."

"That would make me a pretty stupid operator, besides being a jerk. This isn't the endgame. This is the just the beginning. We have a lot more work to do together."

Quintero's nod was noncommittal: whatever you say. "On the other hand," he went on, "I must trust you not to lose your nerve."

Chapel didn't answer. He glared.

Quintero returned his gaze steadily, unimpressed. "You are going to commit the greatest act of terrorism your country has ever experienced. And yet you call yourself a patriot."

"I'm doing this to save my country."

"It became necessary to destroy the town to save it."

"Fuck off."

"Innocents will die."

Did Quintero really believe he hadn't thought of that? Did he believe Chapel was sleeping the sleep of the just at night and keeping himself warm with the thoughts of vaporized children? Before he could reply, Quintero spoke again.

"Let me guess. It's for the greater good."

"Yes it is, goddamn it!" He stopped himself. He'd let Quintero goad him with clichés. "My country," he said, when he felt calm again, "is on the brink. It needs saving. Sometimes the surgery has to be drastic. I'm not happy about this. But if I didn't think more lives, and a way of life, would be preserved in the long run, then I wouldn't do it. Believe me, I've weighed the consequences."

"I'm very glad to hear you say so."

Quintero's tone was neutral. Chapel couldn't tell if he was being sarcastic or not. He let it pass. "Your men know what to do tonight?"

"Don't worry. And after tonight, what? We sit at the SOA until our master calls us again?"

"Down, boy." He watched Quintero bristle at the "boy."

Good. The man needed to be slapped down a notch or two, be reminded who was running the op. "Your muscle is still going to be needed. If not here, then in Venezuela. You won't be forgotten."

"Good." He was speaking quietly again, calm. Unreadable. He should relax, Chapel thought. They were all going to win.

Chapel headed upstairs to change for the party. Quintero watched him go. The man, he decided, was insane. The plan was one thing. Quintero admired its audacity. He revelled in the punishment he was going to help deal out. He saw no reason why it wouldn't work. It was Chapel's motivations that worried him. Chapel was a true believer. A power grab was one thing. Quintero knew from coup mentalities. Revenge was something he could work with, too. That was one of his big pleasures. It was driving Chapel, Quintero knew. He wanted to stick it to Korda and Reed. But he was talking virtue. If the ideological purity was a pretence, Quintero wouldn't worry. He didn't think it was. Chapel believed in what he was doing. Dangerous.

He headed outside. The van was being readied for its cargo. Maldonado was overseeing. He sauntered over to Quintero. "You've been talking to the Chief," he said. The upper case was contemptuous.

"How did you guess?"

"You look worried."

Quintero glanced up at a second-floor bedroom window. It was open. He kept his voice down. "We'll have to be careful."

"Can we trust him?"

"Of course not. But we can trust him to see the operation all the way through."

"There might be a way of having the detonation come a bit early. Let the hero have his martyr's death."

Tempting. Tidy. Useless. Quintero shook his head. "And then what? We'd be stuck here without a sponsor. The bomb is a means to an end, remember. We punish, and in the long run, we get *our* country back."

"That's putting a lot of faith in him."

"That's the nice thing about ideologues." Quintero smiled. "They follow through. Venezuela is part of his reclamation project, didn't you know? He's going to save the whole world from itself."

Luzhkov brought the materials down from New York. An hour before meeting Hallam for the second time, Blaylock prepared the conjuring act at the warehouse. Flanagan and Luzhkov watched. Flanagan didn't seem confident about the quality of MOTF's work. "Is that safe?" he asked.

"It's safe."

She put her accessories together. They all went into a small handbag, which was part of the misdirection itself. She'd made a point of having it over her shoulder when she was on the Hill the day before. It was part of her look. It was normal. She worked on her makeup. She was textbook harmless. Each touch of lipstick, each whisper of blush, was so much sleight of hand. Ladies and gentlemen, boys and girls, for my next and greatest trick...

The journalist showed up at his office a minute early. Hallam shook hands with her. He was struck by how dry her palm was. "Thank you for doing this," she said.

"I must be crazy."

"You can change your mind."

"I'd be irresponsible not to see this through."

She fell into step beside him as they walked the corridors of the Capitol. Baylor took a bottle of hand lotion from her purse and rubbed some into her hands. "Nervous?" Hallam asked.

"Should I be?"

"Given what you're maintaining, implying and hoping to accomplish, I would say yes. I am."

"Is that on the record?"

"No," he said sharply, brought up short by the risk he was taking. Humouring a member of the media. One he knew next to nothing about. This was nuts. But then, so was Pratella, he reminded himself. He'd always thought the man was dangerous. Not necessarily because of ideology. Hallam didn't think any of Pratella's convictions went beneath the surface. The man was dangerous because he was completely unprincipled. Nothing that kept him in power and granted him more would make him blink.

They reached Pratella's office. Baylor fumbled with her purse and Hallam held the door open for her. "Thank you," she said, blushing.

Pratella was waiting for them. He nodded to Hallam as they stepped in. "Daniel," he said. "Nice to see you."

"Mr. Speaker." Hallam nodded back. They were keeping the dance civil, but only just. They had plenty of shared history. None of it good. Their Senate-Congress collisions had been Godzilla versus King Ghidorah, and cities had been levelled. On TV, Hallam worked as hard on Quiet Dignity as Pratella did on Down Home. He didn't rise to baits, and he kept his attacks on political opponents within what passed for restraint in the new millennium. But on the subject of Pratella, the gloves were off. The man was a racist demagogue, as far as Hallam was concerned, and he let it be known. Pratella returned the salvos and fought just as dirty. In politics, there was a lot of show, but there was also real hate. Hallam and Pratella had something pure.

Pratella turned on the Down Home with megawattage for Baylor. "A real pleasure to meet you, dear," he said, and shook with both hands. She responded in kind, her smile just wide enough for Hallam to catch its irony. Clutching both of Pratella's hands with both of hers, she was sending his gesture right back at him. They stood in that position just long enough to look like a wedding portrait, just askew enough to change into caricature. Pratella broke the pose first. He wiped a palm on the side of his pants and gestured to the chairs in front of the desk. "Do sit down," he said. "We won't be standing on the horse's toes here." He moved around the desk and took his own seat a second after Hallam and Baylor did theirs, giving himself a moment to tower. Look at you, Hallam thought. You just love this. You would love to be in the Oval Office with all those toys, wouldn't you? At that moment, Hallam believed everything Baylor had told him. Pratella was a canny operator, a political survivor of the highest degree, and when it came to reacting, he was the best in the business. But he had never *initiated* anything. He was far too conservative for that. If there was a coup going to happen, there was someone behind Pratella, calling the shots. Bet on it.

"Now," Pratella said. "How can I help?"

"Mr. Speaker," Baylor began, "how well do you know Joe Chapel?"

Pratella blinked. He had started to lean back in his chair and fold his hands on his stomach. Instead, he sat up straight. "Why do you ask?"

Wrong answer, Hallam thought. The correct thing to say would have been, "We've been friends since childhood." Or some other such nonsense. Something that conveyed absolute and innocent confidence in the man. Something that showed he had nothing to hide.

"I have reason to believe he is plotting to overthrow the government."

There are lessons you learn after only a short time in politics. Basic stuff. If you last a long time, that's because you remembered those lessons and put them into practice. One of the most important: never give anything away. That didn't mean keep a poker face at all times. The show of emotion was a vital tool, used almost daily. The *show* of emotion. Not the genuine article. If you're caught out on something, never let on. Never, ever, ever show a break in stride. Those were hard and fast rules. No one could live up to them absolutely. Hallam had blinked yesterday, he knew. Every so often, someone got that perfect shot off. The bullet penetrated through the best armour plating, blew apart the soft matter inside. Hallam saw that happen to Pratella. He blanched. The worst loss of control Hallam had ever seen. No explosion, no expostulations, no stuttering. But the man went white white white. Enormous fear. And still he managed to speak. He kept up his role that much. Hallam almost admired him. "That's a grave accusation." Flop sweat on his face. "What is your evidence?"

"It's circumstantial." Baylor wove a web of conjecture and

innuendo around Chapel, leaving Pratella out of it. He was still terrified, Hallam saw.

But the show went on. "What you tell me is very serious indeed. As we say back home, we can't let the fox have all the chandeliers, now can we?"

"I should say not," Baylor replied, and Hallam almost laughed.

"I will look into this. Immediately. You have my word. Thank you for bringing this matter to my attention."

"You're welcome."

Silence. Baylor was forcing Pratella to end the meeting. She's good, Hallam thought. Nasty. But good.

Pratella stood up. "Was there anything else?"

"No." Baylor rose, too, and accepted both of Pratella's hands again. "Thank you, Mr. Speaker."

"No, again, thank you. You've done your country a great service."

Hallam saw something flicker over the woman's face. It might have been amusement, but it was too ugly for that. It might have been hate, but it held too much joy. "Just doing my duty," she said.

Pratella saw them out. Baylor was quiet until they were back in Hallam's office. There she asked, "Well?"

"I think I believe you," Hallam said. "I also think you've made a very powerful enemy."

"Am I in danger?"

The question sounded odd to his ears, as if it were an act. That made no sense, so he shrugged the impression off as a mistake. "I don't want to accuse anyone…" he began, then realized what a crock he was speaking, and this wasn't the time to cover his ass at her expense. "Yes," he said. "I think you are."

"What about you?" she asked. "You're next in line for the throne."

"I'll be fine." Though he felt the cool trickle of worry.

"I hope so. Good luck, Senator." She walked away, disappearing down the first staircase.

After a moment, Hallam realized that she hadn't asked him what he was going to do about Pratella.

He roamed the office, cursing Chapel. The woman knew, and Hallam knew. No question. Did they have proof? Not if they'd come to see him, though he could feel a noose closing around his neck. Round his desk he went, round and round, trying to find a solution. He could guess what Chapel would suggest. Kill the reporter. After all, what was one more corpse? The body count for the good of America would be huge by this time tomorrow. Fine, take her out. What about Daniel Hallam? The man was sharp enough and honest enough to be dangerous. He'd felt the senator's eyes on him. Hallam smelled a rat, no question. So? Take him out too? How? Another convenient terrorist strike? Messy. Everything becoming too messy.

There was another option. Sell Chapel out. Take the moral high ground and all that, root out the evil conspiracy as the first significant act of his about-to-be-born presidency. There was real appeal in that. Removing Chapel's shadow from behind him wouldn't be a disappointment, either. The trick was to guess which way the winning wind was blowing. Chapel still scared him. He didn't want to take him on without the knowledge that he was betting on a sure thing.

Round and round. He couldn't decide. He'd speak to Chapel. See what he had to say. If nothing else, he expected to see the man squirm. That would be fun. Enjoy that show, then worry about making a choice.

Good. He could live with that. Pratella sat down, a bit calmer even though he knew he hadn't done a damned thing to shield himself from the shitstorm. Ten minutes later, the convulsions began.

Daniel Hallam was in his office. He was at his desk. His computer was on. He had a half-dozen subcommittee reports requiring responses. His eyes were on the screen. His mind wasn't. Arms folded, he pretended to himself that he was trying to work. He pretended that he wasn't thinking about the meeting with Baylor and Pratella. He pretended that he wasn't tasting sour bile at the back of his throat, that his heart wasn't skittering nervously, and without even the common courtesy of telling him why. He made the deliberate movement of uncrossing his arms and placing his hands on the keyboard. "Work," he muttered, but all he did was notice that his palms were sweating. He couldn't work. Not when he was soul-deep engaged in waiting.

Waiting for what? he wanted to know.

Something very bad.

He heard the pounding of many feet in the corridor. He knew it for the sound of something bad.

Flanagan sat in the Watergate lobby. He was on a couch near the entrance. He was waiting for his Angel of Death to return. When he saw her approach, he jumped to his feet and opened the door for her. "Hi, honey," he said, tongue in cheek as he played the middle-class hubby. "How was work?"

"Piece of cake," Blaylock said. She followed him to the elevator. Flanagan pushed the button to call it, hit the button for their floor, held all the doors. Just another day at the office for his sweetie, except for the fact that she couldn't touch anything at all. On Blaylock's face, the satisfaction of a smooth operation. And outside, the wail of sirens. Lots of them. Flanagan didn't know if he should link the two. He did, anyway, and was hit by a blast of vertigo as they entered their suite. He stumbled. Blaylock bent to catch him, realized what she was doing, and backed off. Flanagan hit the floor on all fours, giving his left knee a good bang.

"Are you all right?" Blaylock asked.

"Yeah." No. Maybe. He took some deep breaths. His head settled.

"What's wrong? Are you sick?" Big worry in her voice. She was thinking about the chemical on her hands, he realized.

"No, no, I'm good. This has happened before. I'll be fine." The spell was passing. He sat against the wall for a moment, then stood. The world was stable again. He'd had some bouts with vertigo before, but this was the first time it had been strong enough to knock him down. The diagnosis was easy. It was a symptom of the slide he was taking with Blaylock. PTSD, without the "post," because the trauma kept happening, and was it really fair to call the blows traumas when they had almost as much in common with orgasms? The vertigo came with every encounter with Blaylock's war scenes. A collision with the sublime: awe and terror. Ecstasy and the need for more. He had told her that he wanted in. He wanted to be part of the war. He wanted to be a creator, not just a spectator. He wanted to feel the high-voltage of power course through him. So he was getting his wish. He was living and feeling the enormity. And with it came consequences, implications, responsibilities. The price of admission. He knew Blaylock was feeling the cost. She had to be. But she wasn't letting him see what it took from her. She was the point of the spear, never flinching. He wasn't strong enough, yet. Making the link between his lover's face and the scream of sirens had brought home a sharp chunk of that enormity. This wasn't the same as standing before the flaming wreckage of a war zone. This was the knowledge that he had directly participated in a political assassination. It had been his idea that Blaylock had acted on. One word, "poison," and the ground under everyone's feet had shifted once more. The scale of his responsibility made him dizzy.

Enough of that, now. Be strong. Be steel. Love the rush. And get on the ball. "Let's take those things off," he told Blaylock.

In the washroom, he had a clutch of garbage bags and sets of rubber gloves ready. He donned the gloves. Blaylock held her arms out, raising them to shrug her blouse sleeves back. Flanagan pulled the material back further, revealing the seams on her arms. He dug his fingers into the seams, and peeled off the chlordane-drenched prosthetics. The hands were very convincing. Blaylock had suddenly turned serpent, and was shedding skin. Underneath the impermeable MOTF hands, she was wearing surgical gloves, playing it safe. She took them off. Flanagan dumped the hands into a garbage bag, put that bag in another, then added his and Blaylock's gloves. Blaylock tossed in her hand lotion bottle. The chlordane concentration of the liquid was huge. Pratella had been dead the moment he shook hands with her. The whole package went into yet another bag. "What do we do with this stuff?" Flanagan asked.

"Drive it out of town tonight. Burn it good."

He shook his head, impressed. "So those hands worked."

"I'm still alive, so I guess so. Anything on the news yet?"

"Not that I heard." He waved at the window. "But it worked. Can't you hear it?"

She nodded. "I can feel it."

"So now what?" he asked, knowing the answer.

"Now I have to hurry. Party to go to."

He felt the dizziness build again.

19

Night on the Fourth of July. Fireworks time.

The equation was becoming firm: parties = mass death. In New York, the birthday party of Danny "Little Forks" Petraglia. She'd wiped out the birthday boy and his buddies, then burned his house to the ground. In Davos, the World Economic Forum's gala dinner. Not her fault that time. Sherbina had had dirty bombs go off all over town, throwing a damper on things. Now Reed's do. Time for some wet jobs she should have dealt with in Davos. And if I don't, Joe, she wondered, will you instead?

Party on, people. Wonder how many of you will be alive tomorrow.

Reed's property had few approaches, which was the idea. It was on Independence Street. On Petersfield's pyramid of privilege, this was the peak. The few estates were Gatsby-big and old-money private. They fronted on the bay, and kept themselves to themselves with the help of high walls. Independence was a dead end, and taken as read was the rule that any car on that road was a car that lived at an address on that road. Sightseeing tourists and curious locals from further down the pyramid were an evil that happened, but wasn't really tolerated. On days like today, though, with the company that was expected, the rubbernecking annoyance was accepted with a resigned shrug. Blaylock was counting on that shrug.

Then there was Independence Forest. It wasn't so much a forest as a collective turning of the back on the rest of the community. It was a strip of woodland that ran the length of Independence. From verge to verge, it was barely a hundred yards wide, narrow enough to be a very boring stroll. But it cut Independence and its homes off, and from the other side of the forest, it was easy to forget that the road existed.

Blaylock was up in a tree with Jamba. They were high, and at the opposite side of the forest from the gate to Reed's estate. They didn't have a view of the grounds. No way of being any closer without committing suicide by Secret Service. That was fine. All Blaylock wanted was for Jamba to have the approach in his sights. They had waited several hours before coming in even this close. The president was helicoptered in. When he was safe and sound within the walls, the security perimeter contracted slightly to concentrate its forces. With snipers no longer a possible threat, the goal was to completely seal off unauthorized access. The cordon was very tight. No one was going to sneak through. Blaylock had no objections. She wouldn't even dream of trying for stealth.

"So?" she whispered. She adjusted the wig. She was going as a redhead.

Jamba was looking through the scope. He moved the barrel of the rifle back and forth over a narrow arc. The gun was a heavy-barrelled Remington M24 sniper rifle. "Lots of foliage in the way," he whispered back. "Can't see much."

"This is as good as it gets. Sorry." The branches higher up wouldn't support Jamba's weight, and he'd be more visible from the ground. "What can you see?"

"The gate. A little bit to the left and right."

Not quite good enough. "And down the road?"

Jamba swung right. After a minute he said, "I can just make out a spot near the south corner."

"What about the causeway?"

Jamba's shoulders moved, noncommittal. "I can see it."

"Well enough to make out traffic?"

"Yeah."

"Then that'll do. You're spotting, not shooting." Unless her master plan tanked and she needed her back door to open.

"If you're near the gate," Jamba said, "we're good."

"Awesome." They touched fists and she began to clamber down from the tree.

"Don't get your clothes dirty, now," Jamba admonished.

"Thank you, mother." She couldn't see his grin in the dark.

She reached the ground, slipped a receiver over her ear, her hair over the receiver. "Okay," she said.

"Are you receiving?" Jamba's tinny ghost spoke in her head.

"Like fine, fine crystal." She moved through the trees, cutting a diagonal away from the entrance toward the south. She took it slow, kept it quiet, watched for patrols. Ten yards from the road, she froze. A Serviceman was walking the forest, his path crossing hers. Her cover was mediocre. She was standing straight, only partly covered by low hanging branches of the oak beside her. If she tried to step deeper into shadow, she would be eye-drawing movement. If he saw her, her masquerade would be over before the curtain rose. She stood still. She became the night. The man passed six feet in front of her. His gaze slid over her. She waited five minutes before taking another step.

She reached the end of the tree cover. Ahead of her was the road, the Rubicon waiting to be crossed. "Any prospects?" she asked Jamba.

"Not yet."

She waited. She held her impatience down. This part of the operation was completely subject to blind luck. If chance didn't deliver, she could still go ahead, but her disguise would be far less solid. She was gambling on the thorns in the side of Independence Street's privacy. Unwritten rules were well and good, but the president was in town. There were going to be the curious and, more importantly, the curious and stupid. The pains in security's ass. So she waited.

"Got one," Jamba transmitted.

"How does it look?"

"A live one. Red Prius. Packed. They look young."

She blew a kiss down the road. You crazy kids. You're perfect. She strode out from the trees, crossed the road, and walked quickly in the direction of the gate. She glanced over her shoulder. Headlights in the distance, coming closer. She picked up the pace. A security agent looked up at her. Moment of truth, she thought. She nodded in greeting. He nodded back. The costume was holding up. She was in Secret Service uniform: black jacket, black slacks, white shirt. The receiver on her ear as close to regulation as made no difference. "Minor issue coming up," she said, and hooked a thumb back. "Spotters say they're young. Probably nothing, but…"

The agent nodded. He started to say something, but his words were drowned out by the arrival of the car. Its windows were down, and the sound system was broadcasting drum-and-bass loud enough to shift tectonic plates. Blaylock felt the beat more than she heard it. It blocked out all other sound, took over the rhythm of her pulse, vibrated her bones. The subwoofer sounded continent-huge. The agent's eyes popped. "Jesus!" he yelled. Blaylock barely made him out.

"You got this?" she shouted back. "I have to check in inside."

He nodded and flagged down the car. Blaylock touched a finger to her forehead and marched through the gate.

"You're good," Jamba said.

"Glad you saw that," she muttered. She was in, on her own now. She'd needed Jamba as a spotter and backup in case the bluff had gone wrong, and to start shooting and cover her run. She might still need him on the way out. She hoped not.

She crossed the grounds. She walked fast, keeping up the look: a professional on the job, with somewhere she had to be. She ducked her head down slightly, letting the long hair of the wig swing forward and shadow her face. She scanned the layout as she approached the house. Japanese lanterns were strung along the sidewalk, illuminating a buzz-cut lawn, the lawnmower tracks runway-straight. More agents roamed the perimeter of the wall. No action here. The security streetside was too obvious. A few guests loitered, catching smokes on the porch, but the sounds of the party were coming from the beach side of the house. Reed's home looked new. He might have been old money, and Blaylock knew he'd grown up here, but the original house had been erased. What stood in its place was contemporary and assertive about being so. It had the clay colours of adobe, and some of the boxy look of traditional Spanish, but it also made Blaylock think of a fortress done over for comfort. Its two wings, squat towers, were taller than the main body. Where the ramparts would have been, there was a rooftop sundeck. It was lit up, and Blaylock saw plenty of movement. Her first destination, she decided. She passed under the porch's overhang, excused herself as she passed the smokers. They gave her one glance, but not two. Good.

The interior of the house was clean, spare, would have been sterile if not for the generous expanse of the French windows, almost a full storey high. Reed had expunged the past here, too. The furniture was black leather and glass-topped tables, set out with regimental precision in the middle of the living room. The space was huge, reaching up two floors, ringed by a balcony. Under fluorescent lights, the room would have had the warmth of an operating theater. But the bright white of the lighting was just soft enough to convey comfort. It was ordered, almost dictatorial comfort, but it was comfort. There were more guests here than out front, but not so many that they weren't swallowed up in the space. They stood in small groups as they spoke. No one sat, as if they were avoiding contact with the exhibits at a cutting-edge installation.

Blaylock made a guess and took the staircase up to the balcony. At the top, she turned left into the house's north tower. Bedrooms here, and a bathroom. She checked over her shoulder. No one paying attention. She stepped into the bathroom, locked the door. She shed wig, jacket, slacks. The top, which had passed as a dress shirt under the jacket, was a sleeveless blouse. In the suit jacket was a nylon miniskirt. She slipped it on. The slacks had also disguised the footwear, turning the party knee boots into work shoes. Transformation complete, she waited five minutes, flushed the toilet and ran the water for sake of appearances, and left the washroom. She wasn't armed. She didn't have to be. Time to get the party started.

Disgusted whine on the phone: "Krys-*taaaaa*, come *onnnnnnnnnn*."

"I don't know," Krysta Edgerton said. Staying at home was a nice, safe option.

Marnie MacBryce said, "You've been no fun at all since your birthday. You don't go out. You're turning into a hermit, girl."

I'm not a hermit, I'm goddamn scared out of my goddamn mind, she wanted to say. She wanted to tell Marnie about the woman with the dark hair, darker eyes, and darkest threats, who might spring from the shadows and gut her. The woman had done that enough times in her nightmares, when she wasn't squeezing that man's throat again. Krysta wanted to say these things. She didn't. Doing so would summon the woman, she was sure of that. So she said, "No, I'm not," even though Marnie was right. "Anyway," she continued, "aren't we a bit old for that sort of thing?" Marnie was pushing for a drive-by rubbernecking of the Reed estate. See what there was to see. Go for the gatecrash.

Marnie hooted. "Oooh, listen to Krysta, all growed-up and big like." She dropped the kiddie voice. "Are you seriously going to hide at home for the rest of your life?"

"I'm not hiding."

"Right. You say no to partying with the president all the time."

And with the word "president," bright stars of terror linked up in a terrible constellation. The woman was a killer. She'd warned Krysta not to say anything. Plus, there was at least one scary man helping the nightmare woman, so she wasn't working alone. And now the president was in town. Krysta's throat was suddenly sore when she swallowed. "Oh shit," she whispered.

"What?"

The thoughts she wanted to listen to: Run. Hide. Cover your ears and eyes and it will all go away. You don't have to do anything. The Secret Service knows what it's doing. Leave this to the pros. It's none of your business. No one would listen to you anyway.

The thoughts she didn't want to listen to: It *is* your business. You have a responsibility. How will you feel if you turn out to be right, and she kills the president, and you did nothing? Can you live with that?

No.

So what do you do? You tell someone. Maybe someone whose job it is to make sure nobody kills the president.

"What is it?" Marnie pressed.

Krysta cleared her throat. "Nothing. Just spilled something." She took a breath. It shuddered badly. "Okay," she said. She tried to sound light. "You win. Let's go."

"I don't believe I know you," said the sheep.

The predator looked to her left to scan the sheep, but didn't turn her head. "That makes us even," she said. She was standing on the sundeck, leaning forward on the railing. She was watching the grounds below for prey. Big game. She didn't have time for the sheep.

The sheep was slow and didn't take the hint. She didn't go away. "Who are you?" the sheep demanded with the tone of an imperious iceberg.

Blaylock sighed and faced the woman. She traded ice for ice. "Who's asking?" *And try not to piss me off more than you absolutely have to.*

The woman was short, barely reaching Blaylock's shoulder. She was wearing a teal dress that managed to be ostentatious in its simplicity. She wore no jewellry, and somehow Blaylock felt that a point was being made there, too, as if no bauble were in the same league as this woman. Her eyebrows were a sharp arch of permafrown. Her face was a clench on the lookout for outrage. She drew herself up. She'd taken offence, but clearly relished the opportunity to announce herself. "I'm Anna-Louise Rutherford," she said. The implication was that her name said it all.

Blaylock made her expression look even blanker than she felt, and said nothing.

"My husband is Howard Rutherford."

Work that blankness.

"We own the house next door."

"Congratulations." *We can all die happy now.*

"I know everybody in this community," Rutherford explained.

"Which is why you don't know me."

"We can fix that now, can't we."

It wasn't a suggestion. It was an order. Blaylock opened her mouth. She was about to say, *You DON'T want to know me.* She stopped herself. Pissing off this woman might draw her the wrong attention too soon. Caress her, and she might be useful.

Blaylock forced a smile onto her face. "I'm sorry," she said. "I didn't mean to be rude." She pulled a name out of the air. "I'm Alexandra Harrison." Blueblood enough? "From Hartford," she added.

Rutherford held out her hand. Blaylock shook, but wondered if she shouldn't have kissed it instead. Rutherford said, "Were you looking for someone?"

You bet. No luck so far. No Korda, no Chapel, no Reed. The party was a big one, the grounds and the house even bigger. Easy for people to disappear, especially if they weren't into the mingling. Everyone Blaylock could see was enjoying the mingling just fine. The faces were politics and money. They were weathered and jaded with experience. Blaylock didn't see that many faces under forty. Under thirty was rarer still. Reed's guests were using the relaxed setting and the alcohol to lubricate the networking. The Washington game carried on without skipping a beat. It was art. It was impressive. It was brittle. Peter Pratella's name floated in the air, deep anxiety transformed into desperate gossip. No one had heard anything other than natural causes as yet, but the fear was there. It was present in the too-sharp glitter of eyes, in the too-emphatic laughter at jokes too-enthusiastically told. It was present in the Secret Service's lack of subtlety, its agents trying to reassure through visibility and a free-floating alertness. They were on the alert, but for nothing in particular. Too much ignorance, too much gossip. The game fed on both. Blaylock joined in, adding her own touch of the trivial. "No," she told Rutherford. "I was hoping *not* to see someone."

Rutherford's eyes, promised gossip, promised the vital reassurance of the inconsequential, sparkled. Her face relaxed, as far as it could, into practised sympathy. She took Blaylock's upper arm in a grip that was supposed to be one of comfort. "Someone who did you wrong?"

Blaylock nodded, suppressed a smile, looked mournful.

"Then the best thing for you, my dear, is to mount the best revenge by having fun. There are plenty of new people here to meet, I don't mind telling you." The grip on Blaylock's arm tightened. "Come with me."

Blaylock let herself be led into the action. As searches went, this was pretty indirect. But Rutherford at her side was cover that couldn't be beat. She smiled and nodded and how-do-you-doed to all the faces and wattles to which she was introduced. Rutherford's tour of the sundeck was thorough as a grid search, and then it was time to descend to the lawn, and the full force of Reed's barbeque.

On the deck, there was a bar with enough staff to make sure every guest had a drink in hand. Caterers moved through the throng, their cornucopia of appetizers bottomless. On the grounds, Blaylock saw at least two more bars set up at strategic distances from the house. There were also a half-dozen grills. The aroma of ribs and hamburger was heady. Blaylock wasn't hungry, but her stomach growled. There were hundreds of guests, each one, she knew, triple-cleared by security. They moved under the red, white and blue firefly glow of the lanterns. Blaylock looked down towards the waterfront as she and Rutherford passed by Reed's dock. She counted one pleasure yacht and three motorboats. At least one, she guessed, was part of the security detail.

Rutherford took her through so many introductions Blaylock began to believe Alexandra Harrison really was her name.

She tried to match faces with her knowledge of Washington and Langley power players. She didn't have much luck. Too many also-rans, too many hangers-on, and far, far too many brokers who never moved out from behind the scenes. She recognized some names. Some were almost important enough to rate as potential targets if they continued to be naughty boys and girls. To those, she was very friendly. How are you? I'm so pleased to meet you. I've heard about your work. I admire what you stand for. We should meet again. Do lunch.

Would you like to suck the barrel of my gun?

"And you have, of course, met the president before," Rutherford said, expecting a negative.

Blaylock gave her the truth instead. "Just once," she said. "Briefly."

"Oh." Disappointed. "And what did you think?"

"That I'd like to know him better."

The right answer. "You leave that to me." Pat on the arm.

That's good, Blaylock thought. She wondered what kind of social radar Rutherford was blessed with that she could find a specific target in these numbers and in this light. Blaylock had been scanning for a Roman turtle formation of Secret Service officers. The only agents she could see were on the dock. She assumed there were others, beyond her sight, at the perimeter of the grounds. There were no groupings around an individual. Either Reed was somewhere inside the house, or he had confidence in his safety around these people. She hoped for the latter. That would be just touching.

Rutherford marched her along with purpose. She knew where she was going. How? Blaylock wondered. Not possible, she thought. Then she saw the group they were heading for.

Brilliant, Blaylock thought. A reminder: there were gifts out there. There were incarnations. She was one. Rutherford was another.

They were standing a few yards ahead, still in the middle of the throng, but apart from it. The other guests gave them a respectful extra few feet of space. Sam Reed, Jim Korda, Joe Chapel. Cozy. Chapel looked up as Blaylock and Rutherford approached. He grinned. "Well, well, the gang's all here."

The other two turned her way. Reed looked startled, but the expression passed almost immediately, replaced with one of speculation and interest. Korda looked puzzled at the reaction of the other men.

"Mr. President," Rutherford began, "this is—"

"Yes, we've met," Reed said. His smile wasn't plastic or political. He had never mastered that art. It was genuine. It was edged.

"Ah," Rutherford said, her sails slumping as the wind died.

"You have a good memory," Blaylock said. "There was a lot going on in Davos."

"You make quite the impression."

Blaylock bowed her head in acknowledgment. She cocked an eyebrow at Chapel. "And how are you, Joe?"

"Never better." She believed him. The happiest man in the world was standing before her. He leaned on his cane, his stance jaunty.

"I'm sorry," Korda put in. He was missing information. He was close to panic. "Who…?"

"I'm forgetting myself," Reed said. "Jim Korda, Jen Baylor."

"Oh, no," said Rutherford. "I don't mean to contradict you, Mr. President, but this is—"

Reed cut her off. "Ellen," he called to someone behind Blaylock. She saw his lips tremble as he fought down a laugh.

The First Lady joined them. She was about Reed's age, and almost as tall as her husband. He was craggy, a hair's breadth from outright ugly. She was contained elegance. Her dress was more elaborate than Rutherford's, but seemed simpler. "Yes, dear?" she said.

"Wasn't there something you were wanting to ask Anna-Louise?"

If Ellen Reed objected to being her husband's social hand puppet, she hid it well. "Yes, there was," she said, no hesitation, no batting of an eye. She touched Rutherford's shoulder with a finger, a light contact but no more to be denied than Rutherford's grip on Blaylock's arm had been. "I heard how you whipped those decorators of yours into shape," she began as Rutherford followed her away. "I need to know just how you did that."

They waited until Rutherford was out of earshot. Korda spoke first. "Anyone going to fill me in?"

"You may not know this woman," Reed said, "but you know *of* her. Do you ever." No anxiety in his tone. Plenty of amusement. Something else, too. Was he *glad* to see her?

Korda paled. "Oh." He looked completely terrified. Blaylock couldn't figure it. He wasn't on her hit list. Not yet, anyway. But she was seeing the face of a man witnessing the becoming-flesh of a recurring nightmare. He started to back away. She thought he was about to call out.

Reed stopped him. He draped an arm around the smaller man's shoulders. "I don't think there's a need to call security, is there? We're all friends here."

"Absolutely," Blaylock said, scanning back and forth between Reed and Chapel. Such happy guys. That made her nervous. Then there were the different shadings to their joy. Reed was a man about to grasp an unlooked-for opportunity. Chapel's happiness was much scarier. His expression wasn't anticipatory. It was satisfied. It was job-well-done. Against the back of her neck, Blaylock felt the breeze of a mousetrap slamming down on her. She didn't know if she had any moves left. She would make sure she did. I'm taking you both down with me, she promised the happy guys.

"So?" Chapel asked. "Now what? We're a foursome now. Anyone for bridge?"

"Good to see you boys are making nice again," Blaylock said.

"The country before everything," Reed explained.

Chapel nodded. "Couldn't agree more."

Korda said nothing. He didn't want to play anymore. He didn't want to be hurt. Blaylock sympathized. The game was becoming tiresome. She wanted to kill Reed and Chapel where they stood. Not the best plan. She had to play a bit longer.

Music from up above. A band had set up on the sundeck and was playing an electric guitar arrangement of "In the Mood." Reed said, "Would you care to dance?"

Too funny. Big double entendre. But his look was steady, direct, serious now below the amusement. "Of course," she said.

Reed bowed to the other two. "Gentlemen. You'll excuse us?" He gave Blaylock his arm. They walked toward the house. Halfway there, Reed said, "I don't remember inviting you."

"No, you didn't."

"You're here for unfinished business."

"That's right."

"With Joe Chapel."

"Right again." But only half-right. "And you're not really bosom buddies again."

"Are we that obvious?"

Blaylock snorted.

They reached the house. Inside, they climbed the staircase to the upper floor, but instead of heading out onto the deck, Reed led her down the hallway toward the bathroom.

"What kind of a girl do you think I am?" Blaylock asked.

"A smart one, who understands the need for privacy on certain occasions."

"And this is one?"

"I think so." Reed held the bathroom door open for her. "Shall we?"

Blaylock checked behind them. The corridor was empty. There were no curious eyes watching them from the mezzanine. "Thank you," Blaylock said, and stepped inside. As Reed closed the door behind them, there was the quiet buzz of Jamba's voice. "New arrivals. Civilians. One of them looks excited. She's talking to security."

The Secret Service man looked, Krysta thought, like a wall in a suit. He wasn't wearing dark glasses, but his eyes were so heavily lidded the effect was the same. He was cold, implacable. Not friendly. "I'm sorry," he said, though he wasn't. "If you're not on the guest list, you're not going in. Simple as that. Go home."

Before Krysta could speak, Marnie was in like Flynn. "Come onnnnnnnn," said the Marnie wheedle. She took a step closer, leaned forward slightly to give the agent a flash of cleavage. He was unmoved. She didn't notice. She kept at it. "I mean, do we look like *terrorists*?"

Krysta was scared. Her pulsed was so screwed, she hadn't been able to think of a good approach. So she just blurted. "I think there's a killer in town," she said.

Bad judgment. Coming on the heels of Marnie's crack, her warning sounded like a weak party ploy. The agent said, "Get back in your car, girls."

"Asshole," Marnie muttered.

"I'm serious!" Krysta shouted. She grabbed the man's sleeve. He reached to pry her hand away. "She killed a man," she said.

The agent hesitated. "Who did?"

"I don't know." Don't cry. Don't cry. It was hard not to. Her voice trembled. "I was in a nightclub. She killed this guy with her bare hands. She told me not to tell or else."

"*Krysta?*" Marnie bug-eyed and near-ecstatic. "Holy shit!"

The agent had raised his lids. He was looking at her, all attention. "Did she threaten the president?"

Krysta shook her head. "No, but..." Her shoulders slumped. "I thought... I don't know... I thought I should..."

"You did the right thing," the agent said. He spoke quietly into his radio. Krysta looked around. She saw other agents look sharply in their direction. Some of them began to run towards the gate. Down the road, a van was approaching.

Someone raising the alert? Blaylock wondered. Who? Didn't matter. Her window of opportunity was shrinking to nothing. Take the big risk soon, or give up on it again. "So?" she asked Reed. Find out what's on his mind. Might be useful.

"You hate Chapel."

"You can tell?"

Reed's smile crawled with vermin. Blaylock could almost respect him. "We have something in common. He's my own troublesome priest."

"And no one will rid you of him."

"The deniability is never plausible enough."

"But if a third party, unknown, unconnected to the warring sides, stepped in…"

The light of joy in Reed's eyes. "Exactly."

Blaylock gave him the light of joy right back. It was war's purifying beam. "Consider it done," she said.

"You could name your reward," the politician promised.

"I already know what I want."

"Oh? And what's that?"

"Your guts for garters."

The joy winked out of Reed's face. He took half a step back. Blaylock was already moving forward. She shot her hand into his throat, killing his air and his cry for help. He choked, stumbled. His old training came back, and he blocked her follow-up. She kicked his feet out from under him. His head smacked the side of the bathtub as he fell. Blaylock rammed her knee into the small of his back, pinning the bug. She yanked his head back. She lowered her face to his and whispered into his ear. "Are you frightened, Mr. President?" She used the title as a curse. "Or are you still hoping for rescue? These things don't happen to you, after all, now do they?" Reed tried to croak something out. "Shut the fuck up," she said. One movement, then: a hard, snapping turn. She heard the crack of his neck going. She felt for his pulse. Where it should have been, bone was pressing out against the skin.

Blaylock stood up. She checked herself in the mirror. Nothing out of place. No dishevelled hair or outward signs of murder. She heaved the corpse into the tub, drew the shower curtains across. She opened the door, checked the corridor. All clear. The door had a spring lock. She pushed it in, then pulled the door shut. That should gain her a few minutes.

She trotted down the stairs, heading for the back door. She saw agents running toward the house. Countdown almost out. No point trying to leave by the front. That left the water. And then there was Chapel. The boy was too happy. Flanagan's warning that she might be doing the man's dirty work for him was real and present. She began to loop back toward where she'd left him and Korda. More people running. She was hanging by a thinning thread. But the party was still going on. No one knew anything definite yet. An agent shoved past her on his way to the house. She heard him ask, "Found him yet?" into his communicator. Use those seconds. Locate Chapel.

There. Towards the dock. Looking her way. When she saw him, he began to run. Shit, she thought. Bastard, she thought. Idiot, she told herself. She took off after him. Around her, the vibe of Reed's party was turning sour. The sheep were picking up on the anxiety. They were ready to bolt.

Chapel ran with a limp, but he was still fast. He jumped into a speedboat. It almost leapt out of the water. He must have had it idling. She wondered when he'd slipped away to prep it. There was another motor boat, a rich man's toy, tied to the dock. She found the ignition, started it up, tossed the line and gave chase.

The agent had disappeared into the gate. He had told them to stay where they were. No problem. Krysta's feet might as well have been sunk into the sidewalk's cement. Marnie was still eyeing the grounds, though. She took a few steps away. "*Marnie*," Krysta hissed.

"But I want to see what's going on."

"*Don't.*" She glanced around, half expecting gun-toting authority to descend on youth that couldn't follow orders. She noticed that the van she'd seen arrive was now parked by the side of the road. Its cab was empty.

Chapel's wake glowed white in the moonlight. Blaylock had her boat's throttle on max, and she was bumping over water, teeth rattling in her head. She was losing ground. The wake was spreading out before her, losing definition. Chapel's craft was very fast. She wouldn't catch up. Already, she couldn't see him, could only hear the buzz-saw whine of his engine. She checked over her shoulder for signs of pursuit. Nothing yet.

She'd been chasing for a few miles, and was well into the bay, when the engine of Chapel's boat changed timbre. It dropped octaves, slowed down. The wake became more precise. Blaylock strained to see ahead. She willed the darkness to part. Ahead, she saw a larger shape on the horizon. Another boat. She slowed down she approached. It was a fishing boat. Chapel's speedster was tied to its starboard. Blaylock cut the engine back to a crawl. She ducked low, feeling very exposed. No cover and no gun. She watched for movement. Nothing on deck. The cabin windows were dark. Crosshairs could be on her forehead, and she wouldn't know.

She drew closer. She killed the engine. Still no sounds from the fishing boat. She brushed up against Chapel's boat, climbed into it and moved to the side of the larger vessel. She grabbed the ladder and hauled herself onto the deck. She listened. The ship creaked and muttered to itself in the slight swell. It felt dead, empty. Crouched low, she moved to the cabin door. She pulled it open and rolled in fast, jumped up for combat, faced nothing but air and night. The cabin was dark. A green light was blinking next to the wheel.

Blaylock began to creep towards the stairs leading below deck. She had a foot on the first step down when she heard an engine start up port side. She backed up and ran to look outside. A second speedboat was tearing away. From the wake, Blaylock guessed Chapel had rowed the boat out a hundred yards before starting it up. It made no sense. Why use the fishing boat to switch rides? Why be coy about the departure? Creating a delay? No point, given how much of a lead he'd built up in the first place. She would never have caught him. The only reason to sneak away would be to keep her on the boat.

The blinking light.

She turned her head. She saw it flash red.

She banged out the door and dived off the side of the ship. She went deep, but wasn't deep enough when the ship exploded. The blast was a big one. The water lit up, and the pressure wave slammed into her. It knocked the air from her lungs. A vortex took her, worried her like a dog with a bone. She gasped, pulled in water. She flailed her limbs, didn't know which way was up. She tumbled in a whitewater froth. She fought back the panic, but her lungs needed air. Consciousness went grey and fuzzy. Her body betrayed her and she inhaled again. More water. Then, at the edge of final black, air, scraping in like savage glass. She gagged, breathed again, screamed, thrashed at the surface. She threw up, but began to breathe properly. She saw the flaming wreckage of the ship going down. The waves caused by the blast began to settle.

And then the night was torn apart by the incandescent rage of day.

20

One hundred kilotons. Small. Big enough.

Close your eyes. Fear the light. Hold your breath.
Maelstrom came. Sucked her down again.

The seconds before.

Korda was numb. His right hand was still holding a drink,
but he couldn't feel his fingers. His brain was neither sending messages to, nor receiving them from, his body. People
were shouting things at him. He couldn't hear them. The
rising nightmare blocked their voices. It had uncurled in
his stomach when the woman had arrived. Intuition fed by
a recurring dream he couldn't quite remember froze him.
He did nothing but watch. He couldn't speak. He watched
Chapel walk away. He watched the man make his way across
the lawn, then begin to run towards the docks. He saw the
woman follow him. He didn't see the president. And then the
shouting began.

And the nightmare came for him. The killing light flashed. Time gave him an eternal last moment of full knowledge.

The van became the sun. The air became bright fire. It expanded, spreading millions of degrees millisecond by millisecond. It announced its Armageddon presence with three horsemen: radiation, heat and blast. Reed's home vaporized. Beyond, in the town, the dragon didn't kill as cleanly. The heat was no longer enough to disintegrate. Now it killed with pain. Buildings and trees flashed into flame. The blast knocked them into hurricane shrapnel. Bodies burned and smashed into shattered walls. The dragon scoured the earth with its claws. It ate Petersfield. Millisecond by millisecond.

Down. Stay down. She tried to dive. She tried to flee the dragon. But the waves raised her up and she saw the fireball. Huge. Perfect. The icon of absolute art. She was several miles away, safe from the dragon breath, but she felt its blessing as a wave of heat on her forehead. She tasted lead. And there was the sound. It was thunder that filled the world and filled her head. It surrounded her, pushed out on her skull and squeezed her tight. There were no other sounds left in the universe. This one sound was too big. She opened her mouth wide. She couldn't scream, but she wanted to let the thunder out before it killed her.

Chapel sat in the stern of the boat. He watched his act of enormity. The bay here was untouched. Night surrounded him. But in the distance, it was day, then sunset as the heat of the fireball faded. The mushroom cloud rose. That is what history looks like, he thought. That is its shape.

He had given it this form. He didn't feel horror. He had already worked through that. He had already embraced the scope of his crime. What he felt instead was the orgasm rush of omnipotence.

The blast dissipated. The heat calmed. The dragon lost its energy. Half a mile from its birth, it killed the last of its initial victims. But its legacy sank into the ground. It rode the air as the cloud began to disperse, spreading its poison dust downwind. The sound went on, too. It changed, though. The thunder faded. The sound transmuted as eyes and camera lenses saw what had happened and the knowledge spread. It took only minutes for the sound to become the scream of an entire nation.

They heard the scream. Everyone did. In Washington, Flanagan and Luzhkov had hit a bar a few minutes away from the Watergate. The big-screen TV in the corner had been silently playing a Lakers game. Then it was showing a mushroom cloud. At first Flanagan thought he was seeing an ad. Then copy began crawling across the bottom of the screen. Silence in the room. A man in a business suit five years too small for his waistline stood up, shaking, and turned the sound up. The noise of the scream filled the lounge. Flanagan turned to Luzhkov, saw the man mirror his own loss and panic.

They made land at Hither Hills State Park. Quintero was waiting there with the rest of the fleet: two more fishing boats. One of them was held together by rust. They were both last-word inconspicuous. "Did you see the show?" Chapel asked, as he hopped aboard the more seaworthy of the two vessels.

Quintero clapped slowly.

Chapel felt his face shape a grim smile. "So we're off to the races."

"And what now?"

"Back to Fort Benning."

"Is that wise?"

"Turn a radio on. We'll know definitely before we get there. But yes, that's where we should be. I have to be where I can be reached, after all. I'm going to be needed."

"Nothing went wrong, then."

"No. One thing I need checked out, though." He called across to Maldonado on the other fishing boat. "Head back to where the decoy ship was."

Maldonado stared. "*What?* Why?" The two men standing beside him didn't look happy, either.

"Scan the bay. If there's a survivor, kill her."

"Go look yourself, *mamagüebo.*"

"Don't worry, it's safe. The boat was far enough away from the blast, wind's blowing the other way. No radiation."

"I don't see you heading there."

"I didn't see you at ground zero. I might have to be in front of cameras within the next couple of hours. I can't be futzing around in the bay. Nobody's going to look twice at you. Now quit jerking me off and go."

Maldonado glanced at Quintero. The general shrugged. Maldonado muttered something about Chapel's mother.

Wreckage floated past her. It had been part of the boat's gunwale. Blaylock grabbed it. She climbed on top, resting her torso on the flat surface. Experimentally, she stopped kicking her legs. The planking was big enough to support her weight. She thought about striking for shore. She couldn't start her legs again. They had turned into lead. They hung down in the water, useless as pillars. Exhaustion pressed her to the wood, turned her into flotsam. She drifted. She didn't think. She dozed. The water slowly leeched her warmth. Defeat weighed her down, tried to pull her under.

A sound made her snap to. It was the distant roar of a boat's engine. She raised her head. She saw lights heading her way. She looked around, oriented herself from the glow of Petersfield's flames. The boat was coming from the same direction Chapel had gone. Didn't necessarily mean anything. As the boat drew nearer, she saw that it was using a searchlight on the water. Why? she wondered. No reason to look for survivors in the water. The disaster was on land. There *were* good reasons, though. And they were bad for her.

War returned. It poured some warmth back into her limbs. She let herself slide down the wreckage, lowered herself into the water, hung on with one hand. She waited. The boat's light swung in erratic half-circles, insect-searching. It passed over the wood, came back and stayed. She let go, began treading water gently, keeping just the top of her head and eyes above water. There was a shift in the quality of the engine noise as the boat changed direction and slowed down. It came closer. Blaylock went under and swam toward the noise. The underwater night lit up as the light passed over her and moved on. She surfaced portside aft. She hugged close to the boat, looked for a gift. She saw the silhouettes of three men on board. One of them was leaning down, peering at her wreckage. He shook his head. "*Nada*," he said.

As the engine began to rev up again, Blaylock saw her gift. The boat's fishing camouflage was complete, and a net hung down over one corner of the stern. She hooked her left arm through it. The boat sped up, took her for a ride.

The nation screamed. It howled. The world echoed as the sound spread over the globe. The nation, screaming, stretched out its arms, pleading (and screaming) for a leader. Within an hour of the blast, the death of the president was known, and the rules of succession suddenly were headline-important as the full meaning of the death of the Speaker of the House hit home. The Secret Service beat the cameras to the president pro tempore of the Senate by less than five minutes. Daniel Hallam was found in his office. He was pale, but spoke calmly. The Service wanted to spirit him away to Cheyenne Mountain. Hallam refused. The last thing the country needed was an invisible president.

And so Senator Daniel Hallam emerged from the Capitol, stood on its steps, faced the cameras. He'd had the time it took to walk from his office to here to think about what he was going to say. He opened his mouth and spoke for the first time as president to a traumatized nation. His speech began with "My fellow Americans," as all such speeches must. He was aware of the cliché. He didn't fight it, not when it was a simple truth. The simple truth was what he kept to. "I am as shocked as you are by today's events. I'm not going to stand here and tell you comforting lies. I *will* tell you something you already know: that it is when we are tested in this way that we learn our true character as a nation. I will also tell you that we *will* get aid to those who need it. And we *will* find and punish those responsible for this unfathomable crime. Do we know who those people are? No. Not yet. And I cannot emphasize too strongly that we cannot, now of all times, afford to jump to easy, wrong conclusions. We know, to our cost, the consequences of hasty decisions. Rest assured that it is fact, not rumour, that will guide our hand." He paused. Did he have to descend to the expected bromides of "strength," "hope," "faith," and "God"? He supposed he did. However meaningless, the words were the sound of reassurance, and could do no harm. So he did what he could for his wounded, screaming nation.

They had a laptop set up in the barracks. It was streaming the speech. Chapel stared. Then he was calling Felix Jurado. He tried to ignore the look Quintero was giving him. "Pratella," Chapel sputtered to Jurado. "What the fuck?"

World-weary patience and despair in Jurado's tone. "I tried to call you."

"I was busy. What happened?"

"He was poisoned. With chlordane."

"The hell is that?"

"A pesticide," Jurado said. "Loves the fatty acids. Clogs up the heart, lungs, brain and spinal cord. Causes convulsions, miscellaneous other fun things, and death. Doesn't take much. His hands were coated with it, like he was using it for soap. Only took a couple of hours to identify it."

"I doubt he committed suicide. Where did it come from?"

A grunt from Jurado. It was the laugh of the completely pissed-off. "God knows. There's no trace of it anywhere in his office except on him."

"The dumb bastard had to get it from *somewhere*."

"So tell him."

Chapel closed his eyes. "Talk to you later," he said, and hung up. He could see the rabbit holes that were going to swallow up the investigation. It was a classic, freaky, locked-door murder case *plus* political assassination. The leaks would come, and the conspiracy theories would mushroom. Some of those theories might work in his favour. At the end of the day, though, he didn't care how Pratella was murdered. He cared a lot about who killed him. The move was a perfect counter to his agenda. It might as well bear a signature. But the woman was dead. He'd killed her at least three times tonight. She was radioactive dust over the Hamptons or a floater in the Atlantic. She was dead.

Dead, but still screwing with him. He threw the phone at the computer screen, smashing it. Quintero said, "We just detonated a nuclear weapon for nothing, didn't we?"

"No." Chapel turned the muttered word into a heartbeat of rage and desperate urgency. "No, no, no, no, no, *no*." He heard in Hallam's cautious statement a repudiation not only of the rumour he had planted, but of American strength. The new president was the embodiment of every weakness he had struggled so hard, sacrificed so much, to save his country from. Save the nation he would. He still had a card to play. "No," he said again, this time out loud, firm, and to Quintero. "We didn't do it for nothing."

"Really." Skeptical.

"Really. And guess what? You're going to save us all."

Heavy drinking in the lounge. Flanagan and Luzhkov found a table at the far end of the room away from the TV. Vandelaare joined them. The two mercs were playing it stoic. Flanagan wasn't buying. He saw Vandelaare biting his lip. There was a muscle in Luzhkov's cheek that kept moving, as if he were chewing something, or biting back a roar. They were hurting. They had begun, he suspected, to believe in a dream of usefulness and bloody redemption. Waking up was nasty. Luzhkov seemed to be taking it hardest. When he wasn't pounding back vodka shots, his left hand was rubbing the white-knuckled fist of his right. Perhaps his dream had been the most vivid.

Flanagan's throat had constricted around a steel burr of grief. He was feeling the same disconnections from light and hope he had experienced when his sister died. There was also the impotence, a raging, acid-spewing, hate-defining impotence. This was worse than when Holly had been killed. Back then, he had always known he was powerless. Trying to avenge her death had been his first stab at any kind of genuine action. But with Blaylock, being swept up in her war, he had tasted agency. He was running InSec now. There was enormous power there. Only there wasn't. Without Blaylock, he was the hollow shell of a rotted figurehead. He had no direction. He didn't know what to do.

"So what now?" Vandelaare asked, eyes focused on nothing. The question was rhetorical. Flanagan felt it was aimed at him, though. What now? What now? He didn't know.

Luzhkov was frowning, as if trying to give Vandelaare a real answer.

Flanagan felt panic flare through the grief, pierce the anger. He was about to lose something else.

Do something.

The boat must have been slowing. Its wake was dropping. The net dug into her armpit, doing its best to amputate. She felt heavier than an anchor. She half-wondered why she didn't drag the ship down. She had almost blacked out several times during the ride. Each time, she had managed to shake off unconsciousness. Each time, her reserves of adrenaline had dwindled. War threatened to succumb to a killing peace.

Slower yet. She blinked the fog from her brain. The engine noise dropped enough that she could make out snippets of Spanish conversation above her. A man laughed. She wanted to eat his throat. She twisted around to face the direction the boat was heading. She saw a darker mass in the night. They were close to land. The engine went from growl to mutter. It was time to move. Her arm was dead. Her brain sent it signals. The arm didn't want to know. She couldn't tell its circulation numbness from the hypothermic chill in the rest of her body. She looked at it, ordered it to move. She heaved with her shoulder. A constellation of incandescent needles stabbed into her arm. The pain was so ludicrous she had to stifle laughter. Her arm shifted an inch. She strained again. This time, she had to choke back a scream. She pulled herself far enough out of the net for gravity to take over. She slid free. The boat left her behind. Swimming was hard with one arm immobilized. It was even harder not to thrash. She made the arm move. It howled at her. Its gestures were wooden. She kept going under. The flexibility gradually returned. She was able to move forward, barely. Exhaustion and cold made her a crippled frog. Just ahead, she saw the boat's lights illuminate an old pier. She reached the far end as the men finished tying up the vessel and shut it down. She hugged a piling and listened. More snatches of conversation drifted her way. All in Spanish. She heard an English word: "Benning."

She swam under the pier, closer. Two of the men were walking away. The third was still fiddling with the boat. She poked her head out long enough to catch a glimpse of him, in silhouette, rubbing a cloth over a railing. Wiping down the fingerprints. His companions disappeared into the woods. She heard a car start. She had a few minutes alone with this man. The impulse, the desire: rise up and Scylla-snatch the man, squeeze him for knowledge, then squeeze him for blood. The reality: she couldn't take on a preschooler in her state. Even if she could, taking the man down would be a mistake. A missing man would be a red flag for Chapel. Right now, for the second time, he would consider her dead. That was a better edge than one man could give her.

After ten minutes, the cleanup was done. The man left. Another car engine fired up. She waited another quarter of an hour, fighting sleep. No one else showed. Blaylock crawled up on the shore. She dragged herself into the underbrush, out of sight. And that was it. She didn't have any more. She curled up in ball. Shivering, teeth chattering, she slept.

21

Flanagan sat in the hotel room, trying to decide who had won. He had the TV on. He was surfing the news networks, which today meant every channel in creation, including the Cartoon Network. The coverage had his stomach twisting with so many snakes. He couldn't sit down. He couldn't watch one station for more than thirty seconds without wanting to punch walls. He couldn't look away. Chapel's dominoes were mesmerizing. They had fallen in a pattern whose perfection would have been the elevation of Peter Pratella to the presidency, and thank Christ that Blaylock had killed that scenario. Even so, Chapel's narrative was a strong one. Most of the commentators were marching in lock-step behind it. Hallam was already seen as weak, possibly dangerous, and that was on MSNBC. Fox already had him hanged as a traitor for not going after the terrorists.

Those terrorists. My, they were a hateful bunch. All eyes were turned to the Middle East, especially to the perfect dystopia of Iraq. Here the commentators were split. We must go back, sang one choir. We can't go back, sang the other. So much for unity. The patriotic vitriol flew. That was, for Flanagan, the most impressive touch in Chapel's masterpiece. He'd set the terms for a pointless argument. The discussion was whether or not to put boots to ground once again. The origin of the terror strike was never questioned. Across the globe, the potential targets of the wounded eagle's wrath were doing themselves no favours. At least a half-dozen separate al-Qaida cells and wannabes were scrambling to claim responsibility for the nuke. Flanagan wondered how many of them were in a blind panic, wondering who it was who had raised the bar so unreachably high.

And through the hurricane of raging bullshit, Hallam was holding firm. The evidence was not in, yet, he said. There would be no talk of invasion when, for all anyone knew, the terrorists were homegrown. The fact that he would actually say that sent his opponents rabid. Flanagan saw what was coming. Chapel wouldn't stop. He couldn't, not with a result that, from his perspective, was even worse than the starting point.

Luzhkov and Vandelaare were at battle stations in the city. They were keeping the troops in line, keeping all the communication lines open. A decision had to be taken. Action had to be taken. For the moment, Luzhkov and Vandelaare were deferring to Flanagan, as the right hand of Blaylock. He wanted to be the right one. He wanted to honor her memory. He wanted to hang on to the strength.

The goal was simple: stop Chapel. The means were harder to grasp. He didn't even know where Chapel was. His impotence gnawed at him. It made a lie of his power. His self-loathing roiled.

The sun was the promise of life. It was the rebirth of warmth. Blaylock was still shivering when she woke. The mercury climbed quickly. The sun rose, and the day was hot. Fast as that. Blaylock made her way out of the woods, found a road, and walked down it, soaking up the heat. Life spread through her limbs. Her clothes were ragged, but they dried.

She headed west. There was no traffic. She covered several miles without seeing a single vehicle. What she did hear was the distant drone of helicopter rotors. She saw the choppers once she was out of the park. Clustering flies, they circled the festering wound of Petersfield. They were a visual warning for Blaylock: stay away from here. She wondered how she was going to get off Long Island. There would be no land route back to the mainland.

The first town she reached was Amagansett. It was supposed to have a population of just over a thousand. Blaylock saw no one. The evacuation had been lightning quick, she thought. She walked the empty streets, eyes open for military patrols, but not expecting any. Access from the Hamptons east would be blocked. There was no need to waste anything more than token manpower protecting the area from looters who would never come. Then she noticed just how many windows had been left open, how many tires had burnt their traces into the pavement. There had been no evacuation needed here. There had been flight. She imagined the scene. A good chunk of the population outside to watch the fireworks. Check out the small-scale local show, perhaps see what they could of the spectacle a few miles away being put on in honour of the president. Oooooh, and aaaahhhh, and then the fireball and mushroom cloud finale. Only one sane response: run like hell.

Blaylock approached a generous bungalow. She tried the door. It was unlocked. She went inside. The TV in the living room was still on. She sat down on the couch, rested, and saw what the news had to teach her. She saluted Chapel's accomplishment, promised him a century in hell for every victim of his bomb. Krysta's face kept intruding on her mind's eye. Petersfield's population refused to reduce itself to a statistic she could mourn in the abstract. She knew a face and a name. She knew a frightened young woman, terrified because of her. She knew a dead young woman, and how much Blaylock was responsible for that, she was afraid to contemplate. I tried to stop Chapel, she thought. You went to that party bringing war, her conscience responded. Then there was Jamba. She sighed. She acknowledged her encrustation of filth. She stood up, leaving the TV chatter to its imprecations and looked for the bedrooms. The first one she looked in was a young boy's. Action figures of a Covenant Elite and the Master Chief were locked in combat on the bed. No peace for the two until their God returned. The second bedroom was the parents'. Blaylock opened the closet door. She grabbed an oversized T-shirt and a pair of women's jeans. The pants were too big for her. She cinched them with a belt. They would do. She bundled up her rags and left the house.

At the outskirts of the town, she paused. She visualized a map of the area. She had a rough sense of the geography of this end of the island from some of her more wide-ranging searches for Chapel's army. She didn't want to go any closer to Petersfield if she could avoid doing so. She knew there were ferries to Shelter Island and from there to the northern arm of the island. It was a possibility. It was also the only option.

She left the road and cut across country north and west, dumping her torn clothes in a ditch. A couple of miles brought her to the north shore. She followed the beaches until she reached Sag Harbor. There was activity here. From a distance, she'd been able to hear the garble of loudspeaker announcements and the anxious murmur of a crowd. There were helicopters overhead. She didn't try to hide. She was a civilian. She was a refugee. She needed help.

The eastern population of Long Island had flooded into Sag Harbor, creating a bottleneck on the only road north, over bridge and via ferries, to a way off the island. The army was here, keeping order and bringing calm. Blaylock joined the crowd. She saw families and singletons, the beautiful people and the overfed middle-class, the drones from the service sector and the domestic help from the immigration grey zone. They wore jeans and skirts, shorts and slacks, business suits and bathing suits, anything and everything they happened to have on when the terror had come calling. Every face different, every face same: stamped with the mark of nightmare. She heard children crying about abandoned toys. One little girl sobbed over a dog left behind. Blaylock's heart thumped. She had a mad impulse to ask the girl where she lived, run back and get the dog. The evacuation won't be a long one, she told herself. The bomb wasn't a big nuke. They'll be letting people back soon, if only to get belongings. It was the fear that had its spurs into the flanks of the crowd, driving it forward, casting all other considerations to the winds. She tried to block out the sounds of fear and tears. She narrowed her vision to the head of the person in front of her. She slumped her shoulders, falling into her role. She shuffled slowly down the road, baking in the heat, waiting for her turn to be helped.

The troops had all come home. There had been no casualties. They were safe in their tent barracks. That made Quintero happy. His entire force was in one spot, at the pleasure and whim of Chapel and the Fort Benning commander. That made him less happy. The risks Chapel was asking him and his men to take made him even less happy. "You are asking us to sacrifice a great deal for your country," he said. They were strolling the grounds of Fort Benning.

Chapel stopped in the shade of a cypress tree. In the distance, there was the *pop pop pop* of military exercises. "I need you to fix my country," Chapel explained. "Fixing my country means fixing a lot that's going on in the rest of the world. Fixing yours is part of that." He spoke quietly. His sincerity was bedrock-hard.

He isn't simply a believer, Quintero thought. He's a fanatic. He wondered how he had ever doubted Chapel's willingness to detonate a nuke in his own country, and kill thousands of his own citizens, for a principle. "So tell me," he said, "how you propose to fix mine. Your country's attention right now is focused on the Middle East, not the south."

Chapel waved the concern away. "That's just the first act. That's the set-up. Of course the bomb came from the Islamic world. No one would believe anything else. Not at first."

"At first?"

"Second act revelations. Look, everybody is burning mad, screaming blue murder for payback. Right?"

"Yes. And look what happened last time."

"*Exactly*. No one wants to go through that again. Sooner or later, we're going to have to go in and sort that hellhole out once and for all. Do it *right*, for Chrissakes. But this isn't the time. We'll find a training camp somewhere, lob a few missiles, put on a good show with all of our boys and machines coming home in one piece. That's about it."

"I still don't see—"

Chapel held up a finger. "Remember, I said second act revelations. I said no one would buy the bomb coming from anywhere other than the Middle East. But someone else *arranging* for the bomb to come from there? That's conspiracy gold. I doubt I'll even have to start the rumour. It's probably already out there, spreading over the Net."

Quintero was beginning to see the shape of the plot. "It will turn out that the person behind the bomb plot—"

"—is the president of Venezuela. Why not? Makes sense. It's no secret that he's no friend of America. It's a point of pride for him. He wants to dominate South America. He wants us out of the picture. Everybody knows he's really a communist. It's perfect."

"The Islamo-Communist Axis?"

Chapel guffawed. "Sure, why not? It's not that far from the truth, when you look at what goes on in the world. Anyway, the nation will demand that the bastard responsible for this atrocity be taken down. But our military is still recovering from being overstretched, and everybody's antsy about a new invasion."

"So we go in."

"With big-budget tech support. One mother of a sound-and-light show."

"And when will all these wonders come to pass?" His question was flip, but Quintero was feeling the excitement. Chapel was mad, but he was good mad. Brilliant mad.

"They won't, not with Hallam minding the store."

Flanagan sat on the floor of the hotel room, back against the bed. He had a notepad beside him. Half its pages were filled with ideas and sketches on how to flush Chapel out. They reeked of the half-baked and the desperate. He sucked. He had InSec in his hands. He had megaton clout. He had no idea how to use it. Give me a couple of days to work this out, he'd told Luzhkov. The man had agreed, understanding, patient. Not taking over. Not yet. But Flanagan had nothing to show him but a sheaf of abandoned schemes Wile E. Coyote would have dismissed as unworkable. He stared at the wall. He should have been working. He should have been thinking up the better plan, the better mousetrap. He couldn't. The emptiness was taking him again. He'd done his best to hold it at bay. He put on the good show of stoicism for the benefit of the mercs. He had tried to follow Blaylock's example. What would she have done? Lose herself in the work. He couldn't. The emptiness was a cancer, eating him hollow. He couldn't stop waiting for her.

Knock at the door. He blinked, groaned to his feet and looked through the peephole. He looked for longer than was necessary. When he opened the door, his jaw still hanging slack, Blaylock said, "Sorry I didn't call."

And he was safe again, in the arms of war.

22

His last night in his private residence. Hallam could feel the presence of the Secret Service phalanx on the other side of the apartment door. It had taken much persuasion and a full security sweep to be granted this much privacy. He stood in the living room, feeling the clammy tingle of unreality crawl over his flesh. He should be helping Norah with the packing. They were putting enough in suitcases to have something of the personal in the White House until the rest of their belongings were shipped over. He tried to head to the bedroom. He couldn't make his legs move. The TV was on. When they weren't attacking his patriotism, talking heads intoned, full of solemnity and self-pleasure with their originality, about his out-of-nowhere and out-of-ruling-party arrival as the new Most Powerful Man on Earth. If true, he wondered, why did he feel like a pawn? Pratella's death so soon after he had seen him couldn't be a coincidence. He wouldn't be the only one to realize that. The reporter had used him somehow. But he was still inclined to believe her about Chapel and Pratella.

He just didn't believe in her reporter identity anymore. He was exposed to the crossfire of two adversaries with no way of ducking. So he had to fire back. He had one visible target. He would worry about tracking the other threat once he had neutralized the first. His legs unlocked. He moved towards the bedroom. He could be productive again. He was composing a statement for the next day's press conference.

Two visits to make. Two ladies to see this evening. Chapel was the man.

First up, Meredith Leadbetter. Next in line to the ephemeral throne. Her house was in Georgetown, big enough to signify wealth, small enough to avoid ostentation. Leadbetter met him at the door. It was just dusk. "A bit early for an assignation," she said.

"Double duty tonight. Your husband home?"

"Yes." All appearances and proprieties still observed. What Chapel knew: the marriage was a useful lie, its continued existence a tribute to the secretary of state's will. What Chapel didn't know: the true nature of the sexual orientation of Jordan Leadbetter (fourth of that name). What he suspected: that Jordan Leadbetter didn't know either. What Jordan knew or wanted was beside the point. He came with an old name, one with generations of Washington politics behind it, and which had not hurt his wife's rise in the least. Between Meredith and Jordan Leadbetter (third of that name), he was kept on a short leash, out of the spotlight, but just present enough to provide the right optics. He was presentable. He was pleasant. He knew to keep his mouth shut and his head down. The perfect Washington spouse.

Chapel followed Meredith Leadbetter into the living room. It was a space of clean lines and studied power. Chapel took the offered seat on a couch that was just a bit less comfortable than it looked. "Guess why I'm here," he said.

"You want to talk about our latest commander-in-chief."

"Your thoughts about him?"

"Quit being coy, Joe. You know damn well what I think. His party wasn't elected to the White House. His being at the helm is contrary to the desire of the majority of American voters. His ideas are dangerous, particularly at this time."

"So he should be removed."

Leadbetter let the silence become uncomfortable before speaking again. "I very much did not say that."

"It's the logical conclusion of your observations."

"Removing presidents is what we have elections for. I realize that's hard to remember these days, but there it is."

"And you think the country can survive under Daniel Hallam until the next election."

Another pause while she gave him a laser-scan stare. "What, exactly, do you want?"

"I want to know if you're prepared to fulfill the duties your country might ask of you."

"That's a rich way of phrasing your own self-interest."

Chapel felt a vein pulse on his forehead. "Everything I have ever done has been for the good of my country." He held her gaze until she nodded.

"All right," Leadbetter said. "I'll grant you that. So you grant me the fact that whatever your actions have been lately, things are worse now than they've ever been."

"There are reasons—"

Leadbetter held up a hand. "I really, truly, deeply do not want to know. I know you and Pratella had something together, and whatever it was, I'm not part of it. Clear?"

Chapel nodded.

"Good. Get this clear, too. I really don't believe the country can survive still another Chief Executive taken down by force. The perception is already out there that we're turning into a banana republic. One more and we might well be."

She was wrong, he thought. The republic was more resilient than that. As long as the leadership was strong, it could survive almost anything. "I'll tell you what I believe," he said. He spoke with, and from, conviction. "I believe that things are an unholy mess now, and that we're on the edge of the abyss. Having the wrong hand at the tiller will sweep us in. One more change right now will hurt, yes, but like removing a bandage quickly hurts. Control needs to be re-established, and Hallam isn't the leader who can accomplish that."

Leadbetter's face was noncommittal, but Chapel liked the glint in her eyes.

Anticipate and counter. Luzhkov sat in a car a block down from Leadbetter's home. The car was a Lexus, upmarket enough to be anonymous on this street. They'd kept surveillance on Leadbetter from the day before Blaylock took out Pratella. Chapel wasn't staying in his home anymore, so Blaylock had ordered a watch on every player he might want to contact. Leadbetter's position had made her the smart money bet. Luzhkov called Blaylock. "He's here," he said.

"Alone?"

"He seemed to be."

"Assume he isn't."

Luzhkov glanced around. It was Petersfield all over again. Washington crawled with warriors. His position, best for observation and positive ID, was the most vulnerable. He knew he had friendly eyes on his back. Blaylock was right, though. Chapel wouldn't move without his destination being seeded with his boys. He wondered how many unfriendly eyes were on him, and he wasn't even counting the beefed-up security outside Leadbetter's house. He wondered how many opponents had made each other. "Can I take him?" He knew the answer. He had to ask, anyway.

"No. I want his army when we nail him, and you're useless to me as a martyr."

Chapel stood on Leadbetter's porch. The door closed behind him. He listened to the street and the night. There were feral beasts in the jungle. He could feel their gaze. He waited another few seconds, dangling himself as bait. Try it, he thought. Come out in the open. His system buzzed high with risk. It felt good. He had killed the woman, but he guessed her organization would be looking for payback. He dared her men to come for him. If they killed him, good for them, but they would make him a hero. Hallam's goose would be just as cooked. Jurado and Leadbetter knew what to do if he was out of the picture. Quintero would back them. He knew where his interests and his duty lay. Chapel inhaled, taking the air's tension deep into his lungs.

In the distance, sirens. So many these days. He wondered who was being arrested now. The momentum of the police and the FBI was huge. Good luck to Hallam trying to stop it. There would be arrests, and arrests, and arrests, until the country felt safe again. By that time, every enemy of the state, down to the last cranky letter writer, would be neutralized. The wailing Chapel heard was the purifying sound of a slate being wiped clean. It was the cry of a nation's rebirth.

For a few moments more, Chapel listened to his work, and knew that it was good. Then he walked down the sidewalk to his car and got in. No one took a shot at him. You can't, he thought. You killed my pick for president, but there's always another one to take his place. God Bless America.

He started the engine.

"He's moving," Luzhkov reported.

"Track him," Blaylock ordered.

Luzhkov gave Chapel a couple of blocks' lead and pulled out. "Remember," said Blaylock's voice in his ear, "don't make it too clumsy."

"Understood." The delicate balance of disinformation. Luzhkov wanted to be spotted. He wanted his own tail. But if he were too obvious a bait, the play would fail. His mistake had to look legitimate. He kept one eye on Chapel, the other on his rear-view mirror. Nothing at first. Chapel turned south onto Thirty-fourth Street. Luzhkov followed, watched for another set of lights to make the turn behind him. No joy. There might not be anyone, but if there was, and he hung back with his lights off, Luzhkov could easily miss him. Or the potential tail didn't know yet that Luzhkov was there. Ahead, Chapel kept on the straight and narrow. Luzhkov waited for the opportunity to make the fumble. It came as Chapel was crossing O Street. The light went orange while Luzhkov was still a few car lengths from the intersection. He stepped on the gas and barrelled through half on the red. Behind him, a car leapt forward, but then stopped, a bit too quickly at the light. Clumsier than me, Luzkhov thought. His own move must have been a surprise. So now his presence was known and would be tracked. Good.

Chapel led the convoy to M Street, where he turned east. It wasn't until that turn that Luzhkov was able to make a solid ID of that car that was following him. He called Blaylock. "Got me a live one?" she asked.

"Yes."

"What's your evaluation?"

"He's careful, but he's an amateur or a bit rusty."

"I don't think tailing was one of the SOA's graduate courses. Where are you now?" When Luzhkov told her, she said, "Let me know if Chapel takes Pennsylvania."

A minute later, Chapel did just that. "He's probably looking for PR advice," Blaylock said. "Confirm his stop, then head for the decoy point. I'll be there."

Luzhkov hung back a bit further. Chapel's route was becoming obvious. Luzhkov could afford to be less conspicuous, look smarter, more professional, more convincing. He followed the enemy into the West End. Chapel's car pulled up to the curb outside the expected apartment building on L Street. Blaylock had already placed assets at this location. It was under all the surveillance it needed. Luzhkov drove past as Chapel mounted the steps to the main entrance. Luzhkov muttered, "Bang." He carried on. Behind him, the sheep followed, waiting to be fleeced.

The waves of security Chapel moved through worked against the new home's anonymity. They flagged the high value of the potential target. He wondered if Charlotte Taber had thought of that. His impression was that she wasn't thinking consequences and implications out too carefully these days. He had his doubts about her usefulness. His hope: that the talent was too strong to be completely buried. That it could still be tapped.

He had to get past two guards outside her apartment door and another one just inside before he could speak to the woman herself. She had changed. She was still Charlotte Taber in the same way that she was still nominally the undersecretary of state for Public Diplomacy. She hadn't really been either since the assassination attempt at the State Department. Her face was an eggshell-fragile collection of lines and hollows. She greeted Chapel with a nothing voice. Beyond her skin, there was only void. When she walked into the living room, the air rushed to fill her vacuum. What a waste, Chapel thought. She'd been the best. He had admired her work when they were allies, had bled from it when Sam Reed had used her against him. Now she didn't look capable of writing a used car commercial.

"What do you want?" she asked. She stood at a liquor cabinet, pouring Scotch onto ice. The bottle was two-thirds empty. She didn't offer Chapel a glass. In the opposite corner of the room, the TV was tuned to the Shopping Channel. The volume was just low enough to be incomprehensible. White noise company.

"I was hoping to convince you to do your job," Chapel said. He sat on the couch, uninvited.

She snorted, knocked the glass back. Ice clinked in unison

with her bracelets. "You think the job is still going to be mine this time tomorrow?"

"Your duty, then."

Another snort, turning into an exhausted laugh. "Christ, you really love that word, don't you?"

"I love my country."

"I love my life. So whatever you want, Joe, shove it up your ass."

"I'm not asking you to take any risks."

"I help you with whatever this is, and my neck isn't on the chopping block? How are you going to pull that miracle off?"

"You would only be working in an advisory capacity. You give me your expertise. I put it into action. If you don't want any credit—"

"Or blame," she put in.

Chapel ignored her. "Your name doesn't ever have to come up." He tapped a rhythm on the briefcase at his feet, drawing her attention to it.

She finished her drink, poured another. "Tell me what you're after."

"I want to nip Daniel Hallam in the bud. And don't tell me you can't see how dangerous he is."

Taber said, "What's in the briefcase."

"Information about him. Dots that I want you to show me how to connect publicly."

"And whatever I tell you now, it's all your idea, right?"

"Right."

She sighed. Chapel thought he saw a stirring ember of strength. "Show me what you have," she said.

Good enough.

Luzhkov tracked his tail. The other car was staying with him. It was staying in the background, but its persistence made it stand out. Somebody was determined. Somebody was going to make good with the boss by finding out where the opposition hung out and slept. Somebody was jut the right kind of sucker. Luzhkov led the mark from the West End to downtown, backtracked to Foggy Bottom, and over to downtown again, making a show of precaution, of taking turns without signalling and running lights, the standard trick bag for throwing off followers. He was playing the role of the man who didn't think he was being tailed but was playing things safe anyway. Then he pulled into the parking lot of a Marriott. He walked into the lobby. He and Blaylock had made sure the decoy was a convincing one. He even had a room. He took the elevator up to the twentieth floor, unlocked his room and sat there until Blaylock called. "I'm on him," she said. The baton had been passed.

Blaylock hung up and followed Luzhkov's tail. She weighed options. If her target reported what he thought he'd discovered, it might be in her interests to maintain the fiction that the Marriott was a base for a bit longer. It was important that Chapel believe he had the advantage in the surveillance game. The other option was to see that Chapel never received a report at all. The trick there: make sure he didn't think information of his own had been compromised. Decisions, decisions. She'd let the battlefield dictate her course.

Her target was either cocky or playing the same game her team was. After sailing past the hotel, he stuck to major thoroughfares and straight lines. He was a man heading for home, not trying to shake a tail. The odds that he was leading her to a decoy safe house too? Minute. The coincidence would be too close to farce. The driver headed to the city's southeast, kept moving south. He turned off Capitol Street into the Congress Heights neighbourhood. Blaylock liked the location. It was ethnically diverse, so Chapel's boys wouldn't stand out. It was the kind of urban mixed bag she used herself. Some gentrification was taking root, but poverty and the hard rules of the street weren't going away yet. The target took one of the more depressed streets. It was an extended cul-de-sac. Runners hung from telephone wires. Streetlights were out. The wildlife on the sidewalk was sparse, most of it slumped deep into a fix, or twitching-begging for the next one. The car slowed. Blaylock hung well back, turned her lights off. At the moment, they were the only cars moving on the street. She crawled forward, a shark cruising the summer night. Ahead, brake lights flared. She stopped a hundred yards away. There was just enough light coming from the windows of the skin-shedding houses and sullen walk-ups for her to see which house the man walked up to. It was the biggest one on the block. It might once have had ambitions. Two storeys high, obese in its spread on the lawn, its bulk was surrounded by the wreckage of a veranda.

Taps on her driver's side window. Tock, tock, tock of a gun barrel against glass. She turned her head. The man was in his early twenties. His eyes were dead. His body was steroid-huge. Behind him, a posse of the discarded and violent waited. The battlefield was dictating.

Blaylock scanned, evaluated. Her right hand was resting on the seat. It brushed against the bulge of the pistol in her jacket pocket. She had plenty of ways of taking the threat down.

None of them was good for maintaining camouflage. She noted the way the man's squad was positioned. She counted six. The three nearest were moving to surround her car, but the others were hanging loose on the sidewalk and lawn of the house on her left. She spotted yet another man sitting, arms, folded, on the porch. She lowered the window.

"You be lost, honey," the man said. His tone was cold menace.

"Then maybe you could point me on my way," she replied, as if he'd offered to help.

She saw him blink. She'd thrown him. The absence of screams and quavering didn't compute. He recovered. He snickered. "Oh yeah, bitch, I show you the way I like it." He yanked open the door. "Get the fuck out."

"You'll show me the way you like it," Blaylock repeated. "Okay, that's a bit forced as a comeback, but I guess it'll do." She climbed out, stretched, her shirt pulling across her breasts. She triggered a ripple of confusion around her. She wasn't playing by the rules. Not fair. "You taking me inside?" she asked.

Ting. She was sure she heard it: somewhere, a pin dropping into the silence. The boys weren't up to ad libbing. They believed in sticking to the script. The gunman tried to steer things back on course. "Hell yeah, we're taking you inside," he said. Four of the gang closed in around her. Three started checking out the car. The tough on the porch didn't move. He was impassive as mud.

One of the boys standing near her, his breath hot against her neck, said, "Sweet ass."

One of boys at the car said, "Sweet ride." Then he started

jumping on the hood. Another had a baseball bat. He went to work on the windshield.

This was just the kind of ruckus that might draw the wrong set of eyes. "So," Blaylock said, "we going in or not?" She brushed past the man in front of her. Startled, he stepped aside and let her go up the sidewalk. At the porch, in shadow now and unrecognizable for anyone watching from the safe house, she paused and spoke to the seated figure. "Nice place. Yours?"

The man slowly rolled his eyes her way. He didn't answer. In the murk, she could just make out faded tattoos against the needle-tracked pallor of his skin. A sheathed hunting knife hung from his belt. He stroked its length. "Let me know how that works for you," Blaylock said, and mounted the porch. She pulled open the screen door and marched inside the house, the gang members at her heels. On the street, the demolition of her car gathered momentum.

The entrance corridor was narrow. It stank of shit and piss and rotting food and old beer. It was dark. It was dank. The walls pressed in like mossy skin. Despair and old sins oozed from the plaster. The house was a sore. Blaylock stopped halfway down the hallway. It was a fine bottleneck. There wasn't room for two people abreast. She held her arms loose, slightly away from her body. She waited for her cue.

"Not so full of yourself now, are you, bitch?" the ringleader said behind her. He poked her lower back with the gun. "Better be ni—"

He didn't finish. He'd given Blaylock her cue with the nudge. She whirled, trapping his gun hand against her body with her left arm. Her right hand straight-fingered a blow to his throat and closed it forever. She leapfrogged over his body as it slumped. The man behind him was outlined by the faint light of the street. He didn't see her kick. She shattered his kneecap. He grunted, caught her fist in his gut, lost any air to cry out. He fell, and she brought her heel down on his temple. Blood sprayed the dark. Two more, and still minimal noise. The boys were starting to react, but were confused and slow. She had her knife out and slit the next man's throat while he fumbled for the gun tucked into the back of his jeans. Her movement was a wide slice, and her arm was on the way back in as the last man lunged for her. She angled the knife and buried it in his ear. The air in the house had turned slaughter-house-humid with blood and voided bowels. She hauled the corpses deeper into the house, stacked the flesh cordwood in the living room. She returned to the hallway, knife in hand, gun in her pocket as a loud last resort, and waited, the dark within the dark.

The car was good and trashed. "Lighting up," Roaster warned.

Dickerkiller and Road Ice stood back. Roaster stuffed a rag into the gas tank, touched his Zippo to one end, and they watched the show. Good flames on this one. The thought crossed Road Ice's mind that they could have sold the Corolla. He didn't care. Rich bitch tourist had to be taught a lesson. He turned to look at the house, where the lesson was being taught. Or supposed to be. It was taking longer than usual. Way quiet, too. "Blitz," he called to the sentinel. "'Sup with those guys?"

Blitz made the effort to turn his head and look at the door. When it had nothing to say to him, he slow-moed his gaze back to Road Ice. He shrugged. "Shit," he said, very slowly, and with absolute unconcern.

"Well go check it out, man," Road Ice told him, exasperated. Always had to spell everything out for the dumb asshole. "Find out when it's our turn."

Blitz's face spoke his martyrdom. He rose to his feet, the weight of the universe on his shoulders, and shuffled into the house.

"Dipshit," Dickerkiller snickered.

"Watch him take his turn now," Roaster said.

Road Ice rolled eyes with them. The minutes ticked by. The crew started to laugh. The bastard was living up to lazy form. The car's pyre was boring now. "Fuck this, them, and the world," Road Ice said. He marched up to the house, the other two right behind him. Their turn, for Chrissake. He threw open the door, almost tripped over a shoe someone had left at the entrance. He bit his tongue hard as his right foot jarred against the floor. The house hadn't had electricity for over a year. He still wasn't used to it. He moved down the darkness of the corridor. Black closed around him like a womb. "Yo!" he called. "You dogs done yet?"

There was no answer. Roaster stumbled over the same shoe, and that was the only noise. The house was still. Road Ice paused. Something wrong. Where were the sounds of struggle? Where was the muffled weeping? Where was the rhythm of the gangbang? His eyes strained against the dark. It pressed back.

Then the dark bit him. It slashed into his gut with poison fangs. The pain was deep and long, a burn that sliced from right to left. His legs turned to water. As he fell, the dark bit him again, in the throat this time. Warm spray tried to comfort the silver agony. He couldn't breathe. His chest bucked. His head lolled, turning his eyes back towards the entrance. His vision was turning grey. The only light was a flickering sheen from the fire outside. He saw shapes he knew were Dickerkiller and Roaster. He saw another shape that was the biting part of the dark. He watched it tear into his friends. It mauled them. They went down. Eyes badly blurred now, chest giving up the fight for oxygen. The warm bath of his blood felt good. The burning in his stomach and throat was receding into a distant core of ice. He was still afraid. He was afraid of dying. He was afraid of the moving patch of darkness. It towered over him, blocking out the light. He moved his lips, grasping for a plea or a prayer. The shape noticed. It crouched over him. It said, "Quiet." It touched his throat again. The ice flared bright, and then the dark was everything.

Blaylock found a collection of flashlights at the base of the stairs. She grabbed one, used it as little as possible to avoid signalling activity to outsiders. She moved the bodies to the basement. She checked the pockets, found some cash, knives, and a set of car keys. She threw a tarp over the corpses. If her forces used the house for long, they'd need a better solution, but she didn't think Chapel would wait much before acting against Hallam. She looked out the back. There was a pickup sitting on the gravel that substituted for a lawn. Beyond it, an alley. She could come and go without alerting Chapel's safe house.

She climbed into the truck, started it up and drove off. She was pleased with the night's work.

23

His first day in the Oval Office as the lord of the manor. Hallam was reluctant to take the seat behind the desk. The presence of the last two occupants still filled the room. Presidents Campbell and Reed, both consumed by fire. The older history of the room faded into a sad background. There was no room here for anything other than current upheavals. The Republic was fracturing beneath his feet. His job was to halt the movement of the tectonic plates. Piece of cake. Nothing like being at the right place and time of history.

He wanted to go home.

But there was no home. Home was where he stood, like it or not. Home was duty. Home was under siege. Home needed protecting. He needed protecting, too, from more targets than he could identify and whose motivations he didn't understand. Trust was the currency of fools in this town, but he had never felt the need for it more acutely. It was a need he had to trample. Survival demanded he do so. There were so many demands. He had to answer some of them now. One was that he meet with Ryan Cracknell, director of the FBI.

So Daniel Hallam sat. He felt the mantle of power settle around his shoulders like lead wings. He pressed the intercom and asked that Cracknell be sent in. The director entered the office. He was in his late fifties, soft with age but not fat. He had a tiny fringe of grey hair left that he kept cut close to his scalp. He wore bifocals. His heavy-lidded gaze was caution and evaluation. They shook hands, and Cracknell took a seat. He clasped his hands. "I'm sorry that our first meeting isn't a happier occasion," he said. His voice was soft, as concealing as his gaze.

"Can't be helped," Hallam replied. "These aren't happy times. How can I help you?"

"I have a few questions about the death of the Speaker of the House."

"Isn't it a bit unusual for the FBI director to be taking an active role in the investigation?"

Cracknell unclasped his hands an inch, rejoined them. That was his shrug. "The situation is an unusual one."

"True enough."

"It's also a delicate one."

"I appreciate that. And the fact that you do. So what did you want to know?"

Cracknell settled more comfortably in his chair. "You're aware that, as far as we can tell, your meeting with Senator Pratella was the last one he had before he died."

"Yes." The cold stone in his gut hadn't budged since he'd made the connection.

"And you know that the cause of death was a toxic chemical applied to his hands."

"Yes. I was tested yesterday to see if I had come into contact with the same poison."

Cracknell nodded. That wasn't news to him. "I'd like to know more about the woman who was at this meeting with you."

And now he was dancing with extreme caution, calculating risks to himself and to the country, hoping that seeing their interests as mutual wasn't a selfish delusion. "I thought she was a reporter." That was true, as long as the past tense was respected. "Isn't she?"

"We're not sure. We've found plenty of articles with that byline, but nothing else. Those pieces are the only evidence that a Jennifer Baylor even exists."

Hallam frowned. "She had to get paid somehow."

"Yes, and she was. I wasn't entirely clear. There are all sorts of accounts and PO boxes in her name, but it's a closed circuit of mutually reinforcing, and thus useless, evidence. Every institution we've consulted relied on another to confirm her good standing. But there is no primary source. No birth certificate, for instance."

"What about fingerprints?"

"She left none here, none in your office, none anywhere."

"I see." Carefully now, carefully. "Do you think she's the assassin?"

"I don't know. But we don't have even a glimmer of a lead otherwise. She shook the Speaker's hand, didn't she?"

"Yes."

"What about yours?"

"Yes, she did." Big rush of relief. She wasn't the killer. He wasn't connected.

Cracknell looked unhappy at the enormous hole that was opening in his theory. "You're sure?"

"Positive. It was the first thing we did when we met that day. I remember thinking that her hands were unusually dry."

"Then Peter Pratella's and your hands are the only things she touched." Cracknell's own hands unlocked, then jammed together in a tighter vise. Thought travelled behind his unmoving eyes. At last he asked, "Would she have had any opportunity to apply the chlordane to her palms?"

"Without dying herself?"

"I'm not worried about that, for the moment. She may be dead. This might have been a suicide mission." Cracknell looked at him. "Well?"

He thought for a moment. He remembered the woman putting on hand lotion. The sense of relief shrivelled. His calculations hit lightspeed. If he told the truth, there would be a hard link between himself and the presumed killer. There was no love lost between the FBI and the CIA, but that wouldn't stop Chapel from having that nugget of information within minutes of Cracknell leaving the room. If he lied, he was protecting a murderer to save his political skin, and if it ever became known that he lied, his crash would be a Hindenburg and destroy everything he was trying to save. "No," he said. "Not that I noticed." He lied. He lied because he still believed the woman about Chapel. He lied because the enemy of his enemy might yet be his country's friend. This was what he told himself. This was what he hoped very much he could believe.

Cracknell nodded, unhappier by the second. He stood up. "All right then. You'll let me know if something comes to mind?"

"Of course."

"Thank you, Mr. President."

They shook hands again. Hallam looked for significance in Cracknell's grip and in his gaze. The man's eyes shut him out. He made another decision. "There is something," he said. "The reason why she said she wanted to meet with the Senator Pratella in the first place."

"Oh?" Nothing given away.

"It's about Joe Chapel," Hallam said, flying blind and diving in.

In the House of Representatives, Congressman Christopher Davidson of Utah claimed the floor. Meredith Leadbetter had phoned him the night before and called in a favour. What he was about to do would hardly wipe his slate clean. She knew where too many of his skeletons were buried. He didn't mind. When she'd told him what she wanted, he would have paid her for the opportunity. He cleared his throat. He adjusted his glasses. He kept his eyes on the papers he held. He didn't deviate a single comma from the speech Leadbetter had dictated to him. He cleared his throat a second time. The history of the moment was drying his mouth. He began to speak. There were too many serious questions surrounding the death of Senator Pratella, he explained. Too many that spoke to the matter of trust in the commander-in-chief. And so Congressman Davidson called for the impeachment of President-Designate Daniel Hallam.

David Annandale

"I want your resignation," Hallam said to Chapel.

"You can't have it," Chapel answered, and hung up.

Blaylock watched. She watched Chapel's safe house. When she wasn't heading the surveillance team there herself, she had Luzhkov, Vandelaare and Mark Vrenna spell each other off. When she wasn't at the Congress Heights house, she watched the political battle. She couldn't see all of the actual moves and countermoves, but she could see the explosions. They spread their flames across the media. The challenge there wasn't too little information; it was too much. She had to work to filter out the noise from the intelligence. The trick wasn't just deducing what Chapel and Hallam's respective plays were. The trick was anticipating what each would do next, and that depended on the currents of the battlefield, on who was winning.

She and Flanagan turned their Watergate room into a media centre. TV, radio, Internet, papers: a 24-7 info-barrage. They tracked multiple targets. One was the investigation into Pratella's assassination. There was plenty of shouting about Hallam having been the last to see him alive. There was no mention of her. "You'd think they'd be looking pretty hard for you," Flanagan said.

"They are." Either the agents of retribution were playing their cards close to their chest, or they were genuinely confused. It was in Hallam's interest to cast doubt on her involvement, since that would clear him, too. Chapel wouldn't be looking for her if he thought she was dead.

As the day moved towards the six o'clock news climaxes, Meredith Leadbetter spoke out. "President Hallam has lost the trust of the American people and their elected representatives," she said, with the Lincoln Memorial as a backdrop. "If he truly loved this country as much as he says he does, he would step down and spare the nation this prolonged agony."

"Ouch," Flanagan commented. "That's a pretty good one."

"She had to say something while she was still secretary of state," Blaylock said.

"What do you mean?"

"Hallam has time on his side. The impeachment process will take months. In the meantime, he replaces the cabinet."

"Getting his appointments ratified won't be easy. That will take time too."

"Yes, but the current slate will be wiped clean this time tomorrow. Bet on it."

"Which means…"

"Which means Chapel has to win right away or he loses."

Leadbetter's speech didn't tip the balance. By eight, another narrative had begun to surface: Daniel Hallam as the underdog, surrounded by a cabinet entirely composed of political enemies. "Americans love an underdog," Flanagan said.

"Chapel has to move soon," Blaylock said. She left for Congress Heights.

Chapel hit Fort Benning. He had marching orders for Quintero. He had a favour to beg from Bill Eastman. He met the camp's commander at his digs again. The night was beautiful, but Eastman wasn't stargazing. He ushered Chapel inside. He had his shutters closed. No prying eyes. The visitor wasn't a point of pride. "You're letting me down, Joe," Eastman said. He leaned against a wall, did not ask Chapel to sit, did not offer a drink.

"This isn't over yet."

"It looks like it might be. I didn't let you and your boys camp here just to get that goddamned liberal into office. Your work is messy."

"So was the War of Independence."

Eastman snorted. "There was a time when I might have bought that line of thinking. Point of fact, that time was not that long ago, when I was talking to a good man under the stars just outside. But that good man proved me wrong. The Hamptons get nuked and what's to show for it? The same old media war." He shook his head. "Don't mind telling you, I'm in something quite a bit like despair."

"Don't be."

"Why not? For all your effort, look who's in office now."

"He's about to leave it."

"That right? The hand of God going to reach down and smack him?"

"No. Mine will."

That raised a chuckle. "Want to believe you, Joe. Really do."

"Then do. And listen for the revolution. I do need more from you, though."

"Such as?"

"Uniforms. Materiel. Vehicles."

Eastman's eyes narrowed. "That's funny."

"No joke. Get them for me, Bill."

"Forget it."

"Not likely."

"I don't want anything more to do with this."

"Too late. We're going down together if it comes to that. You can't be so dense you don't realize that."

Eastman turned away from Chapel and walked to a corner of the room. He raised a fist. Chapel though he was going to punch the wall. He did, but in slow, weak movements that admitted defeat. "You can't have any of my men," he said.

"I don't want them." Chapel didn't trust the ability of any American soldiers to obey the orders that would be given.

Eastman faced Chapel again. He drew himself up. Hang on to that pride. "You take what you want, and then I want you and your men off my base. We clear?"

"Understood." Chapel saw a man grabbing at fig leaves to cover his ass. Pathetic. Understandable.

"What's going to happen?"

Chapel snorted. He didn't answer. You don't want to know, he thought. You don't have the guts for it.

"I want to be involved," Flanagan had said. "The sidelines suck."

A slight twitch in Blaylock's eyelid. Unreadable. Hurt? Worried? What? No way of knowing. Something bothering her, but nothing she would confide out of consideration for the war strategy. Nothing was allowed to interfere with that. Particularly nothing so trivial as her emotions. "You're moving off the sidelines," she said. "You're going to be our public face."

"Our what?" Wondering about the wisdom of his demand.

And now he was being hustled through the studio, on his way to cock-block Chapel, if he could. Give the president enough of an excuse to take him down publicly. Flanagan had called the network less than an hour ago. His call had met with an enthusiastic reception and whirlwind-speed reaction. He turned around, and there was limo waiting for him outside the Watergate. (Nice location, the flack rid-ing with him had said. We should try to work it in.) Turned around again, and he was in make-up. Another turn, and he was on his way to the set. It was the simple desk-and-black-background combo that signified serious discussion even if the topic du jour was celebrity prison weekends. Flanagan waited backstage for his cue. He watched the monitors. He saw tickertape infobytes scroll by under the host. The music of urgent but cool apocalypse played. The director gave him his cue, and he walked to his seat. The host was wrapping up the introduction. He spoke with his elbows on the table, hands clasped, leaning towards the camera with avuncular intensity. "With us now is Michael Flanagan, acting CEO of Integrated Security." He turned to face Flanagan over the desk. His expression shifted slightly, became a different con-figuration of granite. Now he was radiating deep concern that could turn into accusation on a hair. "Mr. Flanagan, remind our viewers what InSec does."

"We are the world's foremost arms dealer."

The host made a noise a bit like a snort, suggesting cynical surprise. "You don't believe in sugarcoating, do you?"

"What we do shouldn't be sugarcoated."

"I should say not. InSec has had its share of headlines in the recent past hasn't it?"

"Indeed it has, and before you ask, no, they haven't been pleasant. But I'd like your audience to know… I'd like America to know that there has been a change of corporate governance and corporate philosophy at InSec. We are a good corporate citizen, and that is why I'm here tonight."

"Yes." The host pretended to consult the papers in front of

him. "You're here to present some very disturbing information, as I understand it."

"That's right. Recently, we received orders for some unusually large shipments. The weapons were to be delivered to various locations within the United States. This order raised alarms because, for very good reasons, InSec is prohibited from engaging in such traffic within the country unless it is with an official body."

"And no such body placed these orders?"

"No. So we have recently discovered."

"Do you know who actually did?"

"Our indications are that the orders originated from rogue elements within the intelligence community." Flanagan hoped Joe Chapel was watching. He had a mental picture of the man choking on his drink.

The host jumped on the question. No pause. No moment for the audience to digest Flanagan's statement. Instead, a picking up of the pace. Slam home that terror. "You realize how serious that accusation is?"

"I wish I didn't have to make it."

"So what rogue elements are these?"

"We're still working on the evidence. We want something that will stand up in court before being more specific."

"So you're not going to name names."

"Not at the present, no."

"All right." The host shifted in his seat, put a bit more weight on his left elbow. He was signalling a pretence of a change in subject, one that wasn't supposed to fool anyone. "Let me ask you something else. Is it true that Joe Chapel has shown a lot of interest in InSec?"

"Yes. For a while, he was a frequent visitor at our headquarters in New York." Are you watching, Joe? Do you see what I'm doing to you? Flanagan was enjoying himself. He didn't have Blaylock's war genius or Luzhkov's training. He survived in the field more thanks to dumb luck than anything else. But here, he was finding a gift. He felt the currents of nuance and opportunity course through his nervous system like an electric field. He felt powerful. He loved it.

It still wasn't enough.

"And what were the reasons for Mr. Chapel's visits?"

"At first I assumed he was there for official reasons, during the transition period after the death of Arthur Pembroke, our founder."

"You then became a subsidiary of Kornukopia."

"That's correct."

"Which has since been revealed as a corporate front for Russian organized crime."

"We are no longer affiliated with them. But yes, that's right."

"And what was Joe Chapel's role in all this?"

The perfect question. Flanagan worked to keep his face serious and worried. He wanted to high-five the host for his phrasing. Not "Was Chapel involved?" Not "Has Chapel been on-site since Kornukopia?" No. The questions assumed guilt. Beautiful. "I wish I knew," Flanagan said. His voice shook slightly. It was with excitement, but it would pass as the anxiety of a deeply troubled man. He heard the *boom* of the torpedo hitting home.

Chapel felt the torpedo. He caught the interview, saw the best part of his media war take a serious hit. This ship's hull was gutted. Another day, and important allies would swim away, lifeboats or not. He frowned at Flanagan's image. He hadn't tagged the man for a player. The move had someone else's fingerprints all over it. The thought that she might be alive sent spider legs of dread down his spine.

He blinked the nightmare away. There was no problem. He didn't need more than another day. He'd checked schedules. The Hail Mary was on for tomorrow. He would save the country, whether it wanted him to or not.

24

"Sir," Gary Bankhead said, "I really must advise against—"

"Against what?" Hallam interrupted. "Against leaving the White House? Against setting foot outside? Would you be happier if I holed up in Cheyenne Mountain? And for how long? The length of my term?" The Secret Service agent said nothing. Hallam saw a man with the delicacy not to contradict his boss in the middle of a high rant. Hallam felt small. He calmed down. "I'm sorry," he said. "I know you're doing your job, and I'm also sorry I can't make it any easier."

"Not even for a little while?"

That made him chuckle. Sadly. "I wish I could. I know there are risks. But there are risks too in having the Chief Executive seen to be cowering." Anyway, he thought, the current attacks are refreshingly non-violent. Chapel might bring him down, but he was trying to do so the old-fashioned, political way. "Do you understand?"

Bankhead nodded. "Yes, Mr. President."

"Thank you, Gary. In return, I promise to behave. Do what

you need to do to secure the site." But there was no way he was cancelling the day's event. He was speaking to veterans at Arlington Cemetery. Ducking out would be a huge gift to Chapel and Leadbetter. His standing with the vet demographic, and, by extension, those who revered them, was shaky enough as things stood. So he was going for a drive.

He told himself he wasn't nervous.

"Are we using uniforms?" Maldonado asked.

Quintero shook his head. "The man doesn't want to give the wrong idea just yet." Generic fatigues and balaclavas were the order of the day.

Blaylock was at the Congress Heights house. She was there to relieve Vrenna. "What have the boys been up to?" she asked.

"Not much."

"How many of them?"

"Five. They're being very low-profile."

Five was a small number for a house that size. Chapel could stash a much larger contingent than that in the place. There had been up to two dozen the day before. A change in pattern. Something up. "Let's fortify this position," she said. "I want twice as many personnel here as they have at all times."

A big day was happening, and it began with a parade, as all big days should. The parade wasn't strong in floats or fun, but it was long and it snarled traffic in a wide area. Police sealed off the intersections along the parade's route. They planted sharpshooters on top of buildings to pick off any party crashers who might also be thinking of roofs. Sewer access hatches were welded shut. Nobody was going to rain on the parade.

The parade left the White House. It looked like an aggressive funeral procession. Police motorcycles and cruisers led the way and brought up the rear. In between: a black python of secret service vehicles and limousines. One of them held the man in whose honour the parade was held. He sat behind tinted windows and felt both invisible and vulnerable. He rode in deep air conditioning, and sweated.

Luzhkov passed the word to Blaylock that the parade had begun. He stood on the sidewalk on Pennsylvania Avenue, watched the fun go by, was frustrated. He heard similar tension in Blaylock's voice. "Cross your fingers." All she could say, he knew. The move was Chapel's. They could only react, and hope they didn't have too far to run to catch up.

Flanagan appeared at Luzhkov's shoulder. Luzhkov nodded to him. "Nice work last night," he said.

"Thanks." Flanagan watched the stream of black cars. "You think something's going to happen?"

Luzhkov shrugged. "You tell me."

"What are you going to do if Chapel tries something?"

"Stop him. If we can."

"That's the plan?"

"That's the plan." It was all the plan there could be until Chapel let everyone know what sort of game was being played.

"Jen's doing improv again." Flanagan's smile was small, rueful, fond.

"Yes," Luzhkov agreed. He read a need in Flanagan, couldn't put a name to it yet.

"She's good at that."

"She is at many things."

"Too right." He cleared his throat, still looking at the street. "When it all goes down, I want in."

Luzhkov played for time and comprehension. "What do you mean?"

"I mean I want to be part of the action."

"Hasn't Jen given you a role?"

"That was the show. I want a combat role."

"Have you spoken to her about this?" First instinct: do *not* violate the chain of command. Second instinct, in perfect accord: do *not* stick your oar into a relationship.

"She wants me safe."

"Of course she does."

"But I want to help."

"You did last n—"

"That isn't what I mean." Flanagan sighed. He faced Luzhkov. There was something in his expression. It wasn't quite desperation, but it was travelling that road. "I have to be part of what she is." Not, "what she does," Luzhkov noticed. He was comfortable with English. He knew his way around. There were nuances and variations, though, that could throw him. He didn't grasp Flanagan's choice of words. He did hear the hunger in his tone.

Luzhkov remembered the nights in Petersfield, returning to the hotel from the hunt, high on combat adrenaline, and seeing the excluded hurt on Flanagan's face. The wince and worry on Blaylock's. "You aren't going to lose her," he said.

Flanagan's eyes dropped to the ground for a moment. "I know," he said. "Still. I need this."

"What do you want me to do?"

"Give me something. Improvise. You're good at that, too."

Chapel had left the planning in Quintero's hands. "This is your area," he'd said. "Do your thing."

"Any restrictions?" Quintero had asked.

"Just get it done."

"It will be messy."

"I think we're past worrying about that. Just do it."

So they were doing it. They pulled out of Fort Benning, for the last time, according to Bill Eastman. They hit the highway in a convoy of twenty LAV-25s. Six armed passengers in each armoured personnel carrier on top of the gunner, driver and commander. Most of the APCs were packing chain-gun turrets, but Quintero had spiced the mix with a few variants. The full contingent didn't go far. Quintero pulled them off the road, in the woods, within easy striking distance of the capital. He ordered his army to put itself undercover. He packed five civilian cars with troops and sent them off to Congress Heights. Maldonado prepared to head off in another direction with six of the LAVs. He saluted Quintero from his perch. "General," he said.

Quintero returned the salute. "Good luck, soldier."

Maldonado nodded. "Thank you for the honour of this mission."

"Teach them to respect us."

Grin. "I will."

He left, and Quintero prepared one more group.

Thirty minutes later, Maldonado's team, split into two, rumbled the streets of Washington and Arlington. Nothing subtle about his tour. Plain sight camouflage. Pairs of APCs roaring through the urban scene were an anomaly that registered as official. Civilians watched nervously and cleared the way. Police waved hail fellow well met, basking in reflected phallic glory. Security at the cemetery smiled at the arrival of extra help. Two of Maldonado's LAVs reached the Arlington Memorial Bridge on the cemetery side five minutes before the president's fleet was due. The audience of vets looked startled as they drove past. The third LAV held back a couple of minutes. Jose Cabezas was heading up the other team. Two in a pack, one in reserve. He came up behind the tail end of the escort. He didn't close distance until the bridge came into view.

The motorcade passed. Luzhkov checked in with Blaylock. "Follow," she told him. "I'll hook up with you." Luzhkov looked at Flanagan. "Where are you parked?" he asked. Flanagan pointed to a lot a block up. The car was closer than Luzhkov's. He made a decision, improvising. "All right," he said. "Let's go. You drive." He left the rest of the White House team in place. A judgment call. There were only a few men in the area; the White House was so well protected as a matter of course that neither he nor Blaylock could imagine it being a target. There was just enough personnel assigned here to keep track of comings and goings. There could still be some surprises in the president's absence. So only Luzhkov and Flanagan followed the parade. Just to see where it might be off to, and who might come to see it go by.

Blaylock signed off with Luzhkov. She thought for a moment. The house across the street all but empty. The president out in the open. Bad thoughts, bad thoughts. If I had Chapel's goals, what would I do to accomplish them? Worse thoughts. She turned to Vrenna. "Sorry, Mark. I need you to hold the fort here a while longer. You good?"

"Always."

"Thanks." She left, following the bad thoughts, the action, the thrill.

Hallam read over his speech. He took out a pen and made a couple of revisions. He didn't need the notes. He had the talk memorized. He could and would improvise as the spirit moved him. That was his strength. The more he played with the script, the stronger and more convincing his message became. Going over the speech, though, gave him something to do that wasn't looking out the window and imagining the horrors Gary Bankhead had put in his mind. He glanced up as they began to cross the Arlington Bridge. All six lanes were closed to traffic. It was a deserted runway on low arches, pointing straight to the cemetery and his rendezvous. He looked back down at his notes.

Then Bankhead said, "What the hell?"

Hallam's eyes front, full attention. "What is it?" The limousine's driver took his foot off the accelerator.

"I'm not sure."

Hallam squinted, made out two APCs blocking the far end of the bridge. "What are they doing?"

Bankhead shook his head. He lifted his radio, began to speak into it. As he did, he twisted around to look out the back windshield. He frowned. Alarmed, Hallam turned also. From the rear, two more APCs were heading their way. "They aren't part of the detail?" he asked.

"No," Bankhead answered. Radio up again, "Jimmy, come in please."

In Arlington Cemetery, Jimmy Paxton stood with three

members of his detail a hundred yards from the bridgehead. He stared at the two LAVs. He didn't understand the set-up. From a security point of view, their positions made no sense. And why were their turrets pointing in the motorcade's direction?

His radio squawked. Before he could respond, an engine roared behind him. He turned around. Another LAV was bearing down. It wasn't slowing down. Paxton tried to process and act. Too much disbelief slowed him down. He was in midleap when the vehicle ran him over, crushing chest and legs to pulp. He had a few final seconds of consciousness flooded with explosive pain. As his vision faded, he saw men pour out of the APC and open fire on the vets.

Blaylock kept in touch with Luzhkov as she drove. She made good time and joined up a few blocks away from the bridge. She frowned when she saw what car Luzhkov was in, and who was driving it. She pulled in behind them. She was about to order Flanagan to stop the car and get out. Then she heard an explosion. She accelerated past the two men, racing to war.

"Jimmy," Bankhead repeated. There was no answer. "Stop the car," he told the driver.

"What's happening?" Hallam asked. He cursed every brave word he had ever uttered. His palms were slick with terror.

Bankhead didn't answer. He frowned. He rolled his window down partway. From the direction of the cemetery, Hallam heard what sounded like gunshots. Lots of them, a popcorn rattle of lives being ended.

The first two explosions were in such unison they sounded like a single blast. Behind and ahead, an APC's turret spat fire. The lead and trailing cruisers blew up. Hallam's shoulders hunched in an instinctive, fruitless duck. In front, he saw the wreckage of the cruiser spin and cartwheel back along the motorcade. It clipped a motorcycle and sent it flying off the bridge. It came to a crushing stop on another car. The flames spread. The LAVs moved through them, spitting fury, shredding the motorcade. Hallam glanced back, saw the pincer movement, saw mechanized destruction plowing its way toward him.

"Get down!" Bankhead yelled.

"Why?" Hallam asked. No point. Judgment Day was upon him and his country.

The fireworks bloomed for Maldonado. His LAV was a modified version, the standard turret replaced with a TOW 2 anti-tank guided missile launcher. The LAV still packed an M240E1 machine gun, which was more than enough to turn any non-armoured vehicle into Swiss cheese, but he wanted a dramatic entrance. Nothing like a little shock and awe to cow the enemy. So he and Cabezas opened up with the big flourish, missiles slamming into their targets and breathing hell over the motorcade. Now the machine guns of all the advancing APCs were firing, puncturing metal and shredding flesh. The troops piled out and walked alongside the armour, staying low and taking down anyone who escaped the flaming cars. The bridge was one long kill zone. There was no way off. There was no way to escape the teeth of the trap.

Blaylock took in the scene, processed as she drove. Two LAVs in front of her, spewing lead and fire, a wall of troops marching. They were focused on the slaughter ahead of them. They weren't worried about their rear. She put pedal to the metal,

aimed for the space between the two vehicles. She undid her
seat belt. Ten yards from the machines, she opened her door
and threw herself out. She rolled hard, picking up sharp bruises
and bloody scrapes. The car slowed, but was still packing a
nice speed as it slammed into the soldiers. It veered left and
collided with a LAV, tangling wreckage and wheels. Blaylock
was on her feet and running for the right-hand vehicle. Her
SIG-Sauer P-228 was in her hand. The turret of the right LAV
was beginning to turn back. She flew over the final yards and
jumped onto the APC's chassis. She ducked around the barrel
of the launcher, shot the gunner in the face. She pushed his
body onto the road, took his position, rotated the turret to
face the other LAV. She sat low. The surviving troops were
recognizing her threat. The fire wasn't continuous. They were
still confused, not wanting to take out the rest of the LAV's crew
along with her, not sure who was manning the launcher. The
gunner on the other vehicle knew. As his driver fought with
the controls, reversing and pushing forward in an effort to be
rid of the wrecked car, he raced Blaylock to bring weaponry to
bear. He won by a second. Armour-piercing rounds slammed
into the turret. Something burned her right arm. Blaylock
fired back. Hers was bigger than his. The TOW launched and
exploded. The other LAV blew apart. The explosion washed
over the troops, searing with flames and tearing with shrapnel.
The force of the blast knocked Blaylock's LAV back. It rode a
wave of force, tilted and rolled on its side. It threw Blaylock
out of the turret. She flew over the parapet. The Potomac
beckoned.

The front half of the motorcade was demolished. Surviving agents looked for shelter behind smoking, blackened cars. Maldonado's men took some of them down. The others, the ones who didn't poke their heads up to try to fire back, were torn apart as armour-piercing and incendiary rounds ignored their cover. One limousine was largely untouched. Maldonado was closing in on it when the battle on the other side of the bridge went bad. He saw both LAVs fly away from each other, one of them a ball of flame. Trouble. He still had a few seconds to ignore the problem and complete the mission. He hopped from his LAV and ran with his troops for the president's limo.

He heard a helicopter rotor.

Luzhkov and Flanagan arrived at the bridge as Blaylock was jumping onto the LAV. Luzhkov was out of the car as she opened fire. Flanagan was two steps behind him. He ran towards the fray that blossomed electricity and adrenaline as it toppled into chaos. The fact that he was unarmed was a back-of-the-mind concern, easy to ignore. He saw the explosion. He saw Blaylock sail through the air. The fun leaked away.

Blaylock snatched at the railing. She hooked her elbow around it and arrested her fall. Her shoulder screamed. Her pistol fell. She dangled over the edge. She ignored the pain, brought her other arm up, and began to hoist herself. A soldier swung the stock of his rifle at her head.

Luzhkov saw threats multiply. Blaylock was at bay. The APC she'd been riding had righted itself. He saw men climbing back on to regain control of the firepower. Too many targets, all first priorities. He had his pistol out. In the corner of his eye, he saw Flanagan sprint for the bridge railing. He only had one priority. Luzhkov let him take it. He went for the APC. Choices made, there was no room even to hope they were the right ones. There was only survival and killing. That, and the roar of armed might overhead.

Maldonado crouched and threw himself against the side of the presidential limo. The AH-64 Apache came in low. Too low. It didn't have to. With its Hellfire antitank missiles, Hydra 70 rockets and 30 mm chain gun, it could wipe out everything on the bridge. So bad news: air support had been nearby for the motorcade. Good news: the pilot didn't know the score, saw only equipment that should have been friendly involved in combat, and didn't dare cut loose for fear of killing the president. So he was buzzing, for intimidation and intel.

Better news: no hesitations back at the heavy armour. His gunner on the LAV launched a TOW. The Apache was low and close enough. The target was big, the shot not that difficult, the missile guided. The gunner fired as the chopper crossed the bridge. The TOW hit and blossomed. The Apache spun, wild top, smoke tracing a billowing spiral. It slammed down near the opposite end of the bridge. Maldonado felt like he was bringing on the end of the world.

Blaylock reared back out of the arc of the rifle butt. It whiffed air. The soldier altered his swing and brought the blow down on her right arm. He didn't break bone, but he gave her ecstatic pain. Her arm spasmed and lost its grip. The extra weight tried to pop her left shoulder. The soldier tired of playing and reversed the gun, all business and business end. (Black silhouette of a helicopter in the corner of her eye.) A blur that was Flanagan collided with the soldier. (Explosion. Chaos and a giant flailing in the air.) Both men lost their balance. They teetered. Blaylock reached out.

(A whirlwind of flame and metal.)

The death of the Apache filled the world. Maldonado's ears contained nothing but roar. Still crouched, he yanked the passenger door of the limo open. He fired to the left and up. The Secret Service man lost his face all over the upholstery. Maldonado grabbed Hallam and hauled him out of the car. He dragged him to the sidewalk, glanced over the railing at the river below, and pitched the president over.

Flanagan flew. The storm of the helicopter's death launched him into the air. He was still grappling with the soldier. They grabbed each other in anger and fear as they dropped. The bridge wasn't a high one. The drop was a couple of storeys. Still long enough to make the wind whistle past Flanagan's ears and give him enough time to dread the impact. He also had enough time to see the cluster of Zodiacs that were gathering below. Hitting the water split him away from the soldier. The river punched the air from his body. His fall didn't stop. The river pulled him down. He flailed against his momentum, slowed it, forced himself not to breathe, even as blackout threatened. He rose. He could see daylight. His legs were columns of lead, but he kept them kicking. He broke surface and gasped, loving the air and the pain.

The struggle should have been enough. It wasn't. The current took him.

The bulk of the LAV sheltered Luzhkov from the crash blast. One of the attackers had crouched out of the way of the flames beside him. Luzhkov shot him and took his M-16. He stood and strafed the roof of the vehicle, taking down the gunner. He scrambled on board, reclaiming the firepower. He glanced over the scene as he settled behind the cannon. He couldn't see either Flanagan or Blaylock. A wall of flaming metal separated him from the rest of the bridge. There were only a few scattered soldiers left at this end, most of them caught out in the open between the crash and the APC. The ones who weren't dead were wounded, those who weren't wounded were dazed. He didn't need the cannon for them. He mowed them down with the rifle.

The driver was jerking the vehicle back and forth, trying to turn it around back toward town. Luzhkov shouldered the M-16, stuffed his pistol into his waistband and belly-crawled over the top of the LAV. He hung on to a grip, reached down and opened the driver's hatch. He took the pistol and blind-fired into the driver's compartment. The vehicle's movement stopped. Luzhkov dropped down, hauled the driver out, climbed in. He turned the LAV back in the direction it had been facing. He would mirror Blaylock's opening move, only this time with a serious vehicle. He floored the accelerator. He slammed through the wreckage of the Apache. His wheels bounced over metal and bodies. He emerged from a wash of flame and saw battle aftermath on the other side. Limousines guttered fire and smoke. Corpses lay by their false shelter. There were a number of soldiers still here, and they were dropping lines over the bridge. No civilians that he could see. No president. He swore, vowed to be the worst kind of sore loser. He barrelled down the bridge, dodging cars, and rode up on the sidewalk. He hugged the parapet. A number of the soldiers saw him coming. Some of them jumped into the river. A lot of them didn't have the chance. He ground them into the pavement, smeared them against the wall. He picked up more speed, driving for the two APCs at the other end of the bridge. Chaos was slowing down responses over there. One of their own charging at them was confusing. The fact that there was no fire coming from his vehicle didn't clear things up any for them. Their indecision worked for him. He drew nearer, saw shouting faces, pushed his luck as far as he could, put the LAV in neutral, opened the hatch and jumped to the ground. He rolled, bouncing. He stayed flat as stupidity and panic overtook indecision. An idiot with a jumpy trigger finger launched a TOW at the runaway. The hit was too big and too close. The fireball engulfed all three vehicles.

Hands grabbed Hallam as soon as he hit the water. They hauled him into the Zodiac. He lay in the bottom, sputtering. He saw smoke and explosions spread along the span of the bridge. Men went over. Some jumping, some rappelling down lines, some just falling. Those bodies hit the water and didn't surface. The other Zodiacs cruised to pick up the swimmers. Hallam coughed, grabbed the side of the boat and hauled himself up to a seated position. He was ignored. The boat's engine picked up volume and they began to move. Hallam looked at the river, thought about jumping, realized exactly how far he'd get, and gave up the idea. He held onto the fact that he hadn't been killed outright. These men wanted to keep him alive, at least for the moment. What he didn't know was how strong that desire was.

A disturbance in the water caught his eye. A man in civilian clothes was struggling to stay afloat. As the boat went past, still moving slowly, Hallam reached out and grabbed his hand. He began to haul him in. One of the soldiers turned to see what the added pull on the boat was about. He shifted his grip on his rifle, as if about to smash the butt against the man's head. Hallam glared at him. The soldier stared back. The contest stretched the seconds. Then the soldier shrugged and looked away. Hallam dragged the man on board. The boat picked up speed.

Blaylock weathered the blasts, kept her grip on the parapet. She looked below. She saw Zodiacs moving. She didn't see Flanagan. A terrible fear morphed into crimson rage. She watched the extraction operation. She tracked the currents of war, waited for the movement that would give her the flesh she wanted. She spotted the president, saw him pull somebody out of the water. She crushed the hope as soon as it flared. She couldn't afford the soft emotion. She identified her path, chose her tactics. The rage warmed her with anticipation. The last of the Zodiacs was going to pass beneath her. Five men in it. She let go of the railing with her right arm. She unsheathed her knife. The boat reached her position. She dropped. The air whipped past her in delight.

Perhaps the soldier in the rear of the boat sensed what was coming. It didn't matter. He looked up as she landed on him. The impact hurt, jarred up her legs and into her spine. But she was braced for it. He wasn't. His neck snapped, the *pop* loud as a gun, and his head went ragdoll. She rolled off the body and slashed her blade in a wide arc. She caught the next man in the belly, opened him up large. He emptied himself in a wide pool on the Zodiac's bottom, turning the surface slick. Then the shock of Blaylock's attack wore off, and the other three were lunging for her. The quarters were too close, and no one fired. Blaylock met one attack with one of her own, ramming her head into the man's shoulder. He spun and banged hard into his mate's side. They all went down in a tangle of limbs and smear of blood. The man Blaylock butted wound up on the bottom. She felt him thrash in panic, ignored his threat and stabbed up. She couldn't move her arm much, couldn't get the leverage for the killing stroke, but the blade cut meat. More blood poured into the darkness of the human knot. Hands that had been circling her throat relaxed. She kicked and stabbed, kicked and stabbed. The weight on her was oppressive. It was a constrictor's squeeze, and it stole her breath. There was nothing but black and warm wetness and bruising writhing. She felt her knife sink deep into something soft. Someone starting screaming, the sound high as a screeching cat's. The weight eased. She reared up, felt her skull smash a chin. She squirmed loose, was born into light again. The screaming solider was clutching his face. Blood poured from his punctured eye. He was no threat. One active man left. He struggled to stand along with her. One of his arms was hanging limp, huge red around the armpit. She shoved the knife into his throat. The man she'd been lying on stirred. She stood and stomped hard on his chest, caving in his rib cage. Bone killed his heart. There was only the screamer left. She kicked him over the side. His scream turned into a gurgle and he sank fast. She scavenged weapons, then heaved the other bodies overboard.

Pilotless, the boat was spinning in circles. Blaylock grabbed the steering and aimed the boat after the receding pack. She looked around for a counterattack, but none was coming. Her boat was the last, and she heard no more combat coming from the bridge. There was only smoke and the metal pop-corn sounds of ammunition cooking off. She opened up the throttle, trying to close distance. She wondered if, when she caught up, there would be anything left to fight for, except the catharsis of fire.

25

Luzhkov picked himself up. Wind leaned into the smoke, spreading it over the bridge. He jogged back towards the Washington end. He coughed, eyes tearing, as he ducked around wreckage and fire. He had to be out of the area before the cavalry descended, minutes and years late, with its big guns. He could hear approaching sirens. More than time to blend back with the civilian population in all its panic. Even as he pushed himself to cover the bridge's span faster, he worried about what came next. He didn't know whether either Blaylock or Flanagan was alive. If the operation was decapitated, he and the rest of Blaylock's army were going to face a hard retrenchment at a moment they couldn't afford. Chapel's pace had suddenly gone lightspeed.

He hadn't progressed far when the roar of a boat's engine cut through the smoke and his anxiety. He ran to the parapet. He could just make out the retreating Zodiacs, and one straggler speeding to catch up. The smoke was too thick for him to identify the pilot. He pulled his phone out as he started running again. Playing on hope more than hunch, he called Blaylock. He held the cell hard against his ear, as if driving it into his skull would raise the volume. He could barely hear the ringing over the crackle of flames. Then the ringing stopped. At first he thought he was getting nothing but silence, but when he put another burning limo behind him, and was in a trough of relative calm between the blazes, he heard Blaylock's voice say, "Viktor." He became aware of more noise now, a roar that was coming over the phone.

"Are you on the Zodiac?" he asked. He had to repeat himself.

"Yes. Hit the safe house. Hit it hard."

"You think that's where they're taking Hallam?" He ran past the ruins of the LAVs, tossing his pistol into the fire. No point getting caught with that on his person. The worst of the destruction and noise was behind him. He could hear her a bit better now as she shouted over the wake and the engine.

"It's the only lead we have. I'll try to follow."

"How big do we make this?"

"As big as you have to. Don't worry about subtlety now. Make sure you're strong enough to fight your way back out. Hold enough reserve for a second front. We might need it."

"Roger that." He heard her break the connection. He kept moving, was off the bridge now. There were people around, civilians all, and many of them were running too. Luzhkov thought about taking one of the abandoned cars, decided no. The streets were a study in frozen chaos. The sirens were growing louder by the second. He would be faster on foot. He noticed that not all the civilians were running away from the bridge. Some must have been blocks away when the battle happened, and they were rushing forward to see the proof that war had come to the city.

Flanagan coughed up some river water. He wiped his mouth, tasting filth and defeat.

"Are you all right?" the president asked.

"I guess." He looked around, took in the situation, realized that neither of them was all right in the least. The temptation was to sleep. No strength in his bones. He had to find some. There would be more fighting and pain ahead.

"Who are you?" Hallam wanted to know.

Flanagan lifted half of his mouth in a bitter smile. "Someone who was trying to save you." He lifted his hands. "How am I doing so far?"

The boat slowed down. Ahead, a large outlet pipe, over six feet in diameter, protruded from the riverbank. Its grill had been removed, and the soldiers were filing inside. The rats are going home, Flanagan thought. He worked to keep anger his dominant emotion. If he stayed furious, there wouldn't be room for fear or despair, or even the hope that might bring worse through disappointment. Staying mad was easy. Doing something with the rage, not so much. There was no way to fight. He and Hallam lacked numbers, training, weapons. Not a chance. But he stayed angry. As he and the president were bundled from the Zodiac and into the pipe, he started looking for the chance. It didn't have to be for escape. If he saw a way to bury them all, he would take it.

Blaylock saw the boats bunch up, saw the riverbank swallow up men. She slowed down, then cut the engine. She flattened herself in the Zodiac and watched. If she was seen, she wasn't noticed. She waited until the extraction was almost complete. She thought about confined spaces. She thought about fish in a barrel. When there were only a couple of crews left to pull out, she started the engine again and closed in, giving her enemies plenty of time to think themselves safe and gone, but not so much time that she would lose the scent in the maze they were entering. The last of the men vanished thirty seconds before she arrived at the cluster of Zodiacs. She nosed hers through the drifting boats until she was underneath the pipe. She slung her pilfered M-16 over her shoulder, stuffed her jacket pockets with clips. There were several flashlights in the boat's kit. Nice of the boys to leave that for her. She took one and tossed it up into the dark. She stood, reached up and grabbed the lip of the pipe. She hauled herself up and in. She turned on the flashlight, drew her knife, favouring silence, and moved along the length of the pipe, into the sewer system. She listened, heard marching boots to the right. She followed, walking softly on raised concrete beside a fetid canal. She kept the light aimed low, giving her just enough illumination to see the next few steps.

She followed the echoes, moving as fast as she could without creating her own. The path twisted through one branch after another of the tunnels. After the first dozen, she gave up trying to memorize the route. There would be other exits, and she'd find one when the time came. The echoes grew louder, and she heard snatches of conversation. The men were travelling quickly, but not quietly. If they were talking, they were relaxing. They didn't expect to be followed. No reason why they should, given how little they'd left behind that could still move. Blaylock turned a corner and saw light and shadow up ahead. She killed her light. She closed in, feeling the terrain, tasting the battlefield, serpent zeroing in on prey. The two men bringing up the rear were lagging a good ten yards behind the others. They'd slowed to light cigarettes. No clouds of methane blew up, so Blaylock felt safe enough to cause some sparks of her own, even as she felt a wave of dizziness at the men's stupidity. There was another bend coming up, and the bulk of the forces turned, giving her with a few seconds alone in this stretch with the two stragglers. She scuttled up to them. She swung her knife, and buried it deep in the side of the first man's neck. She pulled the blade free as he dropped. The other soldier was turning, slow with surprise but still raising his rifle. Blaylock crouched low and drove the knife into his kidneys. He gasped, was going to scream, but she caught his head as he fell and sliced his throat. She listened, heard no change in the sound of the march. She checked the bodies, found a couple of grenades. She grabbed an equipment belt and strapped it on. Then she rounded the corner. She still didn't rush.

She closed in on the light, watched the bulk of the forces, gauged the risks. Though she couldn't afford the decadence of hope, she had to assume she was still on a rescue mission. She had to act as if there were people in the sewers she didn't want to hurt. No grenades, then, no scorched earth. The options shrank. The risks refused to disappear. She fingered the rifle.

Mark Vrenna was holding the fort at the observation post. He was in the house's attic room. He got the word from Luzhkov. Major shit all over the place. The Arlington bridge a goddamn killing field. The president snatched. Blaylock in pursuit to parts unknown. Luzhkov was on his way, but only as fast as a convulsed city would let him travel. Same for the reinforcements. Vandelaare was loading up in an InSec warehouse with a second force, but they were going to hang back, wait to see where their strike would be needed. So he was running the front for the time being. He had twenty men in the house. He hadn't seen movement in or out of Chapel's safe house for the last six hours. He didn't know the enemy's numbers. He counted on plenty. If he saw signs of mobilization, he would hit them before they could spill from the house. Box them in and burn them down if it came to that. His palms were damp. His system was jumping like it had during the InSec battle. He was jived by eagerness and anxiety. Nick Haasbroek was stationed at the window. He had a large parabolic microphone aimed at the house and was wearing headphones. He looked a question at Vrenna, who filled him in.

"What do you figure?" Haasbroek asked.

"I figure a big boom today, no matter what happens."

Haasbroek nodded. "What's the ETA on reinforcements?"

Vrenna shrugged. "With this kind of chaos? You tell me. Second quarter of next year?" He gestured at the surveillance equipment. "Anything?"

"Not much. I'm getting footsteps, some conversation."

"Something you can make out?"

"No, more of the same. Sounds like a bunch of guys sitting around a table. It's all white noise."

"Numbers?" Haasbroek wasn't giving him new intel. But Vrenna had to ask anyway. Feel as prepared as he could. The storm was about to break. His palms told him so.

"Don't know what to tell you. Doesn't sound like a shitload. But you *know* they'd be keeping the noise down."

"Okay. Listen for the change."

"You figure it's coming?"

"Guaranteed." He left the room and moved through the house, putting the rest of the troops on alert. He'd barely finished when Haasbroek yelled for him. Vrenna ran up the stairs. Haasbroek was on his feet, eyes excited. He was holding the headphones tight against his head, as if he might physically squeeze more information out of them.

"They're moving," Haasbroek said. "I'm hearing excitement, lots of boots running around."

"You're sure?"

A nod. "I even heard some clips being loaded."

Vrenna peered out the window. The enemy's house was calm on the exterior. No sign of buildup. "Do you know what they're planning?"

"No clue. Too much noise. I can't make out anything specific."

Not that it mattered. He didn't need to know anymore. "Okay," he said. "Let's go."

Vrenna put a call in to Luzhkov, let him know what was going down. Luzhkov was making good time, would be there in a few minutes, but the backup forces were still at least a quarter of an hour away. "Don't let them out of the house," Luzhkov said.

"Don't I know it," Vrenna replied.

They stormed out of the observation post. Vrenna's palms dried as the action began. He felt that good combat high. This was what he'd been looking for when he'd thrown his lot in with Blaylock. The gig with InSec had had its moments, but there had also been far too much sitting around and waiting to be thrown the bone of a contract, or, more often then not, tossed an order. With Blaylock, he'd been involved with one long campaign, first covert, now breaking out into full-on urban warfare. Sweet. He saw the faces of the locals as he and his men charged the safe house. Stricken, holy-shit looks of disbelief. The good people were rooted to their positions on the sidewalk, the street, their front yards and their porches, a study in gobsmacked statues. Vrenna saw a gangbanger piss himself as they ran buy. More than sweet. *Fun*.

They swarmed into the safe house yard and surrounded the building. Plenty of uproar within, but still no one coming out. This was going to even better than fun. It was going to be perfect. Vrenna ran up the porch, flattened himself against the wall between the front door and the living room window. He waited until he heard that the encirclement was complete. He glanced at Haasbroek, on the other side of the door, grinned. "Now," he radioed.

Haasbroek took the door, kicking it open with a boot to the latch. Vrenna checked the window, saw no one in the room, then shot the glass out and jumped inside. Three other men followed. The noise of the assault on the house was huge, cresting over the cacophony inside. Vrenna trotted across the room, then stopped. The roar of his army was breaking up in a rumble of confusion. He didn't hear any shots. There was no combat. But he could still hear the sounds of the invisible enemy manning up. The noise seemed to be coming from the room he was in. His ears registered an off quality to the sound at the same moment that his eyes rested on the speakers.

In the entrance hall, Haasbroek led the way forward. His feet broke an infrared beam.

Luzhkov had grabbed an abandoned car just beyond the gridlock at the Arlington Bridge. He was only a few blocks away from the safe house when he heard the blast. It was a clap of last judgment, of everything gone terminally wrong. Smoke roiled to the sky. Dust billowed through the streets. Luzhkov hit the greyout and slowed down. He turned on the lights and crawled the rest of the way. Anxiety tried to push him faster. Despair told him there was no hurry.

He stopped the car at the head of the street. He walked down towards the dead end. He coughed, held his hand over his nose and mouth to filter out the dust. He picked his way over rubble, unable to see more than a few yards in any direction. The bomb had been massive. The safe house had vaporized. There wasn't much left of its immediate neighbours. Shattered masonry and splintered timbers covered the street. So did bodies. The recognizable ones were furthest from the blast site. They were slashed by glass and impaled by shrapnel. Closer in, Luzhkov saw nothing but parts. Legs, arms, heads, torsos, a scattered jumble of bloody puzzle pieces. And where the house had been, there was nothing that looked like it had ever been human. The only traces were splashes of red and bits of rubble that were soft. There was no sign of the assault force. It had vanished with the house. Chapel had removed twenty-one of his opponents' men from the board with one move. His signature was all over the street. Chapel's pattern: the massive strike, the overkill designed to leave nothing of the enemy behind. And very little of the civilian collateral.

Luzhkov turned his back to the crater. The dust was beginning to settle. The full portrait of the street developed from grey limbo. From his vantage point, Luzhkov could see the ripple fingerprint of the explosion radiating out from an exterminated centre. There wasn't a single intact window on the block. Where Luzhkov stood, there was silence. It was the thick deafness that fills the air after enormous sound. It was also the calm of total absence. Away from the centre of the blast, noise was returning. It was a choral tribute to Chapel's move. It was wails of grief and screams of pain.

The air cleared. The vision seared. Luzhkov began to walk back up the street. The scene triggered memories of Chechnya. His legs became numb stumps with jellied knees. A few feet away, he saw a young boy lying face down on the sidewalk. There was no one with him. Luzhkov crouched beside the child. He was still alive. Luzhkov could see spasms shaking his back. Luzhkov put a hand on the boy's shoulder. He saw blood, dark and deep, pooling near the boy's stomach. There was a deep shudder, a deeper, breathless sigh, and the boy was still. Luzhkov looked up, saw more innocent tragedies playing themselves out. He sank down on the curb, weary with anger and despair. The damage wasn't on the same scale as that done in the Hamptons, but he felt this one more viscerally. He had only seen the coverage of the nuke on TV, had heard Blaylock's descriptions. He was touching the destruction here. He wondered if they could hope to fight a man who was willing to go this far. He wondered if they had already lost. His commanding officer was flying solo on a suicide mission. Their forces were divided across the city, with no targets to fight. And they'd been played but good.

The approach of sirens brought him to his feet. Moving again snapped him out of the reverie. There might be nothing left to hope for, but there was still the fight itself. Even if it was futile, it was still a good one. It was the promise Blaylock had shown him in Geneva. Working for Sherbina, he hadn't even had that. Now, at least, if he was going to go down, he was going to go down well.

Blaylock opened fire. She moved the barrel of the gun in an arc across the width of the tunnel. There were a lot of soldiers. They were bunched together. There were plenty of them to stop the bullets before they reached the hostages. That was her hope and only choice. Her burst was a scythe. Wheat fell. She stopped firing before the buffer of bodies was cleared out, and retreated to the last corner. The first retaliatory shots sang by her as she ducked around the wall. She waited for the counter-charge.

Maldonado was at the head of the march. He heard the chattering of the assault rifle from the rear, heard screams and shouts. He threw himself down with the rest of his men. He gagged as sewer water splashed into his mouth. He scrabbled around to face the way they had come. He saw the president dragged down by the other civilian. He saw chaos traced by erratic flashlight beams. He heard more weapons fire. He didn't know what was going on. There were no bullets flying this way. He stood and shouted for his men to follow. He led an organized rush towards the rear.

Flanagan hauled Hallam to the ground, made him lie flat. The firing stopped, and as the soldiers pounded past them, he pulled the president into a crouching position against the tunnel wall. They curled tight to avoid being trampled. They were ignored. An attack pushed down every priority other than combat. Flanagan tensed to make a run. He exchanged a look with Hallam, saw the same idea reflected in the man's eyes. He looked into the tunnel ahead, noticed how black it was without flashlights to show the way, and hesitated. He turned his head, saw that all other priorities hadn't been entirely shelved. A group of three men were hanging back, keeping close, keeping an eye on them. No go.

Blaylock squatted low just around the corner. The first of the charge came around the wall firing from the hip. If she'd been standing, she would have been cut in half. The bullets were a horizontal rain of metal just over her head. She answered with a quick burst of her own, shooting up and into guts. The men on the leading edge were shoved backward in death, tripping up the push behind as they collapsed. They granted Blaylock a few seconds. The next intersection was only ten yards down. She ran, jigging left and right. The roar behind her said she'd been spotted, that the surprise was over, that the hunt was on.

Good.

Maldonado shoved his way towards the front of the charge, yelling for order. These men were trained. They knew better than to run into an ambush. For some, it had been years since they'd seen any action, and even then they'd always been on the delivery side of an ambush, as they had been on bridge. Being taken by surprise was a new and unwelcome experience. It was against the rules. It wasn't the way of the world. Still, they should know better than this. The second round of casualties smartened them up. They weren't rushing to round the next corner.

Malonado caught up to Cabezas, who had been leading the rear team. "So?" he asked.

"One woman," Cabezas answered.

Well that was a kick in the nuts. Not to be dismissed, though. In these cramped quarters, one person could do a lot of damage. This many men in a tunnel, impossible to miss. So don't give her any gifts.

They weren't coming for her. They were thinking this through, making sure the next move was smart. She had turned off her flashlight. She saw multiple beams crossing and bobbing, their sources just out of sight. They were bunched up.

They were suckers.

Two throws: one light, one hard.

Bank shots.

Maldonado wanted two firing positions, one on each side of the intersection. Blind fire around the corner would provide cover. He was about to give Cabezas the signal when he heard *clunk* and *clunk* against the left wall. A flashlight beam caught the spin of grenades. One landed just this side of the intersection. The other flew hard to the rear. Maldonado threw himself into the sewage canal. The explosions went off a second apart. They were a roar and a fist together. They took him, shook him, squeezed him and worried him. No, not a fist, but the jaws of a wolf shaking his life loose. And then there was no wolf, but a bell with him as the clapper. Iron resonation pummelled his bones to powder. He held his breath. He was blind from sound and pain and drowning. He held strong, fought back, fought to find surface in a world turned vortex.

The tunnels boomed with a double thunderclap. Pressure drove into Flanagan's head. His ears popped and his eyes watered. The three guards staggered. The sewage canal foamed with momentary rapids. In the wake of the battering ram noise, silence. No shouts. No gunfire. The soldiers radiated confusion. He felt their gaze and indecision. He glanced at Hallam. The man was slumped against the wall, full of his age. His head hung down. His face was slack and grey. A wash of water rushed over his feet. He didn't move them. As Flanagan looked, Hallam opened one eye. The look was sharp, completely awake. He was playing possum. Flanagan caught the strategy and sagged more heavily. The soldiers said something to each other in Spanish. He caught the gist from their body language. Through hooded eyes, he saw them judge the prisoners and shrug their unease. But they left, heading in the direction of the blast, taking guns and flashlights with them. Their logic was sound: the prisoners were out of it, and they weren't going to go far in the pure dark. Made sense. Screw that.

"Are you all right?" he asked Hallam. His own voice sounded far away.

"Still drawing breath, thanks."

Flanagan helped the president to his feet. "Let's go."

"Where and how?"

"Away, and as best we can."

"Works for me."

Flanagan went first. "Hang on to my shoulders," he said.

Hallam did. Flanagan started forward. He held one hand against the wall. He shuffled quickly. They stumbled away into a dank void.

Blaylock stayed low and against the wall for the blasts. They were around the corner from her, but in the constricted space they were brutal enough. A subway train made of air buffeted her. Her ears rang. She stood and ran into the cloud of dust and vapour and blood. It settled over body parts. The sewage roiled. The casualty rate was total. She didn't see any survivor with enough intact limbs to be a credible threat. She heard boots on concrete, fast tempo in her direction. She raised her rifle. At her feet, the water exploded.

Maldonado surfaced. He lunged forward into air, realized there was a figure standing before him, and the only thing that mattered was to bring the agony.

Maldonado's head came up and knocked Blaylock's rifle and flashlight out of her hands. He slammed into her. She tumbled off the walkway. She grappled with him as the waters, thick with sludge and corpses, closed over their heads. He grabbed her throat. She knocked his hands away, grabbed a handful of uniform. He rolled, and her hand tangled in the clothes. They surfaced for a moment, writhing against each other like lovers. She saw three men arrive, arms at the ready. She didn't give them a target. She held her breath and sank hard. Maldonado punched her in the gut. She gasped the good out, drew the bad in. Control out, desperation in. She thrashed, animal. And then they were surrounded by feet and hands. Maldonado was pulled off her, away from her grasp. Another soldier, instead of stomping her into the shit, made the mistake of lifting her up from behind. Her hands ran up his legs as she rose. Her fingers closed around the knife in his ankle sheath. She dug her feet into the ground, found enough purchase. She became a rocket. Her head rammed against her captor's chin. He grunted and his grip loosened. She held the knife straight in front as she rose. It plunged into Maldonado's groin. She used both hands, slit him high. He opened wide. He spilled himself onto the floor of the tunnel. The soldier behind Blaylock tightened his grip again, going for the bear hug. He forced her arms down. She let him. She flipped the knife around and jammed it into his right thigh. This time he let go for real. She pivoted on her heel, pulled the knife from his leg and thrust it under his chin as he jackknifed forward.

Another quick turn. The other two men were letting go of Maldonado's corpse. She made a linebacker lunge, plowed into a lead bag full of guts. Everybody went down. She slashed the left-hand soldier's throat. The other grabbed her arm, started to pull her down. She slammed the pommel of the knife against his elbow, hit him again until bone poked through. He started screaming. She was about to put a stop to that, too, when she heard a metallic click. She looked down at his other hand. She wasn't the only one packing grenades. He'd pulled the pin. The grenade lay in his open palm. He grinned through his pain. She threw herself backward, into the water, swam for the tunnel intersection. Explosion. Wave. She didn't fight it. It rewarded her by slamming her into the channel wall. Air out, but she fought the instinct to breathe in.

She emerged into air, darkness, and the rumble of collapsing stone. She waited for stillness. When it came, she felt her way back through the velvet dark. Her hands touched rubble. She moved them up the pile. There were no gaps. The blasts had brought down the roof of the tunnel. She was blind, unarmed, and not going any further this way. Flanagan and Hallam were somewhere she couldn't reach. Buried or not, she didn't know. Prisoners or not, she didn't know. Safe or not, that she knew: not. Some rescue. What the hell was that? Charge in like the angel of death and hope for the best? Stop and think.

She confronted the twisting fear of terrible mistake. She made the worst possibility a strategic consideration. She stomped the grief, anxiety and self-loathing. The effort came with the ease of heavy practice. She populated the darkness with the state of things. She'd taken a bite out of Chapel's forces, but had only partially disrupted the specific operation. She didn't think he had Hallam, but nor did she. The fight had been huge and public. Chapel was making his moves in the open. He felt either desperate or unstoppable.

All right. That was the picture. So now what?

So Chapel wasn't about to slink back into the shadows. A visible hand was an easier one to counter. So leave the dark. Find the light. Find Luzhkov. Find the fight. Find Chapel. Burn the fucker's dreams to the ground.

26

Chapel met Meredith Leadbetter in Pratella's old Senate office. It hadn't been reassigned yet. She hadn't been spending a lot of time at the State building lately. Especially since he'd told her to stand by. "Your nation's going to be calling on you," he'd said. He'd been smiling, so she hadn't been able to tell if his phrasing was genuine or a put-on. He was unreadable, yet open. His every word was either sincere or cynical, depending on what the listener wanted. Brilliant. Christ, the man was good. She pitied the politicians who tried to fight him.

Now, he asked, "Ready for your close-up?"

Leadbetter flipped through the hard copy of her speech. The sheaf of papers was a prop. She had the thing memorized. The sheaf was a crutch. She feared a memory blank during the performance of her life. "I'm ready," she said, and knew she was. The nerves were there, but the resolve was, too. There were also some doubts. Not about the cause, not about the ends. The means and methods were another story. "Are you sure you know what you're doing?"

"A bit late to be asking me that." He wasn't smiling. He was judging.

"Maybe. But I'm asking. Is all this necessary?"

Chapel checked his watch. He opened the office door and invited her through. She stepped into the corridor. At the far end, she saw a man in military fatigues. He was cradling an assault rifle. He was not one of the security guards she knew. Chapel began walking so aggressively and so close to her that he forced her to fall into step as effectively as if he had grabbed her by the arm. "Yes," he hissed. "Yes, it's fucking necessary." Each consonant was a dagger thrust. "Why are you so concerned, now? You swallowed the Hamptons being nuked just fine. Don't answer. I'll tell you why. You have to play for real, now. No plausible deniability. No hiding behind me. This fails, and I go down, then you go down, too."

The blows struck home. She didn't answer.

Chapel continued. "Think carefully. If we fail, do you really believe that the country can survive?"

Silence. He was waiting. The corridor stretched endless, echoed hollow, ended in a gun. Her heart pounded. "No," she answered, frightened but honest. "It can't."

"So grow a pair," Chapel snapped. "Because if you're not up what has to be done, I'll find someone who is."

"Get out of my space and let me do my job," she said. Resolve and conviction were ascendant.

Blaylock moved through black, found light again, followed it until she reached the outlet pipe's opening. She looked toward the bridge. It was still shrouded in smoke. It was becoming indistinct as dusk fell. Media and police helicopters were flies buzzing a corpse. She read confusion in the movements. This was all reactive. There was no direction. Chapel still had the advantage of chaos and surprise. His hand was free.

She dropped from the pipe and let the current carry her downriver. She pulled herself ashore on the Mall near the Fourteenth Street bridges. She was a sodden, filthy mess. She was a sight. Two middle-aged tourists were staring at her. After a moment, the woman asked, "Are you all right?"

"Fell out of my boat," Blaylock explained.

"Are there rapids near here?" the man asked. He was taking in her cuts and bruises.

"Got a phone I can borrow?" she replied.

Chapel stood in the Public Gallery, watching the Senate Chamber fill for its emergency session. He was trying to temper his elation. It was an exalted mix of triumph, vindication, pride, and love. The love was what opened the door to the necessary humility. Love for his country, for the beautiful dream it represented. He looked over the Chamber. He saw history and tradition made concrete. The classical lines of the architecture were the bedrock of history and the grandeur of the American Experiment. This was the majesty of democracy. The mahogany desks, arranged in a close-packed semicircle around the dais, were tactile tradition. The names of senators were carved inside drawers, but the desks had indentities that transcended the individual politicians who sat at them. If one became the Chamber's storehouse of candy, no senator would dare break the pattern. That was the force of tradition. That was what Chapel was saving. The surgery was radical. The patient was on life support. But Chapel was cutting the cancer out, once and for all.

He had no illusions about what he was doing. He was staging a coup. He was dealing his country a harsh blow. But America had survived a civil war. It would survive this. It wouldn't survive *without* the coup. The Turkish army had preserved that country's secular state by force. This was the same principle. He hoped Leadbetter appreciated the importance of her moment. It was far more than the installation of a sensible president. She would be providing constitutional sanctification to his extra-constitutional manoeuvre. Her speech would be the seal on the event. The coup would enter the mythology of the nation as the necessary evil that preserved its institutions. The message from the centre of power would be one of stability. From the heart of the nation, the news would course along the arteries of the media, and the bodies politic and public would know that the right measures had been taken, and that the dark crisis had passed.

It was hard not to feel proud.

Then his phone vibrated, and it was Quintero on the line, and Chapel knew he was calling to spoil things. "What is it?" he asked.

"Something happened to the snatch team."

Chapel closed his eyes for a moment, breathed heavily through his nose. You mean some*one* happened to them, he thought. The bitch was immortal. "How bad is it?" he asked, and hoped that their scrambler was up to the job.

"I lost contact with Maldonado shortly after they entered. When I couldn't raise him, I sent another team back for a look. There had been a firefight. The tunnel collapsed."

"Survivors?"

"None that could be found."

"What about Hallam?"

"I don't know. He's either under the rock, or on the other side of it somewhere in the sewers."

"The woman?"

"No sign of her."

Too much to hope that she'd been crushed. She might have Hallam. Act on the worst-case scenario. "Is the perimeter secure?"

"Soon."

"Send whoever you can spare to Pennsylvania Avenue. And no one gets in here. Kill anyone who tries."

"Anyone." The word wasn't a question. It was an anticipation.

"That's right."

"And anyone includes…"

"It's getting dark. Tragic mistakes happen."

"Yes, they do."

The dark was tangible. It pushed back against Flanagan. It slowed him. It confused him. Each step was a frightened prayer. He kept one hand against the tunnel wall and shuffled along like an old man, moving his feet no more than a few inches at a time. If the ground was going to vanish, he didn't want it to be a surprise. He and Hallam took their awkward parade down the tunnel for a hundred yards, and then Flanagan's hand lost the wall. He fumbled in air.

"What is it?" Hallam asked.

"Just a second." He found concrete again. He held on to the corner of the wall. They were at a branch. He felt around with his foot. He couldn't tell if the path continued on as well or not. "We have to make a decision," he said.

"Do you have any idea where we are?"

"Do you?"

"That's what I thought. Any suggestions?"

"Well, I don't know what's ahead. If it's all the same to you, I'd like to stick to where I can feel a wall."

"No argument there."

They followed the wall left. This path lasted a few hundred yards. They hit another intersection. "If we go left again, we're going to be doubling back," Flanagan said.

"We'll have to risk getting wet."

"Yeah."

They formed a short human chain. Hallam kept one hand on the wall, and stretched the other out to hold Flanagan's. Flanagan shuffled out into void. His toes curled as he found the end of the walkway. He used the president as a pivot point and edged from left to right. His feet touched metal. He reached down, found a railing. "Here," he said. They crossed, and carried on forward. So far so good.

"We could be down here a long time," Hallam commented, bringing down the mood.

"We'd better not be," Flanagan answered, thinking of the train wreck going on upstairs.

"No," Hallam agreed.

Half an hour later, they found rungs leading up. Flanagan climbed first. The ladder ended at an access cover. The first light he had seen since the explosion came through the holes. It was dim, little more than a dirty grey. He thought it was about right for the state of hope. He heard foot and vehicular traffic. The sounds broke the wall of darkness. He reached up and pushed against the metal. It gave him nothing. He braced his feet, leaned against the wall, and heaved with both arms. Nothing. Implacable. "Shit," he muttered.

"Is there room for us both?" Hallam asked.

Flanagan moved to the left. It was a squeeze, and he only had one foot firmly on a rung. But the pipe narrowed, and he was able to lean against it. Hallam clambered up next to him, and the two began pounding the cover. It took them a few tries to get their blows synchronized, but then they had the rhythm. After the first dozen hits, Flanagan heard the first scrape of shifting metal. They hit harder. The cover jerked. They pushed. It groaned. They heaved it out of the way and climbed out onto the pavement. They were on a sidewalk. People looked at them, gave them a wide berth. The president was unrecognized and anonymous. For the moment, that was a good thing. Flanagan looked around. "Where are we?"

"Constitution Avenue, I think."

There was a *what now?* moment. Then Hallam said, "I have to get back to the White House."

Flanagan tried to think like Blaylock. She would see the strategic angles. She would play at being the enemy, decide what she would do if she were Chapel. "I wonder if that's a good idea," he said.

"What do you mean?"

"That ambush was very, very public." He worked through the implications. "The people doing this aren't afraid of being seen, which means they feel strong. They want you badly, or at least they want you out of the picture. If they're looking for you, what's the first place they would expect you to head for?"

"How would they stop me? The Secret Service—"

"—thinks you're either dead or abducted. Your people sure aren't expecting you to come strolling home."

"The army—"

"—isn't here yet. Assuming it's going to be."

"You think it won't?"

"I don't know. I don't know how far the conspiracy goes. Given some of what's gone down, the roots must run pretty deep. There must be a lot of players out there, even if many of them aren't directly involved. But they can do you a lot of harm just by doing nothing, or by acting slowly."

"Well, fuck," said the president. He turned on his heel and took a couple of angry strides towards the street. "This goddamn well *can't* be happening here."

"You have no idea how long I've been saying the same thing to myself."

Hallam stood, fists to hips, head down. After a few moments, without raising his head or looking back at Flanagan, he said, "All right. The first thing we need to do is find a TV, see what the story is."

Good, Flanagan thought. That made a lot of sense. Learn the narrative. See how they could work with it. If they could.

They started down the sidewalk, two men in ragged, toilet-reeking clothes. "I doubt anyone's going to put out the welcome mat for us," Flanagan said.

"No," Hallam answered. He pointed. "But *they* won't yank it away." A block down, neon beer ads blinked in a bar window. Blake's, the bar was called. The sign would have been an antique if it weren't so thuggish in its decrepitude. The bar was the sort of establishment that hadn't been typical of Foggy Bottom for decades. Somehow, it had withstood a half-century of revitalization. It crouched with misanthropic pride on its corner. It wasn't going anywhere, and would take on any comer who thought otherwise. As they approached, Flanagan caught the blue flicker of a screen.

"Think they'll turn off ESPN for our sakes?" he asked.

"Ten dollars says they're watching the news. It's been a big kind of day, wouldn't you say?"

Flanagan would. And Hallam was right. The box was tuned to CNN. The clientele was a good match for the bar, as if hand-picked by the building. There was no boasting, brawling or pool going on. There was very little drinking. All eyes were on the screen. The volume was up loud and the chatter was down. Flanagan could hear the TV from the doorway. The tone of the anchors and reporters had a comrades-in-arms urgency. There was genuine fear. They were freaked. They didn't know what was happening. They needed reassurance just as much as their audience. The hairs on the back of Flanagan's neck stirred. The psychology was worrying. It was the need that alarmed him more than the fear. He wasn't sure why. Then the scene shifted to the Capitol and the Senate Chamber, and his alarm took on definition. An emergency session of the Senate was in progress. Secretary of State Meredith Leadbetter was expected to make a speech very shortly. The anchor reminded his audience three times in two minutes what the rules of succession were, and what that meant about Leadbetter. Flanagan heard the desperate hope in the man's voice, and his skin prickled cold. He saw the same frightened-child hope in the faces of the bar's patrons. The TV was going to comfort them. It was going to tell them that things were under control. It was going to tell them that everything would be all right. There were people in charge. They were going to end the nightmare.

And that was all that mattered. Who the people were, what their goals were, and what responsibility they might have for the nightmare were irrelevant issues. Don't think about them, and you'll be warm and cozy in your bed tonight.

Flanagan saw a maw open wide to swallow the last traces of the American Experiment. It took an effort not to scream. He looked at Hallam, and saw the same horror etched on the man's face.

"We have to stop this," the president said. There was a payphone beside the entrance. He and Flanagan had enough change between them for a couple of calls. "I'll damn well get straight through to the Senate," Hallam said. "Get George Lind to raise hell and sound the trumpet that I'm safe." He punched the numbers. Flanagan watched him listen, frown, hang up and try again. And again. And again. "I can't get through," he said. "To anyone. All their cell phones are off."

A coincidence Flanagan didn't buy. "We should find the nearest television station," he offered.

Hallam shook his head. "That wouldn't be enough."

"You don't think your being alive after all would prompt a cutaway or three?"

"Assuming they can in the first place." Flanagan hadn't thought of that. "Even if they could, no, it wouldn't be enough. A single network wouldn't be. Didn't you notice what station that box is set to?"

"CNN."

"Look again."

Flanagan did. "Oh, no." The feed was CNN, but the logo at

the bottom right of the screen was ESPN. *Everybody* was airing this.

"If their little game plays out, I'm finished. It won't matter if I'm alive or not. There will be an official story, and no one is going to want to see it changed."

"What are you saying?"

"I have to be there. In the Senate. I have to stop this thing myself, and I have to be seen to do so."

"Is that all?"

"That's all."

Sweat ran rivulets through the grime on the man's forehead. He was caked in filth. His eyes were red. He looked ready to drop. His face was a mask of grief and fear. And to Flanagan he suddenly looked ten feet tall. "You know," Flanagan said, impressed, "I think my girlfriend would really like you."

"That's nice. Would she have a plan to get me into the Senate?"

"She just might," Flanagan said to Hallam's surprised face.

Luzhkov picked Blayock up on Fourteenth Street. "Anything good?" he asked.

"More casualties on their side. Everything else is bad. What can you tell me?" When she heard about the safe house, she asked, "How badly are we hurting?"

"It was a strong hit. We still have a good strike force in the city."

"You're gathering them?"

"That's where I'm taking you."

"Good."

"What do you have in mind?"

"I'm not sure. Stop that somehow." She pointed at the radio. Luzhkov had it on, and the airwaves were singing with Leadbetter's approaching coronation.

"How?"

"I'm working on that." Meaning she didn't have a clue. She felt like a blunt instrument. A hammer obsessively turning the world into nails. She refused to acknowledge Chapel's tactical superiority. War was hers. No one else could have it. But her imagination was stymied.

And then her phone rang, and it was Flanagan, and everything changed. Inspiration blossomed. The energy surged back. War embraced her.

Leadbetter was taking her time. Chapel watched the senators becoming restless. When he had left her to head for the Public Gallery, he thought she was going to march right in. That had been twenty minutes ago. If she was having cold feet, he would kill her and work his way down the line of succession until the job was his, if he had to. He stroked the cell phone jammer on the bench beside him. The Senate would be getting no information that he didn't control. No more phone calls for anyone. Beside him was the field radio he would use to communicate with Quintero.

He saw George Lind, senior senator for Mississippi, make a show of shifting his bulk to his feet, and just as loudly begin stuffing papers into his briefcase. Matin Poole, his Junior, leaned over and said something Chapel didn't catch. "I don't care," Lind declaimed. "I surely don't. I'll read about it in the papers tomorrow, and then maybe we can rise from our cushy asses and actually do something for the suffering nation."

Cute speech, Chapel thought, as he thundered down the stairs. Always play to the cameras. They're always on. You should be, too. Good, good, good, but time to spoil the grand exit. Lind was just stepping out of the chambers when Chapel reached the door. The senator stopped when he saw Quintero's men. Chapel walked up to him. "I'm sorry, Senator," he said. "But I'm going to have to insist that you remain at your desk."

Lind tried to bluster. "By whose authority?"

"Senator, there has already been one terrorist strike today. We have credible information that suggests all of you would be targets as well should you leave at this time." He wasn't lying. Quintero's shoot-to-kill orders applied not just to anyone approaching the Capitol.

"Oh," Lind said, at a loss. "I see." Pale, he turned around and went back inside. Good little lamb. Chapel watched him through the doorway. Lind had just settled down, his bulging briefcase a forgotten pet at his feet, when Leadbetter entered. As she approached the podium, Chapel saw that he was stupid to have worried. Her face was set, driven. She'd been creating anticipation through delay. Good move. Everyone would *really* be listening now. Chapel ran in his limping hop back to the Public Gallery. Leadbetter was still staring at her notes when he arrived, as if this speech were the last one she would ever want to make. Oh, you're good, Chapel thought. This was someone he could work with.

She began to speak.

They didn't have long for their moment, but at least they had it. What Blaylock saw in Flanagan's face was complete absolution for her clumsy rescue attempt. It was a forgiveness she wasn't sure she wanted. She didn't like the excitement that radiated from him. "Are you all right?"

"Good to go." He sounded almost cocky.

"Did you enjoy what happened?" she asked, stern.

He calmed down. "Of course not."

"Good." She touched his face. "I need you to be okay."

"I am. I'm getting the hang of this thing, wouldn't you say?"

A wrench in her heart. "I wish I couldn't."

Flanagan spread his hands. "It's what you promised, Jen."

Blood and fire. All I can promise you is blood and fire. "I guess it is." He was fine. He was swimming in the element. He was alive. They were together. Where was the problem? She kissed him.

The problem was in what he might become, and what she would miss if that happened.

But for now, there was more blood and fire to be had.

Hallam knew he should be beyond surprise. He was doing his best. The day had thrown enough at him to jade him into catatonia. So when he and Flanagan were picked up by the woman who had passed herself off as a journalist and, he was sure, killed Patrick Pratella, he had only been half-surprised. His current surroundings were harder to take. He'd been taken to a warehouse. It was an arsenal and a mustering hall. He saw automatic rifles and RPG launchers, Claymores and machine guns. He saw many objects he didn't recognize, but whose black metal was enough to mark them as killers. The air was filled with the clash of a global village of accents. Men stripped weapons, applied camouflage, loaded up for battle. He was surrounded by the United Nations of professional warriors. In every face, he saw the same passion, the same joy. It was the fierce love of battle for its own sake. There was something else, too, that he couldn't identify.

"What do you think?" The woman had appeared at his shoulder.

"About what?"

"About the army that's going to save you and your country."

Hallam weighed his answer. He decided on honesty. "It's not what I'm used to," he said. He thought about the troop reviews he had attended over the years. He thought about the faces there, and realized what was missing from the faces here. "These men aren't what I'd call patriots."

"I should damn well hope not."

"Then what are they fighting for?"

"It's what they do, and they do it well."

"That isn't enough."

"Isn't it? You prefer your soldiers to be ideologically driven? You prefer a level of fanaticism? Isn't that exactly what you're dealing with now?"

"You might be right." He was deliberately noncommittal. He didn't want to get into an argument with her. He didn't agree, though. These were more than just soldiers for hire. They might have been at some point, but he didn't smell a profit motive now. There was just as much belief here as in any national force. He didn't know what the belief was, and that disturbed him.

"Excuse me," the woman said. She made her way forward, to a raised platform at one end of the warehouse. The room fell silent as she mounted it. Preparations ceased. She started to speak. The address was no St. Crispin's Day oration. She didn't promise glory. She laid out the situation. She called the odds as she saw them. The only thing she offered was slaughter, and she wasn't guaranteeing whose. Hallam didn't hear a single phrase of boosterism. Yet his skin prickled. His pulse quickened. He felt a stirring excitement at the prospect of battle and blood. His vision tunnelled, the woman and her words becoming his only focus. She presented the facts calmly, clearly, and each datum was another promise of gigantic war. In Hallam's chest, an awful joy ignited.

He blinked, shook off the spell. His skin prickled even more, this time from fear. He looked around at the faces again, and this time put his finger on what he hadn't understood earlier. These men weren't fighting for God or country. They weren't fighting for an idea. They weren't even fighting for money. Despite what the woman had said, he thought those might be the less frightening alternatives. No, they were fighting for her, and for the thing she incarnated. They might not think so. He suspected some quite honestly were touched by some form of idealism, a desire to do the right thing. He saw that in Flanagan. He saw it in Luzhkov. But it wasn't all, and it wasn't enough. It was a veneer, a lure that pulled them over the woman's event horizon. He felt the tug, was struggling against it. He didn't doubt that he needed her. He wanted to believe that she knew right and wrong. It was the core that terrified him, her singularity. If he reached it, if he stripped away the framework of morality, he didn't know if he would find anything other than pure war. Then, even through his fear, the undertow took him. He watched her pace. He listened to her speak. He saw shadows gather around her, making her grow in stature until she filled the room. He saw her transformed into an angular demon, a patchwork of movement and sharp edges that stalked the parapet of hell. He saw the war machine, and her quiet words were the clanking roar of a juggernaut.

27

Quintero sealed off the Capitol. To the north on Constitution, and to the south on Independence, he had APCs barricade every access to the Mall between the two First Streets. Heavy patrols marched north and south on that perimeter, blocking the western access at the end of Pennsylvania and Maryland Avenues, and cutting the Capitol off to the east from the Library of Congress and the Supreme Court. He kept the largest part of his defence on the terrace itself. He walked the length of the West Terrace, behind the stone railing he had turned into the crenelation of a fortress. He had enough mounted machine guns to turn the ground below into an echo of Flanders. He had the commanding heights, and only one building to quarantine. Not hard. More than enough men and firepower. And triple the caution. There had been enough surprises, none of them good. He understood Chapel's anxieties about the woman. He shared them. Any detail, any movement that he hadn't specifically authorized was presumed hostile.

The first civilian casualties happened a few minutes before Leadbetter began speaking. Quintero had swept the immediate grounds and the interior, but he couldn't prevent every idiot in God's creation from coming up the Mall to see what all the fuss was about. He allowed exactly one loudspeaker warning. Then exactly one warning shot. Even those courtesies were on the edge of acceptable risk. Most of the tourists and gawkers took the hint. There were a few whose lives were defined by the ironclad faith that rules were for other people. They died for their belief. Quintero left the bodies where they fell. They made for perfect scarecrows. He didn't worry about political fallout. That was Chapel's field. Anyway, the whole purpose of this exercise was to change the way of things once and for all. With that change, there wouldn't be any chance of repercussions over the breaking of a few brain-dead eggs.

Word reached him that Leadbetter was speaking. So the show was almost over. He felt a twinge of disappointment at the anticlimax. He felt a great deal of relief.

"I don't need to rehearse the day's events for you," Leadbetter was saying. "All of you are acutely aware, as am I, of the crisis our nation is facing. You also know that, following the rules of succession, it is my painful duty and humbling honor to be acting president in the absence of President Hallam. My first, and right now, if we are honest, my *only* responsibility, is to see us safely through this storm." She had been standing military-straight, with her reading glasses on and her head lowered, pretending to read from her notes. Now she took her glasses off, leaned forward and rested her arms on the podium. She looked directly at her audience. She looked directly into the cameras. "I cannot do this alone," she said, so her listeners, in the Chamber, in their homes, in the bars and streaming her on the Internet, would see her humanity, the terrible weight on her shoulders, and sympathize. "I need your help," she said, so they would feel the tug of duty, of patriotism, of brotherhood.

She held the moment. She looked down, put her glasses back on, and straightened. She opened her mouth to speak, but then stretched the silence a few moments more, so they would see her reluctance and feel the importance of her next words. She said, "Though every effort is being made to find the president and bring him safely home to his wife and to us, we have so far been unsuccessful. His kidnappers have not yet made any demands. We do not even know whether or not he is alive." Let that one sink in, too. "While I pray with all the strength of my soul that he will be delivered, my first duty, as it is for us all, is to the nation. The stranglehold that his kidnappers have over us is due to the enormous importance of one man." Pause. Take a shuddering breath. That breath was one other reason she had kept the Senate waiting so long. It had taken her almost twenty minutes of practise before she could do the breath on command, with conviction, and without theatricality. She went on. "If we were to take away that man's importance, the risk to both him and the nation would decrease enormously." Eyes back to the senators. "So there, ladies and gentlemen of the Senate, is where your responsibility lies. Our country needs, as never before, security, strength, stability, and the means to achieve those goals. A house divided against itself cannot stand." She finished. She was pleased with her wrap-up. She never asked the Senate to declare her president. She emphasized their own power to act, but presented them with only one viable conclusion. She tossed in the final cliché as a reminder to her party that Hallam was of the enemy, and a unity of Oval Office and Senate majority was a pretty fine thing.

It was a grubby world, politics. But it was hers, and she loved it.

The op was barely more than improv. Far from the ideal. They were going in with no recon beyond the satellite view on Google Maps, Blaylock could see there was no good approach, and she was launching an assault with prep that wouldn't fill a napkin. She had the enthusiasm and faith of her troops. She had also had their training and resourcefulness. It would have to be enough.

They came in from the south, up Capitol Street. They travelled five to a car, interweaving the massive convoy in the civilian traffic. They were on foot by D Street, splitting into two strike forces. Blaylock led one, Luzhkov the other. The scene on the streets was a montage of the absurd, a collision of mundane and crisis. There was no sign of the Army or the National Guard yet. Blaylock read in their absence how many powerful friends Chapel still had, or at least how many commanders were happy to sit back and let his game play out. The police were out in force, racing sirens and erecting barricades with urgency, but without direction. Blaylock couldn't see any strategy behind which roads were blocked, nor any real attempt to restore the status quo. They seemed to have been given deliberately flawed orders. The main result of the effort, in the end, was to keep the police themselves from going too near the Hill. When Blaylock and her passengers piled out of her car, bristling with guns and wearing balaclavas and dark fatigues, the officers standing around the single cruiser at the intersection of D and Capitol reached for their pistols. Then they recognized Hallam, and stood down, confused. One stepped forward, an offer to help in his expression. "Just try to stay alive, officer," Hallam told him. "You'll be needed when this is all over."

The civilian population was beating a retreat. There was still vehicular and pedestrian traffic, but it was moving with the relentless avoidance of blinkered horses. Don't see trouble, and it won't see you. The people who were off the street were hiding, at home or at work, huddling close to the comfort of the media drone. Blaylock could imagine the seductive reassurance of Leadbetter's speech. That she was addressing the nation at all was almost all that was needed for her to hit a home run. Blaylock had to shatter the comforting lie. It was not going to be a popular move.

More cars arrived. Her force built to full strength. She led them in their dozens, west down D Street, then up a short spur to C. They were facing Rayburn House. No signs yet of the opposition. They were keeping their strength up through a concentration of forces. A reminder that Chapel didn't have unlimited manpower, either. Good to know. She sent the bulk of her forces back east along C, where they readied the assault. With a squad of five surrounding Flanagan and Hallam, she ran up to the entrance of Rayburn House. There was a security guard behind the doors. His complexion turned a sweaty pale as Blaylock approached. She tried the doors. They were locked. She cocked her head at the guard. He hesitated. His hand hovered over his holster. Then he opened the doors. He gaped when he saw who was standing behind Blaylock. "Sir—" he began.

Hallam waved off his apology. "This is how you can help. Keep quiet and out of the way for now. If something bad happens, tell as many people as possible. Okay?"

The guard nodded and stepped aside.

The marble halls echoed with the sounds of marching boots. They were sounds the walls were never meant to hear. Blaylock felt the tension of lethal contradiction grow the closer she came to the Capitol, the closer she came to unleashing the very thing the building and what it stood for were meant to prevent. It wouldn't be the first time, she reminded herself. Sometimes, shock treatment was the only recourse.

The north exit gave onto a courtyard flanked by east and west wings of the building. It had a view of the near approaches of the Hill. There was spotty tree cover from here to the terrace itself. The distance was something Blaylock would have to live with. "Wait here," Blaylock told Hallam and Flanagan. "We'll clear the way as best we can. When I call, use the cover you have, and move as fast as you can."

"Leaving me out again," Flanagan said.

"This isn't about taking turns in the playground," she said. It was a half-truth.

"I know," he said. His tone chilled her. It was an expression of love, but also of desire. Blaylock knew what lay ahead. However victory fell, it would do so in a torrent of blood. She and everyone in her vicinity would be drenched in it. Not that many months ago, Flanagan would have recoiled. He was sinking deeper into her morass, and she wanted him too much to save him from herself. She surprised herself with honesty. "I want you there, too." She didn't care enough about consequences to deny the emotion. "But this is a question of training."

"How long are you going to use that excuse?"

"For as long as it's true." She noticed Hallam following their exchange. The worry on his face went beyond the moment. He could see the moral abyss she had fallen into. He could see Flanagan opening his arms to release his grip on the high ground and embrace her as they plummeted together. She shared his worry. But there was an exhilaration in the fall, too. It felt a lot like flight. The rush was enormous. She looked hard at Flanagan. "You're not missing out," she told him.

"Promise?"

She kissed him, the brief touch of carnage on his lips.

He smiled. "That's a promise."

Blaylock left them there, Flanagan smiling behind his face mask, Hallam grim. As she ran back to the street and her troops, her energy soared, and through the tension and the uncertainty came a flash of a thought. It was brief, a strobe just long enough to illuminate but fast enough to vanish without guilt. One thought.

This is *fun*.

Quintero thought he heard artillery fire. The APC barricade at the corner of Independence and Capitol was being hit. The explosions merged into a continuous thunder. He ran to the side. It could be the attack. It was loud enough, and the north and south flanks were harder to defend than the east and west entrances. He looked down the slope, saw smoke and flames rising, heard automatic weapons fire. He called for more reinforcements on the south end of the building. He did not send any to the front. It didn't matter if the enemy came at him from this angle. Sooner or later, she was going to have to try for the main entrance. Good luck.

She modelled the tactic on the slaughterhouse of the First World War: a heavy-gun barrage followed by an infantry charge. She counted on a significant absence working in favour of the move: the opposition didn't have any trenches. She didn't have any cannons, but her artillery was also her infantry. They stormed around the corner onto Capitol. The rear fired grenade launchers at the barricade. There were three direct hits on vehicles. Fire bloomed and then the light vanished in the eruption of concrete dust. While the enemy coughed and burned, the next group ran forward and lobbed grenades by hand. The blasts were still echoing down the length of the street as she led the charge, assault rifles chattering bullets into the billowing grey. Return fire was sporadic and blind. Blaylock reached the barricade. She saw soldiers scattered in pieces. She smelled barbecued flesh. The air was dry with dust and humid with blood. It slicked the lungs. One man staggered in front of her. He was holding his gun but his eyes were shut. He was shaking his head, trying to shake the tinnitus roar and shock. She shot his face away and pulled another grenade from her belt.

Quintero saw the explosions march his way. A herd of invisible monsters smashed the road and threw up clouds of deeper night. The enemy was coming to him, and she was cloaked in apocalypse. "Fire!" he ordered. His men rained a leadstorm into the advancing cloud, even as it spat its first hail in their direction.

In the Senate Chamber, Meredith Leadbetter was still trying to get her motion to a vote. Chapel put each senator who stood to speak on his shit list. Pro or con, it didn't matter; every yammering contribution was another goddamned delay. Then he heard heavy weather outside. The moment he realized the sounds must be something worse than a cloudburst, he saw the same knowledge spread across the Chamber. George Lind, who had found his stride again far too quickly, the old toad, had been holding forth, but now he trailed off and turned his head in the direction of the distant rumbles and pops. The political action ground to a halt. No, Chapel thought. Leadbetter looked up from her chair to the Public Gallery. Even from this distance, Chapel could read the worry in her eyes. He knew what she was calculating. She was weighing what she had said and what she hadn't, looking for anything irrevocable. She was checking to see if she had condemned herself. She hadn't. Not yet. If the production stopped here, the third act reversed by *deus ex machina*, she was not beyond the pale. She was no Brutus. She could yet switch to Octavius and throw the mantle of damnation to Chapel alone.

Oh yes, Chapel could see all of this in the shadowed caution of her face. She might believe in what they were doing, but she was a politician first, last and always. He knew how far he could trust any of them. And if she thought she could back down now, if she thought any of them had any choice in how the play was going to end, she hadn't read the script. He would allow no revisions.

He lifted his radio receiver and hailed Quintero. He had to know what his options were down to.

"Busy," Quintero said, out of breath and out of sorts. He was hard to make out over the battle din.

"Tell me," Chapel demanded.

"Big push on the south flank."

"Only there?"

"So far."

Too straightforward. The woman always came in sideways. Guns blazing and subtlety be damned, but sideways. A single massive charge? No. "It's a diversion," Chapel warned.

Explosions and gunfire merged into a single blast of static. Chapel jerked his ear away from the phone. Then Quintero was back. Chapel could only make out fragments: "sniper" and "north." Jackpot. "That's it!" he yelled. "That's the real attack! Block it, man, block it!"

Luzhkov thought about Jamba as they prepared to take out the Constitution Avenue barricade. He would have loved the action. It played to his strengths. He was missed. Let this blow be his tribute, then. On the rooftops overlooking D Street NW, with a clear view south to the barricade, was a phalanx of snipers. They waited until Luzhkov and his two fire teams, running southeast down the diagonal of New Jersey Avenue, had reached the green northwest of the Mall itself. By then the uproar of Blaylock's assault was shaking mountains. The first volley sounded like a single shot. The men at the barricade dropped, and Luzhkov's squad was through. The fire teams split off into two directions, each into its own copse. There they stopped. Their equipment was standard. Rifles all. Luzhkov's was fitted with an M203 launcher. Sid Wilson had the SAW on his team. Every man was also lugging a second rifle, a Remington M24. None were snipers by training, but at this distance, a cross-eyed nun could do the job. The potshots began. More of Quintero's troops down. Good times. But come on. Notice us. Notice us. And there: activity on the terrace. A scurrying and a deployment of forces. So there. Attention was being paid. The easy part was over.

Blaylock crouched against a tree. The trunk was blocking bullets for now, but bigger rounds or a well-placed explosive would put paid to her cover. Her initial push had carried them far, up to the last stand of trees. But Quintero knew his thing, and wasn't running. He set up a massive counterfire, assault rifles and mounted machine guns chewing up the night with cheese-grater coverage. Between her and the Capitol was a large stretch of bare, suicide ground. The advance halted. They needed to clear out the defenders. Quintero was having none of it. His men were behind sandbags, hunkering low, and there were plenty of them. A few lucky grenades weren't enough. She could throw up all the smoke she wanted, but Quintero's constant fire meant he could cut her to pieces even if he couldn't see her.

The fire slackened. It dropped from torrent to steady rain. She radioed Luzhkov. "That you?" she asked.

"I think so. Looks like a hornet's nest."

"Watch yourself. They'll be angry."

"I hope so."

Heavy calibre fire swept above her head, punching out fist-fuls of wood. That bad luck grenade came in for her tree. She leapt backwards as her shelter disintegrated. The trunk fell her way and she rolled. The ground banged her hard, shocking a laugh out of her. Bullets *thunked* the ground around her and shot off branches from the fallen tree as she scrambled to the next patch of cover. She crouched behind a larger trunk. Vandelaare was there, laughing himself sick. "And the horse you rode in on," she told him, grinning.

"Is Viktor hitting them?"

She nodded. "Let's do this now." She signalled the retreat.

Quintero saw the wave break against his defences. The tide stopped. Gunfire and the occasional grenade still came from the leading edge of the advance, but not one of the enemy dared set foot in the open. He had achieved complete denial. Then the rate of fire picked up again, but it was coming from further back. It was covering a withdrawal. Chapel was right. The big assault was a diversion. He was more worried about the north flank. The numbers were smaller, but their fire was more accurate. They were taking down clutches of his men, then changing location and firing again. The return fire couldn't pin them down. They were being backed up by the rooftop snipers. Quintero's mobility on that side was compromised. There was no good defensive posture. Any man staying put long enough to get his bearings would take a bullet in the head before he had a bead on the enemy. He was forced to take refuge on the West Terrace itself. He lost the advantage of being able to see the battlefield directly. The open ground, at least, still worked in his favour, but not as well as to the south. The trees ended at an L-shaped parking lot, but the long spur of the L, running the length of the north face of the Capitol, had a cluster of three low buildings. They were the perfect approach for a small team. The enemy hadn't moved in yet, but meantime his attrition was starting to hurt. If it kept up, Quintero would be on the losing side of a numbers game. He had to counter with mobility and cover.

He still had ten LAV-25s, and close to 150 men. That made for a hell of a fist. He ordered half of them to load up and take twenty four-man fire teams into the target area. Blanket the zone with death. Flush the bastards out.

The run-and-gun was a good time, but the spoilers were on their way. There was plenty of cover, but not a big area. Luzhkov heard the rumble of engines. The time open to him contracted. He waved his team forward. They took fewer shots. They headed for the relative shelter of the outlying buildings. They moved fast. So did Quintero's forces. By the time Luzhkov reached the narrow strip of open terrain between him and the nearest wall, he could hear the APCs on either side and behind. Quintero had thrown a noose around his movement, and was cinching it tight. He radioed Blaylock. "Now would be a good time."

Quintero listened to the radio traffic as his cordon drew in on itself. The area on the outside was clean. The area inside was growing smaller. The snipers beyond the Mall were still stinging, but his troops were less vulnerable as they kept their movements aggressive and entered the cover of the trees themselves. He thought about telling Chapel that the end was in sight. He decided not to, leery of his own confidence. Then, from the south, came hell.

Western military strategists talked about the human-wave assault deception as part of the Asian box of tricks. Launch what looks like a massive attack, draw the opponent's attention, then hit him in the rear with special forces to do the real damage. It was a good tactic. It could work very well. Blaylock knew it. But so, she assumed, did everyone else. That wasn't a problem. That was her opportunity. She counted on Chapel and Quintero to be smart and anticipate the tactic. They had. So she struck with her double bluff. The human wave wasn't a deception. It really was the main assault. And it really was going to be a wave.

She waited on Luzhkov's signal. She worried he would let things develop until he was in real danger of being over-whelmed. But she willingly took the gift he gave her: a massive proportion of Quintero's troops drawn away to deal with the special forces incursion. Quintero wasn't being stupid. He was doing exactly the right thing, because if he didn't, Luzhkov and his men would punch through in no time and be on their merry way to the Senate Chamber. By mounting the insane charge, Blaylock was screwing Quintero. She was taking away the possibility of a correct decision.

She had solid numbers. Close to fifty strong, even after losses in the initial push. They weren't quite in the Passchen-daele league, but they were enough for a massive show of brute force. They were her battering ram, and she was on point. They launched grenades again, a heavier volley than before, and the rear echelon kept up with the barrage, not to stop until they ran out or the southern terrace of the Capitol was reduced to rubble. Into the mix this time came smoke grenades. The cloud they generated was even thicker than before. In the night, it rolled in on the Capitol like a freight train of dark-ness. Blaylock ran with it, holding fire. She was blind, seeing nothing but black and the streak of tracer fire. She held herself low but ran straight. There was no point trying to avoid fire from equally blind gunners. Before, the assault had been impossible with the countermeasures Quintero had thrown up. Now, he had diminished his forces, and her artillery was raining harder on the defenders who remained. Their fire was wilder, more sporadic.

It was still dangerous. She heard screams behind and to the side, knew she'd lost more warriors. A big sound, then, as a machine gun opened up and swept the ground. She dropped flat. The noise hammered the ground close to her. It stopped just short, cut off by a new blast. A lucky hit. She scrambled up and ran forward again, faster now, feeling the charge of armed violence at her sides. She was leading an unstoppable wave. Through the roiling cloud, she caught glimpses of the terrace and the movement on it, and now it was time to start firing.

The explosions again hemmed Quintero in, trapping him on the West Terrace. He'd only had a glimpse of the juggernaut thrust of the new attack. He had a vague impression of an endless stream of men storming the ramparts. He hesitated, delaying his response by terrible seconds as the dilemma split him. He had to stop the assault. But he couldn't leave the north open. He couldn't tell which strike was the bluff. He compromised, feeling control of the battlefield leak away, and sent half the remaining defenders to the south. He heard screams and thuds, but no concerted counterfire, and knew he'd made a mistake. He'd turned his men into cannon fodder. They had run into a grinder of rubble and gunfire. The defences were already broken. His troops couldn't regain the advantage. They couldn't even slow down the wave. He yelled for them to pull back to the west side and defend the doors themselves. He called off the north hunt. If he could bring those forces back fast enough, he might yet trap the southern attackers in a crossfire.

No more firing, now. That would give away his position. No more run and gun for Luzhkov, only run and hide. The noose was a good one. He heard firing to the northwest. He recognized the short bursts of assault rifle, the *whump* of a grenade launcher, and then the sustained chattering of a vehicle-mounted gun. A moment of silence, then, and there was the other fire team gone, simple as that. He and his team were sandwiched. They had been driven from the woods, and were crouched in the narrow alleyway between two of the buildings next to the Capitol. The passage ran north-south. At the southern end, it opened onto a narrow band of trees that nestled flush with the terrace. For the moment, the darkness of the alley and the shadows of the trees hid the fire team. Luzhkov figured another couple of minutes would see them located. They weren't going to be flushed, he decided. From these confined spaces, they could inflict some bad pain on the enemy before they were taken down. The attack, when it came, would be mostly from the north, and he was giving orders to concentrate fire in that direction when he heard a change in the enemy's movement. For the first time, the engines were moving *away* from his position. He was no longer in the centre of a shrinking, concentric circle. He exchanged a look with Sid Wilson. He'd heard it, too. "What the hell?" Wilson asked. He sounded almost disappointed to be deprived of his Alamo.

Luzhkov shrugged in reply and moved to the north exit. He risked poking his head out. He took a mental snapshot of the scene. He saw APCs grouping together and charging hard for the West Terrace. Luzhkov visualized Quintero's next move on the chessboard. He saw where Blaylock would shortly be, and what might happen. His move, then. He signalled his team to move out. Wilson's smile was a white smear shining from his balaclava. "What's the plan?" he asked.

"As much harassment as we can provide."

"Sounds nutty." The smile didn't falter.

"What isn't?"

They ran from cover, guns up. Luzhkov watched for infantry. He didn't want them as targets. It was the LAVs that had to be distracted or taken down. The big firepower.

Blaylock's wave crested the southern defences. The assault had created a ramp of rubble and bodies, and she barely had to break her stride as she ran, rather than climbed, up onto the terrace. There had been no enemy fire for the last minute. Her foe had retreated, leaving her that section of the field that she wanted more than any other. She turned to Vandelaare. "You know what might happen," she said.

"We've been through this. Let them try."

"You guys, try not to die too much."

He saluted. "Yes'm."

Vandelaare took over his part of the next phase, and Blaylock called Flanagan.

They ran through the forest. Daniel Hallam felt his age. It had been a long time since he had run. His body's gears ground and howled. And the night grew darker with every step. It might have been because of the trees, blocking the lights of the buildings they were leaving behind. It was certainly because of the smoke, the memory of fire and grenades, that lingered over the battleground. But the real darkness was made up of more than that. The night had its depths more for what it revealed than what it concealed. Each step was another rung down into the Inferno. Capitol Hill was heaped with shattered trees and pockmarked with craters. Hallam had to sidestep and leap over bodies, whole and scattered. He was running through two photographs that had no business being superimposed. One was a shot of every battle-scarred military high ground he'd ever heard of. The other was of the place he'd known, worked at and for, and loved his entire adult life. At its best, it represented the opposite of what the other photograph stood for. Now everything it was and could be was being demolished.

Every step, another rung down. The closer he and Flanagan came to the Capitol, the more choking the smoke, the louder the explosions and roars of fighting, and the more heart-stabbing the sights became. Now they emerged from the trees, and he could see the damage done to the Capitol. The building was still monumental in its presence and solidity, but its pride had been savaged. Stonework lay in tumbled heaps. The walls were scarred with an acne of bullet holes. Most of the windows on this side were shattered.

He glanced at Flanagan as they ran. He wanted to know if the other man was seeing what he was seeing. He thought he saw his eyes flinch. He thought he saw some frightened awareness, even if only for a moment. But then Flanagan's attention shifted, and his eyes flooded with eagerness. Hallam followed his gaze. The woman was standing on the terrace, at the head of a sloping heap of rubble. She was waving to them. She wanted them to climb. Hallam did. Around the corner to the west, he could hear the gigantic clash of many men killing each other. He looked up at the woman. She was kneeling, holding a hand out to help him over the top. In the dim light, she was a black silhouette against the moon-grey glow of the Capitol's marble. For a frozen moment, Hallam saw her framed by the wounds of the building, embraced by the roar of the night. He again wondered what demon he was now in thrall to. Would he have a soul left after this alliance? He had no choice, he knew, and Chapel must be stopped. But the cost was so high, it was beyond bearing.

"Come on," said the woman, snapping him out of the reverie. "Work to do."

That was what he feared.

The woman led the way to the Capitol's south wall. She stood beneath a broken window. She had already thrown up a rope ladder. She turned to the group. There were six of them all told, three soldiers in addition to her, Hallam and Flanagan. "Leave Chapel to me," she ordered. Flanagan and the other men nodded, and she climbed up and through the window.

Hallam watched her go. The last thing she'd said made the bottom fall out of his stomach. In her tone, he heard how *personal* this battle was. Was it for Chapel, too? Were all these people dying, was the country dying, for the sake of a vicious feud? He saw the truth of his role. He wasn't a great man of history. He was one of the little people, a cog, a puppet, a pawn. A peasant under the rule of a dragon. The knowledge did him no good at all. So he climbed up after the dragon's crimson daughter.

28

There was the way in that had a chance of preserving the way out. There was also the quick way. Vandelaare started in with the first. He rounded the southwestern corner of the terrace with blitzkrieg attitude, a lightning strike with all guns blazing and to hell with cover for those first few seconds. The SOA forces fell and fell back. He tried to push the advantage, but the defenders found their feet. They had cover. He didn't. He dropped flat behind a corpse and kept firing. His men had the expanse of the staircase to spread out and angle fire in. The enemy could only fire out from within the doorway. Worse lines of sight, fewer positions for men to shoot from, even if they did hold the high ground. Bullets chipped the ground near him. Something flashburned his right cheek. His face felt too loose. He ignored the sensation and crawled forward to the next body. The sound of engines behind him, *that* he couldn't ignore. He saw the bad shit about to rain down. His position was untenable unless he changed it fast. So he called for the second way in, the messy, risky, quicker one. A fire team that had been at the rear during the southern assault ran forward. The men dropped to their knees. Every man on the team had been tasked with becoming Blaylock's mobile artillery. They had limited themselves to hand grenades and launchers during the first phases of the battle. Now they brought out their reserve: each carried an M47 Dragon anti-tank missile. There were no tanks ahead. Didn't matter. They'd seen service in the Gulf War as just dandy bunker busters.

Simultaneous launch. The sixty tiny rockets of each missile's propulsion system fired. The Dragons streaked into the portico. They breathed a terrible fire.

Leadbetter could see a filibuster in the making. It had been less than an hour since she'd spoken, but already she was seeing the signs. That special momentum was building whose only effect was inaction. One senator after another felt the urgent need to speak on her motion. Each speaker was more loquacious and bereft of point than the last. They fed on each other's ramblings, going over the same ground, raising the same objections, repeating the same pieties again and again and again. And it wasn't just the Democrats. She had expected that: having recaptured the White House, however unfairly, they were hardly going to let it slip away without a struggle. But she was getting flack from her own party, too. Grand Old Men and Young Turks alike were rising to be recognized, and if they weren't all in outright opposition to her, they were sure good at raising obscure hypotheticals that somehow made everything she had said sound dubious. They were scared. They were turtling. They were hoping to do nothing until the crisis took care of itself. Her pulse throbbed. They were pissing away precious moments.

She seized the floor. "Honoured colleagues," she thundered, "do you really mean to throw our nation away?" Stunned silence. She had used language blunt with apocalypse and accusation. It simply wasn't done. Not like that. There had been plenty of blood, thunder and accusations of perfidy and weak sisterhood blandished in this room over the decades. But to cast aspersions on the entire assembled body was unheard of. She didn't care. If she had to grab the old boys' club by the balls (and most of her audience was still made up of old white boys), she would. She would squeeze blood from them if that's what it took to get these spineless teat-suckers to act.

Before she could continue, Alice Simone stood up. No balls to grab but plenty of spine, she'd been an early intruder to the old boys' club. She was also a member of Leadbetter's party, and though she represented a faction that had been increasingly sidelined since the Reagan years, she still commanded respect. She was a wired and wiry eighty-five, and had marked the usual age of retirement by renouncing every last iota of bullshit tolerance. Leadbetter despised her. "We're taking the time precisely to make sure that we don't," Simone said, every implication very much intended.

"Time that we do not have, and that our country doesn't have," Leadbetter countered. She waved her hand at the walls, beyond which came the faint sounds of gunfire. "Can't you hear what is happening out there? Do you honestly think that the solution is to do nothing? Do you think that if you wait long enough, the problem will take care of itself?" She was conscious, at the upper periphery of her vision, of Joe Chapel gazing down from the Public Gallery. If the debate went against her, she wondered, what would Chapel do? He would not concede defeat and walk away, she was certain of that. Right now was the moment of perfect opportunity, the golden second that, if grasped, would set America down the right path for good and all. If it was missed, then everything would grow worse. She didn't doubt Chapel's patriotism, his commitment, or the truth of his beliefs. What she doubted was his ability to refrain from the reckless pyrrhic gesture.

"What would we lose if we made the wrong decision?" Simone fired back.

And then George Lind was on his feet, *again*, and taking his own tangent that, for once, tied horribly well into the doubts Simone was raising. "And perhaps the esteemed Secretary of State," he said, "might be so kind, so considerate, as to inform the House exactly who these people are who are watching over us in so heavily armed a fashion."

Well, shit. "They are the bulwark between the government of the people and absolute chaos," Leadbetter said. If she thought she'd committed herself before, boy was she ever in deep now. The senators gazed back at her. They weren't buying. "How, in the name of our Lord, can you delay voting any longer?" She tried reversing the meaning of their inaction in the face of the din of war. They weren't ignoring it. They were being cowards. "Will you tell your grandchildren that you let the terrorists frighten you out of your duty?" That rattled them. No one spoke up right away. No one returned her gaze this time. They were unsure. But that wasn't enough. She knew, with a certainty that filled her with dread for herself and her country, that she was going to lose the debate. She needed new ammunition. She needed more than the muffled sounds of war. The human animal was too accomplished at denial. With the noise at a distant remove, the politicians could still maintain their self-delusions of immunity. Nothing could touch them, not in this building, of all places. She had to prove them wrong.

The sound of the explosion was much, much closer.

Quintero had his back to the western doors. He stood behind a pile of sandbags. He watched the impact of the attackers against his forces. His men fought back well, but they were in a bottleneck. The LAVs were slower to return than he wanted. They might still create the vise that would crush the invaders. They might. In the meantime, half a pincer was an invitation to slaughter. The enemy pushed forward. His front lines collapsed. He accepted the inevitable: the enemy was going to breach the Capitol. He didn't accept failure. The game would be different inside. Everyone would be fighting in constrained spaces. If he could hold the woman's army at bay long enough, the political magic might work itself. He took a dozen men through the doors with him to add to the contingent already inside. His standing orders for the rest were to fight to the last man. He reinforced the orders by locking the doors behind him. He had just started down the hall to the Rotunda when he suddenly went deaf. And he was flying.

Vandelaare ducked low as limbs and fleshy chunks blew past him. The Dragons punched the doors off their hinges. Marble became a choking cloud. He stood and ran into the cloud. A foul rain of blood and bits of stone fell around him. The charge took him to the doorway. There he had to pause. There was so much wreckage, it had become a new obstacle. They were going to have to clamber over the rubble of the doorway. Not so quick after all. And behind him, the roar of the engines was louder yet, and then it became the killing chatter of heavy machine gun fire.

Quintero grabbed a wall, hauled himself to his feet. He could hear nothing but ringing. Dust from the explosion drifted down the corridor. He didn't look back. He ran forward, saw his stunned troops follow his example. Abandon the entrance. Take up better positions further inside. In some of the narrower corridors, numbers would make less of a difference.

His ears began to clear, and he smiled as he heard the sounds of his pincer movement completing itself.

There was a narrow line of trees marching up Pennsylvania Avenue to the West Terrace. Luzhkov stood behind a trunk and saw the SOA troops pull out all the stops. He couldn't get near enough to slow the counterattack down. The infantry had formed a loose circle around the LAVs, with most of the guns facing away from the Capitol. The protective perimeter kept him at bay. He and his team sniped targets of opportunity, but there were too many of them, and the vehicles were untouchable. The gunners stayed inside and protected until they were in position. Then they were up, jack-in-the-boxes, and firing on Vandelaare's positions. Luzhkov looked through his scope, saw how long the process of getting inside the Capitol was taking. Vandelaare was on the receiving end of the same type of slaughter he had just perpetrated. Luzhkov sighted a gunner, took him down. He was replaced within seconds. Luzhkov kept firing. Nothing came back at him.

"Bastards are ignoring us," Wilson said.

Luzhkov grunted. They were. His team were gnats, dishing out damage to be absorbed until the main force was wiped out. He shot another gunner, but it was a drop in the bucket and the killing was huge. Men dropped, pinned to the staircase by the torrent of bullets. Luzhkov saw, to his horror, that two of the APCs were the same model that had been on the Arlington Bridge, armed with TOWs. He concentrated his fire on those. He swung his sights back and forth between the two vehicles, dropping a continuous stream of gunners. And meanwhile, Wilson was yelling with frustration, fuming at the insult of being considered irrelevant. He stepped out of cover. He shouted, "Come on you motherfuck—"

They weren't being completely ignored. The bullet tore the top half of Wilson's head off. He remained standing for a moment, mouth slack with a look of dumb surprise. Then his knees buckled. He collapsed like an accordion. Luzhkov blinked Wilson's blood out of his eyes, and when he was back the scope, the first TOW was flying.

Vandelaare was in. So were a half-dozen other soldiers. They provided what cover fire they could. The troops trickled in. He saw the flash from an APC, had time to think a complete, bitter thought about irony as he threw himself to the side, and then the missile had shot through the doors and exploded against the interior wall. Enormous light, enormous sound, and then darkness, and enormous weight.

Another explosion, worse than the last. Leadbetter straightened. "You hear that?" she thundered. "That is the sound of what could be this body's finest hour."

This time, the eyes that met hers were buying.

They were in the House Reading Room. Despite the bombardment, the power was still on throughout the Capitol. Enough of the electric candelabra had survived to show off the damage. The racks of newspapers were scattered dominoes. The deep blue mosaic tiling was fading under dust. Near the new entrance in the wall, the tiles had been gouged away by the blast. The gilt panelling had been chewed up by weapon fire. Antique wood tables and chairs were overturned. Some were shattered. The room, Blaylock thought, was an elegant ideal chewed by the jaws of an unforgiving reality. She was part of that reality. So were Jean Decaux, Phil Lambeck and Tony Earl. Their expressions were neutral but alert. They were looking for the next round. They weren't interested in the pathos of the setting.

Blaylock turned to Flanagan and Hallam. She had half a victory in getting them this far. She wanted to know what costs she had incurred. The president was looking at her with undisguised horror. To him, she said, "Did you have a better way of making it inside?"

"No."

"This can be rebuilt, you know."

"The building can, yes."

There wasn't time for this. But still she asked, "Meaning what?" She asked because she needed to see herself through other eyes. She needed to know exactly what she was, and what, if anything, she had left. For informational purposes only. It was interesting to track the descent. Not *to* Hell. *Through* it. She'd burned past Dante's door a long time ago.

"Why is all of this happening?"

"Because Joe Chapel made it necessary."

"And you didn't?"

"Maybe I did, by letting him live." Her answer was too quick, too glib, too pat. Especially for herself. She drew Flanagan aside. "How are you doing?"

"Pretty good." A little too cheerful. A little bit forced.

She wrapped her hands around the back of his head, touched his forehead to hers for a moment. "Mike," she whispered, "tell me why you're here."

"To fight, of course, what else would you—"

"Why?"

"Because it has to be done."

She didn't think that reason would be quite good enough coming from her. It definitely wasn't coming from him. She had her eyes closed. "Tell me the truth," she insisted.

Seconds passed. She heard him breathe. She heard his effort as he dug through his adrenaline to find his own fanged but vital reality. He said, "To be with you."

And that was beautiful. It really was. There was much that was awful about it, because of what he was doing to himself, how he was changing who he was in order to be her partner, but oh, how she loved the beauty and wonder of those four syllables all the same. Only they didn't make her feel better. She had heard a fifth syllable. It had come in the form of a pause just after "be." It was so brief, she wasn't sure Flanagan had been fully aware of how he had corrected himself in mid-sentence. Maybe he hadn't. Maybe she was imagining things. But for a ghastly moment, she thought he'd been about to say, "To be *like* you."

Well. Another of her own pretty rooms being trashed. There would be time to rebuild or demolish later. Now, she'd spent too much time not killing. "This is your turf," she told Hallam. "You guide us. But you don't set foot over a doorway until I give the all-clear. Yes?"

He nodded, still willing to follow orders.

To the others, she said, "Keep him alive. If we don't, this has all been for nothing." More nods, with Flanagan looking pleased to be included. "So lead us," she said to Hallam.

The Senate Chambers were in the north wing of the Capitol. They were going to have to make their way along the entire length of the building. The time involved bothered Blaylock. Nothing to be done. If they rushed, they'd hand Chapel his victory. She rationalized the slow progress by telling herself that nothing that happened in the Senate would be irreversible. There was nothing that Chapel could make that she couldn't destroy.

Her great hope: that she had enough of Quintero's forces tied down outside that there would be limited numbers in the building itself. If so, tactical necessity would limit the number of patrols. Quintero and Chapel would have to concentrate what force they had near the Senate Chambers, and not dilute their strength trying to keep track of non-vital areas. The endgame was being decided in a single room. Everything else could go whistle.

The route Hallam suggested was the simplest. Once they were past the House Chamber, it was a straight line down the centre of the Capitol to the Senate. Between the House and the Rotunda, they saw no one. Blaylock couldn't believe the building was as deserted as it appeared. There had to be cleaning staff and late-working politicians caught short by the war. But if they were around, they had gone to ground and were staying there. Good for them, and an easier path for her.

They heard the explosions as they approached Statuary Hall. Blaylock had been waiting for them. She started to smile, bit it back when she saw Hallam blanch. Their bootsteps echoed on the black-and-white checkered marble floor, bounced up the columns to the arc of the roof, but were swallowed by the growing noise of gunfire. Blaylock thought she heard running footsteps further ahead. She halted the march at the exit from the Hall and looked ahead. Dust filled the Rotunda. She didn't see any movement. Then came another round of explosions, ones she hadn't expected, and she knew she wouldn't be getting any reinforcements. She waited for the blasts to finish reverberating, and for the dust to settle. She tried not to think about what the sound of sustained heavy machine gun fire meant. She led the party forward again, stopped just before the Rotunda. She poked her head in and out quickly. She took in the vastness, the dome, the friezes, the balconies. Deserted, the Rotunda made her think of a tremendous bell. It was waiting for her to set foot inside before it pealed.

Flanagan had come up behind her. He was following her gaze. "Um," he whispered.

"Yeah," she agreed. "Shit." Sharpshooter's paradise. She and her charges were going to play the wooden ducks. There was no good way across. All Quintero would need was two men in balconies on opposite sides of the Rotunda, and they would command the floor, each having prime line of sight on the only area—straight down—that would be awkward for the other shooter. If they'd been watching, they would have seen her. They would be waiting for the ducks to emerge again. Nice.

"Take the long way round?" Flanagan asked.

"Maybe."

They tried. There was a corridor that ran west, and promised a detour through offices. They didn't get far. They ran up against a wall of fallen stonework. The damage from the dual assault on the main entrance was more extensive than she'd realized. There was no way past. As they returned to the Rotunda entrance, she had a sense of having funnelled herself into a prime kill zone. Under cover, she stared down the hall to the slice of the Rotunda visible through the doorway. It was a space of majesty, calm and marble. Not an enemy in sight. The Dome called to her. She had wounded the Capitol, and stood now at its heart. She didn't trust its invitation, though its vengeance would be justified.

The far doorway was an abyss away. It waited. Blaylock visualized the run, assessed the risk, came up with the best countermeasures. She checked her belt. Plenty of ammo for her c7 and sig, three frag grenades, and a couple of special gifts that she wanted to hold back. "Anyone still have smoke?" she asked.

A silence, meaning negative. Then, "A couple of flash-bangs," Lambeck offered.

Inadequate and silly in a lit space this big. But they might be enough to momentarily dazzle eyes looking through a scope. "First one just as we start," Blaylock said. "Second when I call for it." Lambeck nodded. "Mike and the president in the centre," she went on. "And make sure you keep your running random. The rest of us in a square. Three-sixty covering fire. Aim up, spray wide. Cross your fingers."

"Are you sure someone's there?" Hallam asked.

"I would be."

Blaylock and Lambeck ran in first, a second behind his grenade. They ran with their eyes closed, so they were already on the move when the flash went off. The concussion of the blast was stunning, but they could all see their goal when they opened their eyes, and they stayed on it. They split away from each other as they left the shelter of the doorway. Flanagan and Hallam came next. Blaylock heard them doing their best to zigzag unpredictably. Earl and Decaux forming the rear now. They were all firing in jerky, wild bursts, filling the Dome with bullet-song. They reached the centre of the Rotunda. "Two," Blaylock yelled, and Lambeck threw his second flashbang high. Eyes shut, *wham*. The deafening peal of the bell. Fight the buckling knees and keep going. Spray the bullets. Bob and weave. Two thirds of the way there.

The first shot came. Marble exploded a foot away from the president. Blind luck. He had just changed direction. If he had taken another step the way he'd been going, the bullet would have gone through his skull. Flanagan lunged in his direction, knocked him off balance and his stagger took him out of the way of the second bullet. It stabbed down between the two men, a final judgment missed by inches. Then Blaylock was throwing herself at both of them, self-preservation overwhelmed by the deeper terrors of defeat and bereavement. Both of them leaped aside to avoid being hit by her locomotive charge. Two bullets this time, from opposite directions. The first went wide. The second streaked down her side, white fire close as a lover's finger. It sliced vertically down her jacket. Billions-to-one, it clipped off her belt and knocked free a grenade. Blaylock fell. She'd seen one of the

443

muzzle flashes. Lower balcony, above the southern door. In the corner of her eye, she saw Decaux direct his fire behind her. He'd spotted the north shooter.

A glance down. On the floor, an arm's length away, a live grenade with no pin. She scrabbled forward, electric heat on her side, grabbed the grenade, twisted and flung it up. As she did, the muzzle flashed again, but her throw had startled the man out of his precision. The grenade exploded as it hit the balcony. Figures on the frieze discovered violent motion, their limbs and heads flying outward.

Blaylock on her feet again, running for the exit. Behind her and above, a keening. Someone was broken badly. Good.

Earl and Lambeck had taken the lead. A short corridor now led to the Small Senate Rotunda. Flanagan and Hallam stopped, boys being good, well before the doorway. Earl and Lambeck had the momentum. They barely paused. A lightning check of the room and they were in. Blaylock saw the mistake coming, but was too late in catching up.

The Senate Rotunda was made up of two circles: an outer perimeter and a ring of thick-pillared arches. It was a wonderland of concealment. The mistake took Earl in the eye as he ran in. His head jerked. The exit wound blew grey matter, blood and bone shrapnel back at Blaylock. As his body crumpled to the ground, Lambeck threw himself right, behind the nearest pillar. "Guard the entrance," Blaylock told Decaux, and took the left pillar. She checked her flanks. No one coming her way. "Lambeck!" she called.

"Clear my side!" he yelled back.

The enemy, however many there were, had to be towards the north exit, then. Maybe not that far, though. Her field of vision was extremely circumscribed. The curve of the wall was tight, the space between the two rings a shadowy tunnel. "Pincer!" she shouted to Lambeck. She was also telling the opposition. So she stayed put, edged around to the right side of the pillar until she could see into the centre of the room. She saw Lambeck dodge from arch to arch. He was two-thirds of the way towards the north end when she saw a man flit out from behind the arch nearest that exit. He scuttled low and quick, sticking close to the east side of the room, invisible to Decaux back at the entrance. Blaylock applauded his move. He was going to avoid the pincer movement and come up behind them. Too bad she had lied about the movement. She shot him in mid-stride. He fell forward, sliding on his own blood. "Lambeck!" she called again.

"I'm at the door."

"Keep coming."

He did. They didn't flush any more rabbits out. Blaylock moved to the centre of the room, nodded to Decaux. She checked the body, scavenged a couple more frag grenades from it. When the others had joined her, she asked Hallam, "How close are we?"

"Close," he said.

Noises came from the direction of the Rotunda. It sounded like a heavy hammering and moving of stone. Like the clearing of rubble, she guessed. "We'd better be."

Luzhkov swore. Under his breath, he found the comfort of his mother tongue in a glossolalic rant of sublime profanity. It was the most productive thing he had left to do. There were three of them. No way to get at the APCs. He and the remainder of his team circled and strafed. Given time, they would make their presence felt through sheer attrition, but there wasn't time. The double slaughter on the West Terrace was done, and the last men standing, still a force of a few dozen, were working to get past the wreckage. He whittled their numbers. He slowed their work. He tried to act as a decoy. They didn't bite. The orders must have been firm. And the work progressed, no matter what he did.

Ron Cohen took a bullet in the throat. He died with his face frozen in indignation. Luzhkov sympathized. The bullet had been a stray. It had ricocheted off a concrete wall. So now random stupidity was taking them down. He had one man left, Oleg Chelishchev, another Kornukopia refugee.

"Feels bad," Chelishchev said in Russian.

Luzhkov nodded. His hands squeezed his rifle as if to bend it. He flushed with a mixture of helplessness, impotent rage and, most of all, shame. He had let Blaylock down. He was staring at a battle he could not affect. He couldn't imagine Blaylock standing here with her thumb up her ass. Each second of inaction compounded his shame.

"Must be something we can do," Chelishchev said, echoing his thoughts and driving the shame in deeper.

There was an action. It was better than nothing. There was the other entrance, created by Blaylock. "Let's go," he told Chelishchev, and set off at a run. He began to feel better. Inside, close quarters, he could lose the sniper and turn to his AK-74, which still had plenty of rounds. Inside, close quarters, the numbers would shift again. Back and forth, back and forth, the math of the battle was as fickle as it was symmetrical. Luzhkov radioed Blaylock. "Want some backup?"

"Couldn't hurt."

Results of the final equation? Spin the wheel.

The explosions ended the arguments. Denial was no longer an option. Leadbetter had her vote. Down the alphabet went the calling of names. One by one, the senators rose and gave their answers. Chapel watched. Leadbetter had her vote, but she didn't have her unanimity. There were nays. They didn't respect party lines. Chapel saw as many Republicans turn against her as Democrats join her. Halfway through, and the tally was in her favour, though the margin wasn't big enough to be definitive. He felt his jaw tighten another notch with each vote con. Was this what he was fighting for? A country that could vote to destroy itself, even in the face of the most incontrovertible evidence that that was exactly what it was doing? Why bother?

Because of how things could be, he reminded himself. Because of how things had been, and how they would be again. That was just as incontrovertible. He was going to win. The alternative possibility simply didn't exist.

Even so, with each "nay," his pistol grew a little heavier, a little more insistent, in his shoulder holster.

The next two rooms were clear. The lack of opposition bothered Blaylock. The skirmishes so far had been small-scale. Not enough men. Quintero had to have more strength than that. Which meant he was holding it back. The longer he did, the bigger it would be when she encountered it.

Hallam was looking cautious and eager at the same time. There was a short corridor leading from the gallery they were now crossing. Beyond it, space opened up east and west, but straight north was a door. The distance was small. Hallam was staring at the door. Blaylock called a halt. "Where are we?" she asked.

Hallam pointed. "That's the door to the Senate cloak-rooms," he whispered. "And through them is the Chamber."

"Tell me about the space I'm seeing."

"It's a hall. A big one." He wasn't stupid, then. He saw the danger.

Blaylock filtered out the noise of the SOA soldiers clearing fallen marble. She listened to the silence of the hall. She visualized her own defence of the territory. She saluted a fine opponent as she promised him a terrible death.

She looked at the door. She took the ambush for granted. She factored in the crossfire. She rehearsed her steps. Reaching the door herself wouldn't be hard. Getting Hallam across and alive, that would be a bit more difficult. She saw how it would happen, every movement choreographed to a specific second and no other. She turned to the others. To Hallam, she said, "Memorize where the door is. You'll be going for it blind. When I call, you run, and you stop for *nothing*. If you hesitate at all, we lose everything. Clear?" He nodded. To Flanagan and Decaux, she said, "You two do the same. And you..." Her throat dried suddenly. She swallowed. "You flank him," she finished. She stared at the ground. She had just ordered Flanagan to make himself a target. Tactically, it was the only thing to do. She fought the urge to vomit. Flanagan leaned in. Kissing through their balaclavas wasn't easy, but he managed it. "Thank you," he whispered, making her feel even worse. *You're willing to sacrifice the man you love for the good of the mission,* she thought. *Do you have anything left?*

There was no answer but the humming of her machine.

29

It was a long run. Luzhkov and Chelishchev moved at a fast jog back down the length of the Capitol, up into the breach on the south flank, and then back again inside. No one bothered them. The exterior forces were entirely concentrated on getting in. Inside, all they found was bodies. Luzhkov didn't worry about a careful check of each room. He followed Blaylock's bloody trail of breadcrumbs. From the moment of decision to the arrival at the Rotunda, it had taken five minutes. The scrape of stone on stone was loud. Quintero's boys were going to be coming through. They turned left and raced for the entrance. There was the crumbling sound of a small rockslide, a puff of dust, and Luzhkov felt night air on his face. He hugged the right wall, Chelishchev the left. The first of the SOA men crawled through a hole that had been punched through the rubble. Luzhkov took him, shot him to dead meat, dead weight, partially plugging the hole that had just been made. The next soldier made the mistake of clambering over the body, gun in hand, firing blind and uselessly. Chelishchev finished that one.

Now they had a barrier again. Luzhkov waited for the corpses to be pulled out so they could start again. The set-up was good. The wreckage still formed a large, sloping pile, perfect cover, great obstacle. They could keep this up indefinitely, unless the enemy grew tired of the game and decided to fire another few missiles and close up the entrance once and for all.

He'd have to watch for that.

The bodies were dragged out. Luzhkov and Chelishchev stayed low. No one else was coming through just yet. Maybe the enemy had already found a workaround. Bad news. Then he heard a groan. It came from within the rubble pile, near his feet. He looked at Chelishchev. He'd heard it, too. "Don't let them through," Luzhkov said.

"Not likely."

Luzhkov crouched. "Hey," he said.

The groan came again, slightly to the right. It didn't seem to be coming from too deep within the heap. Luzhkov began hauling stonework away. He started higher up the pile than he thought he had to go, to reduce the chance of more rock falling down and further crushing whoever was below. It had to be an ally. The collapse had happened during the SOA counterattack.

Chelishchev let off a burst.

"What?" Luzhkov asked.

"Nothing. Just trying to get their attention. Didn't want them to get bored."

"What are they doing?" He dragged a particularly heavy chunk out of the way.

"Not much. Talking. Waiting for something."

"Orders."

The voice from the rubble, a croaked whisper: "Viktor."

He thought recognized it. "Peter?"

An affirmative grunt from Vandelaare. Luzhkov dug faster. The rubble shifted and he almost fell through. He'd found a hollow where two large pieces of marble had fallen against each other. They formed a low tent over Vandelaare's chest. He cleared the chaos away from the South African's torso and face. "How bad?" he asked.

Vandelaare blinked, wincing in the sudden return of light. "Bad. Can't feel my legs. Can you get me out of here, man?"

"Yes." Still, mindful of time and priorities, he radioed Blaylock. He would free Vandelaare. There was just the little question of when the success of the mission would let him.

"Where are you?" Blaylock asked.

"In the Rotunda. Found a man down here, but we can extract him." No names. Better for security, and better for a clear-eyed judgment call.

"What's the status of the enemy?"

"Pending. If they try to come in this way, we can keep them out, for a good while anyway."

A pause. Then, "Leave."

"What?"

"Win or lose, this will be done in the next few minutes. You bought the time I needed. Now take our man and get out before the real army shows up."

"Roger that." He started digging again.

"We're going?" Vandelaare asked. His voice was so weak, he sounded sleepy.

"We're going."

Blaylock began the dance. She lobbed a frag against the door to the cloakrooms. As the explosion punched the way open, she took out the gifts she had been hoarding: two thermite grenades, held back for the chance she would need to bring a fire to the party. The incendiaries had served her well in the past. She trusted them to do so again, and their light would be at least as important as their heat. Right hand at her strapped C7, with her left she popped the pins, one, two. She released the handles. One, and she was running. Two, she threw herself down and rolled diagonally into the hall, to the side of the door, leaving the way clear. Three, she sent one grenade skittering left on the floor. Four, twist of the body, and the other incendiary bounced to the right. And on that "four," the last second before she shut her eyes tight, she saw the nature of Quintero's ambush, saw that it was good. Then her eyes closed, as the first bullets flew overhead, where they had expected her head to be.

And she yelled, "*Now!*"

And the grenades went off, giant, brighter-than-sun flashes one after another. They shone red through her eyelids. The heat baked her cheeks. She was still finishing the movement that had brought her into the room. She tucked in as she went forward and was on her feet before the light of the first blast faded. Before the second was done, she had her C7 raised above her head and angled down. She spun, firing full-auto bursts at her memory of Quintero's emplacements. Covering fire for the blind runners.

The red faded. The heat didn't. She felt the wind of passing bodies. She opened her eyes. Liquid flames had spread across the floor and were licking up the walls. The carpet was raging.

To the east, her timing had been perfect, and the front line of the ambush was a twist of writhing limbs and screaming flesh. To the west, the damage wasn't as full, but the line was being driven back by the fire. She had her seconds of total chaos in the enemy ranks. Her charges ran for the door, Flanagan and Decaux faithfully flanking Hallam. She concentrated her fire west, punching lethal holes in dazzled men. She disembowelled the ambush. She turned men into fountains of blood and heaps of useless, torn muscle. She howled her triumph.

But war was chaos that belonged to no one, and there was discipline and training in the enemy ranks. There was return fire. In Blaylock's precious seconds of surprise and fire, the response was disorganized, badly aimed, and dangerous all the same. Three steps from the doorway, Flanagan stumbled. He pitched forward. Hallam, his eyes still closed, must have felt the movement and he paused a split second. Only Decaux kept a steady pace, so only his head was where an experienced shooter might have predicted it to be. So only his head took the bullet. It entered his temple and mushroomed inside his skull. Blood erupted out the other side like the blast from a rocket engine. His body spun on momentum and severed strings. It fell against Hallam. The president tripped and tangled with Flanagan. The two men tumbled through the blasted door and into the cloakroom.

Blaylock saw the game of random luck. She saw how much she had almost lost. She was vaguely aware of yelling, "*Go!*" and then there was no mission, no strategy, only the need for total retribution, the absolute necessity of becoming nothing but war. She crouched and kept firing east, the direction the shot had come from. The flames were high enough for visual cover, and the advantage was now with her as she scuttled left and right, strafing the end of the hall with bullets. She was only one target. She was firing at a concentration. She could hardly miss. When there were no more screams or bullets from that direction, she turned her attention west, just in time to see a tapestry thrown over the flames. There were four men charging her way. She leaped right, still firing. Her bullets marched over the line, chewing two of them up. Their own shots screamed around her. One slammed into the wall beside her face and spat marble shrapnel at her. The side of her head burst white with dozens of tiny daggers. She staggered. As she dropped to her knees, she grabbed and tossed the last of her frag grenades. It fell behind the attackers. The explosion shot them through the air at her. One landed with a groan. The other somehow stayed on his feet and kept coming. The pain in her head was so enormous it yanked her lips wide in a sardonic grin. She was laughing with agony as she rose to meet the soldier and slammed the butt of her rifle against his chin. His neck snapped. He dropped, and she shot him in the chest for good measure.

She turned to the last man, trying to see clearly through her wince. Her every exhalation was a growl, equal parts rage and pain, all animal. Through his bruises, burns and cuts, she recognized Jorge Quintero. With talon hands, she grabbed him by the collar, hauled him to his feet, and shoved him ahead of her through the door to the cloakroom.

Meredith Leadbetter had her vote. She had her victory, by a tiny majority. She had history, she had a legal improvisation, she had the future and salvation of the nation. Then everything went wrong, wrong, wrong, and it wasn't right, wasn't right, not fair, not fair, *not fair*. She hadn't even been addressed *once* as president when explosions and gunshots erupted just outside the Chamber. The Senate rose as one, a herd catching the stench of panic and ready to stampede. Smoke billowed into the Chamber. And there, running in with a man in a facemask, was Daniel Hallam.

The moment was pivotal, and stretched to an agonizing eternity. Leadbetter had all the time in the world to see the constitutional nightmare that had just bloomed, and to know how it would be resolved. She would lose, it was that simple. As the moment rolled on, she raised her eyes to Chapel in the Public Gallery. He was standing straight. He was rigid. He was vibrating. He looked ready to leap over the low balcony to the floor of the Chamber. Then the moment was suddenly rushing to its conclusion, and she hadn't had the time to find the right strategy. So she said the most pathetic thing imaginable. "Mr. President," she began.

"Do shut up," Hallam snapped. He turned to the face the Senate, his face haggard and dust-streaked. "Do you have any idea what has been going on here? Any of you? Do you care? Do you know under whose protection you have been?"

His speech gave her the opportunity to find the kernel of a strategy. "Mr. President," she began again, "you are the one who is the company of a masked man."

He whirled on her with a rage in the same league as Chapel's, but she saw a weakness there, too. This was a man who hadn't been in control of his own destiny, never mind the country's, for some time, and he'd been damaged. Before he could speak, there was a crescendo of violence outside the

prop himself up against a wall. His face was pale agony, but he was grinning.

"So," he said. "Do we call it a draw?"

(*Blood and fire.*) Images of all the people he had killed. Kelly Grimson blown apart for trying to save her from herself and *trying to save this man.* The thousands in the Hamptons vaporized for ideological wet dreams. (*Blood and fire.*) She didn't shoot him. She put her rifle and her knife down and took another step towards him. Chapel sniffed the smoke that seeped into the Chamber. "I think this is where we came in," he said. He was right. Geneva all over again, with her confronting his broken body in a shattered seat of power.

"Never too late to correct a mistake," she answered and snatched his cane. Worry crossed his face. "I bet you thought that beating they gave you in Switzerland hurt." Her voice was coming to her from a huge distance. Her consciousness was filled with the womb-beat of lava. Far, far away, she was shaking her head and saying, "Sherbina was a fucking amateur." Up close, in *bloodandfire* detail and the erotic perfection of war and rage, she swung the cane and broke Chapel's right knee. He slid down the wall. She broke his collarbone. She stomped on his wrist, snapped it, and laid in to his kidneys. When he started to scream, his blood was already pattering against her chest and face. She swung and swung and swung, bursting organs and sending teeth flying. She corrected the mistake of Geneva, and snapped his spine. When the cane broke, she picked up her rifle and used the butt. He was unrecognizable and still screaming when she hauled his soft weight up, leaned his head nose-first against the wall, and drove her boot against his skull until his shriek hit a keening climax and cut off, and there was nothing solid left to beat.

The red haze parted. As it did, she became aware of a rhythm that had accompanied the execution. The rhythm became a voice. It was Hallam, hoarse, desperate, still begging, "Stop, stop, stop, *stop!*" She stepped away from Chapel's corpse, faced the president. He was being supported by George Lind. His expression was a withered mix of weakness and horror. His voice fell to a whisper, but was determined. "I have to stop you."

It was time to go. At her back, the shadows and smoke that filled the Capitol called to her, promising concealment. Still, she gazed back at the man she had saved, the man whose principles had marked him as someone she would defend and fight for. The man whose principles now demanded that he become her adversary. Stop her? Stop war? "Try," she said.

And pitied him.

acknowledgments

Writing, let's be frank, is, by its nature, just a teeny, tiny, little bit self-indulgent, and I am enormously lucky to be surrounded by people who are so completely supportive of my obsessions. And so to my wife, Margaux Watt, and to my stepchildren, Kelan and Veronica Young, my thanks for love, support, feedback, patience, and so much more than a simple thank you can express. My gratitude also to my parents, my sister and my brother for always being there, and always believing.

I am incredibly fortunate to have the editor and the publisher that I do. Thank you, as ever, to Wayne Tefs for his unerring eye and judgment. To Jamis Paulson, Sharon Caseburg and Christine Mazur at Turnstone, my thanks for continued support and for showing me just how exciting and collaborative the publishing process can be.

For website help, hosting, support and presence, my thanks to Gino Sassani of Upcomingdiscs.com.

Research for this book was made easier by a number of texts, and I owe a particular debt to *How to Build a Nuclear Bomb* by

Frank Barnaby, *Coup d'État: A Practical Handbook* by Edward Luttwak, *Phantom Solider: The Enemy's Answer to U.S. Firepower* by H. John Poole, *Combat Techniques: An Elite Forces Guide to Modern Infantry Tactics* by Chris McNab and Martin J. Dougherty, *Deadly Doses: A Writer's Guide to Poisons* by Serita Deborah Stevens and Anne Klarner, and *The Elite Forces Handbook of Unarmed Combat* by Ron Shillingford. As always, any inaccuracies are entirely my fault, and not that of my sources. On that note, I should add that I have taken some dramatic licence with the city of Washington, DC (especially with its sewer system). Petersfield, of course, exists only in my imagination.

And finally, my thanks to you, the reader. Without you, this self-indulgent profession really is a little bit pointless, now isn't it?

Crown Fire

the battle begins

The police finished with Flanagan sooner than he had expected. Now he was sorry that they had. He was standing in the kitchen of his Hudson Tower apartment in Battery Park City. He couldn't remember why he was there. He hadn't come for food, he knew that. It was eleven o'clock, he was completely freaked, sleep was a very distant option, and he didn't want to be alone. He walked to the entrance hall and stared at his coat. Go out? Go out where? Call Holly? Call Harland? Again? No. They'd already done their time on the phone with him this evening. They were probably asleep now, and how much further could he justify bringing murder into their homes?

Okay, so go out. Just go where there are people. There was a bar a block up at the corner of Albany and South End. He didn't go there often. It was called Characters, but that was a lie. It was about as generic as you could get, but that was probably for the best right now. Tonight the bar was practically deserted. Flanagan had hoped for more people. He counted six. Still, better than nothing. And now that he was here, he wasn't interested in socializing. He just wanted evidence of other lives, of the world continuing on as usual. He sat at the bar and ordered a boilermaker. He would deal with the hangover tomorrow. If he had to, he'd even call in sick.

Two drinks in, the buzz wasn't happening right. It was as if the adrenalin from earlier was still hanging around, burning off the alcohol almost as fast as he could down it. He could feel his body begin to lose precision, but his mind wasn't getting any of the benefit. Solution: order a third drink.

"Hard day at the office?"

Flanagan turned his head to the right. A woman had come in and was sitting two stools over. She was smiling, and she had a nice smile, but her eyes almost made him look away. Dark eyes, very dark, matching the raven of her short hair. They were deep, dangerously so, glittering, and he could feel targeting lasers coming from them, painting the terrain, evaluating and moving on. Caught in their search, he felt a scan take him in, size him up, and download everything worth knowing. Already vulnerable enough, he broke gaze. But when he looked again, the eyes had accomplished their mission, and there was only the smile. He smiled back, trying to place the other thing that was striking him about her. He couldn't put his finger on it. She was dressed in a black wool pantsuit and a white cotton blouse, pumps. The Career Woman, courtesy *Vogue*. And that was part of it: the clothes were perfect, but sat on her as if they weren't quite sure what they were doing there. But there was more. What, what? He could see the faint trace of a scar running a diagonal from her hairline, over her left eye, to her cheek. But still, so what, none of his business. Something else was hitting an off key, though, something else…. And yet there was that smile. It said, Talk to me. It said, Relax. It said, No fear. It said things he really needed to hear. "You don't want to know about my day," Flanagan said, now very much hoping that she would disagree, that she would get it out of him, that he could spill his guts yet again tonight.

"Why don't I be the judge of that?"

"You always this sympathetic with strange men, Ms. ...?"

"Baylor. Jen Baylor." She shifted over to the stool next to his. "And you are?"

"Mike Flanagan." They shook, and the off-key something now rang home. Those were not Career Woman hands. Strong, calloused, strangers to manicures. Weird.

But the grip was firm, and had the same Trust Me message as the smile. Flanagan decided to go with the good instincts.

"Pleased to meet you, Mike," said Baylor. "And to answer your question, let's say I feel pulled to tend wounded animals. And you look hurt."

Flanagan didn't object. He hadn't wanted to in the first place. "I saw my boss get shot and killed today," he said, and out the story all came again, but this time with none of the shakes and the hesitancies and cries of Jesus and God that had punctuated his monologues to Holly and Harland. Each sentence was as flat, calm and simple as the first. Each sentence went out for the last time, the desperate need to repeat and relive winding down. And it was all thanks to Baylor. He had no idea how she was doing this, but he was sure she was. As he tried to describe the chaos of his emotions as he saw someone he knew and (well, yes) liked blown to meat, he felt an understanding deep and absolute radiating from her, and he plunged into it, a balm. When he finished, he felt so calm he wanted to curl up and sleep on the bar floor. He didn't, though. Instead, soothed by a temporary closure, he waited through a brief but comfortable silence, and changed the subject. "And what about

465

you?" he asked. "When you're not playing ministering angel to complete strangers, what do you do?"

"I write freelance."

Bang, the tension started ratcheting up again. He had sudden visions, dark and tabloid-red. Baylor must have noticed. "Relax." She laughed. "I wasn't pumping you for a scoop. I don't do that kind of writing. I do corporate stuff: copy, pamphlets, manuals, speeches, annual reports. That kind of thing. Most thrilling. Anyway, you're not interested. No," she shushed when Flanagan started to protest. "What you are is exhausted. Go home. Sleep."

Flanagan surrendered. "Can I see you again?"

She gave him an appraising look that turned stern. "Depends. If I say yes, and you turn up looking hangdog again, then I might come to the conclusion that you like feeling sorry for yourself. And then I'd have to cross the street to avoid you." She gave him a quick, tight grin: joking but not really.

Flanagan nodded. Message received. "Stiff upper lip. I promise."

She appeared to think about it for another moment or two. "Well, you might be worth one shot, anyway." Sharp twinkle in those black eyes. She got a pen and a scrap of paper out of her purse. "Give me your number."

Flanagan did. "Can I have yours?"

"Not yet." Twinkle again, diamond hard and sharp as wit.

Flanagan stood up. "In that case, it's been a pleasure, Jen. Thanks again." They shook hands again, and he caught himself hoping she wouldn't squeeze too hard. "I hope you do call."

Jen Blaylock watched Flanagan leave the bar, and felt no guilt. Assessment: mixed. The pick-up couldn't have gone more smoothly. She had the man hooked, and could reel him in at her leisure. She had to be careful, though. He didn't seem dumb, and if he felt the tug of the line at any point, the game would be up. The big problem was his value: how much did he know? Was she wasting her time and putting the operation in jeopardy for nothing? Hard to say. But he'd been having drinks with Smith, and that had to be worth something. Flanagan might have access to things he couldn't imagine yet. If so, she'd have to help him rise to his full potential.

After she'd shot Smith, she had ducked back down the corridor to the washroom and out the fire door. It opened into the stairwell of another part of the building. No one around, so she'd doffed the dark clothes she'd worn over her civilian outfit, stuffed them into the gym bag, and sauntered outside. Across the way from the Baying Hound was an atrium. White pillars, twice the height of the potted trees, held the ceiling high over a big space. The white walls and white ceiling were delicate steel grids, and made the space seem even bigger. White metal tables and chairs were arranged along the periphery. People ate lunch at the tables or sat taking catnaps on the raised bases of the pillars. Blaylock had sat down on a base. She could watch the entrance to the Baying Hound from here, and she did, taking in the parade of sirens she'd triggered. She had wanted to see where Smith III's friend went. She wanted to get to know this guy. If she was going after Pembroke next, she needed a conduit to get information out of InSec, and to let her poison in. She waited until she saw Flanagan totter out, face pale, knees soft rubber. Then she followed him back to

467

his apartment and staked it out again from the Battery Park City promenade until she saw him leave for the bar. After that, it had been easy-breezy. Problem: he seemed nice. He wasn't hurting for money, not if he was living in a riverfront building. But he gave all the signs of the genuine innocent, and she hadn't counted on Smith keeping such company. A lesson learned on the dangers of assumptions. Too late now, as far as Flanagan was concerned. She was committed to this course of action, and determined to make it work. She felt no guilt. Some regret, maybe, but limited and contained. She could allow herself that, but no more. Especially now that the war had begun.

In Jen Blaylock, Annandale has created a tough, morally aware hero, someone who has the will to survive the worst. One can only hope she'll be back in another black comedy of political terror.

—National Post

ISBN: 9780888012920
Price: $10.99

Kornukopia

the battle rages

Davos' history was the shifting desires of wealth. Before skiing, the town's industry had been recovery. The resort had been sanatorium central, with twenty-nine institutions. Tuberculosis became passé, gave way to the lure of the ski runs. The hotel took over. Then came the WEF, born to Davos thanks to esthetic inaccessibility. The Congress Center, at the midpoint of the town, was a sprawling collision of disparate wings, half warm wood siding, half institutional concrete. It bridged the slope between the Promenade and the Talstrasse, the two parallel arteries that stretched the length of Davos. Without the forum, the Center would have been a middle-of nowhere aberration, grotesque for a town this size.

Thanks to the forum, it had a glove-fit perfection.

Blaylock reached the Center. She showed her pass, went through the fine-tooth security check. She was unarmed.

This was becoming a habit. She strolled through the main lobby, and flipped through a program. There were over three hundred sessions during the forum's weekend. They were deeply Serious, deeply Worthy. There were quite a few self-consciously progressive panels, well-meaning hand-wringing over the developing world. One was titled *HIV–AIDS: Is Attention Being Paid?* Blaylock wondered if the presenters had delivered the same talk for the last ten years. She counted at least a dozen sessions that worried the bone of the Ember Lake fire. Most of them plotted out the ongoing economic meltdown. There was one, though, that asked, *Are Leaders Expendable?* The big keynote was at one. President Sam *Not on My Watch* Reed was promising to storm the barn.

Blaylock arrived at the lecture theater early, and it was already stuffed to standing room and beyond. Reed was a hot ticket these days. Threats of hellfire and crackdown could do that for a guy. Then there were the leaks. His staff had been busy, hints of big policy pronouncements falling like pigeon droppings. Everything from internment camps to war on France was suggested. Lots of selling going on, but Blaylock wasn't buying. Reed's talk was a good place to track the scent of a big show, though. Better yet, Reed wasn't just delivering a speech. He was also going to have a debate. With Lawrence Dunn. Welcome to superstardom, Mr. Dunn, Blaylock thought as she looked for a vantage point of the stage. She found a perch behind the last row of seats. When Reed walked onto the stage, he looked grave. He gripped the lectern, and looked at the audience for fifteen solid seconds before he said a word. The silence was so pregnant, Blaylock began to choke on a suppressed laughing fit. "We are at a critical juncture," Reed said, and Blaylock thought, Is that the best opening you can come up with? Reed began a catalog of the world's hell-in-a-handbasket condition.

Blaylock's attention went AWOL. Her eyes wandered over the audience. She spotted Joe Chapel. He was sitting in the middle of the back row.

Blaylock shuffled her way left until she was standing behind Chapel's seat. She crouched and whispered into his ear. "Bang, he's dead." Chapel jumped, whirled his head around. She made a gun with thumb and index finger, blew smoke from the barrel. She winked. Chapel glared.

"These are our challenges," Reed said, and Blaylock listened again. She rested her chin on Chapel's shoulder, which went neurosis-rigid. Malice warmed her. She tickled the back of his neck with her fingernails. "We face them, not as individual nations, but as a world. So how do we, the world, respond? Not, I am afraid, through the United Nations. That body has failed all of us one too many times. Our nation, for one, will no longer be held hostage to its whims. True, the UN was founded with the noblest of dreams. So was the League of Nations. Dreams fade. So where do we turn? Is there a concrete, *practical* alternative to the UN?" Blaylock's fingers froze. "There is. Sometimes, when we set dreams aside, we find that reality has already provided us with what we need. There is no more effective means of bringing countries together in stability, mutual interest, and peace, than trade. And there is no more effective a body for bringing nations together in trade than the World Trade Organization. It is time for the WTO to realize the full potential of its name."

Bang, Blaylock thought. You're dead.

David Annandale presents Blaylock as a female Jason Bourne, a war machine crusading for the truth as she sees it. ... Kornukopia is a perfect winter vacation read.

—Winnipeg Free Press

ISBN: 9780888013033
Price: $11.99

David Annandale was born in Winnipeg and has lived in Edmonton, Charlottetown, and Paris. He did his MA on the Marquis de Sade at the University of Manitoba and a PhD on horror fiction and film at the University of Alberta. Currently, he teaches English and film at the University of Manitoba in Winnipeg where he lives with his wife and family.